DAWN
OVER KITTY HAWK

DAWN
OVER KITTY HAWK

THE NOVEL OF
THE WRIGHT BROTHERS

WALTER J. BOYNE

A Tom Doherty Associates Book
New York

Boy

This book is respectfully dedicated to all the pioneers of flight, from before the Wright brothers to those who are still pushing the frontiers of aviation forward.

DAWN OVER KITTY HAWK: THE NOVEL OF THE WRIGHT BROTHERS

Copyright © 2003 by Walter J. Boyne

This book is printed on acid-free paper.

Book design by Michael Collica

A Forge Book
Published by Tom Doherty Associates, LLC
175 Fifth Avenue
New York, NY 10010

www.tor.com

Forge® is a registered trademark of Tom Doherty Associates, LLC.

Library of Congress Cataloging-in-Publication Data

Boyne, Walter J.
    Dawn over Kitty Hawk : the novel of the Wright brothers / Walter J. Boyne.—1st ed.
        p.   cm.
    "A Tom Doherty Associates book."
    ISBN: 0-765-30471-6 (alk. paper)
    1. Wright, Orville, 1871–1948—Fiction.   2. Wright, Wilbur, 1867–1912—Fiction.
3. Kitty Hawk (N.C.)—Fiction.   4. Aeronautics—Fiction.   5. Inventors—Fiction.
6. Brothers—Fiction.   I. Title.

PS3552.O937D39 2003
813'.54—dc21

2003040020

First Edition: May 2003

Printed in the United States of America

0   9   8   7   6   5   4   3   2   1

ACKNOWLEDGMENTS

The author wishes to thank all those who helped him with this book, particularly Rick Young, who carefully reviewed all of the technical elements relating to the Wright gliders, Flyers, and their methods of flight. Rick is an expert in the field who has not only studied the many aircraft of the Wrights, but has also meticulously reproduced and flown them. Thanks also to Philip Handleman, Gregory Alegi, Guillaume de Syon, Doug Culy, Wally Meeks, and Loyd Carr, for their help with research. I especially appreciate the efforts of Martin Greenberg of Tekno Books, Bob Gleason, my editor at Tor, and Brian Callaghan. There are many excellent nonfiction books on the Wright brothers, but my central, indispensable source is *The Papers of Wilbur and Orville Wright, Including the Chanute–Wright Letters*, edited by Marvin W. McFarland of the Aeronautics Division of the Library of Congress.

CAST OF MAJOR CHARACTERS
(In Order of Appearance)

Augustus Herring. A very intelligent aviation pioneer with more of a taste for unorthodox business matters than for the pursuit of flight.

Bishop Milton Wright. A devoutly religious man and the revered patriarch of the Wright family. He had decidedly rigid views on the role and prerogatives of the head of the family.

Wilbur Wright. An ascetic loner, wracked with emotional and physical problems, but with a mind peculiarly suited for both inductive and deductive reasoning.

Samuel Pierpont Langley. Secretary of the Smithsonian Institution, this esteemed scientist was fully committed to solving the problem of manned, powered flight. His success with his model Aerodomes inspired the Wrights and many others.

Octave Chanute. A generous, successful man, Chanute invented some early hang gliders. He also served as an information-distributing facility for pioneer aviators.

Albert Blohm. A wealthy man with slightly more ambition than talent.

Katharine Wright. The Wright brothers' sister, a charming, vivacious girl who was more independent of their father than her brothers were.

Glenn H. Curtiss. Originally interested in bicycles, like the Wright brothers, Curtiss went on to become a great aviation pioneer, and the Wrights' most competent competitor in the air and in the courtroom. Well supported by his wife, Lena.

Orville Wright. Wilbur's working partner, who joined with him to solve the problem of flight. More outgoing than Wilbur and better with his hands.

Charles Manly. A mechanical genius and the "engine man" for Samuel Pierpont Langley. Manly was also the designated pilot for Langley's creation, the Great Aerodrome.

Annette Coujade. Albert Blohm's lover, confidant, and unwitting agent.

Alexander Graham Bell. The inventor of the telephone, and founder, with his wife Mabel, of the Aerial Experiment Association, which would prove to be a formidable rival to the Wright brothers' business efforts.

Henry Cleaver. Devoted friend of Katharine Wright.

Thomas Baldwin. A pioneer balloonist who joined forces with Glenn Curtiss to create the first airship purchased by the U.S. Army.

Lorin Wright. Another of Bishop Wright's sons and the designated publicist for the Wright brothers' success at Kitty Hawk.

First Lieutenant Thomas Selfridge. A rival to the Wrights in the Aerial Experiment Association, and, sadly, the first man to be killed in the crash of a heavier-than-air powered aircraft.

Minor characters will include most of the aviation pioneers, among them Clement Ader, Ernest Archdeacon, "Casey" Baldwin, Louis Blériot, John McCurdy, John Montgomery, Charles Renard, and Alberto Santos-Dumont. Important supporting characters include Carrie Kayler, Charley Taylor, Charles Furnas, Hart Berg, Léon Bollée and many more.

PROLOGUE

As the sun glanced off the rolling silver sand it turned the early morning dew into a field of diamonds, bright against the waving shadows of the beach grass. Pausing to savor the moment, he laughed to himself—more than diamonds would be mined from this morning's work. All his years of effort and study had funneled down to this. He was going to fly.

There had been so many pitfalls, so much to learn. So many people had been so wrong about flying—even the greatest of them all, Otto Lilienthal, had made mistakes, and the last one had killed him. He looked around slowly, checking the two long wings one more time, admiring the taut white cloth curving over the ribs, the slight droop of the tail-plane. He had made many glides in similar craft; this would be the first time he—or anyone else—would fly with an engine giving power instead of just the wind or gravity.

He waited, enduring the familiar apprehension before a trial glide, sensing the impatient tug of the wind on the wings, running through the litany of cautions about not over-controlling, keeping your balance, not landing on your nose. One final long look at the engine and two propellers and he nodded. The engine started, sending a comforting rumble through the wood and wires, and he was off against the sand-laden wind, flying under power, sweeping along a few feet above the ground, heading toward the water, doing what no one had ever done before. Time froze as he sailed inches above the rippling surface, his body moving to control the machine, his eyes staring straight ahead at the thin line of the horizon where the water met the sky. Touching down in a spray of sand, he felt the whole wood and wire structure bobbing and twisting with the shock, then looked back to see his grinning witness sprinting toward him.

The flight had lasted only a few seconds, but it was enough. He had done it! He was the first man in history to fly a heavier-than-air machine, and the date, October 11, 1898, would live in history. Now he, Augustus Moore Herring, ranked with Alexander Graham Bell, Marconi, and the other immortals who had been first in their field. All his competitors, crazy John Montgomery, that cheap stiff-necked academic Langley, all of them with their government money and their fancy laboratories and their fortunes, could never take it away from him. He was first and he would always be first.

Herring stood up, his muscular forearms pushing the two wings up. He had flown with the machine draped about him like a horizontal sandwich-board sign, his legs hanging down. Now he ducked his head and pushed his way out, glancing at the drooping, sand-sprinkled wings with affection. The machine—his flying machine, nobody else's, it was a Herring Flying Machine, by God—was un-damaged, ready to fly again. In layout it was like the many hang gliders he had built and flown, but with one great addition—power. He had wanted to install a small gasoline engine, but time and finances had forced him to compromise, as they had so often in the past. Money—he always needed money, and now he could make some. He patted the tank of compressed air, cold to the touch from the rush of air it had delivered to the small motor that drove the two propellers. It was not ideal, but it worked—and a gas engine could be installed in the next one.

Big Charley Morton stood waiting next to him, hand extended, a smile stretching across his normally dour face. Herring turned, grabbed his hand in both of his and yelled, "We did it, Charley—that's the first powered flight in history. You'll go down in the record books with me."

Morton shrugged his shoulders. "Its only about fifty feet, Mr. Herring. Is that enough to really be called a flight?"

"Of course it is, you damned fool. Did you expect me to fly across Lake Michigan in it? All I needed to do was to get off the ground and power myself through the air, and I did that and then some."

Morton's smile evaporated. "No need to cuss me—if you say it's a flight, it's a flight." He scuffed his toe in the sand, debating with himself about just smacking this smart young college boy in the mouth. He shook his head and asked, "What's next?"

"What's next is we take this back to the shed and store it. The next time I fly this I want Octave Chanute to be here. And I've got to get to the *Detroit Post*—I've a friend there, he'll be glad to have this story."

They each grabbed a wingtip and moved back up the dune; the machine weighed only eighty pounds, about half Herring's weight, but it was sturdy, the wings braced in a Pratt truss with wood and wire.

At the shed, Morton was slow in opening the door, and Herring yelled, "Come on, can't you do anything right?" Morton stepped back and let him shoulder the door open. This was the last time he'd ever work for him. Just get back to Detroit, and that would be it. Herring might have flown his machine, but he had no right to be so mean all the time. Especially for what he paid his help. Morton guessed that Southerners were used to cheap labor.

PART ONE
THE CALLING

A wise man learns from his experience; a wiser man
learns from the experience of others.
Confucius

CHAPTER

1

She'd been dead these seven years, but the image of Susan Wright still loomed large in the Bishop's consciousness. She had been a good wife: docile, obedient, and handy around the house. And she knew how to take care of her husband's needs—she had given him pleasure in bed, decorous but spirited, able to take part in God's gift of marriage with a good will and even sometimes with a laugh. She'd delivered seven children and five had survived; he still regretted the loss of the twins and celebrated their birthday every year, just as he did for the other children.

Even at seventy, Milton Wright still had urges, and it was more than a decade since he had possessed Susan. She had been so vital in her youth, so strong, able to work hard all day and still welcome him at night. Sometimes when she was feeling reckless and he was tired, she would seek him out, boldly reaching for him beneath the nightshirt. He never knew how to feel about that, didn't know till this day. He always liked it at the time, but afterward would feel guilty for her. She, however, never seemed to feel guilty. Even later, when the consumption had her, she would sport with him on occasion. But the long years of illness wore her down—him too, when he was home, which was not often. The church took him away for weeks at a time, sometimes preaching, sometimes fighting to keep the doctrine pure and legal, free of the growing Masonic influence.

Susan had been an invalid for the last part of her life, and the children at home, Wilbur, Orville, and Katharine, had rallied around to take care of her. He was happy that they were such good children, so much alike in their ways that they might have been just one person. He thought about that for a minute—three people with just one personality. Was that a spiritual quality, sort of like there being three Spirits in the Lord? Now the question troubled him—maybe it was blasphemous to even think like that; they sure didn't show any spiritual qualities. He'd pray on it.

Milton moved around the Sunday parlor, glancing in the mirror over the dark walnut fireplace mantel. The fireplace was built of good wood he had selected and Susan had sanded and stained. Then she had polished it every week all those years so that the grain still gleamed. It was solid like he was solid; both could stand the knocks of time. He passed his hands over his gray-white hair, thinner now, and smoothed the beard that a parishioner had once called "Lincolnesque." He paused as he always did to gaze at the framed photographs of his family, all standing in perfectly straight lines on the mantel. No picture of the twins, of course, they were taken away too soon, but pictures of all the survivors, and of Susan and him. It gave him pleasure to look at the photographs, to see the meld of him and Susan in them, in their eyes, their brows, their noses. Fine-looking children, not handsome nor pretty, but honest looking. Not pious, either, no good Lord, not pious, he'd done something wrong there for sure.

A thin patterned rug covered the pine floor of the parlor that was still, by far, the finest room in the little house. Susan had loved the place, and it still pleased him; it was meet and fitting for a bishop to have just such a home. He'd bought it back in 1870 for eighteen hundred dollars, stretching their budget, for that was twice his annual salary then as a preacher. But Orville had been born here the following year, and Katharine three years later. Then a few years ago, when he was away on church business, Wilbur and Orv had added the shutters and the long L-shaped covered porch. It was vanity, pure vanity; they should have known better. Putting in those curved columns and turned posts—it was like a Greek temple, not an honest minister's house. He picked at this old sore, looking for more to complain about, then came up with a new morsel as he realized that the porch roof cut down on the light coming into the house, made it dark inside. That's why he did not like it, that's why it bothered him: there was less light. And their workmanship was terrible, not like their mother's. He had pulled more than one splinter from his hand from the rough railings. One day he'd have them tear it down, maybe have somebody just put a little stoop by the door, let the light back in.

He picked up his favorite photo of his wife. She was staring fixedly at the camera, her left arm folded awkwardly across the waist, her right arm poised self-consciously on the chair arm. He remembered the dress very well, black silk and white lace and too expensive. The photo made her look prettier than she really was, but it told nothing of her confidence and her quiet capability, nor did it give any hint of her sweet dark scent that he loved and missed so much. He kissed the picture hard, pressing his lips and beard against it, then took out his large white handkerchief to polish the glass and the silver frame.

One more look and he turned to walk up the closed stairway to the second floor, murmuring, "Thank God for Wilbur." Like all the children, Wilbur needed a lot of direction and control, especially after his accident, when he was sick for so long. "Not really sick," he said aloud, "Sick in the head maybe, but not in the body." But when Susan had fallen really ill, then Wilbur had seemed to come out of it. He had been a godsend, nursing his mother for the last two years of her life, carrying her up and down these same stairs every day till the day she died. A good boy. Maybe too good. He worried about that sometimes, too. Sin was bad, but not having any sins at all, that wasn't right, not for a young man like Wilbur.

Despite his age, Bishop Wright still possessed a ferocious, combative energy and an awesome will that brooked no opposition. He'd spent his life fighting the wishy-washy compromisers in his beloved United Brethren Church, and it looked as if he would have to go on fighting them till the day he died. He'd held the upper hand for a while, but they had nibbled away at his position with their lying and their cheating, and now he was fighting back.

The Bishop paused on the stairway for a moment, his hand clasping the railing. Wilbur had surprised him in the church battle, studying his case and writing well-reasoned arguments that should have devastated the opposition, and would have too, if the blasted Mason-lovers had not been so devious. The liberals in church had forced him to spend more time lawyering than preaching; sometimes he felt he'd had the wrong calling and that he should have studied law. Too late for that now for him, but maybe not too late for Wilbur. He had to get Wilbur going, get him started on something. His life was wasting away, and so was Orv's. Katharine, at least, had completed high school, and would get a degree from Oberlin in two years. It pained him to have her out of the house, but he had to have one college graduate in the family. All of the boys had disappointed him so far. The oldest, Reuchlin, "Roosh" they called him, had abandoned them, scarcely writing from time to time, and the second, Lorin, was a cipher, never going to be much. How could it be? How could all his energy, all his brains, all his prayers, have been so poorly rewarded? They were good children, respectful and obedient, he'd give them that, except maybe Reuchlin. But none of them could get going—they were not lazy, they just were not effective. Not as he understood being effective.

And worst of all, none of them were real believers. The two older boys, Roosh and Lorin, would put on a show for him, pretending at least to be honest churchgoers, but Wilbur and Orville and Katharine did not even go through the motions anymore. It was an embarrassment with his fellow ministers. They never mentioned it, but he knew they talked about it, and it probably hurt him in the church council.

Somewhere, somehow, with all his preaching and all his talking, he had failed all his children, but especially the youngest three. He'd spent his life trying to straighten out the United Brethren, and driven his own family from the faith. He'd have to pray about this; it was serious and sad.

At the top of the stairs he roared, "Wilbur!" and his son popped out of the tiny bedroom like a cork out of a bottle, his pale face expectant, hands trembling slightly. About five foot ten inches tall, with a muscular frame gone slightly soft, still not recovered from his wearisome illness, he was nonetheless an imposing figure. His face was long and narrow, the length accentuated by closely set eyes and a finely shaped nose. His mouth was little more than a slit, nervous tension keeping his lips tightly compressed against the bridge of false teeth, a souvenir of the field hockey accident many years ago, the one that had started his illness. He was, as his father had confided in him, "Not handsome, but acceptable looking. A good enough match for a serious young woman."

"Yes sir, what is it?" Wilbur knew what it was—it was the same thing every day.

Milton gave him his usual tight little smile. "You think you know what I'm going to say, don't you?"

"Something about getting serious about life, about stopping reading and thinking and working in the bicycle shop. Maybe something about getting a job with the railroad?" His tone was jocular, friendly, respectful—but his mouth was dry, ready for the daily formula of question and answer. Sometimes he got relief, when his father was called away on church work, but that happened less and less since the big blow-up. Bishop Wright had challenged the United Brethren council on matters of religious law, and had lost both times. Tired of his clamoring all the many years, they had stripped him of his work and his privileged place in the church leadership, left him with a title and a miserable little salary.

"Not the railroad, this time. How about reading for the bar? You could pick up some courses at Oberlin, and I could get you in to read at one of the firms in town. The good Lord knows I've spent enough money on lawyers—they owe me a little something. Then maybe you could save me some money later."

Wilbur was quiet; this old graybeard was planning lawsuits four and five years in the future as if he would never die, as if he would just go on running everybody's lives and suing everybody that disagreed with him. But he sensed this was different somehow. Normally his father just complained, without offering any kind of alternative. This time he at least was talking about some schooling—that meant spending some money, and that was rare for his father.

"Going back to school might be good. I don't think I have the stomach for being a lawyer. Maybe I could be a teacher. I'm not cut out for business, that's for certain."

"You just don't have any gumption, you don't stick to it. Do you think I liked my first years out preaching, starving to death? Do you think I liked traveling up in the Oregon backcountry, where there were still Indians out to kill me?" He warmed to the old story, one he'd told a hundred times, but one he liked, him against the Indians.

Wilbur shook his head, listening to the familiar cascade of words, feeling sympathy for the Indians, sensing his father's presence swelling, filling up the narrow hallway, shutting off any escape. Sometimes you could divert him if you could come up with something different, something outside the usual line. "Do you remember" was always a good start—his father remembered everything, every detail, every date.

"Father, do you remember once, when you came back from a trip, you brought Orv and me a little toy flying machine?"

"Of course I do. It was 1878; it cost me half a dollar, lots of money then and now. They called it a 'Penaud helicopter' and you boys played with it quite a while. You even tried to make some like it, didn't you? But what's that got to do with the law?"

"Nothing, really, but I was at the library, reading in the *Scientific American* about a flying machine built by a man at the Smithsonian a couple of years ago." It was a good ploy; his father's face shifted and lit up. He approved of all three—going to the library, the *Scientific American*, and the Smithsonian. Wilbur decided to go on.

"It was just a model, didn't carry a man or anything, but it flew for almost a mile, and came down without breaking. If you can make a model to do that, you should be able to make a machine that would carry a man."

His father stared at him, giving his best bishop look, the cold, wise stare that said, "The good Lord says I've got to be compassionate so I won't tell you how stupid I think you are."

"Anyway, I thought maybe I'd like to find out more about what he did, and maybe experiment a bit and try to make one."

"One what? A flying machine? You and Darius Green?" He knew it was one of Wilbur's favorite poems from his childhood.

"Well, I was thinking, maybe it would make life at the shop a little more interesting. We've done about as much as we can do with bicycles, making them, selling them. Competition is getting fierce, too."

The light died out of his father's face. "Ah Wilbur, you and Orv are just not steady. You had a printing business, you got it going, you gave it up. You started your bicycle business and you are doing pretty well—got a new store, and all. Now you want to give it up, not for a profession, but for a folly. What's Orv got to say about this?"

"Nothing. I haven't talked to him. He's pretty content with the shop, and maybe I could be too, if I could fiddle with this flying machine stuff on the side. A hobby, you know."

"Will, I know I'm about ready to give up on you. You are thirty-one years old, and I cannot tell you what to do. But you need a profession. If you don't want to lawyer, maybe you should think about being a teacher."

Wilbur felt his stomach relax. He'd eased through this one—there would be no tirade, no jeremiad on all the sacrifices his father had made, no fervent calls to his mother to look down from heaven and forgive him. It was important to stop his father's spiel early like this or there was no holding him. But once he proposed an alternative, his father was ready to stop the arguing. Wilbur knew he was getting free and they would only talk for a little while longer.

"I'll see, father. Let me look into it."

"You do that, and you get Orv to look into it with you. I'm not worried about him, he can do anything with his hands, but you are a dreamer. I need to get you started in something you can make a living in. I'm not going to be with you forever. I'll be joining your mother, sooner than you think."

The thought flashed, *but not sooner than I want*, but Wilbur suppressed it, saying only, "Now, Father, not for many years, you know that."

Milton turned into his bedroom, shutting the door quietly. Wilbur raced down the steps, headed for the library again. He resented the remark about Orville being good with his hands, but his father was right about Wilbur being a dreamer. He dreamed of getting away, of breaking out from his father's domination every moment of every day. So did Orv and Katharine too, but not so much as him. His father pushed down on him like a cider press, snuffing out the air, the weight gnawing at him inside and out.

CHAPTER

2

Just over four hundred miles to the east, Samuel Pierpont Langley, third secretary of the venerable Smithsonian Institute, sat at his paper-encumbered desk, the long delicate fingers of his left hand idly waving a letter as he struggled with a new challenge.

At fifty-four years old, he was still a powerful bear of a man, with big shoulders and the deep chest of a lumberjack. His white hair receded only slightly above his broad forehead, while his bold, determined jaw was concealed by his graying beard and mustache. His face might have been considered handsome except for his heavy-lidded, protruding eyes and a fixed, condescending smile that could quickly turn into a snarl if he was provoked. That was easy. One had simply to walk down the stairs or turn into a hallway ahead of him to catch his wrath. His staff had quickly learned how capricious his imperious nature could be; he demanded perfection and immediate obedience even when he gave, as he often did, contradictory instructions. He was king in this Smithsonian Castle, and he let everyone know it.

Except important visitors, of course, to whom he tried—often failing—to be the soul of courtesy. The most welcome were those who contributed money to finance his experiments. None were coming today, so, instead, he waited with good grace for visitors of the second tier, scientists who could advance his claim for solving the mystery of flight.

Langley's office, furnished richly but overcrowded with scientific instruments, books, and stuffed birds, was nestled in one of the crenellated towers of the red sandstone building. It was impressive, but he much preferred to be "out back" behind the Castle, in the South Shed, the spartan two-story laboratory where he had carried out two decades of experiments in flight. There he had assembled a good staff, sullen and resentful sometimes, but capable of good work when prodded to do it.

And there he had succeeded, against all odds, against all charges of humbug and fakery. Two years before he had flown one of his experiments, Aerodrome Number 5, and now it was suspended in the South Shed.

Alexander Graham Bell himself had witnessed the flights and took a photograph of Aerodrome Number 5 as it made a beautiful half-mile flight over the Potomac River, landing so softly that it was able to fly again a few hours later.

At the end of the second flight of the warm May afternoon Bell had said the words he wanted to hear—"The problem of flight is solved." He needed Bell to be there, to see the flights and to understand their import, for the critics were on him like hounds from hell. Colleagues from the scientific community, the internal back-stabbers for which the Smithsonian was famous, all of them had written him off as either a charlatan or a fool. Yet even after Alexander Graham Bell told everyone that the problem of flight was solved, and that Langley had solved it, he had not received the credit he was due. He'd made another flight with the Aerodrome that fall, just to get some additional data, but he was finished working with models. Since that time he had wanted to build a man-carrying Aerodrome, and had lobbied unceasingly to get federal funds for the project. Now the letter he held was promising the funds, sending a stirring within him.

There was a knock at the door and Ross Robbins, his assistant, glided in. Langley glanced at him with unveiled contempt. The unctuous Robbins was part of the Institution's bureaucracy. Langley had inherited him, there was no way to get rid of him, and therefore he had to be endured.

"They are here, sssir." One of the things Langley hated most about Robbins was the snakelike way he hissed the 's' in sir, always smiling an oily smirk that never left his lips in the presence of a superior, yet incapable of being genuinely courteous.

Langley rose to greet his guests, calling out, "Octave! So good of you to come. And Albert! You didn't have to travel so far, but

I know how busy you are. Thank you for coming. I need to get your opinions, your vote of confidence."

The portly Octave Chanute was puffing from the climb up the stairs. Fashionably dressed, with a gray goatee and mustache, his remaining white hair slicked back against his head, Chanute's bright eyes beamed at Langley, the man who had come closest to solving the problem of flight. At his side, the Cassius-lean Albert Blohm moved slowly, his every gesture showing deference to the two great men in whose company he was—and in whose company he felt he more than belonged. He ran his hand over the back of the chair in which Langley was sitting. He would sit there one day, if things went as well as he knew they could. And Octave would help him get there. He was only thirty-three; he had plenty of time.

Blohm fussed about in his usual agreeable manner, pulling out chairs and generally being helpful. A good scientist, he was a better organizer, a facilitator able to motivate people and get bureaucracies to function. He'd hit Catholic University like a whirlwind when he offered to build the biggest wind tunnel in the world at his own expense. Students demanded to get into his classes, and he spread goodwill by funding other department projects. Blohm's personality glowed with an infectious, self-deprecatory good humor. He always gave the impression that whoever he was talking to—student, bus driver, college president—was the most important, most interesting person in the world. Good listening—rare enough in the scientific community—long training, and a natural knack permitted him to pick up on a conversational tidbit and then feed it back in a complimentary and amusing turn of phrase that flattered whoever was speaking.

When they had gone through the conventional comments on the beastly August weather in Washington and on President McKinley's handling of the war with Spain, they settled down and Langley spoke in professorial tones.

"Gentleman, I have a letter here that I want to discuss with you. But first I wanted to ask you what was going on in the world of aeronautics. Is there anyone out there who is doing anything worthwhile?"

Blohm was silent, deferring to Chanute, who over the last few years had become a clearinghouse for aeronautics. He gathered information from all over the world, recording the data carefully and dispensing it freely to anyone who asked, meantime using what he had learned to design gliders of his own.

Chanute chuckled. "Well, there is Herring, of course."

Langley knew Herring, having employed him as an assistant in the South Shed for a few months. He sputtered, "An impossible little man, always knew it all, would not take direction. Not unintelligent, quite bright in fact. But unreliable. There are still some questions about some missing tools."

He hesitated, then went on, "He actually claimed that he had made important contributions to the design of my Aerodromes. Pure lies, of course."

Chanute sat smiling, saying nothing. He too knew Herring, had employed him twice, and knew that he had been of real importance to Langley, solving in just a few months problems that Langley had worked on for years. But Herring could not endure Langley's imperial ways, and had left, coming back to work for Chanute.

Calming down a bit, Langley asked, "Well, what has Herring done? Or rather, what has he claimed he's done?"

"He says he has flown under power, using a compressed air engine."

"What kind of machine?"

"One of my two-surface models. As you know, we worked together a few years ago on the shores of Lake Michigan. Herring made some good glides, up to three or four hundred feet in my machines."

Langley leaned forward, eyes bulging a little more as his face drew taut. "Do you believe he flew under power?"

"Not for a minute. He asked me to come out to watch him do it again, and of course there were problems. He never got off the ground. Somehow he has acquired another backer, some dupe named Mathias Arnot. I think the whole thing was a charade to milk Arnot for some more money."

Langley relaxed a little. "Has that Montgomery fellow been doing anything?"

Professor John Montgomery claimed to have flown a glider out in California. There were no witnesses, and Montgomery had made a fool of himself when he attempted to explain his theory of flight at a Chicago conference, but he seemed to have a following, nonetheless.

"No, I talked to him while I was writing my little book. He claimed a long six hundred–foot glide, but he hasn't done anything else. I don't think he will."

Chanute's little book was *Progress in Flying Machines;* it was the bible of all the experimenters, for it covered everything in the field from Leonardo da Vinci's sketches to the magnificent work that Lilienthal had done. He'd published it in 1894, and it had made him an instant celebrity among fellow researchers in aeronautics, who typically were not generous about sharing their secrets. Chanute was different. He did not believe any one person, except perhaps Langley, could, on his own, solve the problem of manned, heavier-than-air flight. He was sure it would take a team approach, over many years of effort.

"What about Europe? Has anyone picked up poor Lilienthal's mantle?"

"No, quite the contrary. His death seems to have squelched interest. There are a few people flying Lilienthal-type gliders—Herring flew one for me—but I don't know of any serious experimenters. Lots of work going on in lighter-than-air, of course, but I think that is a dead end. You, sir, seem to have the field to yourself."

Langley sat back, relieved. He waved the letter. "This is from the Board of Ordnance at the War Department. The war with Spain taught them that they could have used a flying machine. They want me to build one." He passed the letter to Chanute, who read it quickly and gave it to Blohm.

The young man whistled softly. "Fifty thousand dollars. That's a lot of money, but is it enough to build a flying machine? And who will fly it?"

Langley nodded. "Fifty thousand dollars is a lot, but it is probably just enough, if I can find an engine that is not too expensive. My Aerodromes have flown. I plan to just scale one of them up so that it can carry the load of a man and a gasoline engine. The key factor will be the cost of the launching mechanism. It has to be scaled up as well, and that will be expensive."

Blohm smiled. "From little acorns, great oaks; from little Aerodromes a Great Aerodrome, eh? Can I help you with my wind tunnel?" He watched Langley closely; the man had been unbelievably lucky. Not even a college graduate, he had moved like a sleepwalker from one position to another, before winding up in this toy store, this playground for academics. Langley had spent twenty years creating a flying model of an airplane, something that Blohm felt he himself could have done in three years with the same resources. And the "Langley Law"! What nonsense! Only someone with Langley's reputation as an astronomer could have published such piffle and gotten away with it. Langley's Law proclaimed that the faster a surface moved through the air, the less power was required to move it! It was absurd on the face of it, yet he had had honors heaped upon him from all sides. Blohm considered him a lucky charlatan whose intimidating imperial air had gained him a position he did not deserve.

Chanute cleared his throat, a nervous habit signaling that he was going to say something that might be construed as disagreeable. "My dear Langley, do you feel that simply scaling up your Aerodrome is wise? I learned a few things building railroad bridges and one of them was that every time you change the size of a project, you have to change the materials and the way you put them together. And that's especially true if wind is a factor." Chanute's mind went back to some suspension bridges that he had built that had suffered terribly from wind-induced oscillation.

"Perhaps for bridges, Octave, but not for flying machines, not in the size I plan, anyway."

He stood up suddenly and moved around the desk. "Come with me, I'll show you." It was a not a request but an order; Langley was at the door before either Chanute or Blohm had risen from their seats. He led them down a short back hallway and sprinted down the steps two at a time. At a landing, a surprised clerk plastered himself against the wall like a West Point cadet, white-faced and obviously terrified. Blohm shot him a smile as he went past on the way into the yard behind the Castle.

As Langley approached the two-story South Shed, laughably plain after the ornate Smithsonian building, the entrance door sprang open and a short, bald man cowered half-hidden behind it. Langley swept to the center of the room and pointed up, looking as much like a biblical prophet as Blohm thought he might ever see.

"Look above you." He pointed to the Number 5 Aerodrome, slung from the ceiling by a web of guy-wires. There had been four men in the room; two slipped quietly out another door and the other two seemed to melt into the woodwork, staying as far from Langley as they could, obviously not expecting to be introduced and pretending to study the papers in front of them with fixed intensity.

Blohm followed Chanute around a table in the center of the room, staring up at the beautiful Aerodrome. There was no denying that it was an elegant machine, as intricately made as a chronometer, its polished copper fittings gleaming amidst an intricate spider web of bracing wires. Every wire was connected with tiny brass fittings, each one hand-machined by a veteran craftsman. Two curved surfaces, each about fourteen feet long, were mounted one each at the front and the rear. The gossamer wings had their tips elevated to form a shallow V. Out of sight, nestled in the tubular maze of the fuselage, was a small gasoline-fueled steam engine that drove the twin propellers, just two twisted slabs of metal and fabric. They were mounted between the wings and driven by a system of shafts and bevel gears. At the rear there drooped a cruciform rudder that served to stabilize the craft in flight, much as feathers stabilize an arrow. It was a metal sculpture, a tribute to the master metalworkers that Langley employed, for he directed the work—he did not do it. His style was to give instructions on a concept, then monitor and pick at the results, complaining constantly, and changing things as his own ideas evolved.

"As you can see, my Aerodromes had wings about fourteen feet long. I can build a man-carrying machine with wings no more than fifty feet long. All I need is the power, the engine. Obviously, I cannot use steam this time; it has to be internal combustion."

Chanute's face was not impassive; his jaw dropped a bit and for a moment the customary twinkle was replaced with a steely hard look of disbelief. But he was too polite to argue. Instead he took another tack.

"Surely you do not intend to pilot the machine yourself? We are of an age, you and I, and I do not do any gliding. You can hire younger men for that."

"No, no, I'd break my old bones for sure. But I'll hire someone, a river pilot, a chauffeur, someone who will be able to steer it well enough. The air is too turbulent, too filled with violence, for a man to be able to react quickly enough to steer the Aerodrome. It has to have automatic stability so that it can overcome the vicious shifts of wind."

Chanute and Blohm exchanged glances. Both were familiar with gliding and neither had ever heard of such tumultuous winds. Chanute, at least, deferred to Langley's long history of experiments, but Blohm persisted.

"Would you like to have whomever you hire do some gliding with my people? It might be good experience."

Langley looked benignly at him. "My friend, I know the Aerodromes glide; I saw them glide down safely, lightly into the Potomac, with no damage. No, I don't need to have them do any gliding."

Blohm watched the two men intently. Langley looked down on Chanute as an inventor, but valued him as the middleman of aeronautics, a distribution center for knowledge and for ideas. He did not think much of the crude gliders Chanute had built, not the ones with two wings, nor those with twelve.

Blohm dared to repeat himself, asking, "Sir, my tunnel will be ready in a year or two. I'd be honored to have you use it for any purpose you wish."

"That's very kind indeed, Blohm; you and Octave are both so helpful. But I think my Aerodromes have flown in the best wind tunnel of all, the sky. To scale them down and put them in your tunnel would not reveal much. I'll leave your tunnel to another investigator. Now, let's go back. I've ordered tea for us."

The trip back was equally swift, and Chanute was breathing heavily when they were seated again. Langley held up his hand for silence, then motioned them to the window. "Look there, just outside the ivy." They watched as two, then four hummingbirds darted in and out of the foliage, their wings beating feverishly.

"I keep some sugar water in inverted retorts there—they come back every year in greater numbers."

Blohm and Chanute tried to watch as appreciatively as Langley, then edged back to their seats. After a moment, Langley returned to his own and picked up the letter again, reading it once more before speaking.

"The question for me is an ethical one. I believe I can build an Aerodrome—"

"A Great Aerodrome," Blohm interjected.

Langley smiled. "A Great Aerodrome, indeed, and my dear Blohm, I will call it just that if I build it. But I cannot determine if it is morally correct to do this for the War Department."

Chanute hesitated. The statement was more than disingenuous; it was deceitful. It was common knowledge that Langley had a network of people lobbying for him with the president and had gone before the Board of Ordnance himself with an impassioned personal plea. But there was nothing wrong with that—why dissimulate? Langley coughed and Chanute realized he'd delayed too long.

"Of course it is. Do you believe that Great Britain or Spain or France or Germany would not develop a flying machine if they could? They would in a minute. You owe it to yourself, and to the country, to do it."

Langley suppressed a smile. Now he had what he wanted.

"Would you mind if I put that on paper, quoting you, when I go to the Smithsonian regents? I'll have to take time from my duties here, of course, so I have to have permission. Your word will carry great weight."

So does his chair, Blohm thought, but he said nothing; he never made audible jokes about people who could help him.

Chanute's high-pitched, almost girlish voice cut into his thoughts. "Certainly, Mr. Secretary, I would be honored. You have a duty to your country. I've monitored the field of aeronautics very closely for almost twenty years, and no one has come close to your success."

"Hear, hear!" Blohm was not going to be left out.

Langley slammed his fist into his palm. "Then it's done. I've got to find an engine, and get my men started on the new machine."

"Sir, I think I can help you with the engine—I know a few people in the field. There is a Hungarian, Balzer, who has some promising ideas."

"Thank you Albert, please let me know what you find. And Octave—I feel much better with your vote of confidence."

They parted with many expressions of mutual esteem, and the two visitors walked slowly down the winding marble staircase, picking their way past worn spots in the carpet runner. Once outside the door to the Castle, Chanute turned to Blohm and said, "He's a stubborn fellow, isn't he? Did you understand what I was trying to tell him?"

Blohm seized the opportunity. "I believe I know exactly what you were saying. The metal tubes and fittings he uses in the smaller Aerodromes are strong enough for the stresses put on them. But if you just scale them up, they will not be able to stand the strain of the greater speeds and the greater weight. That's one of the reasons I kept suggesting the wind tunnel."

"Exactly. And the gliding?"

It was time to show a little modesty. "You are the expert in that field. I've done a little gliding myself, but nothing to compare with your experiments. If you think gliding would be worthwhile, he should do it. And what would it cost? A pittance."

Chanute turned, then said, "Well, perhaps it will work out. The Lord knows he has time, and money, and the backing of the Smithsonian. Now he even has the War Department behind him. He is already far ahead of everyone else. But he is mule-stubborn."

CHAPTER

3

The male anatomy held few secrets for Katharine Wright. She had grown up in house filled with young males, none of them too careful about modesty in the little house out back or during their Saturday evening baths in the tub in the kitchen. And it was mutual: they had learned about female anatomy, for they had not been shy about bursting in on her, especially Orville. Orv, as she called him, took a fiendish glee in coming in just as she was stepping out of the tub, especially when Father was on the road. It was part of their special secret relationship that went back as far as she could remember. Wilbur always shook his head and disapproved, but she knew he was taking a peek whenever he could.

But all that was different from the intense closeness she felt for a man she had known for only a year. The feelings, the good hot feelings, came with the freedom here at Oberlin, a freedom she had never known before, and she loved every moment of it. Katharine knew that she was not a beautiful woman—her father had often told her that. But the mirror told her that her face was pleasant and she knew that beneath the puffed blouse and voluminous skirt she had a good figure. One thing for certain—she had a wonderful smile. It came through even in photographs, and many people had told her so. She was popular with both men and women, for she knew how to stroke egos—living with her family had taught her that.

She walked briskly, stepping carefully over the green moss weeping from the brick path that led down to a grove of trees that edged the campus. Wilbur would have told her immediately that they were a mixture of sycamores, alders, and evergreens, but Henry Cleaver would not know or care what they were. He'd be waiting at their spot, a thicket of evergreen with branches that drooped near the ground, a blanket spread over the deep layer of pine needles, a book of poems in one hand and in his other a jug of something— water, buttermilk, or even homemade wine when he could get it. And he would be ready for her, ready with some more secrets of the male anatomy.

She dropped to her knees, pushed through the branches and into his arms. As she fastened her lips on his, she thought for a moment of what her father would say, and laughed. Henry laughed too, they often laughed when they made love, and liked it better when they did.

CHAPTER

4

When he first swam in it, they called it "Crooked Lake," for the way it bent to hug the land and lap up against the green valleys surrounding it. It looked mighty inviting now as he pedaled down the dusty road from Rochester, heading for home at Hammondsport.

They should have called it Ice Lake, he thought. It was nearly as cold in summer as in winter, when it froze solid. About ten years ago some local do-gooders had the name changed to Keuka Lake, supposedly the original Indian name meaning "lake with an elbow." Changing the name did not make it any warmer—or any less inviting.

Hunched over the handlebars, racing style, Glenn Hammond Curtiss's powerful legs moved like pistons, rhythmic, tireless, never stopping. There was plenty of time, but he liked to go fast, always. Someday he'd bolt a motor on his bike and then he'd really make time.

The road, dusty and rutted from last winter's wagon wheels, began to run downhill and he relaxed a bit, catching his breath and enjoying gravity's free ride. God, he loved the wheel! What freedom; without it he'd never have left Hammondsport to get to a big town like Rochester. And it was a ticket to friends; everybody worth knowing either had a bicycle or was going to get one. Few had a screamer like the lightweight Stearns he was riding, but there were all sorts out there, made by Monarch, Columbia, Fleetwing, and most of them were pretty good. He'd read somewhere that more than a million had been sold in the United States the year before. That meant a million people had more freedom, could go more places, do more things. Steering to keep out of the ruts, he eased off the brakes as the road began to level out.

He made the trip almost every week, shooting down from Rochester, more than eighty miles on early Friday afternoon. Most weeks there would be races on Saturday and Sunday, and then he'd ride back, dead tired, first thing Monday morning. His boss at Eastman was a bicycle rider too, he understood him. Glenn would work extra hours during the week, so he could have a few more hours to himself on Friday and Monday, time to make the journey.

Curtiss began to pump again, enjoying this, the best part of the trip, the last few miles on the way home, when he was still fresh, and he could he could see the lake lapping back into Pleasant Valley, the hills filled with color, with tiers of vines arrayed like ladders on the hills. The dust from the road was thick on him and he licked his lips, rolling the grit back into his mouth, thinking how much he loved this area. He'd been named for it, his first name coming from the craggy glen where the spring water was so cold, his middle name for the town of Hammondsport, inserted like a cork at the bottom of Keuka Lake.

Up ahead, a crew of girls, clad in dusty white bonnets, voluminous skirts and aprons, were working the lower levels of the Pleasant Valley Wine Company's vineyards. The grapes were mostly Catawba, for the white wines and champagnes, but there were other more expensive grapes higher on the hills from vines that had been brought over from France and grafted to American stock. The girls moved quickly and carefully, packing the grapes gently in the baskets so they would not bruise.

Curtiss sped by, but a girl in a light blue smock caught his eye and he slammed the bike around in a quick U-turn, sending up a cloud of dust that rolled back on him when he stopped. She was the most beautiful girl he had ever seen, and he had no idea of what to say to her.

At eighteen, Curtiss was shy. He'd had a few dates with local girls in Rochester, but they had been painful experiences, with no common ground and a terrible tendency on the girls' part to want to spend his money. He was not tight, but he could not afford a night of drinking and dancing, not on what he made as a photographer, and not when he was paying off what he owed on the Stearns bike.

Curtiss dismounted, panting, and rolled the bicycle toward the girl. She had waited for him; the cart where the baskets of picked grapes were placed had moved on, the other girls moving with it, looking back at them and smiling, talking low and laughing in the sun as they picked the long purple bundles.

She spoke first: "Would you like a drink of water?" She shifted her hip and reached down into a fold in the sack she had slung over her shoulder, pulling out a mason jar, capped and glistening with moisture. She unscrewed the cap and held it out, saying, "It's from the spring up the hill."

He nodded, never taking his eyes from hers, and drank. "Thanks, that was delicious. What's your name? I'm Glenn Curtiss."

"I know who you are. My father talks about you. You ride with the Hammondsport Boys, don't you?"

Immensely pleased, he blurted, "I'm the captain," then felt foolish. It wasn't much, being captain of a racing team, not enough to brag about. Embarrassed, he repeated, "What's your name?"

"Lena Pearl."

Curtiss looked surprised. He knew almost everyone in Hammondsport, and there were not any Pearls. She smiled and said "Lena Pearl Neff."

"I know your father. He runs the lumber mill. He's a good man."

"We think so."

"How come we haven't met before? I go to the lumber mill all the time."

"Dad was working here for a while before the rest of us moved in. We were living over in Wheeler."

Her voice was like her eyes, soft, but deep and penetrating. "I'm sorry, I've got to go, I'm picking. Maybe I'll see you tomorrow at the races."

She was already moving away, smiling and nodding as she ran to the wagon, looking back to give a small wave. The other girls were laughing again.

The next morning, Glenn dressed carefully in black shorts, a red short-sleeved shirt and a red knit cap—the uniform of the Hammondsport Boys. They were spiffy compared to most of the teams they competed with because they were sponsored by a businessman, Jim Smellie, who ran a number of businesses, including a pharmacy, a tack shop and a bicycle shop. The talk among his fellow drivers was that Smellie spent the money on uniforms so they wouldn't make fun of his last name.

It was the kind of racing that suited Curtiss perfectly, a five mile run around the roads surrounding the Pleasant Valley winery, with big Bully Hill to start, where his strength would dominate, and finishing in a long, level straightaway where he could really turn on the speed. The competition was strong today, with an eight-man team from Urbana and a six-man team from Cold Springs, all good wheelers.

After the usual milling around, the race started and Curtiss lay back with the pack until they left town. Once on the road up Bully Hill, he rode the only way he knew, full out, legs pumping in a racing crouch that had him bent forward over the handlebars, grabbing the lead and kicking up dust for the rest to eat. There was nobody on the road; people knew the bikers were coming, and they stayed clear. Little groups of people gathered at key spots, the turns and the hills, but for the most part they were racing alone. As they made the final turn into the long stretch back toward town, Curtiss poured it on, legs pumping, breath coming hard, increasing his lead until he flashed across the finish line, two hundred yards ahead of the pack.

As he slowed, he saw her, standing back a little in the crowd, but waving. Curtiss rarely smiled, but a grin lit up his face and he pedaled directly over to her, sweating, still breathing hard, but able to talk.

"Thanks for coming out. Appreciate it."

"Thanks for winning. Tell you what. Why don't you come over to see me tonight, after supper?"

Surprised at her directness, Curtiss hesitated a moment.

"Sure, I'll be there. About seven?"

"That's fine. Do you know where I live?"

They were getting ready to set up the next race and Curtiss backed his bike away. "No, but I'll find out."

They realized they were in love immediately and spent the next several months trying to find out why. Curtiss understood his own emotions. Lena appealed to him sexually in a way that no girl—he had never really been with a woman—had done before. But more than that, she was kind, clever enough to be amused by him and to amuse him, and very levelheaded. He saw in her someone who could balance his own impetuous nature. For her part, Glenn was a romantic ideal, a knight on a bike instead of a horse, but a knight nonetheless. He presented a rough, sometimes gruff exterior, but she soon learned how innately kind he was. One of the things that impressed her most was his affectionate relationship with his sister Rutha. She was almost three years younger than Glenn, and deaf, a victim of meningitis. Her doctor opposed the use of sign language, preferring to teach finger spelling and how to move lips and tongue precisely to enhance speaking ability. When Rutha was taught, Glenn insisted on learning as well. In the early days, when both were learning, Glenn spent hours every day with her, encouraging her and becoming proficient himself. As the years passed, he saw to it that they communicated every day that he was home.

Glenn had told her nothing of this; it didn't occur to him to do so. But Lena picked it up from friends who knew and admired him. So it was no surprise that they would be married, eight months after they had met, in a simple ceremony, done Presbyterian style in the bleak parsonage at Hammondsport. Curtiss kissed his bride with gusto, and she giggled as the fuzz of his embryonic mustache tickled her. It was such a relief to be married; she wasn't pregnant but she surely would be soon, if they kept at it the way they were going.

As a bride, Lena Curtiss was as pretty and innocent looking as Glenn was tough and hard. To her, Glenn was a champion, riding his bicycle like a king, and best of all, seeing something in her no one else had seen.

It had not been easy. Glenn's mother, Lua, objected, said he was too young, and she would not give him permission to marry. Glenn knew that she was more interested in keeping his income within the family than anything else. When the time came, he simply added two years to his age, signing the parish marriage book as twenty-one. On the other side of the aisle, Guy Neff was all for the marriage and all for Glenn, but his wife Jenny was not. Lena was her pearl, that's why she'd named her that; she was only seventeen, two years younger than Glenn, and she didn't like the way Lena had fallen head over heels for a bicycle rider. But when Glenn formally asked for her hand, Guy gladly gave permission, telling his wife, "That boy is going places, he will put her in a brick house someday."

At the moment, Curtiss could not even put her up in a rented room; they were moving in with his grandmother, in the upstairs room where he had grown up. Lying side by side in his narrow bed, Lena was happier than she had ever been. They had been together often before, but always out of doors, sometimes in a carriage, most often between the rows of grapevines in the vineyards. This narrow bed, with its hard mattress and skinny pillow, was sheer heaven. She reached over and traced the scar on Glenn's lip, a souvenir of a racing accident. The mustache was intended to cover it.

"Don't look so glum, Glenn, you look like you have a toothache."

"No toothache, a wallet-ache. I got you to marry me and I don't have any money to keep you the way I'd like to."

He given up his job with Eastman in Rochester and gone to work for Saylor's Photo Studio in Hammondsport. They gave him all the out-of-town assignments; he covered them on his bicycle, staying in shape and carrying his photographic gear stowed in saddlebags he'd made for the rear wheel. Mostly he shot photos of weddings and new babies. That was part of the problem. Pretty soon he'd have some of those babies himself, and he was not earning enough. The job at Saylor's paid seven dollars a week, and he could sometimes make as much as that racing on the weekends, but it was still not enough. He turned on his side and kissed her on the forehead. "Lena, will you take a chance with me?"

"I already have. And my mother says I'll take a lot more. She's not too crazy about you, you know."

"I sort of gathered that when she wouldn't come to the wedding. But I'm serious. You know Jim Smellie, down at the drugstore?"

"Sure, of course, poor man, what a name. I'd have it changed if it were me."

"Well he says it's a good name, nobody forgets him, it's like advertising. He's done pretty well, you know, buying land around the lake and planting vines. He's offered to let me take over the bicycle shop and the tack shop, nothing down, pay it off as I go. It's getting to be too much for him. The only problem is that I've never run a business before."

"You've never been married before, and you are doing a pretty good job at that." Her hands reached out for him.

"Just a second, honey, just a second. I'm serious. I want to give up my paycheck and take a chance on making some real money running a bicycle shop. Everybody is buying bicycles, and there would be money in repairing them, too. I'm doing that all the time anyway, for free. I could run the selling and the shop, but you would have to help me, keep the books, watch the shop when I'm out, everything. Will you do that?"

"It is lots better than picking grapes, Glenn. I'll do anything you want, anytime you want it. You know that. I think I've proved that to you already."

Gratefully he gathered her to him, murmuring, "Many times, many times."

CHAPTER
5

D ayton was a utilitarian city that worked well because it was filled with good workers, each one anxious to carve a little bit more out of the prosperity generated by the big factories. It was tough during winter, when ice storms would glaze every surface with a sparkling crystal wrapper that bent trees to the ground and turned streets into ice rinks. Then a storm from the lakes would smother the city into silence with four feet of snow, brilliant white at first, then progressively turning gray, brown, and black from the factory smoke. But you could work in winter, put on more clothes, move around. It was the summer that stunned, when a burial shroud of humid heat hung over the roofs. The remorseless sun pumped up whirling vortices of dust, spreading the acrid smell of horses working too hard across the still-bustling city, tainting neighborhoods rich and poor. When night fell, people tried to sleep as best they could, crowding porches and even lawns, hoping for some errant breeze.

On South Williams Street, the shop's flat black tar roof sucked in the sun's warmth, bubbling in its embrace before transferring it intact to the crowded workshop below. Oblivious to the heat as he was to any discomfort, Orville hovered over the bench where the components of the next Van Cleve bicycle lay ready to be assembled, his gloved hands deftly moving the steel bars of the frame into place. The Van Cleve was the top of the line, the best bicycle they could make. Last year they sold it for sixty-five dollars, profiting thirty-five dollars on every bicycle. They had to guarantee and service it, but it was good money.

He paused, using a pristine shop cloth to pat his brow. Prices were dropping, and they'd be lucky to get fifty-five for it next season. That's why they had to make more, and sell more. He pressed his tie carefully in place, making sure not to touch his spotless collar, then paused for a second to retie the strings of his long apron. With smooth precision, he placed the angled frame connector in the heavy vise so that its openings were evenly positioned, checking the placement quickly with a level. He inserted the two steel tubes of the frame into the connector, then he warily picked up the electric welding torch—he was always sure it would shock him and it seldom disappointed. Holding it at exactly the correct angle, he tacked the steel tubes into the connector.

Orville paused for a moment, then resumed his work, holding the welding rod at the proper angle to make a smooth bead, first on the left connector and tube, then on the right. The smell of hot metal and oil filled the air and gave him a peculiar satisfaction. He liked this work; it was solid, tangible, and handling the torch and the hot metal gave him a sense of creative power. Orv turned the power off with his usual sigh of relief.

Katharine stood in the doorway, fanning herself with a folded magazine, and watching him with pleasure. At twenty-nine, Orv retained the hard, lean figure of his bicycle-racing days. When he stood perfectly erect—and he always did except when bent over the workbench—he was five feet eight inches tall. He weighed just under one hundred forty pounds, about the same as when he left high school. She loved the way he took care of himself, dressing with meticulous care even to work in the shop, keeping his thinning hair combed, his mustache groomed. Old Orville was a dandy, no doubt about it. Only problem was that he didn't go anywhere where being a dandy would do him any good.

"Drat."

"What's the matter, Orville?"

Orv's blue-gray eyes flashed with annoyance. "Blasted bead has a little dent in it above the connection."

"Can't you just paint over it?"

He pointed to the sign above the lathe that read *If it's not Right it's not Wright*. "No, I'll have to file it down first, see if I can even it out."

"Come on, Orv, you've been at this all day. You've already made one bicycle."

"It doesn't take much when I finally get all the parts together. I need to make a bunch more before spring, or we're going to starve next year."

She reached over and rubbed his shoulder. "Orv, you need to get out, you should start racing again."

"Too old, Sis, too old. Got to put beans and bacon on the table, keep you fed, you, with your high-class college ways."

He gave her a hug and turned back to the bench.

She waited no longer. "Bad news, Brother."

"Don't tell me. Papa's coming back early?"

"Yep, he'll be here tonight, coming in on the five o'clock train. You better put your tools down and get home to wash. You know he likes to be greeted at the station."

"Does Will know he's coming?"

"Will's glad. He's got everything ready, and he's going to tell him that he's off to North Carolina to play with his flying machine."

"Better Will than me. Pop's not going to like that; we'll hear all about railroads and lawyers and Indians and all the rest."

She laughed and they walked arm in arm to the door of the little shop on South Williams Street. At the door, Katharine reached up to give him a peck on the cheek. "Be brave, Orv, we're all in this together." Then she started. "Oh my goodness, I forgot to tell Carrie to put on a linen tablecloth. She'll be setting the table on the oil cloth."

Three hours later they were all sitting around the table, with frightened little Carrie Kayler serving. She'd only been with them a few weeks, and the first hours of his visit had made her more terrified of the legendary Bishop Wright than his children were. From the look of the way they were fiddling with their plates, it was obvious that they didn't like her beef stew, the first she ever made.

The bishop gave up on the stew and buttered some bread. His mind was never very far from his battle with his church, a battle that had changed him. Years before, he had been a leading figure in the United Brethren Church and thought that perhaps the good Lord had selected him to lead it one day. No more. The church was changing, too many young preachers with liberal ideas and fat stomachs, more concerned about collection plates than the good rules of the church, rules that he had hammered into place over many years. But the news was not all bad.

"Think I made a little progress this time, Will, thanks to some of your papers. I think I got the council to listen to me about barring Masons from joining the church."

Will nodded. No one was expected to say much, not till Pop got finished talking and started asking questions. Listening and nodding was the thing.

When Carrie disappeared back into the kitchen, the Bishop put his finger over his mouth and whispered "Katharine, is this how that girl cooks?"

"I told you she was young, Father. I'm trying to teach her, but she's only fourteen."

"No matter, she's got to do better than this, or you've got to get someone else. I don't want you doing the cooking, I want you to run this place like a business." He didn't say what he really wanted. He wanted Katharine to take over Susan's role, do all the things a wife should do, except in bed, of course. Then he'd have more time to fight his battle, not have to worry about running the house.

Will pumped up his courage.

"Speaking of business, Pop, I'm making good progress with my project."

Bishop Wright snorted, knowing what Wilbur was talking about, but leading him on. "What project? You taking up the ukulele like Orv here?"

"Ah, you know, the so-called flying machine. I've studied all the stuff the Smithsonian sent me, and I think I'm ready to do a little testing. Not flying, just testing."

"I thought you did that last year with that kite." The blasted kite had caused him embarrassment last year with the elders, who made jokes about "the bishop getting his own Ezekiel's chariot." It was bad enough that they were always telling him how well their children were doing, this one a doctor, that one a lawyer, none of them flying kites.

"No, I was just working out particulars. This year's will be bigger; I've got some new ideas, something no one else has done yet."

"Orv, what do you think about this? Are you helping Wilbur?"

"Yes, sir, a little bit. I helped him last year with the kite flying. It went pretty well. This year we've just been talking about it a little, 'cause mostly I've been trying to build up the inventory. There is so much competition nowadays that bike prices are dropping, so we'll need to sell a few more next year, to make a profit."

" 'Specially if you are going to pay me back that hundred and fifty I loaned you." He had bailed them out last year when things got tight, and now Wilbur was spending more money on some fool flying machine. Thank the Lord he was blessed with an easy manner and lots of patience.

"Why don't you try perpetual motion, Wilbur? With all the wheels and gears you have in the shop, you could do it pretty cheap, and you wouldn't kill yourself."

"I won't kill myself, Pop. Where I'm going the sand is soft and will break my fall."

The bishop sprang like a tiger on the operative word. "Going? Going where? Aren't you going to fly your machines right here in Dayton?"

"Well, I'm just getting started, and I'll need good steady winds to do the testing. Just don't have them here, not regular. It will be a lot like flying the kite at first, just testing some ideas I have, but then I'll need steadier winds to take it a little further along the way. . . ." his voice trailed off, dry, realizing his father was glaring, sure that what he was saying was nonsense.

"I asked you a question. Going where?"

"There's a place down in North Carolina, on what they call the Outer Banks, sort of like a chain of islands just off the coast. It's a little place called Kitty Hawk, and it has the right winds, almost all the time."

The bishop sat and chewed reflectively. The stew was bad, and the news was bad. But maybe not. At least Will would not be embarrassing him here. And maybe he was doing something to break out of his shell. It couldn't cost too much, rail fare, room and board.

"What do you figure this machine will cost you?"

Wilbur breathed a sigh of relief. His father was going to go along with the idea, just enjoy the complaining for a while.

"The machine won't cost much at all, it's just wood and cloth and wire, maybe twenty dollars all told. I'll have a tent out on the beach and cook camp food. The rail ticket will be the big expense, and I can get one of those round-trip, holiday fare packages."

"Sounds about right. But tell me about what you are doing. What makes you think you can do something for twenty dollars that other men, scientists like Professor Langley, haven't been able to do with thousands?"

Wilbur hesitated. This had to be done correctly, or they would be off in Indian country again. "Well, Professor Langley has come a long way; I told you how he flew his little machines, sort of like sailing model ships. He hasn't flown a machine with a man aboard, not yet anyway. Besides, there must be more ways than one to fly. I think I'm doing it the right way, one step at a time, just easing in."

He took a sip of water, waiting for his father to pounce again. When he didn't, he went on. "But I've got it pared down to the basics. First, you have wings for lift—Langley did that. I've used the tables Lilienthal developed, and I know I can make the wings. Then you have to have an engine to give enough power to move the wings through the air, so they'll have lift. That will be harder to do, but I'm sure I can find a gasoline engine that will do it. Not steam, gasoline."

"Are you going to have them flap like a bird?"

"No, I think that would be impossible. But you've seen birds soaring with their wings perfectly still, somehow getting lift out of the air, so you know we can fly without beating wings. The wings will be simple, almost flat, one on top of the other, like a box kite, but without any side covering. Langley doesn't do it like that, he's set one wing in front of the other. I'm not sure that's the way to do it, it's not as strong. But the most important thing is that there has to be some way to control the machine, to make it do what you want it to do, when you want to do it."

Wilbur's voice had risen and his face took on an unaccustomed animation. "I've just about finished the new machine—I've got the cloth all sewed, and the wood and wire ready for the struts. All I need is the spars, and I'll get them later. I'm going to fly this machine just like a kite, at first, just like I did last year."

Orville chimed in. "It worked pretty good. Will had little control sticks that he used, running a line from them up to the tips of the kite. When you twisted it one way, the tips on one side bent up, and the tips on the other bent down, worked like a charm."

"Get the box, Orv," Wilbur commanded, "it's upstairs beneath my bed." Up and down the stairs quickly, Orville handed Wilbur the box, looking apprehensively at his father. He hadn't asked permission to leave the table, but the old man was too intrigued to object.

The long slender square box still smelled strongly of the rubber bicycle inner tube that it once housed. Now Wilbur held it at arm's length in front of him, facing his father. "Look, Pop, when I twist it like this, one end goes up and one end goes down."

Bishop Wright stared at the box and at Wilbur and bit his lip. This was going to be a flying machine, this bit of soiled cardboard. He gave a quick prayer for patience. He had to take it easy with Wilbur, who had been frail for years after that stupid accident down at the lake at the Soldiers' Home. He'd been skating with the other boys, playing shinny, when he was hit in the mouth with one of the sticks. The blow had knocked out some of his front teeth, but more than that, it seemed to knock the stuffing out of him—he just withered up, heart palpitating, no interest in life. Since then he had wavered back and forth between life and death, sometimes getting lively enough to go out to his old club, the Ten Dayton Boys, other times just holing up in his room, hibernating, not eating right. Did not graduate from high school, wouldn't go to college. That rascal Roosh wrote and asked if Wilbur was going to be a housewife all his life. The only thing that seemed to bring him around was Susan's illness. He came right back to serve her, and since then he had been doing a little better. Maybe this flying machine thing would be good for him, get him out in the fresh air, force him to do some hard physical labor. Orv was much stronger, even though he'd been sick too, just four years before when the typhoid fever got him. When it came to working, if Wilbur was soft, Orville was solid, and he had a good imagination, too; he saw how things fit together.

"That's the secret to flying, eh? One end turns up, the other end turns down."

"Well, it's not the secret to flying, but I think it's the secret to control. I've been watching birds all my life, and this is what they do."

"Don't think I've ever seen a bird with a box for a wing. But you mentioned this German man, Lilienthal; you are using his tables? And didn't he kill himself, jumping off a hill?"

"Yes he did, Father, but his tables must be good, or he could not have made all the glides. His problem was the way he tried to control his machine, shifting his weight back and forth, swinging his legs to keep the balance. That was the problem, he just couldn't control it. With my method, twisting the wing tips, I won't have to do that; I'll just sit there and twist the wings the way I twisted that box."

The bishop stared at him, trying to mask his emotions, sputtering, "Twisted that" as four sets of eyes stared at him, three at the table, one peering in from the door. Finally he composed himself. The boy was daft, but he was his boy, so that was it.

"Ah, then I see. Orv, are you going with him? Can you get away from the shop?"

Orville had been running his finger around the top of his milk glass, making it hum. He started when his father spoke, almost spilling the milk.

"Yes, I've been working extra hard, building up stock. I can take off, and Katharine can keep an eye on the store for us. I'm not much on flying machines, but I'd like to see how Wilbur works it out. And I want to get away from Katharine's cooking and nagging."

She kicked him under the table. "No you don't. I'm going too."

The bishop's hand came down in a tremendous slap that shook the plates, splashing Orv's milk across the tablecloth. "That's the last thing you'll do, young lady. I didn't send you off to Oberlin College to desert me in my old age."

Carrie peeked in from the kitchen. The three younger Wrights were sitting like children, petrified with fear as the Bishop, livid with rage, raised his hand and slapped the table again. "Never, never, never! You can teach school, but you are not going traipsing across the country, out camping and doing the good Lord knows what else." He crumpled the napkin in his hand, glaring at her ferociously, daring her to speak.

Katharine burst into tears and ran from the room, plunging out into the side yard. Somehow, the bishop had learned of her romance with Henry. He had let her know with little hints, but this is the first time he had ever revealed how he felt about it. She felt ashamed and humiliated, and she hated him with a passion she knew was wrong and sinful.

Orv stood up to go after her.

"Sit down, Orville. I'll not have you popping away from the table every two seconds." Then turning to Wilbur, "Son, I think it's a good idea that you go to North Carolina. I want you to take Orv with you. You wouldn't be safe there alone, you could hurt yourself, I know it. Orv will be a big help. He's good with his hands, and he's a better cook than you are."

Shaken, Wilbur nodded. At least he and Orv and his blasted good hands could get away. Poor Katharine.

In the kitchen, Carrie sampled the stew. It tasted pretty good to her. The Wrights were strange. They never used any bad language, not even damn or hell, like she had heard at home, but they got mad at each other much more than her folks did. Really mad. It was all very strange.

CHAPTER

6

From the pitching, sea-swept deck of Israel Perry's flat-bottomed scow, the *Curlicue*, the memory of Carrie's stew caused Wilbur's stomach to rumble with desire. Faint with hunger and dying for sleep, he bent down and bailed, trying to keep up with the water forcing its way between the rotting planks of Perry's boat.

The trip had turned from pleasure to pain. His train had pulled out of Dayton on Thursday night and dropped him off at Old Point Comfort twenty-four easy hours later. He'd loved the ride, watching the countryside go by, knowing every mile was a mile between him and 7 Hawthorne Street and Milton Wright. Then he'd taken a steamer across Hampton Roads to Norfolk, where he'd tried to find eighteen-foot lengths of spruce for the wing spars of his glider. There weren't any, and he had to settle for sixteen-foot lengths of white pine. Now they made his baggage even more awkward to handle.

The next leg of the train trip was short, carrying him to Elizabeth City, where he had to find a boat to carry him and his gear across Albemarle Sound to the outer banks where the by-now-mythical Kitty Hawk was supposed to be.

It took him three days to find a boat, and then it was the *Curlicue*, a dirty hulk with rotting sails, sprung seams, and worn ropes whose rolling movements matched its name. One look at the cabin sent him back on deck in a hurry—he didn't mind a few friendly fleas, but the cabin was crawling with roaches and worse.

At that moment, however, it seemed certain that Wilbur, Perry, his less-than-able seaman, and the vermin were all going to drown together, as the roaring winds—the very reason he was there at all—threatened to swamp the boat with waves that came straight over the bow to drench them, then swapped around to poop them from the rear.

The *Curlicue* had a flat bottom, good for shallow waters, but dangerous on the sound, as the winds grew from strong to gale force. Lightning flashed repeatedly, and first the foresail, then the mainsail tore away, flopping across the deck in the breeze and cutting off movement. As the schooner's nose wandered before the wind, it began to heel over so far that Wilbur was convinced it was going over.

Perry was a better seaman than a boat-keeper, and he managed to keep the hulk afloat, fighting the wind as best he could. Finally he gave in and ran before it, using only the remaining jib to kick around and bring the wind directly on the stern. They reached a point where he could cross over, and Perry took shelter in a North River cove. When the anchor dropped, the three men looked at each other and nodded, knowing they had come very close to dying together on the sound.

Wilbur felt he had become a sailor overnight, and he dropped gratefully to the deck, falling asleep instantly. They stayed in the cove for another twenty-four hours, bobbing at the end of the anchor, wet through and through and still bailing every hour, their knees stiffening from resisting the slap, slap, slap roll of the water. As hungry as he was, Wilbur refused the mess of porridge and dried peas that Perry offered as food, warmed in a dirty pot in the filthy galley. Good old Katharine had slipped a jar of strawberry jam in his bag, and he rationed it out to himself, a jackknife blade's worth at a time.

At nine that night, six days and three hours after he had steamed out of Dayton, Wilbur and his bags, baggage and spars were tied up at a makeshift dock on the Kitty Hawk shoreline. He was cold, cramped, and starving, hankering more than ever for some of Carrie's stew, but suddenly and blissfully happy. There were a few lights visible, but he decided to spend one more night sleeping on the deck, grateful that the schooner was not rolling and that if it started to sink, he could just step off to the dock.

The trip to Kitty Hawk had started in May, when he had written the great Octave Chanute for suggestions as to where the winds could be found to conduct flying experiments. Somewhat to his surprise, Chanute had answered immediately and graciously, suggesting beaches in California and Florida—both too far for a Dayton boy to travel. A letter to the chief of the weather bureau brought different results; it was clear that the winds at Kitty Hawk, North Carolina were perfect. It was the work of a moment to follow up with a letter to the weather bureau at Kitty Hawk itself. Joe Dosher, the telegrapher at the station, confirmed the winds were good and that the beach was perfect, a mile wide with no trees and plenty of sand. Dosher circulated the letter, stirring the little village to a state of excitement usually associated with a hurricane, a ship running aground, or a bit of smuggling. The principal politician in town, William J. Tate, also replied, telling him of an eighty-foot hill that might be useful, and offering to help in anyway he could.

The next morning, Wilbur struggled up the sandy path with his bags, certain that Kitty Hawk was the most beautiful sandy waste he had ever seen, and happy that not only did he have some six hundred miles of reasonably comfortable rail travel between him and his father, he had the rough trip across Albemarle Sound as a buffer. He would have paid a lot to see how his father got along with Israel Perry.

As he reached the top of the gentle rise, William Tate burst out of his door with a cry and ran down to help him, grabbing his bag and talking a blue streak about the beauties Wilbur would find in this paradise, Kitty Hawk. And the first bit of paradise was a meal of ham and eggs, cooked with a smile by Tate's wife Addie. In a few days he would learn just how generous a breakfast it had been, for both ham and eggs were hard to come by in Kitty Hawk, where meat was rarely seen, and fish, fresh or salted, was a treat.

In a way it was like eating at home with his father, only pleasant, for the Tates were dueling talkers, obviously glad to have a stranger in their house, each one grabbing the end of the other's sentences and running with them so that all Wilbur had to do was nod and chew. Addie was nominally the postmistress, but it was obvious that Bill Tate ran his household, the post office, and the entire community with an iron hand, for he was the notary public, county commissioner and part-time fisherman. A pretty woman, plainly dressed, Addie was a housewife, able to help with the fishing if she had to, but mostly concerned about keeping the house clean in the blowing sand and jumping when Bill spoke.

By modest Hawthorne Street standards, the unpainted two-story home was no beauty, but in Kitty Hawk it was one of the best in town. As he appreciatively accepted a second helping of eggs, glistening with bacon grease just the way he liked them, Wilbur listened and looked around, impressed both by the cleanliness of the house after the loathsome *Curlicue*, and its absolute lack of decoration. There were no rugs, no pictures, no paint anywhere—it was as starkly utilitarian as the workshop on South William Street. He soon realized that the Tates and the house had a lot in common—good solid no-nonsense construction with no attempts at adornment. To his surprise, Wilbur judged them to be physically attractive and, despite the simple lives they led, surprisingly well informed. Both took official pride in the simple board sign on the front of their plain wood porch. Hand lettered, it read *Kitty Hawk, N.C. Post Office*, and it conferred status on them.

"You can stay with us for a while, Mr. Wright, till you get your camp set up. The neighbors will be wanting to meet you." And indeed they were; the word had spread quickly through the little fishing village that the flying machine man was in town at last, and everybody who could find an excuse came up the sandy path to the Tate house. Bill took Wilbur around to the lighthouse to meet the crew there, proud members of the United States Lifesaving Service. In a matter of days, he knew most of the villagers by sight. They were all friendly and respectful, calling him Mr. Wright, and pleased to shake his hand. It was novel for Wilbur; he was liked well enough back in Dayton, but no one crossed the street for the pleasure of shaking his hand.

What they really enjoyed, though, was to watch him working in the Tates' barren front yard, using Addie's highly-prized sewing machine, one of the few in the village, to refashion the shiny white French sateen fabric he'd brought along. When he had been preparing the glider in Dayton, he'd figured on making the wings eighteen feet long, to get the lift he needed. Lilienthal's tables had told him that eighteen-foot wings would lift the glider and him in a wind of fifteen to twenty miles per hour. He would need more wind now, with only sixteen-foot spars and he had to redo the fabric covering to fit, splitting it in the middle, cutting off two feet of cloth, then sewing it back together. The village ladies laughed, politely and behind their hands, to see him working the pedal and guiding the fabric through the sewing machine, knowing that there was not one man in the village who would have done such woman's work in private, much less out in front of the house, in plain view. They also knew that not one of them had ever had a dress made out of as fine a material as the flying machine feller was sewing into what looked like a long square bag. It made them like Wilbur even better; he might be crazy about flying, but he wasn't afraid to do a little sewing, and he used good cloth. They were disappointed when he carefully folded the piece he had cut out, and put it away—they would have had a dozen uses for it. Wilbur liked them too, because they kept their distance; the men came up and shook his hand, but the women were shy, and that's the way he liked his women—shy and not too close by.

Wilbur crowded the Tates' residence, and when Orville showed up a few days later, it was time to pitch the tent and start camping out. They selected a sandy rise far enough from the Tates' that they had some privacy—there was no privy, so answering nature's calls had to be done in the open. A pair of windblown scrub trees flanked the site, and for as far as you could see, little clutches of razor-sharp grass tried hard to restrain the wind-drifted sand.

Putting up the tent in the wind was not easy, even after they had anchored one end to a scrub oak. The tent was about twenty feet long and half that distance wide, and they worked swiftly to peg it down, then ran guy wires from an external frame to make it solid. They fixed simple meals on a gasoline stove that Tate had brought back for them from a trip to Elizabeth City, used acetylene lamps for light, and went to bed early. Water was the only genuine problem, for Orville's bout with typhoid fever had put the fear of God in them, and they drank no water that was not boiled. Every time the wind blew they worried about the glider, tethered outside, and more than once they had to dig it out of drifted sand.

Life was primitive, but it was free, and the two brothers were kings in their tent-castle. Orville liked the simplicity of Kitty Hawk, and turned to ordinary camp duties with a good-natured enthusiasm, whipping up biscuits for breakfast, and making good gravy to go with the bacon at night. He still was not as convinced as Wilbur about the practicality of a flying machine, and he would join his brother in watching the buzzards and the gulls circling endlessly above the sand and sea. It beat selling rolls of tire tape and fixing flats back in Dayton. The only thing that would have made it better would have been Katharine's sunny presence; he missed her so much, writing her long letters almost every day, sometimes twice. She would have loved it there, away from home and all the problems, all the dreary housework that she hated. In a way she was here, for he never looked at a sunset or watched a gull twist and turn over the water without thinking of how he would tell her about it in the next letter—she liked him to be funny. He had to be careful, though; the old man thought nothing of reading someone's mail, so he kept the letters light and joking.

Will was itching to get out to test the glider, and by October 3rd it was ready, the thin wooden rods that gave curvature to the two sixteen-foot-long wings inserted, the twelve tall struts in place, the wires guyed up so that the wingtips would bend. Assembled, the glider had a taut appearance, but it gave readily to the touch; the main members were not fastened together with nuts and bolts, but rather held together with stout cord and then tucked into the folds sewn into the fabric. When they had to carry it to the beach, the wind was blowing, and Tate asked one of the men from the lifesaving station to come along and give them a hand. It was a difficult job, for even with four men holding on, wind gave the wings life and the glider reared and bucked, wanting to take off on its own.

Down by the lifesaving station the wind was kicking up a steady twenty miles an hour, just what they wanted. Bill Tate was so ready to help that he was letting his other responsibilities slide, and Addie would not let him forget it. No matter. He was captivated by the flying machine—just as long as he didn't have to do any flying himself. But nobody did any flying at first. The Wrights intended to fly it as a kite until they had gathered some experience—then Wilbur would climb aboard.

The new machine had a simple beauty. Wilbur had rounded the tips with wooden bows, so that each glistening white wing now spanned more than seventeen feet. The front rudder, a smaller flat surface in front of the wing and supported by struts, was intended to control the up and down movement of the craft. Turns would be done by the "inner-tube box" method, with Wilbur moving wires that would cause the wing tips on one side to turn up while those on the other turned down, just like a birdie as Orville always said. There was no vertical rudder—Wilbur didn't see any vertical rudders on birds, and was sure that none was needed.

The first tests were like those of the kite from the previous year, unmanned, using guide ropes to control it from the ground, feeling the drumming wings generate lift that threatened to rip the glider out of their hands and send it tumbling along the beach. Wilbur was satisfied with the instant response to the controls, and concentrated mainly on keeping the aircraft level with the front rudder.

As the days passed, Orv's mood soared with the joys of Kitty Hawk. The meals were pretty bad at first, mostly biscuits and bacon, until they went into the tiny general store that Ben Calhoun ran. The Wrights bought all of his eggs—he had sixteen, ordinarily sold to the locals at one or two at a time—and lots of his canned goods, paying cash.

Always gregarious when there were no women around, Orville joked a bit then asked: "Mr. Calhoun, would you be our agent for food?"

Calhoun looked at them blankly.

"I mean, why don't we give you a standing order to buy anything you can find—ducks, eggs, chickens, fish, canned goods, whatever else you can find—and we'll pay in advance. That way you won't have to carry us and we'll get some variety in our diet. We've had enough biscuits and bacon to last a lifetime."

Wilbur watched him with quiet pleasure and whispered, "Canned peaches and tomatoes, and we're down to our last can of condensed milk. And coffee."

Calhoun puffed with importance. Here were these two flying machine men, doing cash-in-advance business, no questions asked about price. That was something! In the days that followed Calhoun neglected his regular customers, twice making trips to Elizabeth City to be sure the Wrights had everything they needed. For the first time in their lives, the Wrights were the rich boys; they had more money in their pockets than most of the Kitty Hawkers had ever had in the bank. Wilbur worried for a while that other people in Kitty Hawk would be offended when Calhoun went out on his buying spree but strangely enough, no one seemed to resent it. The sheer drama of having two polite strangers from the north choosing Kitty Hawk to try their flying machine was overwhelming. Nothing, not even a shipwreck with lots of cargo to fight over, could be so exciting. They thought it was sort of fitting that anybody crazy enough to come down and try to fly ought to have all they wanted to eat—they might not be eating for long.

But the thing that really lifted Orville's spirits was an increasing interest in the glider. The more he saw it, flailing on the end of the string, the biggest kite he'd ever seen, the more he liked it. And as Orv's spirits rose, Wilbur's sank. He'd worked out what was needed back in Dayton, but there was something wrong. They were flying the glider with weights of chain aboard, and it just was not performing like it should, not even when they built a derrick something like the one Lilienthal had used, using a counterweight to offset the weight of the glider. Theoretically, the more lift they had, the higher the glider would fly. The very first attempts told them it was impractical; they'd kill themselves for sure using the derrick. But Wilbur was in agony. He had made his calculations carefully and checked them over. There was nothing wrong with his mathematics; there had to be something fundamentally wrong in the information he was using and he could not tell what it was.

Months ago Orville had suggested that they build two gliders, each slightly different. Wilbur had said no, and he was glad now. All they had was invested in this one machine, and it alone was teaching them more than they could absorb.

"Orv, we're not getting half the lift we are supposed to. Why, to fly with me aboard, we'll need winds of thirty miles per hour or more, which is too dangerous, it could kill me. Something's wrong. We need bigger wings, or we need to change the curve, maybe get more lift."

"Let's give up on this kite-flying and go on down to the hills, do like Lilienthal and Chanute did, run down a hill and lift off that way."

On October 18th, they carried the glider to a little hill that rose up about a mile away. Wilbur pulled his brother aside and said, "Before I get in that thing, Orv, let's just try tossing it down the hill see what happens. We can fix the front rudder so that it doesn't move."

Grunting, pushing against the soft sand, the two men ran forward down the hill, each one holding a wingtip. "Now!" yelled Wilbur, and they both let go, sending the glider on a smooth glide of thirty feet or so that ended in a spray of sand. They worked hard for two hours, going down the hill, lugging the glider back up, their ankles straining in the soft sand, then tossing the glider again. Sometimes the glides were quite long, reaching out as much as fifty feet, and twice they were much too short, ending in a frame-shaking crash. After one of these, Orville examined the glider closely and glanced up at Wilbur with real appreciation. "Pretty clever, Will, I have to admit it. I thought the way you built this thing was too loose—it would never work in a bicycle, you know that. But it doesn't break, the fabric distributes the load, and the framework just rattles around. I have to hand it to you."

Wilbur flushed; Orville rarely said something so positive. Usually he found something funny to say, some sly dig that made people laugh.

"I've got to keep it simple, Orv, or it will get away from me. I'm just going to take this flying business one step at a time, build on what I know, find out what I don't know."

Bill Tate joined them, and after a few more test glides, Wilbur licked his finger and held it up. "There's enough wind. I'm going to try her."

Pausing only to turn his cap to the rear, Wilbur stood within the lower wing, in an area he had left uncovered, holding onto a rib on each side. He lifted himself up and lay down flat, his hips on the crossbar between the two end ribs, his feet in place on a bar that moved the wingtips up and down, one hand grasping the front spar, his other tight on the stick that controlled the front rudder.

Orv and Tate took their place, one at each wingtip, each man with a twenty-foot coil of rope ready to pay out.

Wilbur took a deep breath, then said, "Let's go." Orville and Tate slogged across the sand, into the wind, until the wind turned the glider from two sagging superimposed flat surfaces into a powerful giant of lift, exerting a tremendous force, something far beyond anything Wilbur had ever known or anticipated. Surprised, Orv and Tate yelled as their ropes ran through their hands, burning them; they gripped the ropes tight, feeling the glider pulling them, ready to yank them off the ground, not willing to let go, knowing if they did that Wilbur would crash in an instant.

In flight for the first time, Wilbur was terrified, overcontrolling on the front rudder, bobbing the glider up and down; he could feel the lift too, threatening to sweep him right on up and over to crash him straight into the ground. If he eased the control bar forward, the ground seemed to slam up at him; if he pulled back, the glider soared, jerking the two men on the ground almost off their feet. It was worse than any horse he'd ever ridden, worse than Perry's schooner in the storm; it was like riding a cyclone bareback.

The glider drummed into the wind, flying fifteen feet above the ground, not moving forward, just trying to go higher, Tate and Orville were more in control now, paying out the rope. Wilbur still could not keep the nose from bobbing up and down, couldn't get the control centered, was unable to smooth out the ride. Suddenly the glider pitched up and Wilbur screamed: "Hey! Hey! Get me down." The two men pulled on their ropes and in seconds the glider was down, with Wilbur's nose inches above the sand.

Wilbur crawled out, face white with fear. "Scared me, Orv. I just got scared, it reared up and I thought I was going to crash."

Orv slipped his hand over his brother's shoulder. "Scared me too! Will, I thought we'd lost it right there, and that you were going to break your neck for sure. Lucky Tate here knew what to do." Bill Tate, accustomed to respect but not to praise, glowed.

"You too, Orv, you both did just right. We'll test this machine a few more times without anybody on board, then I'll try it again."

That night, as Wilbur slept, Orv found his voice again in another of his thousand-word letters to Katharine. He could argue with Wilbur and joke with the Kitty Hawkers, but he could be himself only with Katharine, covering the day's events, pouring out his heart to her about the gliding, about the natives, about the food and the storms. He had not heard back from her from any of his previous letters and did not expect to; just writing her was a joy and a relief. He hoped it would not cause any problem with Pop; Katharine always tried to be the first to get the mail, and she would know better than to let him see the letters.

He thought for a minute, then wrote, "This is just before the battle, sister; just before the squalls begin. About two or three nights a week we have to crawl up at ten or eleven o'clock, just to hold the tent down. When one of these 45-mile nor'easters strikes us, you can depend upon it, there is little sleep in our camp for the night." He liked to mix it up, the way he knew she liked it; a little drama, a little joking about their diet. "We are expecting to have a big blowout tomorrow, when we get those two chickens. We have just appointed the Kitty Hawk storekeeper to buy us anything he can get hold of." He toyed with the idea of writing, "but at least it beats Carrie's cooking," but that might upset her. Carrie was her protégée. He wrote some more about how cold it was, and told her he was coming home Tuesday, then added a P.S.: "Ullam is in bed asleep while I'm writing."

When they awoke the next morning they went through the usual rapid drill of fixing breakfast then washing the dishes in the sand, pure abrasive silica, then wiping the shining plates and pans with a cloth before putting them away. They were quiet, no arguments, no joking, for they knew this had to be the day. Finally, Wilbur said "We need a bigger hill, one where I can actually practice some real free-flight gliding. I asked Bill Tate to come by and help us carry the glider." Four miles south of their camp, on a sandy beach that stretched between Kitty Hawk and Nags Head, were three massive dunes—the Kill Devil Hills. The largest hill was shaped like a half-moon and reached up almost eighty feet above the sea that constantly raged at the shore. One side of the hill sloped gently down, perfect for a glider launch.

Bill Tate showed up early, his regular work either done or pushed aside. He'd hired a rig to carry them and the glider down to the hills. They unloaded near the top of the big Kill Devil Hill. Orv and Wilbur stood side by side for a moment, surveying the long gentle barren slope that stretched toward the water, Wilbur wondering if the combination of slope and sand would be enough to get them airborne, Orv worrying about the climb back after a long glide. Finally Orv nudged Will and pointed—at the water's edge was the little cluster of rough buildings that housed the U.S. Weather Bureau and the lifesaving station. Will nodded and said, "Good, maybe they can be witnesses when I really start flying."

Orv shot back, "They must know some medicine; maybe they can fix you up if you crash."

Their experiments had been safe so far, the greatest risk a twisted ankle in the soft sand. Both brothers knew that when Wilbur climbed aboard, things could change drastically. Wilbur didn't plan to fly any higher than their un-manned gliding flights, but a crash from even ten feet high could be deadly—and they both knew it.

When they transported the glider, the wings went as a unit, the two surfaces stoutly bound together with the struts and the wiring. The front rudder was carried separately, but was attached to the wings easily. As Wilbur climbed on board, lying flat, the sun was climbing toward its zenith, and the wind was holding steady, kicking up whitecaps offshore and blowing a thin, steady stream of sand into their faces.

Orv and Bill grabbed the glider's wingtips and ran forward, letting the glider gain a life of its own, grabbing lift from the air. As they ran, the glider began to pick up speed, flashing over the sand, five feet above the ground, Wilbur watching the front rudder tremble in response to his corrections. When the glider was tugging at their arms, ready to go faster than they could run, the two men let go, and Wilbur flashed on, accelerating still more, truly flying now, holding a fairly steady course for almost one hundred feet before gently dropping back into a spray of sand. The wind streamed sand into his face and emotion streamed through his body in a galvanizing rush. He was doing what he had planned to do, he was airborne, he was flying, he didn't care if it was dangerous, he was flying.

Orv and Tate ran whooping down the hill; this was genuine flying, they had seen it, and Wilbur was up and dancing too, happy with the machine, even though he knew he knew it was flawed, that it had not yet performed as he knew it should. In the course of that one day, Wilbur made another dozen flights, some reaching out horizontally to four hundred feet, as far as many of Lilienthal's flights.

Now Wilbur flew without fear, there was no room for it as he soaked up the sensation of whipping over the ground, never higher than ten or twelve feet, watching the beach grasses fly by, conscious sometimes of the shouts of encouragement from Orville or even of the sudden cry of a gull, but always learning, always fighting to understand just what his control movements did, and what the wind did to the glider. In the few seconds of each flight, he learned a little more; it was like riding a bicycle, you needed very little pressure to make the controls work, and you had to feel like the glider was part of you. Yet when he had touched down, when there was the welcome scrape of sand that signaled another safe glide, he felt a profound relief and a momentary exhaustion. The combination reminded him of how pleased he was to be finished at one of his rare public talks—glad to have done it, happier to have it over, and always sorry that he had not done better. It was exactly the same with the gliding so far.

After the last gliding flight, Wilbur took Orv aside. "Orville, I think we've got all we can get out of this. We've only had this one day of gliding, but I know that there is something wrong with our figures, and we have to sort it out."

Orv lowered his head, drawing a circle in the sand with his toe. It was always like this. Wilbur would drop into the "we" mode when he wanted something. When he was talking about flying to outsiders it was usually just the "I" mode.

"Let's go home and figure it out. Then we'll build a bigger glider, and come back here next year. You can do some flying yourself, maybe."

Orville flopped down on the sand, gazing out at the gulls effortlessly dipping at the shore's edge, his back braced by a log windswept so long that the sand had polished all the bark away, leaving only a shining pocked surface.

"I don't think so, Will; you are doing a good job, and I'm not so sure I want to risk my neck. And I don't think Pop will let both of us come back."

Will bent over and dusted the sand from his knees. "Orv, I'm coming back, come heck or high water, and you should too. This is our chance to do something, to be somebody, to stop being Bishop Wright's boys and start being us."

He waited for the usual argument; Orv was a scrapper, quick on the comeback, and ready to go for the jugular in an instant. They were never closer than when they were arguing, almost on the point of fighting, no matter what the subject. Now, though, Orv didn't speak, just looked miserable.

Wilbur went on. "Well, if you don't of course, I'll understand. You've got a life to live, and the shop can't run by itself. Besides, Bill Tate has come a long way just these few weeks. I can count on him, I know; he's spending more time with us than with Addie."

The words "Bill Tate" ground into Orville's ear like the sand-laden wind—he was not going to let some Kitty Hawker get the glory of flying.

"Don't worry about the business. Katharine can handle it; we'll get somebody to help. I'm coming back with you, and maybe I'll do a little gliding too."

Wilbur bent down to pick up the wingtip—and to hide his smile. Orv didn't get hooked often, but this time, Tate was the bait.

They moved swiftly to pack their things, making many notes about what they should bring next time to live a little better. They struck the tent and moved all their baggage to the water's edge where Israel Perry and the loathsome *Curlicue* were waiting to take them back across the sound.

Back on the low hill at Kitty Hawk, there was one last ceremonial flight of their $14.95 glider. They carried it to the top of a dune, then tossed it. It made a short, erratic flight, twisting to land at the bottom. As they stood there, side by side, they felt both fulfillment and challenge. Unconsciously, they leaned together against the wind, aware that in these short weeks at Kitty Hawk they had grown closer than they ever had during their lifetime in Dayton. Neither man spoke of it, but both felt an almost mystical kinship that transcended their blood relationship, a kinship embodied in the stout white wings of their flying machine.

Addie Tate watched them, hesitating to interrupt, but anxious to make a claim. When they seemed to stir, she asked, "Are you taking your glider back with you?"

Wilbur smiled at her. She had been a good friend, and they had been a bother, he knew. "No, Addie, we're just going to pull a few metal fittings off and leave it here. Will it be in your way?" He was joking; the glider was just a dot on the vast windblown landscape, and it would be gone in weeks, covered by the ever-moving sand that made houses and trees disappear in the course of a year.

Then, sensing what she wanted, he said, "If you know anyone who would like to have the fabric from it, please let them have it." She smiled shyly. That afternoon Addie Tate came out to the glider with a pair of scissors and quickly stripped it of the French sateen fabric. A good hand-wash in an open tub got rid of the sand and dirt embedded in it. By the time the Wrights were back in Dayton, her sewing machine had turned it into two dresses for her daughters, the best they had ever had, and, forever unknown to her neighbors, into two sets of knickers for herself.

CHAPTER

7

The long trip back home was punctuated with eating as much as possible and arguing about what was wrong with the glider. It simply had not performed as Wilbur's calculations had predicted. They had stopped talking to each other by Elizabeth City, picked up the argument again as soon as the train to Dayton had pulled out, and stayed awake the whole time analyzing every one of the flights.

Orv, as always, got under Wilbur's skin with his insistence that he knew intuitively what the problem was, implying that all of Wilbur's scribbled figures were interesting, but not important.

They sat side by side in the day coach, alternately silent then speaking at the same time, their voices raising so that an older man sitting on the other side of the aisle called the conductor aside and talked to him. The conductor didn't say anything, just looked at them meaningfully. For a while they were quiet again, watching the scenery roll by, dreading the return to Dayton, but still chewing over their disappointment in their glider.

Orv stood up in the aisle, not holding onto anything, just spreading his feet to adjust to the rhythm of the rails, turning his back on the old man. He reopened the conversation with a touchy subject—expenses. "What do you think you have invested in this project by now? We know the glider cost a nickel less than fifteen dollars. But what were the other expenses?"

Will nodded at the pertinence of the question. That was the first thing Pop would ask. He consulted his little black book, and added up some figures.

"Everything, including the food we left behind with the Tates, comes to one hundred ninety-five dollars and fifty-eight cents. That's really not too bad, considering our railroad fares, what old Israel Perry hit us for, and the high prices in Kitty Hawk."

"No, that's not bad, especially since we paid back Pop his one hundred and fifty dollars." Orville waited, then said, "Will, on this other thing, how the glider flew. It boils down to size. You didn't have enough wing area. Next time, let's get the spars in Dayton and make wings twenty-four feet, heck, thirty feet long."

With the pained expression that is an older brother's stock in trade, Wilbur laid out the lift figures once again. "Maybe, Orv. But maybe not. I think it's the curve of the wing. We had it too low, way too low. Next time, instead of one in twenty-three, we'll go one in twelve. That's what Lilienthal used, and that's what we should have used." Orville knew he meant that the ribs had curved up one inch for every twenty-three inches they were long. One in twelve was almost the arc of a circle.

"Yeah, and you'll kill yourself just like he did. Too much curve and you'll get no distance in the glide. Would you put up a big shield on a bicycle if you were racing it? No, you'd keep everything clean, wax that bald head of yours, and duck down and pedal. It's the same with gliding; you can't have too much hanging out in the wind, you won't go anywhere. Why are you lying down instead of sitting up or standing? It's to cut down drag. You run the curve up to twelve, it's just like you sitting there all along the wing. Wilbur, you are just not thinking straight, haven't been since you first tried gliding. There's something wrong with your noodle, Will, something that just won't go away."

"I didn't see you rushing to do any gliding."

" 'Course not, I'm too smart for that. Maybe next year, though, if you'll listen to me, if you'll let me get some ideas of my own in it. It can't just be your party, you know. You are always going on about 'my machine' and 'my glides.' "

"Ah, so that's it, I thought so. If li'l Orville can't own the toys, he won't play. You haven't changed a bit."

They started talking again a hundred miles later.

The spat on the train had a lingering effect on Wilbur's thinking, and when he wrote to Octave Chanute, detailing the results of their tests, he was careful to use "we" instead of "I" all through it.

His November 16th letter to Chanute was intended as a courtesy, to tell the man who had been helpful what they had done, but more than that, to get down in writing his insight on what the problem with the glider might have been. Wilbur wrote the letter first on plain paper, than copied it over on the elaborate stationery of the Wright Cycle Company. He wrote in his usual spidery yet legible hand, interspersing the letter with accurate freehand drawings of the ribs and the wing truss, a nice touch, acknowledging that the truss was taken from Chanute's work.

He reviewed the letter, wanting to make sure the main points were clear. First of all, the drag of the airplane, its resistance to the air, was much less than he had thought it would be, and much less than either Chanute or Herring had calculated in their published papers. Second, he thought he had proved the value of lying prone to fly, cutting down the resistance still more. But the third was the most important. There had not been as much lift as he had calculated, and he could not determine why not. Perhaps Chanute could.

After he had mailed the letter, Wilbur walked back into the parlor to find Milton Wright reading the plain paper copy. The bishop was not embarrassed, for his rule was that anything that went on in the house was his business, and any letters were part of that.

The bishop tossed the letter back on the table. "Have you lost what's left of your mind, Wilbur? You are giving this man everything you worked for. All he has to do is copy it, and where are you?"

"Father, Mr. Chanute is an honorable man. He's helped us, like he's helped everybody. I'm doing what I should do to pay him back."

"Everybody's honest until there is a dollar to be made. You wait and see, he'll blab this around, and half the world will be laughing at you for being so stupid as to think you can fly, and the other half will be building a flying machine like yours. The first thing you should have done was take out a patent, before you told anybody anything. After this, I don't know if you could even get a patent."

"There's not much to patent yet, father; we haven't built a real flying machine, we've just built a kite we can glide in for a little way. We are a long way from building a flying machine, and I think Mr. Chanute can help us."

The Bishop's expression softened. "I'm sorry, Wilbur, you are trying to do the right thing, just like I taught you. I was being greedy myself, for you, worrying that you might be cheated. But I tell you, you ought to think about getting a patent as soon as possible. As soon as possible! If you don't, every Johnny-come-lately will latch on to your idea, and maybe even make something better out of it." He patted Wilbur on the shoulder, leaving him standing with the copy of the letter in his hands, furious that his father had read it, yet strangely moved by the pat on the shoulder.

Wilbur was still considering the pat, what it meant, why he felt so strangely about it, when he walked into the bicycle shop to find Orville talking to Charley Taylor.

"Ah, Will, you're just in time, I was talking to Charley here, and he's telling me that he's not too happy with his job over at Dayton Electric."

Wilbur would have preferred to have caught Orville alone and talked to him about his father and the patent, but Charley was related to the shop's landlord, and that meant he had to be kept sweet. "Sorry to hear that Charley, what's the problem?"

Taylor was a workingman, less formal than the Wrights, a plug of tobacco or a cigar in his mouth all the time. He waited a moment, then said, "No problem, I'm just not used to bossing people. I'd rather be working with my hands."

"Will, you know we've been talking about taking on somebody to run this place while we go off to Kitty Hawk. Maybe Charley here's our man. What do you say, Charley, what would it take to get you to come here from Dayton Electric?"

Charley blew a long column of smoke and assumed a thoughtful expression. The Wrights were nice boys but hard taskmasters, he knew that. If he were going to come to work for them, it would cost them.

"I'll tell you what. I'll come for thirty cents an hour, and I get an hour off for lunch every day."

"Let's step outside, Orv, and talk this over. Be with you in a second, Charley."

Outside Orv pinched his nose—neither man liked cigar smoke.

"That's eighteen dollars a week, Will; that's pretty steep."

"I know. I wish someone was paying me eighteen dollars a week. But like you said, we are going to need somebody to run the shop while we go to Kitty Hawk. And Charley's a good worker and honest as the day is long. We both know that."

"What will Pop say?"

"He doesn't come down to the shop too often. I say we just don't tell him till we go over the books next fall. By then it will be too late."

"Katharine doesn't like him a bit, you know that."

Orv stiffened a little. It was bad enough crossing Pop, but they would never fool Katharine; she'd be on them in a minute. Still, they needed someone.

"Let's do it!"

CHAPTER
8

In Chicago, Chanute read Wilbur's letter several times, trying to make sure that he understood what the Wright boy had done and what it was he was asking. If it had been a newspaper account he would not have believed it; it seemed impossible that they could have such success on their very first attempt at flying. True, they had the benefit of his years of experience, and of all the published material, but no one else had ever done so well so swiftly. He had spent years experimenting, and never had he done better than their first effort.

Chanute was good-spirited; he was happy for them, but even happier for the other experimenters, Herring, Edward Huffaker, Blohm and others, who would be delighted to learn what the Wrights had done. Langley, however, might not be so pleased. He'd have to handle that carefully. Best of all, he could use Wilbur's information in the article he was doing for *Cassier's* magazine; it would round out his discussion on his own work.

In the following weeks there was a flurry of letters, and in the first of them, Wilbur skillfully and diplomatically told Chanute what he could and could not say in the article about their work. He sought to excuse the exercise of privacy by stating that he was not sure of the results, but it was evident that he wished to keep secret the heart of their work, the system of control.

Chanute realized then that these were indeed two bright young men from Dayton, brighter than he had first thought, and brighter by far than Herring, or even Huffaker. He knew both of these men well, they had both worked as assistants to him and to Langley. The

Wrights were not scientists like Langley, obviously, but there was something about them, some innate quality of character, that made them vastly appealing. Yet they had pride; Wilbur asked that they not be referred to as "the Wright Brothers" in his article, but as "Messers. Wilbur and Orville Wright." "Messers.," where had a Dayton boy picked that up? And they were confident, Wilbur at least, for he did not hesitate to correct Chanute's mathematical computations in his letter. If the corrections had not been made in such a friendly tone, they might have seemed impertinent. As it was, these were merely letters between two colleagues, albeit one a man with forty years experience in the most demanding engineering, and one a stripling of thirty-something.

Still there was no doubt that the Wrights showed promise. If he could bring them in with the others, get everyone learning from each other, maybe the problem of flight could be solved. With Langley's backing, Herring's energy (put under proper control, of course), and the Wrights' original thinking, they might be able to achieve manned flight. He would have to run the project, of course, as they were all "Chanute's boys" to some degree, even Langley, although he would not admit it.

It all depended on whether he could successfully court the Wrights. Chanute knew intuitively that he would have to make himself indispensable to them. Wilbur's last letter had inquired about an anemometer; he would lend them his own. And a visit, that was the thing; the mountain would come to Mohammed, but in Dayton, not Mecca.

Chanute had arrived after dinner on June 26th, and spent the evening in the parlor chatting with Orville and Wilbur, while Bishop Wright sat in the background, ostensibly reading a book of prayer, but in fact listening to every word of the exchange. Much of it was over his head. The terms—lift, drag, angle of incidence—all meant nothing to him. But he saw that Chanute was taking his two sons seriously, paying them respect. The boys, of course, were attentive and respectful to Chanute, but that was to be expected. If Chanute thought they were sensible, then there must be something in it. The man was a legend in railroading, and had made more than one fortune in a variety of businesses.

It was not so easy for Katharine, for her role was to keep on Carrie to make sure that the house was perfectly clean, and supervise the next day's luncheon—tomato soup, salad, roast chicken, mashed potatoes, and for dessert a melon. As it turned out, she could have served anything, for none of the men paid any attention to the food. Three of them were far too preoccupied with the subject of flying to notice, and the fourth, Bishop Wright, was too busy assessing Chanute's questions and answers. Chanute seemed like a sensible man, and the boys had told him that he was the preeminent authority on aerial navigation, which was not much, given that no one had navigated anywhere by air yet. It didn't bother the bishop that he did not understand any of the engineering issues, nor even that he had to be quiet and listen. What did bother him was that for all their talk, and all their courtesies, it was obvious that his boys didn't understand Chanute, and Chanute didn't understand his boys. There was a veil there, something between them that they could not penetrate and he could not understand. Strangely too, there was no malevolence, no desire for gain, just an impenetrable misunderstanding, like that of married people with their in-laws.

Chanute left at two o'clock to go to his train; the brothers accompanied him, thanking him for coming, and promising to keep him informed. As Chanute's train left the station, he felt dissatisfied. He had impressed the boys' father, he knew, and that had been no easy task. The brothers were as correct and precise in person as Wilbur's letters had hinted they would be. Yet there was something missing. First of all, they absolutely refused any financial assistance, from him or from anyone else. On other matters, such as having him visit when they returned to Kitty Hawk, they were agreeable, but only conditionally so; it was obvious they had reservations but were too polite to refuse him. And they absolutely did not understand when he told them that others had preceded them with their idea of twisting opposite ends of the wing. He could not have made it any more evident, citing Louis Pierre Mouillard's use of differential drag brakes, which Chanute had helped him patent in 1896. The Wrights merely replied that they had read Mouillard's papers, and there was no relationship. It was so odd, so perverse, that they could be so bright in so many respects and so obstinately dull in this one regard.

As the train pulled out, Wilbur stopped waving and tugged Orville by the arm.

"He just doesn't get it, does he?"

"Nope, not by a long shot. He is a very bright man, no doubt, but he never understood a word of what you were talking about in controlling the machine around all three axes. I thought when you used the bird analogy he would understand, but he did not. Never got a glimmer."

Wilbur squeezed his thin lips into a tighter line. "We can't ignore him, of course; he is extremely helpful, and he can advise us on many things. But I can't get over his total lack of understanding. He thinks you can fly an airplane like you use a pole to move a barge along a shallow river. He doesn't see that it's three-dimensional, not two-dimensional. That's his problem." He waited a moment and went on to the really sensitive issue. "And the nerve of him, wanting to visit and bring along friends to Kitty Hawk."

Orville was tired of the talking and aching for exercise; his arm reached out for a signpost on the sidewalk, and he spun himself around in a full circle. Wilbur stopped to wait for him. "I don't see how we can get out of that, Will. It's a free country, they can come down and set up camp next to us if they want to. Might as well bring them in, feed them some of that good Kitty Hawk grub and let the mosquitoes carry them away."

They were silent for a while, then Will went on. "It will be good to have Chanute with us; we can tell him quite a bit, enough to keep him writing and helping others, but we'll keep the real secrets to ourselves, as we find them. I'm worried about Herring and Huffaker, if they come. Who knows what they would do? They could turn around and copy everything we've done. Pop's right, we need to get a patent, but not right away. In the meantime, we can give Chanute enough to keep people satisfied."

Orville considered this and spoke with admiration. "Pretty Machiavellian, Ullam! And it works the other way too. If anyone else does some good work, we can count on Chanute to tell us. Langley, for example, he's our real competition. I don't think Herring knows what he's talking about, or anybody else, for that matter. But Langley, he's serious and well financed. We've got a race on with him, and he's about three laps ahead right now."

CHAPTER

9

Langley had just done three laps around the table in the center of the South Shed, waving a letter and screaming at the top of his lungs at his chief aeronautic assistant, Charles Matthews Manly.

"The engine leaks water like a sieve and we need new castings. What on earth is happening here? We've already spent more than five thousand dollars on this engine, if you can call it that."

His thoughts quickly turned to Albert Blohm, who had gotten him into this mess in the first place. Blohm had recommended Stephen Balzer, a Hungarian who had invented a three-cylinder air-cooled rotary engine that had been used successfully in the first automobiles built in the city of New York. Balzer had agreed to adapt the engine for use on the Great Aerodrome. He proposed a five-cylinder version that would generate twenty horsepower, and cost fifteen hundred dollars. Langley was quick to sign the contract with him, and agreed to have him build the transmission, propellers and the other necessary elements of the power plant.

Balzer's engine turned out to be a complete fiasco; instead of twenty horsepower, the engine could only produce six. In desperation, Manly, by far the most trusted of Langley's long line of assistants, was given the task of somehow revising the engine until it worked.

Manly stood quietly, listening to Langley rant as he had so often. He had lasted longer than the other assistants because he could take Langley's abuse, accepting it as a price to be paid for working at the great man's side. There was also a basic difference in their relationship compared to that of Langley and Huffaker or Herring.

Langley did not care a whit about retaining either one of them; he could dispose of their services in a minute. It was different with Manly; he had grown dependent upon him. And because Langley's interests were so diverse, Manly could stay a few steps ahead of him by always focusing on the Great Aerodrome. More importantly, despite always being deferential and agreeable, he also quietly projected a steely image of courage that Langley instinctively respected—he knew there was a point beyond which he dared not go and still keep Manly on board. The young man had gained his respect, something Langley did not give easily.

As with most difficulties, the real problem was money. And he was desperately short of money. Langley kept exact records in his work diary. The first $25,000 of government money had been spent by September of 1899. Now the second $25,000 from the War Department was gone, and so was almost $20,000 in money from the Smithsonian and various grants. If the newspapers were informed of this before he got the Aerodrome to fly, Langley knew they would run him out of the Smithsonian and out of the city.

Now the chief assistant stood like a man in a cold shower, shoulders hunched, head down, anxious to just get it over with. As he listened, he realized that today's tirade was more justifiable than most. Manly had gone out on a limb for Balzer, because he respected his engineering genius. He had not covered for him at all, and he had encouraged Balzer to persist and convinced Langley to give him more time, until the very end. And the latest fiasco, the leaking water jacket, could not be blamed on Balzer—it was his responsibility.

"What have you to say for yourself, Mr. Manly?"

"Mr. Secretary, I can only tell you that I believed in Mr. Balzer's engineering genius and still do. However, he failed with this engine, and I'm at fault for encouraging you to continue. But I will make you a promise. I will have this engine running by spring, and when it runs it will deliver at least forty horsepower."

The words forty horsepower startled Langley. Twenty or twenty-two had been the projected horsepower. "How can you promise that? The engine has never run to this day."

"With all respect, sir, it has run, but not correctly, not as it should run. I know what the problems are—ignition and carburetion. I can fix those, and I'll squeeze forty horsepower, perhaps more, out of it in six months or less, and the complete installation will weigh less than two hundred pounds."

America's preeminent scientist resumed his pacing, quiet now, thinking. There was no way to recover the five thousand now; that was a sunk cost. The only alternative engine that had been offered had been the one by that unusual Connecticut fellow, Gustave Whitehead.

"Manly, what do you think of the Whitehead engine? He promises twenty horsepower from his calcium carbide engine, and it is supposed to be very lightweight."

"Sir, when I'm feeling kind I think he is an eccentric. When I'm being myself I think he's a fraud. Believe me, we are within six months of having a practical engine. I have no idea how long, if ever, it would take Whitehead to develop an engine, or if it would produce one horsepower, much less twenty."

While he was speaking, Langley realized he had a winning card. He played it.

"Young man, are you confident enough in your engine that you will agree to chauffeur the Great Aerodrome?"

The request stunned Manly, who realized that far from being a step ahead of Langley, he was several dangerous steps behind.

"I've never flown a kite, sir, nor did any gliding."

"You drive a carriage, don't you?"

"Yes, and even an automobile, but—"

"Then you can chauffeur the Great Aerodrome. I've told you about the flights of Number 5 and Number 6. Easiest thing you've ever seen, spiraled around and landed in the river like a feather. All you'll have to do is operate the engine and steer the rudder, just like a boat."

Manly nodded. He should have seen this coming. Yet in a way he did not mind. Langley might make the history books as the inventor of the flying machine, but Manly would make them as the first flying machine operator.

He reached out for Langley's hand. "Sir, it is an honor. I accept. And you will get your forty horsepower."

CHAPTER

10

Albert Blohm was a realist, and never more so than with himself, for he ruthlessly dissected his own failures, follies and fancies with the morbid skill of a physician, noting each transgression and ascribing a probable and usually culpable cause.

One transgression lay next to him, sleeping deeply, her elfin beauty accentuated by the dim morning light peeking through the shaded windows of his Georgetown home. There was no question about the probable causes here, his being sex, and hers being money.

Knowing that he was buying Annette's affection did not lessen his enjoyment of her a whit. How else could he, a short, ordinary-looking man, too preoccupied with wind tunnels and flying machines to charm women, have lured such a gorgeous creature to bed, and by God, to board, for she ate like a horse and never seemed to gain an ounce.

Money. It was so pleasant to be young and to have so much of it. And it had come so easily, after a painful childhood. His father, Albert Blohm, Senior, had been one of the unsung brains behind the investments of J.P. Morgan, and as Morgan had prospered, so had Blohm. American steel, railroads, and oil had all funneled enormous wealth into his holdings. Yet while the name J. P. Morgan was always in the headlines, Blohm remained virtually unknown outside of financial circles. His father had been as clever in marriage as he had been in business, seeking out an eligible heiress, Sarah Bonden, whose familial wealth extended from its English roots in maritime commerce to Pittsburgh steel. They lived in baronial style, with houses in Washington, New York, Saratoga, London, and Paris, a private railroad car, and a magnificent yacht, the *Imperial*.

While neither his father nor his mother had ever demonstrated any affection to Albert while they were living, they certainly did after their death. Both had perished ten years before when the *Imperial* had sunk with all aboard in an ill-advised attempt to cross the Atlantic during a series of winter storms. It was one time Albert was glad that he had not been asked to go along. Blohm sat up, struck by the memory of the two-story library of their New York home, fragrant with a mixture of smoke from the fireplace and the cigars that his father and the yacht's captain, John Avery, were enjoying with some very old brandy. Avery knew his father well, and was dramatizing the dangers of the winter crossing with a big map, to which he had pinned colored pieces of paper showing the probable weather pattern. Two huge pieces, black with bright red centers, were placed on either side of their route. His father had reacted as he usually did, listening quietly, asking questions, then deciding that they would sail. When Avery protested, his father smiled once more and said, "Come along, Captain Avery. I have to be in Ireland, and I have to have my yacht with me. Either take me across, or let me find someone who will." It was his father's style; listen to the information, then decide. It was a style his son had inherited.

Fortunately, his parents had made careful arrangements about their estate, and excepting some small gifts to charity, and even smaller ones to their longtime servants, their combined wealth had passed to him intact and uncontested. Though they had placed no restrictions on the estate—he had inherited at twenty-three—they had been thoughtful enough to have it invested soundly in a broad spectrum of securities, real estate, government bonds, and other things which had no intrinsic appeal to him whatsoever. He was more than content to have the estate continue to be managed by his father's law firm, Creighton, Hastings, and Baake, and scarcely noticed when the checks arrived each quarter to be deposited in a personal account that grew at an embarrassing rate.

His own needs were small, but he had made one extravagant gesture, directing the law firm to seek out each and every one of the many servants at all their houses, and the families of all the crew that had been lost on the yacht. Against his lawyers' advice, he provided them all with decent annuities, based on their salaries. He had ruthlessly sold all the houses except the big one in Georgetown where he now lived to defray part of the cost; the rest came out of "capital" as his lawyers defined it.

It was not a caprice. Blohm did it to make up for the years the servants had spent hopping every time his father coughed or his mother blinked, or just for the endless waiting in homes that were never visited but had to be maintained, ready for a surprise arrival. His lawyers had objected—it was not done, they said, but he had insisted and for good reason. The servants had always treated him better than his parents. He felt close to them, for he had spent his youth in their care, seeing his parents only on those holidays when they were not abroad. Albert had retained a few of the seniors for the Georgetown house: Martin the butler, Mrs. Jensen the cook, and Roland the chauffeur. Even with their annuities, they were glad to have employment, and doubly glad to work for him rather than his parents. It was a happy household now, and he appreciated the fact that they treated Annette so well when she visited, as they did his other friends when they dropped by to spend the night.

Blohm reached over and lightly ran his fingers over the surface of Annette's body, as if he were committing it to memory. She stirred, turning sleepily to him with her usual agreeable receptivity, but he was sated, wanting only to look at her, enjoy her beauty for a few minutes more before scrambling to work at the wind tunnel.

Work was the real seductress, far more demanding than Annette or any of her American counterparts. And while women could be persuaded with money, or with the elusive prospect of someday marrying a wealthy man, wind tunnel work was a hard, indifferent master, one that demanded all his attention and had to be continuously wooed to make it give up any secrets.

The wind tunnel, like Annette, had originated in Paris. After his parents' estate had been settled, Albert finished his graduate engineering training at the Massachusetts Institute of Technology. In 1895, he had gone to France to study, not at a university, but in hard, practical experience at the French Central Military Installation for Ballooning at Chalais-Meudon near Paris. Normally closed to foreigners, Albert had appealed to an old family friend, one his father had supported with campaign funds, Grover Cleveland. The president responded readily, sending a personal letter to the French premier, and providing Blohm with an unsolicited "To whom it may concern" backup letter.

Blohm had gone to Paris with the idea of creating a new and larger version of *La France*, the dirigible that had flown a few years before and seemed to him to point the way to the future. They had greeted him warmly at the historic Chalais-Meudon facility, where the first military balloonists in the world had trained in the time of Napoleon. He was placed directly under Charles Renard, who, with Arthur Krebs, had created the dirigible that had inspired Blohm's trip. Renard had been portly when he and Krebs had flown *La France* on its epochal fourteen-minute round-trip back in 1884. Now the airship would have trouble getting him off the ground. His unceasing love for good wine and rich food had added another twenty kilos to his weight and several inches to his waistline, so that he was shaped like the Army observation balloons that were his primary occupation, training observers for artillery spotting.

It was evident that Renard was tired, however, worn down by a War Ministry antagonistic to his work. Now he amused himself with experiments with model helicopters. Krebs, Renard's longtime partner, was away on official duty. Renard indicated that Krebs had not completely abandoned dirigibles, but was increasingly interested in heavier-than-air flying machines.

Blohm was blissfully happy, living in a small slate-roofed house near the gate, eating in the local restaurants, partying with the officers, and being a generous host to all the enlisted personnel with whom he worked. There were several young women who diverted him, some trotted out by their officer parents who had learned of his wealth, some just young local girls who knew how to enjoy themselves without a thought of tomorrow.

His ardent interest lay within the classic angular gray stone walls of Chalais-Meudon. Musty with history, huge arched rooms that had once held inflated balloons were now jammed with wicker baskets and bolts of fabric, strange machines for generating hydrogen, and the equipment that had been used by Clement Ader to build his flying machines. Blohm admired the beautiful, exacting work of the craftsmen who worked in the experimental shops, but was amazed at the slovenly conditions under which they worked, floors strewn with sawdust, machine tools greasy, and the worst imaginable lighting. He was allowed in most of the rooms, where he saw them building engines, guns, and other warlike devices, but barred from others, which were kept under tight lock and key.

Renard liked Blohm, for despite his presidential patronage and being so obviously wealthy—no one threw parties like he did—he was nonetheless enthusiastic about the work, getting his hands dirty and talking to the technicians as courteously as he did to the officers. He particularly approved of the way Blohm took ballooning seriously, methodically going through all the classroom work with the Army officer trainees and making as many flights as possible. Most of the flights were tethered, but on the free flights, he always tried to get the maximum distance regardless of the weather. And Blohm showed the proper respect for the safety precautions, both when inflating the balloon and around the hydrogen generating equipment. Many young men did not, afraid that caution would be interpreted as fear.

Blohm had been at Chalais-Meudon for just six months when Renard sent him on a mission to Germany to meet an archrival, Count Ferdinand von Zeppelin. Renard no longer traveled if he could avoid it—he was simply too heavy to endure train travel and staying at hotels, and he was still vain enough to not want von Zeppelin to see just how portly he was.

Blohm visited the Count at Friedrichschafen, where he was busy creating the plans for his first dirigible, and at the same time relentlessly lobbying the Prussian War Ministry for the funds with which to build it. Blohm came away tremendously impressed, convinced by von Zeppelin that the massive size of the dirigible assured practical success where others had failed. No construction had begun, but there were various aluminum assemblies that showed how the dirigible would be built, light and strong. The Count was very forthcoming, answering all his questions, and guiding him to those he had not asked. It was obvious that he did not fear competition from Renard.

On Blohm's return to Chalais-Meudon, there came the incident that changed his life. Renard had greeted him pleasantly, asking, "And, tell me, what do you think of the count?" Even after six months, Renard spoke slowly and loudly, confident that doing so would further improve Blohm's quite fluent French.

"He is magnificent!" Blohm replied. "And his airship will revolutionize the world. He will sail it across the Atlantic, to the North Pole. There is nothing it won't be able to do."

Blohm went on at length, describing what he had learned of the construction and the internal arrangements. "He is going to use gigantic rudders to turn the ship, and a weight on a slide to control its up and down travel." Renard listened in silence, encouraging him occasionally with a question.

When Blohm began to wind down, Renard smiled sadly. "I wish I could share your enthusiasm. Believe me, I'm not envious; I've had my time in the sun. Count von Zeppelin is breaking new ground. But he has only tragedy ahead. The concept of an airship is fatally flawed. The bigger it gets, the more dangerous it becomes. And with hydrogen—" His voice trailed off.

"You flew with hydrogen, did you not?"

"Yes, Arthur and I flew, but we risked only our own lives. Zeppelin will be risking the lives of dozens, perhaps more with airships of that size."

"I asked him about the risk. He says, with precautions, hydrogen is perfectly safe. He compares it to gasoline in automobiles: both will explode and cause fires, but you can use them if you are cautious."

Renard shook his head. "A facile argument, but an empty one. And suppose that an automobile does explode, it is carrying only one or two people and it is on the ground besides." He was quiet for a while, then said, "You came back at a good time; there is something I want you to see. Today we are conducting some experiments, using explosive bullets to see if they will ignite observation balloons. The next war will have many observation balloons, and perhaps dirigibles too, and we will have to be able to shoot them down. Come along, I want you to see what happens."

Renard led Blohm out of the huge cathedral-like structure of the school to the field beyond. For decades a military training ground, it had poplar trees on three sides and a long mound of earth on the fourth that was supposed to soak up rifle and machine gun bullets from the firing range. Three observation balloons were tethered at the base of the mound.

Puffing from the short walk, Renard halted and pointed across the field to them. "They are worn out from service, so we use them for tests. We will let them ascend, one at a time, to about two hundred meters, then shoot at them, using a Hotchkiss machine gun. The first trials will be with ordinary bullets. They probably will hole the balloons but not blow them up. Then we will use a belt with the explosive bullets. You will be surprised to learn they are developed from an American Civil War product, the Gardinier explosive bullet. They did not work so well for you, but we have improved them a bit. We hope they will blow up the balloons. It should be interesting."

Renard's jaws suddenly dropped and he shouted, "Stop that man!", waving across the field to a soldier walking under the line of balloons, a thin trail of smoke visible from the pipe he was smoking. It was futile; the people clustered around preparing the balloons were too far away to hear the warning.

Blohm watched as the man reached the second balloon only to disappear in a massive fireball. There was another huge report as the two adjacent balloons blew up, followed by a third tremendous explosion that sent a shock wave across the field, dumping both Blohm and Renard on their backs.

Pale and panting in the sudden silence, Renard whispered, "The last one was the hydrogen generator." Then, "You see what I mean about von Zeppelin's big dirigibles."

Blohm did indeed see, and, in the style of his father, made up his mind immediately. He would give up dirigibles and instead pursue the challenge of the flying machine itself.

In France, Clement Ader was to the flying machine what Renard was to the dirigible, but Renard had been far more accessible. A self-taught engineer, Ader had flown a balloon of his own making during the siege of Paris. Later he had made a fortune with his Theatrephone, a system that allowed music from the Paris Opera to be broadcast via telephone lines to a larger audience in the Palais de l'Industrie exhibition hall, or to coin-operated telephones in the top hotels.

Renard's entreaties and the letter from Grover Cleveland had no apparent affect upon Ader, who for weeks adamantly refused to see Blohm, protesting that he was under contract to the French government, and could not share his secrets. Blohm persisted, writing a weekly letter, and was pleasantly surprised when Renard walked into the shop one chilly Monday morning to say: "He'll see you at two o'clock. He's coming here, and said he would give you half an hour. Be prepared, don't waste any time with pleasantries, go right to the point with your questions."

Ader swept in, immaculately dressed in a gray overcoat with black velvet lapel facings. Almost completely bald, he was as short as Blohm himself, and his olive skin seemed to pulse with energy. His long pointed mustache was mostly gray, and concealed a thin mouth. Beneath his strong chin there was a brilliant red tie in which gleamed a diamond stickpin.

Renard made the introductions and then sat quietly at their left, watching as Ader began the conversation in his usual peremptory manner.

"Are you here to steal my secrets?"

Blohm made a quick choice between sweet and sour, choosing between the servility Ader expected and the confident response of a man wealthy and capable in his own right. In an even voice, he replied, "Yes, and to improve on them if I can."

Renard had rocketed to his feet, certain the interview was over, but Ader smiled. "At least you are honest. What do you wish to know?"

"You flew in 1890. I would like to see the flying machine, if it still exists."

Ader stood up. "Very well, it is here, as you undoubtedly knew. Renard, if you will get the keys we will have a look."

They walked slowly to the locked area of the workshop, Ader being considerate of the corpulent Renard, questioning Blohm on the way about his education, his family, his interests. By the time the adjutant had unlocked the door and rolled it back, Ader was obviously charmed by Blohm.

"Here it is, the *Eole*. On October 9th, 1890, at my friend Gustave Pereire's chateau at the Parc d' Armainvilliers, I flew it for more than fifty meters. It is a little worse for wear now, of course, but it is complete, as you see."

Blohm had seen drawings of the aircraft, with its batlike wings and long snout to which a four-blade propeller was attached, but it was far more impressive in the dim light of the workroom. Ader led him around the craft, pointing out the twenty-horsepower steam engine, once taking a work cloth from a bench to wipe down a bit of oil, showing him how closely the structure, not just the outline, resembled that of a bat. The wings were built up on an articulated, skeletonlike frame and were covered with cloth. They were like a canopy, some forty-five feet across. The *Eole* was huge, much bigger than he had imagined.

"Look here at the ribs, and see how they have been very artfully routed out—they retain their strength, but are much lighter."

Blohm asked a question he thought he knew the answer to. "Did the wings of the *Eole* flap?"

"No, they did not flap, but they did fold."

"How did you make it go up and down?"

"By increasing the turns of the propeller; more steam and you go up, less steam and you come down. Very simple."

"And turns?"

"Ah, my friend, this was a tentative machine only. It has a small rudder, as you see. In time I might have made it turn by folding a wing, as birds do. But my next machine will be larger, and have two propellers. When I want to turn to the right, I will speed up the propeller on the left; when I want to turn to the left, I'll speed up the propeller on the right. And those are all the secrets you will get from me today!"

They moved out of the workshop, Ader watching closely as the adjutant rolled the doors shut and locked them. As they strolled back, again mindful of the puffing Renard, Ader said, "I do not know whether you have learned anything or if I have encouraged or discouraged you. The *Eole* took two years of my life, and cost almost a million francs."

He paused, his voice grave, his eyes seeming to moisten. "But you must remember, my young American rival, that when the flying machine comes, it will revolutionize the world; it will be the supreme instrument in war. That is why it is worth spending your life and your fortune to bring it about." At the moment, Ader seemed to be genuinely wishing Blohm success, a proud older man seeing a younger man coming to replace him in history.

When they parted, Blohm's protestations of gratitude and promises of future service to Ader were genuine. He owed the man a significant debt, for he had shown him several ways not to go, steam engines and folding batlike wings being two of them.

After Ader was gone, Renard turned to Blohm. "I have never seen him so cordial. You touched him, somehow. Perhaps he saw himself in you. Now the important question. Did you learn what you wished to learn from him?"

Blohm hesitated. He could not tell Renard, after all his kindness, that he learned only that Ader was pursuing a dead end; that the *Eole* was interesting, but without any effective means of control, worse than useless—it was dangerous. Instead he said, "He is a great man, and I feel privileged to have met him, and to have seen the *Eole*." Renard nodded, thinking that he understood.

Only a few days later, Blohm left Chalais-Meudon with regret, but Renard's recommendations and the letter from Cleveland now earned him a two-month stay with Gustave Eiffel himself, in his new laboratory in the Tower, and there Blohm had conceived what would become his all-consuming fascination, his obsession; the creation of a wind tunnel large enough to ferret out the secrets of flight.

It was while working with Eiffel that he had met Annette.

CHAPTER
11

The salt-laden wind swept across the deck, depositing moisture on their glasses. He breathed deeply, appreciating the almost violent striations of color, the greenish-blue, whitecapped sea against chalky cliffs that were topped with a brilliant green mantle of grass, brush and trees, all backed by the bright blue Canadian sky. Turning, he took her face in his hands and spoke sweetly, gazing directly into her eyes, infinitely happy as always that she understood him so well. She was the living personification of his work, his calling, and he was fortunate to have married her. His voice, low and mellifluous, said "It is always a double homecoming. This part of Nova Scotia reminds me so much of Scotland."

"You say that every year, Alec, and I love it each time." She spoke with the flat mechanical sound and cadence of one who had learned to speak without ever hearing the voices of others.

They stood holding hands as the little steamer edged toward the dock. They had given their home the Gaelic name *Beinn Breagh* for "mountain beauty" and it was surely that, a turreted French chateau poised on a Cape Breton promontory, far larger than their own needs, but just right for their many visitors. They came to spend six months each year here as Alexander Graham Bell pursued his latest interest, the flying machine.

Mabel Bell quietly accepted his fascination as she had all the others in the past, knowing that only good could come of it, just as only good had ultimately come of what had been a childhood curse, her deafness. Alec, whose mother had also been deaf, had devoted his life to communication. He believed that signing stigmatized the deaf.

Instead, he sought out the harmonic sounds of the living voice and found ways to transmit them so that the deaf could "hear." He had done so with her, and in the process they had fallen in love.

His ideas about using harmonic tones to teach the deaf to hear had led directly to the idea of transmitting voice tones over a telegraph wire—and from this it was but a step to his great invention, the telephone. He had been successful before, but the telephone had provided a welcome wealth, giving them the wherewithal for this lovely sea and mountain retreat and their beautiful home in Washington, and now, for his experiments with flight. Who could tell where they would lead?

She pointed across the waters of the bay to the little town of Baddeck, saying "They'll have their telescopes out to watch you as soon as they see the first kite."

Bell was a source of pride and amusement to the locals, who could not imagine how the famous man could spend long days on the sloping fields behind his mansion, flying kites. They were glad he did, for his kites were large elaborate affairs, clearly able to lift a man off the ground. Between the crashes and the changes, building them had become a local industry, employing as many as a dozen people at the height of the season. This year would bring new demands, for Bell had designed an entirely new kind of kite he called a "tetrahedron," made up of individual triangular prismlike cells joined together in a strong, light structure.

Mabel watched him checking to see that their baggage and his boxes of equipment were all carefully stowed on the dock. Amidst the baggage were the aluminum struts and red silk fabric that he would make into his first kite of the season, and as always, he was anxious to get on with it.

Since 1896 he had grown more impatient every year. It was then that he had seen Professor Langley's machine fly, and though he would never admit it, he was determined to build a better machine than Langley's, one that could carry a man safely in all wind and weathers. His position was delicate; as a regent of the Smithsonian, he was in some way's Langley's boss. But he would handle that, as he handled all the sensitive questions in his life, with tact and dignity.

And she would help him. One of the few advantages of being deaf was that it permitted her to focus her attention on the most important problems, without being distracted by noise or idle conversation. Now she thought about the kind of help that Alec would need. He was not good with his hands, and he admitted that. Nor were his sketches really exact. What was required was a team of young men to help his ideas come to fruition. An engineer, someone with drafting skills, was important. Then a craftsman, skilled in wood and metal, able to translate Alec's ideas into reality. And, she presumed, there would have to be a chauffeur, a pilot, to guide the flying machine. She certainly did not want Alec flying; it was bad enough that he towed his boat with kites, blazing about Baddeck Bay like a madman, within seconds of turning over and sinking.

Last of all, they would need someone who knew engines, about which Alec knew nothing, hating them as noisy, willful creatures that polluted the air with sound and odors.

It would have to be a consortium, where people could express their own ideas as well as listen to Alec's. Otherwise it would be too dull, not sufficiently challenging, if they were just carrying out Alec's thoughts. There needed to be discussions, arguments even, but lots of interchange. Alec had a tendency to pursue odd ideas beyond the point of any rational return, and people had too great a tendency to defer to him.

Mabel Bell looked again toward Baddeck, wondering how she could persuade young people to come to this backwater, this sanctuary, to give up all social life and live with them in pursuit of an idea. Alec himself was the trump card, of course. Any young man with ambition would see the advantage of working closely with Alexander Graham Bell for a summer or two—it would be worth missing a few balls and parties to be able to put that on an application form for a teaching position.

Funding the consortium would be no problem. She would put up the money herself; Alec would regard it as a tribute, and be pleased. But getting him to work with others, to surrender some of his independence, that would be the difficult task. It would require special people, young rebels that still knew how to cooperate.

PART TWO
STEPPING FORWARD

The man who can't make a mistake can't make anything.
Abraham Lincoln

CHAPTER

12

To a boy from Hammondsport, the Buffalo Pan American Exposition of 1901 was simply dazzling—the huge buildings, turrets topped with flags, the lakes, with gondolas and other boats he couldn't name, the flowers, and most of all the crowds of people scurrying from one exhibit hall to the next.

Curtiss was not there to sightsee. He had read in the Hammondsport paper that there was a medical exhibit that featured incubators for babies, and he wanted to see if they might be helpful to his infant son. Carlton had been born in March, and was desperately ill with some sort of heart condition that the doctors could not diagnose. They did not expect him to live, but Lena nursed him fiercely, trying to love and pray him into health. Curtiss wanted to see if the incubators could help. He did not know if they were sold, but he was convinced that if he saw how one operated, he would be able to build one for Carlton.

In the end he was disappointed. The Medical Arts building was temporarily closed. He wandered around the outside of it. A guard warned him off, but when he explained his situation, took him inside and showed him the arrangement. It was clearly too complex; it would require a doctor and a nurse even if he could build it. Discouraged, he thanked the guard, then began the long walk back to the entrance. He was plunging along the "Midway" that ran around the left side of the exposition grounds, his eyes taking in the magnificent buildings, when suddenly he tripped over the legs of a man whose body was stretched in to a vendor's exhibit booth, examining the underside of a motorcycle.

The man rolled over quickly, then helped Glenn to his feet, apologizing profusely. "I'm so sorry, I got so interested in the bike that I forgot where I was."

Curtiss dusted himself off. "No, I've taken many a tumble worse than that, riding my own bicycle." He glanced at the motorcycle the man had been examining, a Thomas Auto-Bi.

"Are you a bike rider? I'm Glenn Curtiss, and I do a little racing."

"Glad to meet you, Mr. Curtiss. I'm Augustus Herring, and I ride a bike, but just for transportation, not for racing. My business is flying machines, and that's why I'm interested in this motorcycle. I need a lightweight engine."

Curtiss hesitated for a moment, wondering if this sharply dressed young man was making fun of him. "Flying machines?"

"Yes, sounds crazy but I'm really not."

Curtiss nodded and they both squatted down, looking at the Thomas Auto-Bi, commenting on the big single-cylinder gasoline engine slung between the wheels and on the cylindrical fuel tank strapped to the bar.

"Look at that—they're using a flat belt to drive the rear wheel. I'd put on a V-belt for sure, wouldn't slip as much. But I'll bet it's fast."

Herring nodded. "No doubt, but I'm more concerned with the weight. I was hoping that it might be light enough to use in my flying machine, but I can tell by looking that it's not."

"Are you serious, about the flying machine business?"

"Absolutely. What line of work are you in, Mr. Curtiss?"

"I've got a funny business, too. I sell bicycles in one part of my shop and tack in the other; you know, saddles, harness, whips, whatever you need to make a horse go from point A to point B. Make one line of bicycles, too, you might have heard of it, call it the Hercules."

"No, I'm sorry, can't say I have, but I'm just a bike user, not a real fan. Ever make a motorcycle?"

Curtiss thought he saw which way the conversation was going, and he liked it. "Not yet."

"Could you make a motorcycle?"

"If I did, it would be with an engine a lot smaller and lighter than this."

"That's what I want to hear. Lets go have a soda pop and talk about this."

As they walked along they exchanged comments on their families. Herring deeply loved his own two children and felt a pang when he heard that Curtiss's son was probably fatally ill. By the time they reached the huge refreshment tent, they felt a kinship and a confidence in each other.

"Have you seen this place at night?"

Curtiss shook his head. "No, I'm just up for the day, to see about the incubator."

"You really ought to see it at night. It's as if they take all the power and energy of Niagara Falls and channel it into the lights that cover everything, every building, every tree. It's really magnificent, a real tribute to Thomas Edison."

There were a dozen restaurants along the Midway, but Herring had picked this one for the music. The tent was crowded with tables, filled with weary-looking visitors, and a band playing some cakewalk tunes. Herring chose a booth whose back divided the sounds neatly; from the left there came a low buzz of conversation, and from the right, the music, which made Glenn sad. Lena used to like to dance, not out anywhere, just around the house when no one was there but themselves. She hadn't danced for a long time. She probably never would again, not for a long time, anyway.

"Moxie or Orangeade?" Herring was looking at him, wondering where his thoughts were.

"Orangeade, please." He reached in his pocket but Herring shook his head and gave the waiter a quarter when he brought the drinks. "Keep the change."

They sat for a while, Herring knowing that Curtiss was choked up, thinking of his family, no doubt. As he waited a small boy approached the booth, staring intently at them.

"What is it, sonny? Would you like a soda pop?"

The boy shook his head, then asked, "Are you twins?"

Curtiss laughed, the first time that day.

"No, not even brothers. Why do you ask?"

The boy said, "You look like twins," and walked on.

They both took stock, realizing that they were dressed just alike, with tan caps, brown suits, and brown high-top shoes. Physically they were about the same size, Herring perhaps a bit taller, and, of course, Curtiss was distinguished by his mustache.

Then Curtiss looked closer. They were both wearing brown suits, all right, but his was inexpensive, from Sears, and his pants had a clear line where the bicycle clip went around his trouser leg. He didn't know where Herring's suit came from but it was impressive, as was the gold watch he had tucked in his vest. To Curtiss, the suit and the watch went along with Herring's faint southern accent, his urbane manners, and the people he apparently knew. He had only a faint idea of who Octave Chanute was, but he had heard the name, and he knew that Samuel Langley headed the Smithsonian Institution, and he was impressed that Herring had worked for them both. You did not meet many people in Hammondsport who knew real scientists.

"How was it, working for men like Chanute and Langley? Were they hard to get along with, being so famous?"

Herring hesitated for a moment, wanting to tell what he really thought of them. "No, no, both were very nice. Mr. Chanute says I can come back and work for him any time, but I need to move along, and work on my own ideas. And I could work for Langley too, but the pay is low, and . . ." His emotions ran away with him. "And Langley is impossible; he takes the credit for everything, never acknowledges what you do. He would tell different people to do different things on the same project, and then be angry with me when things did not work out. No, Langley was much more difficult than Chanute. I could tell you . . ."

Herring caught control of himself. It was better to be thought of as an associate of Langley than an enemy. "But on the other hand, he is a genius, and his small Aerodromes have actually flown. I am pretty proud of them, myself, for I had suggested to him how the wings should be positioned, and the use of the tail." He pulled a folded piece of paper from his chest pocket and quickly sketched an Aerodrome. "See here, this swinging tail, that is my idea. He liked it, but never said a word to anyone, says it was his own idea. Still, I guess if you are paying the salaries, you get to call the shots."

"Well, what about Chanute?"

"The kindest man in the world, like a father to me. He has difficulty keeping his mind on one project, but other than that he is a perfect boss. In a way he's like Langley, he takes credit for things I've done, like the two-surface and three-surface gliders, but he's generous to a fault."

"Two-surface, three-surface?" Curtiss's face was charged with energy. Herring drew swift little sketches of the gliders, putting down their dimensions. He decided to take advantage of the sudden change in his new friend's mood.

"How much would it cost to make a really lightweight engine to put on one of these little gliders? It doesn't have to be too durable, not the first one, I just need it to run for a few minutes, give me maybe ten horsepower and not weigh more than one hundred pounds."

"I don't have any idea, Mr. Herring, but I'll find out. It interests me. I'm pretty good with my hands, and I have access to a shop with all the tools I need."

Herring considered for a moment telling Curtiss that he had already made a first flight with a compressed-air engine, then decided against it. There would be too many questions, he would wonder why no one had heard of it. Better to keep this going the way it was.

"It can't cost too much. I've got some backers in Denver raising money for my flying machine, but I don't think they are having much luck."

"Let me look into it. Don't worry about the money. My businesses are doing well, and this is something I want to do for myself. There may even be some way to make money on it, who knows. I'll finance the first one, and if it suits your needs, I'll sell it to you for a price you can afford."

Back in Hammondsport, Curtiss told Lena about his disappointment with the incubator system. She understood; her hopes had not been high. But she began to feel an odd mixture of resentment and relief as Glenn talked to her about Herring and building a lightweight engine for the motorcycle. She wanted to meet Herring herself, for no one else had ever made such an impression on Glenn. He was normally suspicious of strangers, particularly if they seemed wealthy. Of all things, Herring's suit seemed to impress Glenn, a man who would wear the same work clothes until she yanked them off him. He was already talking in vague terms of partnering with Herring somehow, to take advantage of his connections.

Over the next few days her feelings were hurt again as Glenn began to spend less time with her and Carlton. Still, she was glad to see him shed the sadness, to show some of the old Glenn Curtiss vitality. She knew there was nothing for her to do but try to keep the baby alive, knowing that she was not going to succeed, but trying anyway. There was one sure thing. She would never have another child. The risk of loss, the sadness was too great. Glenn, at least, could get some relief in his work.

And he did, working long days in the shops to make a living, then spending evening hours trying to design an engine. He was a natural mechanic with an eye for detail. With no more than the information from a few magazine articles, Curtiss had built an acetylene plant to heat and light his shop, and acetylene was tricky. But an internal combustion engine was different, more complex, and he finally gave in, ordering a disassembled engine from the E.R. Thomas Company, the same people who built the Auto-Bi.

Lena's uncle, Frank Neff, was there when it arrived, and he and Curtiss both looked at the opened wooden box with dismay. There was a just a set of rough, unpolished castings: cylinder, piston, flywheel; and no instructions at all. There was no carburetor, no provision for ignition.

"Do you think we can do anything with this, Frank? Do you have enough machinery to lick this thing into shape?"

Neff didn't speak, running his hands over the castings with the familiar touch of a master machinist. He was famous in Hammondsport for inventing the wire hood that contained the champagne corks; in the past the corks had been kept in the bottles— sometimes—by waxed cord. He'd patented the process and even the French had picked up on it. He was, in his business, a celebrity.

Finally he said, "I think so Glenn, but this is not really what you have been talking about. Let's put this one together and run it, learn something from it, and then you sketch out what you really want in an engine."

It took them weeks, but they eventually got the engine running, with a carburetor made out of a tomato can and ignition coming from a sparking coil a local doctor used to give his patients mild therapeutic shock treatment. Starting it was difficult and when it finally lumbered into life it was a noisy, rambunctious piece of ironmongery. They attached it to a bicycle, using belts to drive first the front wheel and then the back.

There were no secrets in Hammondsport, and people were continually dropping by the shop on Park Square to watch Curtiss, always so deeply absorbed in his new project that he did not even hear their greetings or respond to their jokes. They didn't mind; they knew Glenn was a serious man, friendly enough, but when he was working, absolutely focused on the task at hand.

Frank Neff had given the bike the name "The Happy Hooligan" after the cartoon hobo character whose hat was a tin can, and the name suited the bike, which was rough and crude in appearance. Curtiss had not wasted any time on paint or finish: he wanted to get a motor attached to a bike as fast as he could.

Late one Saturday afternoon, Curtiss put down his wrenches, winked at Neff, and moved the bike into the dusty street. They had talked it over, and decided the best way to start it was for Glenn to pedal the bike with its regular pedals and chains until he got up to a decent speed, then clutch in the transmission belt to start the engine.

When Curtiss moved the bike onto the street there were no more than five people anywhere on Park Square. He spat on his gloves, climbed on the seat and began pedaling; when he engaged the transmission there was a loud bang and the bike ground to a halt. He tried again, and by the second bang, Park Square was lined with people, coming out of the stores and the side streets.

Curtiss tinkered with it, playing with the spark, and adjusting the screw valve on the carburetor, then started pedaling again, this time down the hill that led to Keuka Lake. The engine suddenly kicked in and Curtiss placed a little pressure on the brake caliper he had refashioned to act as a throttle lever. The bike picked up speed, shooting out from under him, throwing him off the back and driving itself into the side of the road. Neff was laughing so hard he could barely help Curtiss to his feet.

The next try was better. Curtiss eased the throttle forward and found himself almost out of control, the bike traveling faster than he had ever pedaled. He rode it out to Bill Smellie's track, with Neff following along behind on a bicycle. There he flew around the track, leaving behind the machine a blue-gray cloud of smoke and a roaring noise that startled horses in the next field.

He made two laps, then pulled in to talk to Neff. "Your turn, Frank?"

"Never in your life, Glenn. I'm not going to kill myself on that thing."

Curtiss was elated. He had enjoyed speed in bicycle racing, but that speed came at the cost of aching legs and bursting lungs. With the motor he was experiencing pure speed without the demanding physical exertion, and he loved it.

"This thing could get to be a habit, Frank. I'm going to take her around again."

They spent most of the afternoon at the track, Curtiss gradually increasing his velocity as he became more comfortable. Then on his final run, the engine gave a massive series of backfires that tore it away from the frame and sent Curtiss spinning in the dust again.

Over the next few weeks, they ran it and repaired it, Curtiss and Neff learning from every mishap. In the fall, they found a machine shop that would cast engines to Curtiss's own economic design. He improved his carburetor and put in a new ignition system. The new engine ran smoothly, weighing in at only 120 pounds. After a test ride Curtiss thought, "Well, it's better than the Auto-Bi, but still too heavy for Herring. Still, I need to write him a letter and let him know how we are doing."

CHAPTER
13

Wilbur was embarrassed, too fond of Katharine to let on, but annoyed that Henry Cleaver was sitting on her bed with her, unconscious of how it might look.

It was his fault, of course; he admired Cleaver's command of English and had asked Katharine to invite him to come over and listen to the talk Wilbur was going to give the following evening to the Western Society of Engineers in Chicago. Katharine had insisted on listening, too, and because she was sewing, asked that Wilbur practice in her room. He'd agreed—but he hadn't anticipated that they would sit side by side on her bed to listen to him, Cleaver leaning back, supporting himself on his arms, but holding his right arm too close to Katharine.

Wilbur droned on, his high-pitched voice monotonous, dropping down to a whisper. Katharine called, "Go on, Wilbur, you are doing fine. But speak up. It will be noisy in Chicago."

Wilbur went on rapidly, finishing with, "Well, I don't have the lantern slides here, of course, but that's it. What do you think?"

Cleaver leaned forward; tall and blond, with an open, sunny face, he was everything the Wright boys were not, relaxed and confident, not bothered by the fact that he was sitting with a girl on her bed, genuinely absorbed in Wilbur's talk.

"It sounds fine to me, Wilbur, but I don't understand one thing. You seem disappointed in this year's flights, yet no one else has done so well. Why should you be disappointed?"

Katharine laughed. "Well, one reason is that he lost so much blood to the mosquitoes, and another is that he had to put up with Mr. Chanute's friends visiting."

Wilbur smiled. "She's right about the mosquitoes, Henry. They literally ate us alive, they covered us, we'd lie under blankets and have smoke fires going and they would just chew and chew. I thought we were going to have to leave, come back to Dayton just to get away from them. Then one day, poof, they were gone. It was like a plague for a few days."

Katharine spoke again. "At least they left. Can you imagine, down at that tiny camp, with its little tent, they had three people visiting, eating their food, watching what they were doing. I'll tell you, Henry, my brothers are saints."

Wilbur shook his head. "It wasn't too bad. Mr. Chanute only stayed a few days, and he's been such a help we'd be ungrateful wretches not to have him. I don't think our cooking pleased him, though; I suspect he dines more elegantly when he's at home. But he never complained. But his two friends, they were something else. One of them, a chap named Huffaker, was just a pain, always complaining, always in the way, always writing in his little notebook. The other, George Spratt, was a treat—he was lots of fun, did his share of the work, never complained, always had funny stories to tell. He has some good ideas too. Old Huffaker, he'd made his glider out of cardboard tubes, and the rain just tore it up." He looked away and chuckled. "Cardboard tubes. What an idea! You should have seen his machine after the rain, looked like a safe had dropped on it."

Cleaver asked him again, "But what was wrong with your glider? From your talk, it sounds like you did fine. Maybe you are being too hard on yourself."

"It's hard to explain, Henry, but in layman's terms, we were only getting about one-third of the lift we expected to get. I don't know what's the matter. I feel like a fool, going to the Western Society of Engineers and telling them that we know there is something wrong, but we don't know what. Just so you know how serious this is, when we were coming back from Kitty Hawk, I told Orville that I did not think that we could go on, it was just too tough. I told him that no one would fly in our lifetime. 'Course, we soon got over that."

Will waited awhile, trying to think how to say what was wrong so Cleaver would understand. "First of all, Henry, flying it was entirely different than the 1900 glider. On that glider, you could just move the forward rudder a bit and it reacted. This year, sometimes I had to shove the forward rudder all the way up or down to get a reaction. I came close to killing myself once; I'd tried to get the nose to come down, but it wouldn't, it just kept rising until I was about forty feet up, not moving at all. It was just that sort of thing that caused Lilienthal to crash. But the strangest thing happened. Instead of slamming straight down, as I was fearing, the glider just settled down and hit the ground flat. The forward rudder saved it; it kept the glider from nosing over and killing me. And that was pure luck, we never planned it that way."

"You were lucky!"

"Yes; the good Lord was watching over me that day, for sure. But I think we've got our wing all wrong. We have to make longer wings, and use less of a curve." His voice trailed off as he lost himself in thought.

Katharine brought him back. "Will, go back over the bit about the horse again. That was pretty funny."

He fumbled with his notes. "Remember, I'm trying to make a point about the importance of learning to control and to fly a flying machine. Lots of people just don't understand that, not even Mr. Chanute." He shuffled his notes, then recited, "Now there are two ways of learning to ride a fractious horse: one is to get on him and learn by actual practice how each motion and trick may be best met; the other is to sit on a fence and watch the beast awhile and then retire to the house and at leisure figure out the best way of overcoming his jumps and kicks. The latter system is the safest; but the former, on the whole, turns out the larger proportion of good riders. It is very much the same in learning to ride a flying machine; if you are looking for perfect safety, you will do well to sit on a fence and watch the birds; but if you really wish to learn, you must mount a machine and become acquainted with its tricks by actual trial."

He looked up expectantly, and they both applauded.

"That's good, Will, that makes your point. And it's funny, too. You need a little humor, because it's a difficult subject."

Wilbur glowed in Cleaver's approval. He dreaded public speaking, and had tried to get out of the talk by pleading that he would not wear formal clothes. It did not matter; Chanute was determined to have him speak, and Wilbur felt he owed it to him. And he felt a pride in it too, not a sinful pride, just pride that engineers, men with college degrees, some of them professors, would be listening to what he had to say.

Below them they heard the side door slam. Cleaver shot to his feet, panic-stricken, and Katharine turned pure white. If it were Bishop Wright there would be an ugly scene.

"Will, where are you?" Orville's voice rang through the air, and Cleaver and Katharine sat back down on the bed, weak with relief. Orville bounded into the room, saying, "Will, you have a letter from Chanute."

He stopped, dropping the letter as he took in Katharine and Henry still sitting side by side on the bed.

"What's this? Katharine, what . . ." His voice trailed off and he spun around, racing from the room and back down the hallway and the stairs.

Wilbur looked at them. "Well, at least it wasn't Father."

Later that day, Katharine spent her time outfitting Wilbur for the trip. His old dove-gray suit had to do, but she raided Orville's wardrobe for an almost-new white shirt, a collar, cuffs and cuff links, then topped it off with his handsome topcoat. Wilbur would go to Chicago looking better than he had in years.

As she dusted off his shoulders one last time, she said, "Will, thanks for understanding about Henry."

"Katharine, my dear, I understand about Henry just fine. What I don't understand about is Orv."

She looked at him, her eyes tearing. "There's nothing to understand, Will. Orv misses Mother; he's sort of substituting me for her. He needs me."

Will shook his head, took his small valise and went out the door, glad to be going to the train station.

To his immense relief, the speech in Chicago went well, despite Chanute's lengthy introduction that was both fulsome and faulty. After all their conversations and all their letters, Chanute had told the assembled engineers that the lack of a suitable engine was "the great obstacle" in the path of powered flight. It was disconcerting, and Wilbur had to change his prepared remarks a bit to disagree, stating that stability and control were the most important problems. Chanute did not seem to notice.

As the talk went on, Wilbur realized that the audience was pulling for him. They all seemed vastly interested in what he was saying. The section on "the fractious horse" got a good laugh, and after he had finished, the questions were both worthwhile and courteous. He'd expected to have some sneering naysayers, know-it-alls who believed that flight was impossible. It was quite the contrary; he sensed that most of the audience believed that flight was possible, and more than a few were interested in trying to build a flying machine themselves. He worried that perhaps he had disclosed too much.

Things were back to normal by the time he got back to Dayton, with Katharine and Orville as friendly as ever. He had done a lot of thinking on the 1901 glider on the train, and he realized that before they went back to Kitty Hawk next year, they would have to find the errors in Lilienthal's tables.

They plunged once more into the arguments of flight, with Orville arguing one theory while Will argued another; sometimes they would argue all evening, swapping sides two and three times. It was a process of homogenization, taking the best characteristics of both of their personalities and melding them by this continual engineering dialectic.

"Let's face it, Orv. We've got to go back and check every one of Lilienthal's figures. We'll make us a set of wings, and test them on some sort of a balance."

Orville shrugged. "If we do that, we may find ourselves back where we started. What if he's wrong? Where do we go from there? And it's going to be a lot of work—it's October now—we'll be checking at Christmas, maybe until New Year's. Don't forget we have some bicycle building to do if we're going to be able go back to Kitty Hawk next year."

Lilienthal had used a whirling arm to test his airfoils, and so had Dr. Langley, an enormous affair that must have cost thousands of dollars. Orville cobbled up a simple device, taking the tire off of a bicycle wheel and mounting it horizontally over the front wheel of one of their bicycles. A standard plate with a known lift value was placed on one side of the wheel and a test airfoil on the other.

Wilbur would pedal the bike as fast as he could, and they could get a rough idea of the relative lift of the airfoil. The rig worked pretty well, but it was too haphazard, too subject to ordinary breezes to yield any hard data they could put down in a table and use to design the best wing.

"This isn't getting us anywhere, Orv. It looks like Lilenthal's figures are wrong, but it's all subjective. Let's bite the bullet, build a wind tunnel, and see if we can get some hard data on this wing."

Orv was already moving toward the stack of lumber piled in the corner of the shop when he called back over his shoulder, "If we are going to do it, let's do it right. Let's test a whole lot of wings, and see which is the best."

Later that morning, Charley Taylor looked in on them.

"You gonna bury somebody in that thing?"

They stopped and looked; the box they had built was about six feet long and a foot-and one-half square.

"That's right Charley, you guessed it. There's a circus coming to town, and they asked us to build a coffin for one of the midgets." They laughed harder than Charley thought was reasonable, but to them the joke had a double meaning. Down Kitty Hawk way, it seemed that every other family was named Midgett, and the boys had often laughed about it before. Today it helped break their building tension over the failure of the 1901 glider to deliver the performance it should have.

Most of the wind tunnel came together rather easily. Charley lent a hand shaping a metal hood shielding the two-bladed wooden propeller that provided the wind. The propeller was driven by a gearbox from the system of belts that ran all of the machinery in the shop. The belt system was powered by a homemade one-cylinder engine. Fueled by natural gas, it was noisy, smelly, and reliable.

The outside of the tunnel looked crude, but the inside was as delicate as the flying machines they were building. A system of vanes and balances was installed; test airfoils could be placed inside, and positioned in a variety of angles. They could watch through a glass panel and make very accurate measurements of both lift and drag. Working feverishly, they were soon able to insert a new wing profile, test it at fifteen angles ranging from zero to forty-five degrees, and then tabulate the figures.

By November they were convinced that Lilienthal's figures were basically flawed. By December they began to see that a totally new wing shape was required, much longer and narrower than they had tried before, and with a relatively small curvature. On the seventh of December, Katharine came in the door of the shop and signaled to Charley Taylor to shut off the wind tunnel. The two brothers looked up in surprise.

"Enough's enough, boys. Its time to get back to business. You've got to start building bicycles again, or we'll go broke next spring."

Wilbur glanced across the still buzzing wind tunnel. "Orv, I think we've got enough for now, don't you?"

"I've had enough for about two weeks. I know just how we should build the next glider, and by golly, I'm going to fly this one." He walked over to the table where all of the airfoils were laid out in the order they had tested them. He picked up one, "Number 12" on its tag. It was long and narrow, and he said, "This is it, Will; we'll show those Kitty Hawkers what a real glider looks like."

CHAPTER
14

Octave Chanute always rose early to go over his correspondence before breakfast, but lately the flood of long letters from Wilbur Wright was shifting his schedule. He read Wilbur's letters before, during, and after breakfast, and he was not getting to work on his own projects until almost ten o'clock.

Yet the letters were worth the time he spent on them, carefully going over the calculations, following Wilbur's clear logic. The amount of work the young men were doing was simply astounding; they were generating more data on wing shapes and profiles than had ever been done before, and almost too rapidly to be believed. If he had not reviewed the data carefully, right down to checking the arithmetic and the trigonometry, he would have been forced to assume that it was a hoax. No one else had ever gone into the question of lift and drag with such scientific skill; no one else had ever created tables of such simplicity and utility. The tables on lift and drag became a menu of airfoils—you could pick and choose exactly what you wished from them.

And their intuition had been as correct as his had been wrong. They had sensed errors in Lilienthal's tables, and they had found them. The errors were not as bad as they had first intimated, but it was clear that Lilienthal had overestimated the lift value of his airfoil by a considerable degree, enough to throw others off if they used his figures. This was revolutionary, and would cause a sensation when he published the results. He could already hear the cries of protest from the German Lilienthal loyalists, and from the French! Ader would be furious, he knew, for the airfoil he had been working with for more than a decade was among the least effective according to the Wrights' data. No matter, let them scream; this material had to be given as wide a circulation as possible.

But what amazed Chanute more than anything else was the Wrights' evident lack of interest in grasping a scientific principle from the data. Instead they seemed to be interested only in coming up with the best wing shape. It was as if a Michelangelo had cast his masterpiece, a gigantic bronze statue—and then refused to assemble the parts.

"Mr. Herring, would you come in here please?" Chanute had taken Herring back on the payroll after a series of begging letters. The poor chap had run out of money—again—and despite all his problems, Chanute liked him and wanted to help.

Augustus Herring came in, eager, polite, his rolled-up sleeves held with a green band, a green visor on his head, dabbing at his nose with a handkerchief. Chanute thought, *a little Uriah Heep, straight out of Dickens.*

"Mr. Herring, an old friend is coming to visit today, and I thought you might want to know. It's Professor Langley. He will be here at eleven, and probably stay for lunch. If you want to take a few hours off, it will be fine with me."

Herring blushed. He passionately hated Langley, who had brutally fired him with accusations of incompetence and even thievery. But business was business, and he needed the work with Chanute. Besides, who knew what might come in the future—he might even need Langley again.

"No sir, I understand Professor Langley; he is very high-strung and demanding, and our personalities were too different. But I hold no hard feelings." His tight smile concealed his real thoughts about pushing Langley down the stairs and jumping on his head until his brains spilled out on the sidewalk.

"Good. You will understand if I don't invite you to stay with us? The professor will want to speak privately, I know."

"I would prefer that, I have a touch of the croup anyway. Thank you for being considerate."

After Herring went sniffling back out to his drafting table, Chanute put the Wright correspondence in chronological order and contemplated Langley's visit, truly the mountain coming to Mohammed. The irony was that it was all Langley's doing. The Smithsonian was loosely supervised by a board of regents, nominally headed by the chief justice of the supreme court, with the vice president and some congressmen as members. His mind raced to the recent changes; after President McKinley's assassination, Theodore Roosevelt had become president, and there was as yet no vice president. He would have to ask Langley what he thought this might mean for aeronautics; Roosevelt was one of Langley's backers.

As far as running the Smithsonian, the senior officials ignored the place except for ceremonial occasions, leaving the actual oversight in the hands of a few civilian appointees. Langley had successfully labored to have Chanute appointed as a regent, and in doing so, had changed their relationship. Where before it had been the great Professor Langley speaking down to a mere communicator, a facilitator in aeronautic circles, he now saw him not only as a supervisor, but as his chosen man on the board of regents, someone who would understand how much time and money Langley was spending on his Aerodromes—and perhaps argue for some more.

Chanute recognized both the difference and the rationale for it, and this visit pointed it out. Langley had been to Chicago many times in the past, but never deigned to call. This time he was making a special trip to see him—a real honor, especially from Langley's viewpoint.

Herring was at the door at eleven, opening it just as Langley was about to knock.

"Ah, Herring is it? What are you doing here?"

"Please come in, Professor. Mr. Chanute is waiting for you in his library. I'm working for him now. I hope you had a nice trip."

Langley fixed him with a cold eye and bounded up the stairs, leaving Herring standing holding his coat and hat. Chanute was waiting at the top, "My dear Professor, welcome to my home. I hope you had a pleasant trip."

Langely did not speak until they were seated, then jerked his thumb toward the closed doors of the library. "What on earth is he doing here? I thought you had fired him." As he spoke he glanced approvingly around the room, with its leaded glass windows, walnut paneling, and expensive furniture. Trophies of Chanute's past triumphs adorned the walls, with photos or drawings of his biggest projects having pride of place.

"I did, but I rehired him. He's having a hard time and he has a family. I use him for drafting and computing."

"Well, keep your eye on the silverware; I wouldn't trust his computations or his honesty."

At the door Herring's eyes moistened. He knew how cruel Langley was, but to accuse him like this? And Chanute did not defend him, Augustus Herring, a man who had done what no one else had done: flown a powered aircraft. They discussed him as if he were a criminal. He was back at his desk, still fuming, when Chanute's maid brought up the heavy silver coffee tray, laden with a coffeepot and pastries.

"Leave that here, please. I'll take it in." She shrugged and left. Herring went over to the tray and picked up a spoon. He stuck it in his mouth, licking it on both sides, all the way up the handle. Then he took a cup and ran his tongue around the inside and outside edges. That done, he carefully arranged the place settings, and knocked at the library door.

"Ah, that will be coffee. Come in." Both men looked surprised when Herring walked in. He set the tray on a table, and carefully served Langley with the licked cup and spoon first, then Chanute and looked at them expectantly. When Chanute nodded, he left without a word.

"A strange young man. Quite bright, but impossible to keep on the job."

Chanute chuckled. "You are so right. I've hired him to make drawings of my two-surface and three-surface machines, but half the time he is working on his own projects; a motorcycle, and, of all things, a gold dredging machine."

"Enough of Herring. You were telling me about these young lads from Dayton, the Wrights. What are they doing?"

"Professor, they are astounding. They are generating data at an incredible rate, and with real precision. I would say they have made more progress in two years than anyone else—except yourself, of course."

It pleased Chanute to see the doubt and fear flood Langley's face. He had been so certain back in Washington, so sure that he alone was solving the mystery of flight. Chanute passed Wilbur's letters across. "I'll have copies made of these for you. I'm sure the Wrights would be honored to have you review their work."

Langley sped through the letters, but the data did not speak to him. He was not used to doing the hardscrabble work of computation; he had people for that.

"But what do they say they are proving? What scientific principles are they working toward?"

"You've put your finger on the problem. They are not working for any principle—they are just looking to find the best wing shape, and then use it in a flying machine."

Langley read on, then jabbed at the letter he was holding. "Look at this, I think this exposes them. They claim that Ader's wing profile is not efficient. I can tell you that I visited Clement Ader outside Paris in 1898, and he showed me his *Eole*. It is a magnificent machine, and I have used some of his ideas in the Great Aerodrome. He has a method of routing out his ribs that makes them strong but light. I cannot believe that he has selected an inefficient airfoil."

"Well, Professor, I've gone over the Wrights' tables, and cannot fault them. I have not found a single error. I've checked almost every figure and every one has been absolutely correct."

"But my dear Octave, don't you see? Without an overriding principle, these numbers are just so much gibberish. And I am far from certain that a curved wing is necessary; I believe that a flat surface will get more than sufficient lift, and they are certainly easier to construct."

Chanute was puzzled; he knew the Great Aerodrome was to have curved wings.

Langley's expression went from passionate to crafty. "And when do the Wrights say they are going to fly? Do they have an engine? You yourself know that power is the big problem. The Lord knows I'm having problems with it, even with the best engine man I can find."

"Well, last year Wilbur—he is the older brother—said that after the end of their experiments he felt no one would fly in their lifetime. But lately his letters have been much more optimistic. They are going to take a bigger glider to Kitty Hawk."

"Where?"

"Kitty Hawk, North Carolina. They have wonderful winds there for gliding. He says they are going to take a bigger glider, and if they are successful as they think they will be, they will get an engine for it. Perhaps they will try to fly it under power the next year, 1903."

"Try to get an engine, eh? Good luck. I've got the best man in the world working on an engine, Charles Manly, and he is still a long way from getting the power we need. As you've said many times, the engine is the most difficult task, and we are finding it so. The Aerodrome is virtually ready, but the engine is not."

"If it is not a proprietary secret, Professor, when do you think you will have the engine installed?"

"I wish I knew. Manly—and he is a good fellow, so unlike this Herring person—says next spring or summer. If things go as they have gone in the past, perhaps next fall. It's not Manly's fault. He works hard and is very intelligent. It is just an extremely difficult problem to get power at a low weight."

They went on to other matters. It was Langley's view that as president, Roosevelt would boost military spending. "He'll want flying machines, balloons, dirigibles, everything he thinks might make us strong. You wait and see. We will all benefit from his leadership."

They parted with mutual expressions of esteem, and as Langley left, he said, "Will you be kind enough to remember to have those Wright papers sent to me? I'll just file them away for reference."

When he had seen Langley off, Chanute called Herring back into the library. "There, that was not so bad, was it?"

"No sir, it was a pleasure to bring him a cup of coffee." *And the croup*, he hoped.

"Well, be a good lad, and make a copy of these letters for him, will you? No hurry, if we can mail them next week, that will be fine."

Herring took the Wright correspondence back to his desk, reading it avidly as he walked. "By golly, these chaps are on to something."

The next few days Herring was a model employee, making two copies of the Wright letters. One he copied exactly, for his own files. The other, for Langley, he copied almost exactly, taking care only to change the numbers he thought most significant. "Let us see the old tyrant work with these!" The changes made him feel a little bad about spitting on the professor's spoon. It had been a shabby thing to do, not something worthwhile like this. He comforted himself with the thought that, shabby or not, it was the best he could do at the time.

Just a casual inspection of the papers told Herring that he should find some way to take out a patent based on the Wrights' findings. It was the work of a moment to convince him that the Wrights were merely covering ground that he had long ago explored. After all, he had flown in a powered two-surface machine, and so far they had done nothing but glide, and not much of that. This was worth pursuing.

CHAPTER
15

The only time it was really peaceful at 7 Hawthorne Street was when Bishop Wright was on the road, or when he was with Wilbur in the parlor, working on papers that he was sure would win back his leadership position in the United Brethren Church.

"We've got them now, Wilbur. That scoundrel Kreiter has been stealing funds from the parishioners for years, and all the time railing against me, keeping me from my post."

Wilbur nodded. He was not an accountant, but he had kept the books for their various companies, and it was quite evident that Bishop Millard F. Kreiter had, under the kindliest interpretation, mixed church funds with his personal funds. With less charity, though, it could easily be asserted that Kreiter had systematically dipped into church funds for his own needs. There were several suspicious areas where documentation was completely lacking, even though considerable sums were involved.

"It looks bad for him, Pop, I have to agree. What are you going to do?"

"Do, do? I'm going to take him in front of the church council and demand that he be unfrocked! I'm going to put out so many pamphlets exposing him that he won't be able to get a job taking up a collection, much less preaching. I'm—"

Very Christian, Wilbur thought. *No wonder none of us go to church any more.* "You might have a problem, Pop. Your friends on the council are not going to want to advertise that their leader was a thief."

"Don't you believe it, Son. I've helped make this church grow, and there's no place in it for a thief and a liar. They will have to get rid of him, and reinstate me. It is the only thing they can do."

The bishop suddenly switched subjects. "I saw that last letter you sent to Mr. Chanute. Don't you ever listen to me? You told him everything you knew about the flying machine, and you still don't have a patent. What is the matter with you?"

"Father, I've explained it to you before. Mr. Chanute is a scientist. He has helped us a great deal, and I owe it to him to tell him what we are doing. He will not take advantage of us, and he won't pass the information on."

"Son, son, son, listen to me. Five years ago I never would have believed that a senior in our church would be such a thief and a liar. And here we are, with Kreiter's hand in the cookie jar, plain as day. Believe me, you will rue the day you sent Chanute all this information."

Irritated, Wilbur slyly took the offensive. "Well, Dad, it seems like you are beginning to believe we'll succeed, that we'll have us a flying machine."

The bishop was wary. This could be the prelude to another loan.

"I didn't say that. But if there is any money to be made, it's you that ought to make it, not Chanute and his cronies. These rich people are all alike—they like to keep their money and make some more from other people's effort. How do you think they get to be rich in the first place? Lord knows we're not rich, not rich enough to be giving ideas away, ideas we paid good money to get."

He was off and running. Wilbur lifted up the paper he was working on, listing all of Kreiter's malfeasances, and began to read the one beneath, a letter back from Chanute. It was apparent that Chanute was determined to send people to Kitty Hawk with them again, perhaps even Herring. Even worse, he was going to "give" them no less than three gliders—one each of his two-surface and three-surface machines, and another strange device from some man named Charles Lamson who, apparently not content with mere wings, had oscillating wings that "automatically adjusted themselves." The Wrights were supposed to test them "in their spare time." They were having enough problems with wings that were fixed in position—he had no ideas of the problems involved in wings that oscillated. He let out a long sigh.

"Don't you go sighing at me, Wilbur Wright! I know what I'm talking about."

"Pop, I would never doubt that in a million years. I just wish other people knew what they were talking about as well as you!" And he meant it.

CHAPTER
16

It had been a miserable summer for flying a balloon, with low, cold scudding clouds, lots of rain, and virtually no one taking the streetcars out to Golden Gate Park where the Baldwin brothers were scratching out a living. Mark Twain's joke about the coldest winter he'd ever spent being a summer in San Francisco would not have gotten a laugh from them today.

Tom Baldwin was nursing his back, sprained earlier in the year when the crucial strap that ran from his belt through his crotch and up to the harness had let go when the parachute blossomed. Now it flared up whenever it was cold and damp, which was most of the time. Sam, as usual, told him it was his fault, economizing on materials, spending the money on women and liquor and not worrying about the future. It was a good wrangling brotherhood of a partnership, always at each other's throats, but always back to back in the frequent barroom fights against others. Tom—the Captain, as they billed him—took the risks of flying the balloons and jumping out in parachutes, while Sam watched over their finances, got the bookings, tried to keep the equipment in shape, and most of all, cozened Tom through his cycle of crazy binges and black melancholy.

Now the Captain sat sulking, pulling on a wicked black cheroot, hat pulled down over his eyes, not talking to anyone, working his back with his hands, trying to massage the pain away. He was a big man, with a broad brow and strong marble-sculpted cheekbones. When he scowled he was intimidating, a menacing hulk who looked like he could make bow ties out of crowbars. He rarely smiled, but when he did his entire face lit up, eyes sparkling, a wide grin disclosing some missing teeth. If he was feeling good and had a few drinks and thought something was really funny, he would erupt into a great all-encompassing belly laugh that would invite everyone to join in.

Tom squeezed his back muscles ferociously, trying to be ready, for if the weather broke he was scheduled for a two-thousand-foot jump—and that meant a badly needed four thousand dollars would flow into their empty pockets. Two bucks a foot, that was the agreement they had with the local promoter, Larry Adler. Earlier that week, Adler had told Sam this was their last shot this season; either make the jump today, if the weather was right and the crowd was there, or forget about it until next year. They could not just forget about it—they had to eat.

There were always a dozen people hanging around their stand where the balloon was tethered, no matter what the weather, asking questions, the boyfriends asking if they could have a turn with the parachute, trying to impress their girlfriend; the girlfriends, some of them, trying to flirt with the Captain, making the boyfriends jealous. Today, there was one of the worst, a little fourteen-year-old know-it-all squirt, the kind of kid you'd like to give the back of your hand to if his dad wasn't looking, and if his dad wasn't about six-foot-five and built like a wrestler. He kept asking jeering questions, telling how much he knew, and Sam could tell it was irritating Tom.

The boy sure didn't take after his dad with his build; he was a scrawny rascal, all arms and legs, with a smug confident smile and eyes that darted to his father for approval. The big-ox dad simpered at everything his son said.

"What's your name, sonny?" Sam asked. "You seem to know a lot about balloons and things."

"Puddinghead Tane; ask me again and I'll tell you the same." He shot a quick look for witticism approval from his dad and was surprised to get a frown and a headshake. Quickly he said, "No, I'm Thomas Taylor, Jr., and that's my father."

Sam decided to use the poisonous little runt to good advantage. "Well, Thomas Taylor, you have the same first name as my brother, Captain Tom, here."

Tom Baldwin grunted and looked away.

"Let me tell you something about my brother, maybe it will inspire you to be an aeronaut someday."

The kid was quick to interrupt. "Oh, I'm going to be an aeronaut, all right, I'm going to be like Santos-Dumont." He looked expectantly, waiting for Sam to ask him who Santos-Dumont was. Sam ignored him.

"Yes sir, maybe you can be like Tom here. Do you know the Cliff House?" He had to know the Cliff House—it was the most famous resort in the area. The boy nodded.

"Well, Tom here had a tightrope strung from the Cliff House way out to Seal Rocks, seventy feet high above the water, and he walked out and back on that tightrope. Could you do that?"

Young Tom Taylor was torn between a disbelieving sneer and wanting to hear more. He shook his head no.

"When Captain Tom here was your age, he ran away from home. He was an orphan, his parents killed during the troubles in Kansas." Sam didn't explain that he was an orphan too, no sense in cluttering up the story. "Tom joined the circus as an acrobat and worked his way up to be a trapeze artist, the best in the business, so good he outgrew the big top and had to do his trapeze work on a balloon."

Sam was watching Tom now; applesauce like this usually thawed him out, made him reasonable. He had to get reasonable, for there was a thin glint of sun cutting through the clouds. He might have to fly in a couple of hours.

"Then he invented this special parachute he has; see it up there on the side of the basket? That's what he uses to make his drops. Would you like to try it someday?"

The kid had had enough listening, he was back in his smart mode. "No, I'm not going to fly in a stupid balloon. I'm going to be like Santos-Dumont, and fly a dirigible around, fly it right around the city, no matter what the wind does. This balloon of yours can't go anywhere, just up and down; wherever the wind blows, that's no good."

Now the dad's eyes were misting over with pride. Sam looked at Tom to see if he was getting angry. Instead he was lumbering to his feet, his normal catlike athletic grace contorted into a mincing walk by the back spasm. He spoke for the first time.

"You keep talking about this Santos-Dumont guy. Tell me about him."

It was as if Tom had handed the kid a million dollars. He brightened up and began spieling off stories about this Brazilian, Alberto Santos-Dumont, who had built several dirigibles in France, flew them around Paris, parked them over the sidewalks. He went on and on, talking about other people who had flown dirigibles, Giffard and Renard and Krebs, and prattled on about some count who was building a huge dirigible in Germany.

Tom finally reached out and patted the young boy on the head. "Kid, you are a pain in the neck, but you got my interest." The boy and his father exchanged glances, not sure whether this was approval or disapproval. The Captain went on, "Looks like it's going to be sunny enough for a jump. You come back in about three hours, and we'll give you free tickets."

The two went away pleased, the father's arm looped around the boy's shoulder, the boy prattling on.

"Sam, that obnoxious little bastard has something. We've got to get over to Europe and see what they are doing. I'm tired of just going up and down like a blasted clock weight."

The sun had come out, a big crowd had gathered, glad to be outdoors in the sun, and Captain Tom had made his usual dramatic leap from the balloon, landing safely. They took their four thousand, had a big Italian dinner in North Beach at *La Pantera*, with Tom shocking Sam by drinking only one bottle of the rough homemade red wine. That night in the little suite of rooms they kept on Polk Street, Tom began sketching out his own ideas on what a dirigible might look like.

"Lift won't be no problem, Sam, we can build as big an envelope we need. Power is the problem, and controlling it. I think we can control up and down pretty easy, just walking back on a platform slung under the envelope. But going right and left, I'm not sure about that."

"Steamships go right and left, and they just have a rudder."

"Yes, but they are floating in water, gives the rudder something to push against. We'll be floating in air. And we need a lightweight engine."

"There's no such thing as a lightweight engine. You get pistons pounding up and down, gasoline exploding in the cylinders, crankshaft turning, you've got to have a solid crankcase to hold it. Even the steam engine in the Stanley Steamer you got parked out there weighs six hundred pounds if it weighs an ounce."

Tom glowed with pride. He'd won the Stanley in a card game, drawing a fifth card to fill a flush. "Sam, it's a steam engine, of course it's heavy, the boiler, the water, the condenser, everything. I need to get a gasoline burner, an internal combustion engine, not from an automobile, maybe special built. Electric's no good, that's for sure, can't haul a bunch of batteries around. But I tell you one thing. We're going to France, and see how this Brazilian guy does it."

It sounded good to Sam; they'd just about mined all the ballooning gold in California anyway, and he'd always wanted to see Paris.

CHAPTER
17

Lightweight gasoline-powered engines were not easy to build, not even when you had a brilliant engineer working on them. Especially if that engineer was Stephen Balzer.

In the months that Charles Manly had been laboring over the Balzer engine, he had developed a strong prejudice against engineering brilliance. Balzer had produced a beautiful, intricate rotary engine, where the cylinders rotated in a whirling blur around the crankshaft. Theoretically it was perfect. It was lightweight, and the whirling cylinders insured good cooling and kept the flow of gasoline to the intake valves constant.

The only problem was that it was too elegant, too lightly built, and too low in its power output. After months of negotiating with Balzer, a man he really admired, Manly had decided to start virtually from scratch, retaining only the five-cylinder radial arrangement that Balzer had selected, and a few features such as the automatic inlet valves. The exhaust valves were cam-driven. It was a tremendous risk; he had to tell Professor Langley that his judgment had been bad about Balzer, but was going to be good on an engine of his own design.

The most radical change was that the crankshaft no longer stood still while the cylinders rotated. Instead, as in every other engine Manly knew, and he had purchased and disassembled several, the crankshaft rotated while the cylinders were fixed. The cooling problem that Balzer had solved with rotary motion was solved by Manly with a closely fitting sheet steel jacket that surrounded the cylinders and the valve chamber, and through which water flowed. It was heavier than the air-cooled rotary cylinders, but it was effective. The steel jacket was just one-fiftieth of an inch thick, and molding it to cylinders had been difficult; it had to have enough brazing to be in contact, but enough free area for the water to flow. Just one hot spot would be enough to melt a hole in the sheet steel and send a geyser of steam spouting out.

Manly was a master machinist, and he created steel cylinders that were just one sixteenth of an inch thick, but still extremely strong, able to withstand the pounding they would take. He'd put cast-iron liners in the cylinders, so that the steel pistons, with their slotted piston ring, would have something soft to wear against. The master piston rod was connected directly to the crankpin; the rest of the piston rods were connected by bearings to the master piston rod. This kept friction—and wear—low and made lubrication easier.

Manly knew that he had survived as long as he had because Professor Langley had no interest in the engine; as his memo stated he merely "desired" that it deliver twelve horsepower. But time was running out. He'd wasted months with Balzer before taking over, and he had spent more months developing the engine to its present state.

The blasted thing had never delivered the power it should. He had thought he'd conquered the problem earlier in the year when he devised a new ignition system using a sparking plug in each cylinder. It had helped—the engine ran smoother, not bucking, but still put out only about ten horsepower. The only thing left was carburetion, and Manly thought he had solved that earlier. Obviously he had not, and he had better figure it out now, for Langley was beginning to put pressure on him. The Great Aerodrome was virtually complete, with propellers and drive shafts all ready. All that was lacking was the engine, and all it was lacking was about two horsepower.

Charles Manly stepped back to admire and to curse his work. As it stood on the test stand, the engine was a thing of beauty, five cylinders radiating out from the central crankshaft, where, when the time came, he would put a gearbox to drive the two propellers. It was just shiny black steel and silver tubing, totally inanimate, soulless, a mechanical object of his own creation—but he felt a kinship with it. There was something about it that gave him confidence that it would run, and well. There was no rational reason to be so convinced that he was on the right track, for if Samuel Pier-pont Langley walked through the door and "desired" his twelve horsepower, they would not be ready. But Manly knew intuitively that this engine was right, that when it did run correctly it would deliver far more than twelve horsepower, maybe as much as thirty or forty. That would be something, more than Langley had ever talked about having. If the Great Aerodrome really was a flying machine, this engine would make it fly.

CHAPTER
18

Katharine alternated between elation and despair when the boys marched out the door, carrying their luggage and a few more parts for the flying machine. The rest had been shipped down a few days earlier, through Elizabeth City, all the way to Kitty Hawk, where it would be waiting for them.

It was a good thing that Bishop Wright was traveling. Orv and Wilbur had been fighting like cats and dogs for the past few weeks, as they filled every spare foot of the house with the fabric for the 1902 glider, Orville marking the seams, and Will sewing them, bending over the sewing machine like a factory worker, running off miles of stitching in the Pride of the West muslin that covered the flying machine.

They pretty much had it down to a science, able to work and argue at the same time, never missing a beat. The only time they agreed was when Carrie Kayler would come in and say "Supper's ready" or, if she was feeling real devilish, "Soup's on." Both men would stop wherever they were and march back to the kitchen to wash up, then settle down to the meal, still arguing. They took no notice of Katharine; if she asked a question or interjected a comment, they would respond politely, as if she were a stranger, and then they were back at it, hammer and tongs, arguing about everything from the wing curve, to which hill they should use at Kitty Hawk, to—always—how the new glider would fly.

They never bored her—she followed their progress closely—but they did irritate her when they ignored her, so she tried to have one bombshell for every meal, something to make them sit up and take notice. Today she had a good one, and took her chance when Orville was drinking milk and Will was chewing on the beefsteak.

"Well, I guess you'll be going to St. Louis next year, and if you do, I want to go along."

Orv had recovered first; Will was having trouble with a bit of gristle. "Why would we go to St. Louis? And why we would take you if we did?"

"Well, you'd go because they are going to have a one hundred thousand dollar prize for the best flying machine. And you are going to take me, because I told you about it."

Wilbur whistled. "A hundred thousand dollars. What does it have to do?"

Katharine reached beside her and pulled up the daily paper. On the inside of the front page there was a story of the St. Louis Centennial World's Fair. In the second paragraph from the bottom there was a lead, "Flying Machines To Compete," and then two paragraphs detailing the prize money.

Wilbur read it and passed it to Orville. "Doesn't say anything about what kind of flying machine or what it has to do to win. It's just supposed to be the "best one at the fair."

"Well, are you going?"

"We won't be ready, Katharine—we have at least two more years of experimenting to do, maybe more."

"A hundred thousand dollars is a lot of money. They'll have people coming out of the hills to cash in on that. You ought to give it a try."

"It will be airship people, mostly. Maybe Professor Langley will be ready by then; he's the only one that could have a flying machine ready, at least as far as we know. One thing for sure—we won't be. Now if they were going to do it in 1904—then maybe we'd have a shot."

The two brothers fell back into their usual rhythm, argument and counterargument. When their father was away, they could get quite sharp at the table, raising their voices so that Carrie would look in, all wide-eyed and expectant. When Pop was there, they ate like good boys. It was the same with their speech; when their father was present—or if the subject was critical—their speech became as formal as a church sermon. If their father was gone, or if they were not talking about some critical flying subject, they would joke in

the vernacular. But never a profanity, never anything off color. Carrie had heard plenty of both, and was continually amazed at the
purity of their language.

She eyed their plates, the platter, and the serving dishes. They
were eating everything she cooked now, and apparently liking it.
They never said so, never actually paid her a compliment, but that
was just their way.

Carrie looked with love at Katharine, who had been so good to
her, teaching her how to cook and sew, "making her marriageable"
as Katharine often said. If the boys would not take her to St. Louis,
she ought to go with Henry Cleaver. It would cause a scandal,
Bishop Wright would be all upset, Orville would have a fit—but
Katharine deserved a little pleasure, a little consideration, too. She
was growing old before her time, and Carrie knew it was not right.
Katharine was "marriageable" right now, and Henry Cleaver was her
man.

CHAPTER
19

"This is an omen, Wilbur, I swear to you, this is an omen. We are going to have a good season of flying."

"Pop wouldn't like you swearing, or talking about omens either, but I have to admit, this schooner looks mighty good compared to the *Curlicue*."

The two brothers were exhausted. They had pulled all their gear off the train when it arrived in Elizabeth City—their baggage, the boxes with the glider parts, all of the camping equipment—and stored it at the freight depot. Then they had walked out the double doors of the station to see, bobbing up and down at the dock, the schooner *Lou Willis*, skippered by an old friend from last year, Captain Franklin Midgett. There were whole families of Midgetts along the Outer Banks, and Franklin was one of the best. He told them he was leaving on the morning tide, so they ran back to the depot, carted all their gear down to the wharf, and then went on a shopping spree. Wilbur bought a barrel of gasoline for their stove, and Orv rounded out their grocery list with some cans of his favorite baking powder. It was worth the effort—they might have had to wait for two days until the *Curlicue* arrived, and another two days for it to depart. The *Lou Willis* was a yacht compared to Israel Perry's boat, and Captain Midgett actually served edible meals: bacon and eggs for breakfast and fish for other meals, if they caught any; if they did not, he cooked up a mess of potatoes and canned corned beef that went down pretty well.

There was almost no wind, and the trip took thirty-five hours, twelve of them spent that night at anchor. During the day, Will and

Orv had moved about the deck, crawling under whatever shade they could find, alternating between arguing about the flying machine in their usual fashion and long periods of silence. The silences were the times when they seemed closest, when their minds were working together in almost telepathic harmony. The big question they worried about now was whether or not they had cured the tendency of the 1901 glider to turn about its high wing in some turns, just the opposite of anything they'd ever seen a bird do. That turn was inexplicable; there just was nothing about it in anything they'd ever read or seen or thought about. No numbers explained it, and there was no way to think it through. It was as if you were riding a bicycle, tried to turn left, and suddenly had the back wheel turning you to the right. It made no sense at all.

When the two men talked, they sounded very much alike, using the same expressions, and getting about equally excited. But their minds worked differently. Wilbur thought in abstractions; he could translate the turning of the high wing into numbers, and he tried to decide mathematically what to do about it. Orville was just the opposite, thinking in concrete mechanical terms, visualizing the high wing, the warped trailing edges, the awkward, unnatural turn away from the low wing. As he thought, he saw the wing structure, the wires, Wilbur's movements on the controls. Wilbur did not visualize, he enumerated, seeing every flight in quantitative terms, the lift of the wings, the drag of the forward rudder, the weight of the airframe and the pilot. But he could put his thoughts into words, translating the numbers into ideas that Orville could quickly understand. And it worked in reverse, with Orville putting his mechanical conceptions into words they both used and Will understanding and quantifying them as Orville spoke. The process resembled two mountain streams merging into one swelling river, neither one conscious of the melding, but both raging onward, never stopping for a moment, neither aware that one was different from the other, nor that the two were really one.

As wrapped up in flight as they were, they never functioned better than when getting the mundane things like setting up camp out of the way. The shed from last year had been battered by wind shifting the sand out from under it, leaving the roof as swaybacked as an old mule. This year they were determined to be comfortable, and they had to expand to accommodate their rush of guests—Chanute,

Herring, George Spratt, and even their brother Lorin were all coming down, and for awhile they would all be there together. They had sent down the hardware and the lumber, and had the new building all sketched out in their mind, inside and out.

Orville's handiness showed up in the way the building was expanded, and in sinking a sixteen-foot-deep well. Ever since he had typhoid, he and Wilbur watched their water carefully, making sure it was pure or boiled, or both. They had built their own well-drilling rig, and it worked so well they made up their mind to patent it when they got back to Dayton. Patenting things was heavy on their minds these days.

Their faithful friend Bill Tate was busy politicking, and his half-brother Dan came to help raise the big addition. Dan didn't have quite the love of flying machines that Bill did, and usually was happier when a few dollars came his way for the work he did, but he was still a big help. They tar-papered the roof, and for the first time put wooden strips over the cracks in the boards to keep the driving wind, rain, and sand out. While it was not exactly snug when the wind blew hard, it was still much cozier than last year's shack. The biggest innovation was a foundation and a real floor—it made it seem almost like 7 Hawthorne Place, or at least like Bill Tate's front parlor.

The new "big room" served as kitchen and dining room, with what they called their "patent" beds placed in the rafters above. Orville was particularly proud of them, making them out of wooden frames with double sheets of burlap that were springs and mattress combined, sort of a stiffened hammock. They took a little getting used to, but they were up where the heat was the greatest, and if you didn't thrash around and roll out, they were pretty safe. It was in the furnishings that Orv's artistry excelled. He took excelsior used to pack parts for the flying machine and put it on the chairs, covering it with more of the ubiquitous burlap. Then he made a covering for the table so it was now a fashionable "soft-top."

Wilbur sat down on one of the chairs, giving it a try. "Not pretty, but pretty comfortable, Orv!" It was high praise coming from his older brother.

The two men had pitched in together when more hands were needed, but when Orville could handle the task alone, Will was off measuring the heights of the three hills they used for gliding, using an instrument that Chanute had been kind enough to send them.

The gift was characteristic of Chanute, who was utterly invaluable and utterly annoying, for he helped magnanimously while at the same time imposing on them to have things done his way. Neither brother was looking forward to his visit, particularly with Herring in tow; they could do more in one day alone than they could in five with Chanute and his protégé there. But there was nothing for it—Chanute was too kind and too important not to be treated well.

But he was a logistical nightmare. He had shipped his strange, buglike multiple wing machine along with another weird contrivance built by the kite-maker, Lamson. The peculiar thing was that he insisted that they were "gifts" to the Wrights, who considered them white elephants, demanding work and care, and utterly without prospect of use. Herring was going to have a couple of gliders as well, the kind he called "Herrings" and Chanute called "Chanutes." Kitty Hawk was going to be crowded with flying machines—or at least what people hoped were flying machines.

In the meantime, the two brothers went systematically to work building their 1902 glider, putting it together with the cloth, parts, nuts, bolts, wires, and cords that they had shipped down. Covering the surfaces was the tedious part, with lots of small tacks and many small stitches to convert the Pride of the West muslin to a nearly drum-tight covering that would shed the wind as a raincoat shed rain.

They mixed the gritty work of tacking and sewing with some fun—hunting down mice that were raiding their neatly stacked supplies in the kitchen, and chasing off some ugly razorback hogs that looked like they could eat Orv for dinner and Wilbur for dessert. The best times were the experimenting. As each of the big white surfaces was completed, they would take it out into the wind and fly it like a kite, testing its pull, and checking the angle at which they felt it soaring, keeping it stationary in the wind above the ground, not moving forward but quivering with motion. It was then that the guide ropes became gigantic pulsating nerve fibers, reaching out from the glider and into their hearts and brains and souls, speaking flying to them, communicating the wind and the air, almost lifting them from the ground with an insistent pressure. It was then that the two really became one, anticipating each other's thoughts, moving flawlessly together as if someone had choreographed their movements.

"Orv, this is the best we've ever done. This thing is soaring with the slope at an angle of seven and three-quarters—that is very good."

Orville nodded; he liked the pull of the wing on the ropes that retained it; it was solid, no-nonsense, it was bucking to fly. If they'd let it go, it would have flipped over backwards and soared up the hill, tumbling like a card thrown into a hat.

They were back in their paradise of Kitty Hawk, away from their father; the visitors had not arrived, and so far all their calculations were proving out. The little shack, which Bill Tate had allowed them to build, rent-free, was much more comfortable than their primitive camp of the past two years, and they had a little gasoline stove for cooking and for heat when the nights got really cold.

In the evenings, they would talk over the next day's work, and when moved to do so, Orville played his mandolin, singing along while Wilbur remained sunk in thought.

Once he stopped picking and asked "Will, do you think we have any chance at the prize money in St. Louis? A hundred thousand dollars would fix us all up for life."

"Don't see how. And I wonder if they'll really have the money. Lots of times these fair people put up these prizes, then can't pay off. Besides, we can make a lot more than a hundred thousand dollars if we can get a real powered flying machine in the air."

It was a bombshell. They had never discussed making money before. In the early days, there had simply been no prospect either of success or of a means to make money. But this year it had dawned privately on both of them that they were nearer success than they had ever expected, and that there might be some way to capitalize on it.

"How much money do you think we can make, Will?"

"Can't say Orv, but hundreds of thousands, maybe millions. Think about it; there are people all over the world that want flying machines. If just one government gets one, every government will have to have one, then they will start bidding against each other, trying to have more and more, just like with battleships. You don't think Teddy Roosevelt got his ideas about 'the great white fleet' because he liked boats, do you? No, he was just telling England and France and Spain that we were not going to be pushed around. It will be the same with flying machines. And we will have the patent!"

"You sound like Dad, now. But we don't have a patent yet, and we've got all these visitors coming down. Herring has said he's already flown a powered airplane, and Chanute's got the bee in his bonnet, too, and then there's Langley."

"Don't you worry about Herring or Chanute, either one. They are still barking up the Lilienthal tree, hanging their feet down to control by balancing. Never work, not in a million years. You wait until you feel how powerful the wind is on this glider! Nobody could kick their legs around and control a force like that. You've got to use the power of the wind to control it, tricking the wind with twisting the wing tips and manipulating that front rudder up and down.

"But do worry about Langley! He might be on the right track and we don't know about it. He got his little models flying, and maybe he's got some ideas about control that he hasn't told anyone about. The main thing is, he has money and connections and lots of people working for him."

"How come he hasn't flown yet?"

"Don't know. Chanute doesn't know either, thinks it's the engine keeping him back."

"Might keep us back, too."

"No, we'll build our own engine if we have to. Charley Taylor can help."

Orville put the mandolin away and started to climb up toward his bed in the rafters. "That's right. We can make anything—even an engine. Especially an engine!"

Building the camp and the glider took them almost three weeks, but on September 20th, they were ready for the first flights. Both men were cautious and a little frightened, for the glider was bigger than anything they had ever built, with wings almost thirty-two feet long but only five feet wide. The decision to use long narrow wings had come from their wind tunnel work, as was the height of the wing's curve, one inch in every twenty-five. But the most radical decision was almost invisible to the naked eye. They had moved the high part of the wing's curve back twenty inches from the leading edge. Absolutely no one else would have approved of their design, not Lilienthal, certainly not Ader, and most of all not Langley. Even Chanute, who knew them best, had his doubts.

They had none, for they had an ace in the hole. All their days and nights of talking, all their concerns about the way the 1901 glider had reacted so strangely, turning around its high wing rather than its low wing, had led to an essential new element, one they had previously thought was totally unnecessary: a vertical tail fixed on booms four feet behind the wings. They had had many a hot argument about how it should be made, and finally compromised on a double fin, each one five feet high and fourteen inches wide. It was fixed, and its function was to force the glider to turn around the low wing in a turn. Intuitively, they knew it would work, Wilbur having run all the numbers and Orville having calculated the mechanical actions visually.

To a stranger, the 1902 glider looked much like the 1901—one wing superimposed on the other, connected by struts, the flyer lying down to control the forward elevator with a lever. The most obvious difference was the rear rudder. But to the Wrights there was something else about the 1902 glider, a harmony, an elegance that spoke not only to the craftsman within them, but to the artist that was there as well. It was a beautiful machine, a sculpture of cloth and wood and wire.

For all his determination to do some gliding, Orville was more than happy to have Wilbur make the first few tries. Dan and Orville joked about the walking-gliding ratio; the two of them spent twice as much time walking as Wilbur spent gliding. They would walk the glider into the wind until it had the flying speed to sustain itself and Wilbur for a short glide downhill. There was a peculiar fascination to it; as soon as Wilbur was off and gliding both Dan and Orville would stop and watch, utterly amazed. Then they would run after it and all three of them would walk it back up the hill, their feet sinking in the sand, but aided by the wind that always threatened to wrest the glider out of their hands.

At the top of the hill they paused to survey the shoreline, watching the white-capped waves marching in their endless succession, feeling the stir of sand across their skin, catching their breath and trying not to show how much each climb back up the hill took out of them. Orv looked closely at Wilbur's tightly drawn face.

"Ullam, are you OK?" Will nodded yes, but it was evident he was worried. There was something wrong with the glider, some catch that he could not yet determine. It was clutching at him, he could feel a strange nibble, a slapping of the wing against the winds like water slapped the flat bottom of the *Curlicue*. The noise, the trembling was independent of any control movements he made. He knew there was a monster lurking in that frame of wire, spruce, and muslin, but it had not yet showed its fangs.

It did late in the afternoon. Will made a good launch and was happy with the way the glider was responding; it was "cleaving the wind," to use Orville's favorite phrase, and all the controls were responding well, the elevator not so sensitive as last year, the wings lifting and dropping as he moved his hips back and forth in the new saddle they had devised to control the wing warping.

Will estimated he'd flown more than two hundred feet when the glider began to slide toward the right wing, lowered for the turn, and he felt the "nibble" begin. He waited to see if it would do what the 1901 glider did, suddenly start turning about the high wing, but it did not. Fear clutched at his heart as it began to slip toward the ground in a frightening sideways slide. Overanxious to correct, he jammed the forward rudder to a full up position, and the nose of the glider soared upward, speed falling off. From the ground it appeared to Orville like a great white whale breaching the surface of the water, leaping toward the sun. At the top of its climb, Wilbur struggled not to scream with terror, realizing he had no control anymore and that he was going to crash straight into the ground. For a moment he remembered his dying mother, wondered if he would see her in the next minute, as the glider suddenly slid to the right, falling straight down on its right wing, Wilbur feeling the wind suddenly coming from the rear, then plunging into the ground and swinging around like an augur taking hold.

The sand was still flying when Orv and Tate arrived, looking to see if Wilbur was injured. He was not—and the glider had only superficial damage, easy to repair there in the field.

"What were you doing, Wilbur, digging a well? You had that wing stuck in the sand like a drill bit."

Wilbur was shaking, his face dead white, breath coming in short gasps. Slowly he brushed the sand away, and recovering himself, said, "Can't explain it, Orv; it looks like the rear rudder isn't as big a help as we thought."

They were silent as they climbed back up the hill, lugging the glider, thinking about what was wrong. Wilbur felt weak with fear and the glider seemed to be twice as heavy as before. On the way up he was not sure he could force himself back into the machine for another try.

They said nothing at all as they made the few repairs and tested the controls. Sensing Wilbur's unease, Orville spoke. "Well, we're making progress. It may be in the wrong direction, but we're making progress. Let's not make any more flights for a bit."

They played with the glider for the next few days, tuning it as a maestro tunes a violin, altering the truss wires, tightening the struts and adjusting any bracing that looked like it had been overtaxed by the practice flights. Wary, they test flew it as a kite, no easy task in a twelve knot wind, but gratifying, for it showed the glider soaring at a six-and-one-half-degree angle of descent, better than many a hawk could do.

Orville knew that it was time to relieve Wilbur's flying a bit and he eased into gliding, his ambition tempered by his caution, with Wilbur at his side, shouting instructions. It was not until September 23rd that he summoned up the nerve to try a true free flight, making a glide of one hundred sixty feet down the big Kill Devil Hill.

Wilbur reached him at the end of the glide, still laying facedown, staring at the sand.

Wilbur betrayed his nervousness by asking "You OK Bubbo?" He used "Bubbo" deliberately: it was the name Katharine used for her brothers. Orville turned with a grin and said, "Will, you've been cheating on me, keeping this all to yourself. I think I'm going to like flying this machine!"

"It'll take more than one itty-bitty glide down this hill to make you a flyer, Orv, but it is fun, isn't it?" His voice was not convincing.

Orville's was. "Exhilarating. I never felt so well, so alive, not even when we were doing the bicycle racing. The best thing, you go speeding along, and you don't have to do any pumping, just lie there and steer!"

His confidence back, Wilbur took over for a while, making glide after glide, sometimes 150 feet long, sometimes 225 feet, but always in a straight line, and always landing with a smooth spray of sand.

It was Orville's turn. He made three short glides, then told his brother, "I'm going for the record this time." Halfway down the hill, he tried to trade some speed for height and overcontrolled, shooting the nose up into the air; the glider fell off on the wing and sideslipped straight into the ground, breaking up as it hit and hiding Orville in the center of a ball of broken spars and tangled cloth. Wilbur and Tate raced down the hill sure Orville was hurt, maybe dead. Then they saw the cloth moving and heard Orville muttering. He crawled out, face pale, but with just a few scratches.

"Well, I guess I'm not quite a birdman yet, Will. How bad is she damaged?"

"Pretty bad, Orv, but it doesn't matter. We can fix it a lot easier than we could fix your skull or your backbone!"

That night they veered from sheer delight at the way the glider was performing to utter dismay as they analyzed the two mishaps. The glider was flying as well as they had expected, but the rear rudder had not fixed things exactly as they wanted. They had spoken briefly about their fears, then stopped—they were reinforcing each other's anxieties when what they needed was confidence.

"This is going to take some thinking and some talking, Orv."

"Well, we've got plenty of time. We're going to have to fix this machine, and that will take awhile. In the meantime, we have to figure out what we're doing wrong; I'm tired seeing you dig wells all over Kill Devil Hill. And never get a drop of water, either."

"It's a good thing that you haven't lost a few drops of blood. I thought the last one had killed you."

Orville paused. "Will, there were a few seconds there when I was sure I was going to die. After I hit, there were a few seconds when I thought I must be dead. And after you came up, there were a few seconds when I thought I'd tell you I was quitting. But I tell you what. Right now I can hardly wait to get back up on the hill and glide that fool thing again."

Lorin was there to see the next flights. Lorin was, like Roosh, a breakaway brother, on his own, out from under the domination of his father, and raising his own family. But he loved his younger brothers and had come down to see what they were doing and determine just how dangerous it really was. The day after Lorin's arrival, their good friend George Spratt arrived, full of his usual good-humored yarns, and he and Lorin immediately hit it off. They were both practical jokesters, and they both had a fund of stories to tell. Lorin and George became an all-purpose support team, helping with the glider whenever there was flying going on, out fishing for the next meal when there was not, making everybody laugh all day long.

Both Lorin and George were amazed with the progress Will and Orville made; neither could tell which Wright brother was the better pilot, and neither one wanted to take a test flight themselves, for they could see that the danger was palpably real. But they liked to watch as the big glider flew farther and farther, setting new records for itself almost every day, sometimes going as high as thirty feet and reaching out as far as two hundred yards, a substantial distance that took almost thirty seconds to fly.

They discussed "well digging" with George and Lorin. Lorin did not pretend to understand, but George had some good ideas, and helped them analyze each step of the flight. They sat talking late on the night of October 3rd, drinking too much coffee, laughing, and talking about the last year, when Ed Huffaker had been with them and made so much trouble.

Later, Orville lay in his bunk staring up at the roof only a few feet over his head, listening to the rustle of mice in the cabinet and thinking about well digging. As he lay there, Wilbur's gentle snores coming across the loft, he began to see the solution. Instead of a fixed rudder in the back, they needed one they could turn. When you warped the controls to turn to the left, say, you needed to tip the rudder a little bit to the left, too, to keep the glider turning. It would take another controller, maybe something they could guide with their feet, like they used to use to warp the wings. He was thinking about the new rudder—one in place of two—it would be easier to install, when he finally went to sleep.

Next morning Orville was late getting up, and George, Lorin, and Wilbur were already eating breakfast.

"Come on sleepyhead, better get some coffee into you. We've got work to do."

Orville busied himself at the stove, fried an egg and some bacon, his face knotted in thought. He had to do this cleverly, or Wilbur would instinctively object. If he didn't present the idea on the rudder just right, it would take a week of arguments to get Will to try it.

Orv slid in at the table and winked at Lorin, alerting him to the fact that something was coming and to watch Wilbur's reaction.

"Will, I've been thinking. The problem is that the rear rudder is fixed. We need to get it to turn when we twist the wingtips. Say we're going to turn left, we move our hips to turn the left wingtip up and the right wingtip down. As we do, we push a little lever, and we turn the rudder left too, so it's offsetting the drag of the high wing."

Wilbur sat quietly. Orville kicked Lorin under the table, expecting Will to come back with "Well, I've already thought of that, and it won't work."

Will was quiet for more than a minute, then he looked up, no smile on his face, just concentrating hard. "You're right. But we don't need another control. We'll just wire it into the wing-twisting mechanism. When we move our hips to the left, the left wingtip will turn up, the right wingtip will turn down, and the rudder will turn left automatically. Just the opposite for a right turn. Would you pass me the coffeepot please?"

Orville passed him the coffeepot with pleasure; it was really rare to get approval from Wilbur so fast—it made him proud of his idea, and eager to get to work.

But visitors intervened. Octave Chanute and August Herring arrived on Saturday, October 4th, both weary from the long trip, and both obviously tired of each other already, with Chanute being fairly severe with Herring, and Herring being very apologetic and humble to Chanute. No problem seeing who was the boss and who was the employee—except when the conversation became general at night after dinner. Then Herring was apt to hold forth, interrupting everyone, even Chanute, and putting his own ideas forward. It was as if he gathered courage from the flickering light of the lantern and the warmth of the gasoline stove, fierce up close, feeble a few feet away.

While Orville and Wilbur worked on changing the rear rudder from two fixed surfaces to one that turned, Herring was busy assembling the Chanute multiwing glider. It was hard for the two Wrights to keep a straight face as they looked at Chanute's pride and joy. Chanute had commissioned Herring to rebuild the multiwing glider—they called it the *Katydid*—using the glider they had flown in 1896 as a basis. Chanute was convinced that more wings were better than fewer, despite the fact that more wings meant more weight, for each one had to be attached and braced, each connection adding weight but not lift. Aware of this, Herring had systematically cut down the weight of the wing framing, always getting Chanute's approval before proceeding. As Herring worked to assemble the *Katydid*, it was apparent to the Wrights that it was far too flimsy to take the winds at Kitty Hawk, which had shaken their own sturdy gliders like rags on a clothesline. They could tell by inspection that the fragile glider's wing would twist in the wind, dumping any lift they might generate. Still, they had to be polite and encouraging.

When Herring finished, the *Katydid* looked like a stack of bed frames: eight wings, four on a side, each one precariously attached to a lightweight central cage in which the operator stood, legs protruding so that he could make a running takeoff. Chanute invited them all to watch a test flight. The three Wright brothers stood silently with George Spratt as Herring continued to fuss with the *Katydid*, tightening a wire here, loosening one there. Finally, with obvious reluctance, he placed himself inside the glider and ran a few steps down the hill, then stopped and trudged back to the top, shaking his head. On the second attempt, he ran hard and leapt off the ground, gliding about twenty feet before crashing on the right wing.

Herring crawled out of the glider, obviously furious with himself, and embarrassed about the poor flight. Wilbur and Orville helped him carry it back, keeping quiet, not wishing to spark a quarrel. Yet that night, Herring was again authoritative, putting his ideas forward with clarity and precision. The Wrights listened in silence as Herring went on and on about the *Katydid*, comparing it favorably to the Wrights' glider—which he had not yet seen fly.

Inwardly, Herring seethed that he had done what none of the others had done, flown under power. There was nothing he could say or do to convince them of his primacy in the field; he had been relegated to the status of Chanute's boy, just someone to haul that ridiculous *Katydid* around and attempt to get it in the air. It was mortifying. Particularly in front of the Wrights, nice enough fellows, but with no formal education. He, Herring had gone to school in Switzerland and Germany, and spoke both French and German. He had completed the requirements for a mechanical engineering degree at the Stevens Institute of Technology, a top school. He had built engines, steam and internal combustion, and more than anything else he had flown under power, something none of them had done.

Yet Herring's comments, delivered with his soft Georgia accent and his invariable good manners, did impress the Wrights. He was obviously a serious student of flight, and he seemed to understand them much better than did his mentor Chanute. The only thing that really bothered the Wrights was Herring's notebook. He had recorded everything that had happened so far, including every detail of the 1902 glider. He kept it close to him at all times; once, when Wilbur had asked to see, he had demurred with a flimsy excuse that he was "not neat."

For his part, Chanute was quiet and withdrawn, thinking about the obvious and troubling differences between his glider and that of the Wrights. His *Katydid* was relatively small and obviously fragile; theirs was big and seemed rugged as a bridge with its wire trussing. When he finally spoke, it was to Herring, about reinforcing the wings and trying to find a hill with a steeper slope. It was dark in the little shack, and Orville risked nudging Wilbur in the ribs and whispering "Maybe they ought to go out to the Grand Canyon—pretty steep slope there." Wilbur nudged him back and looked away.

Two days later, as the Wrights continued work on their own glider, Herring tried again, but could not get Chanute's glider off the ground. The two men carried the glider back to the shed, quietly arguing, their voices low but their gestures giving them away. Chanute was lecturing Herring. "I told you not to cut so much weight! But you insisted, you are always putting your ideas first, and not listening to what I say."

"That's not fair, Mr. Chanute. We talked about everything I was going to do, and you approved."

"I did not, and you and your twenty-foot glides are making me look ridiculous."

Herring stalked away, and Chanute climbed up to his bed in the rafters, itself always a comic scene as he warily lifted his portly body up and into his "patent bed."

On balance, Chanute was an easy guest. Orville was doing most of the cooking and the food was necessarily plain, with biscuits and gravy serving as the keel of meals that featured fish when available, an occasional duck brought in by one of the lifesaving station boys, and with precise regularity, either canned corn or canned tomatoes as vegetables. Chanute was an epicurean, and had dined in all the best restaurants in the United States and Europe, but he ate heartily, and always complimented Orville on his cooking, something that no one else could bring themselves to do. Herring, on the other hand, always dabbed at his food, tasting it gingerly and suspiciously and occasionally registering the look of a man who had bitten into a bad oyster.

Chanute's general gentility was why the Wrights were embarrassed that night. Sanitary facilities were nonexistent at the camp, which posed a problem with six people living there. The accepted technique was to take a shovel and some newspaper and move out of sight, well down the dunes from the well. But the Wrights valued Chanute, and, giving consideration to his age and weight, had prepared for him a lightweight wooden seat that he was quietly and privately advised was for his own special use. It did not avoid the use of the shovel, but it was at least a little more dignified and comfortable. Chanute, despite his wealth and fame, had spent many years in the rough, building bridges and dams, and he regarded the Wrights' gesture as a touching and genteel tribute.

The problem was that Herring quickly appropriated the use of the seat, which the Wrights and Spratt regarded as very pushy. Lorin and Spratt took it upon themselves to teach Herring a lesson, making a duplicate seat, but weakening the legs so that they would give way when any weight was placed on them. A routine had developed, with Chanute using the chair first, then going to bed, with Herring following suit. That night, after Chanute went to bed, they substituted the weakened chair for the proper one, in anticipation that Herring would use it. The problem arose when Chanute quietly climbed down from his patent bed, took the duplicate seat and disappeared into the night, heading for the sand south of the well. He came back quietly furious, but not saying a word. The incident was never mentioned—until Chanute and Herring left a few days later.

On the morning following the "great disaster" as it became known, the Wright glider was ready at last. Wilbur tested it very cautiously, unwilling to take chances with the new rudder. But even with the first, cautious glides of only about 125 feet it was obvious that both Herring and Chanute were shaken. The Wrights had moved ahead of them both, and by a considerable margin.

By Friday, October 10th, Wilbur had gained sufficient confidence to fly the glider boldly, crossing the sloping dunes at an angle, meeting winds from sharply different directions and gliding out to 280 feet. Herring watched the glides with such intensity that he seemed to be mesmerized, measuring every flight, recording the wind in the little battered leather notebook that he carried, and jotting down page after page of commentary. Orville noticed his industry and whispered to Wilbur, "There is a good reason to get right on our patent when we get back. He's done everything but pull out a tape and measure your nose."

Chanute had noticed Herring's note-taking as well, and once took his notebook to read, handing it back to him without a comment.

Then the weather went sour, with high winds reaching sixty miles per hour and driving rain that seemed to pack the inside of the shack with gloom and despair. Fierce arguments broke out between Chanute and Herring, Orville and Wilbur, and even Lorin and George, the inseparables. Fortunately, the arguments were kept confined to the pairs, without any crossover that might have led to some real unpleasantness, say Lorin arguing with Chanute or Herring with Spratt. The last one would have been a bad one, because Spratt, a tough farmer, would not have thought anything about punching Herring in the mouth.

The flying, the weather, and the arguments broke up the camp, with Lorin leaving first, followed by Herring and Chanute, both tight-mouthed and brow-furrowed. There was one more storm, and the weather shifted abruptly, with the temperature dropping to near freezing and the wind hitting fifty miles per hour. It was, in Orville's terms, a "five-blanket" night.

CHAPTER

20

Octave Chanute was too much a gentleman to remain angry on the long train ride back, and by the time they left Elizabeth City, he and Herring were once again on good terms, with Herring promising faithfully never to reveal any of the Wrights' secrets.

"You've got a lot of notes in your little leather case there, Mr. Herring, and I hope that you will not share them with anyone. The Wrights have worked very hard to get where they are, and until they want to tell their story, we have to keep their secrets as if they were our own."

Herring's face assumed the intensely honest air he had perfected, thinking, *But they are our own, now*, but saying, "Of course, Mr. Chanute. Would you like to have my notebook? I could get it from you whenever I need it."

Chanute declined, replying, "Just be careful. It is our task to promote aeronautics, not to be first. I don't care if the Wrights fly the first flying machine, or if Langley does—just as long as someone does!"

When Chanute told him that he was going to stop in Washington on the way back to see Professor Langley, Herring immediately asked if he could accompany him.

"No, I'm sorry, Mr. Herring, but we both know you've offended the professor somehow. As a regent, he has to see me; I don't want to put him in an embarrassing position by bringing you along."

Herring nodded; he'd expected to be refused. "In that case, sir, if you don't mind, I'll just go straight on home, and then see you in Chicago in a few days."

Langley met Chanute at the door to the Castle—no sending some clerk to bring him in now that Chanute was a regent. They climbed the stairs to Langley's office slowly and gravely, Langley expounding on recent discoveries by Oliver Heaviside on a peculiar layer in the atmosphere which appeared to assist radio waves, sending them farther out than anyone had believed possible. He asked if Herring had been to Kitty Hawk with Chanute, and clucked when he learned he had, commenting, "I hope he behaved better there than he did here."

Once in his office, Langley came straight to the point. "Tell me, then, how are the Wrights doing?"

"My dear Professor, they are doing superbly well! They are operating under the most primitive conditions"—the thought of the collapsing chair flashed through his mind—"but you would be amazed at the purity, the utter simplicity of their flying machine. They are getting flights up to more than five hundred feet, and they are flying with real control. They can turn left or right, flying in winds up to thirty miles per hour and more. It is really quite phenomenal. I'll tell you frankly, they have beaten me all hollow."

It was not what Langley wished to hear.

"What is their secret? What are they doing that no one else has done?"

By chance, Langley had asked the one question Chanute was not prepared to answer, not because he was reticent, but because he did not know. After all his time in the Wright camp, after closely inspecting the glider and watching the Wrights' mastery of it, he still did not grasp the basis for their success: controlling the flying machine in three dimensions.

"I think it's the superimposed wing. They have such a strong structure that it can take the strong winds, and, just as you have theorized, draw energy from them."

"Can they put an engine in their machine?"

Chanute hesitated, hoping he was not giving too much away. "Not this one; it's bigger than any glider I've seen, but nowhere as big as your Great Aerodrome. No, I think they'll have to build a bigger machine, test fly it as a glider, then find an engine and install it. Seems to me that they have two more years of work, then they'll be flying."

Chanute asked about how work on the Great Aerodrome was progressing and was annoyed when Langley seemed to freeze.

"It's going very well. That's all I can tell you."

"You cannot tell me when you intend to fly it under power?" Chanute's voice had the faint ring of iron used by supervisors; it was time for Langley to remember who was the regent and who was the secretary.

Langley knuckled under. "I don't think it will be ready until the fall of 1903. I'm ashamed to say this, but the engine has just been intractable. I've told you how much I think of Manly, and I still do. He's promising me forty horsepower now—but he doesn't see how he can deliver until well into the year."

Chanute rose, and they talked about other matters on the way out, both men thinking the same thing—this was getting to be a real horse race. It depended upon the Wrights, and whether they could find an engine.

Fifteen minutes later Ross Robbins brought in an envelope, carrying it on a silver salver, as Langley had recently requested him to do. It was from Herring, asking for an audience, and promising "some interesting" information.

Langley sent back a note, sealing it with wax to prevent Robbins's eagle eye from reading it. It read, "Do not come to this office again. Be at the southeast corner of Twelfth and Pennsylvania at four o'clock p.m. today. I will send a carriage for you."

Herring had caught the hint; he was waiting in the freezing drizzle under an umbrella, muffled in a tall hat, scarf, and coat with collar turned up. He scrambled into the carriage like a gopher diving in its burrow.

He began his usual obsequious apologies, but Langley cut him off. "What have you to tell me?"

Without a word, Herring handed over his notebook, opened to the flights of October 10th. The light was poor in the carriage, and Langley had to lean forward and squint, asking Herring brief questions about his abbreviations and what some of the notations meant.

"Sir, the Wrights are quite advanced in their experiments."

"Silence, Herring, I can see that, and Mr. Chanute told me so. When do you think they will install an engine and try to fly?"

"In no more than a year, perhaps less. I wish we could have stayed a few more days and watched how they did. But I had the feeling they were holding back, not doing all they could do while we were there."

Langley looked contemptuously at him, thinking that the Wrights probably had his measure, all right.

"Mr. Herring, you will never mention our meeting today with Mr. Chanute or with anyone else, do you understand me?"

Herring nodded, smiling to himself. He would get something from this meeting, one way or another; if not from Langley, then from the Wrights or even Chanute.

"I hope this information is of some value to you, Professor. If you could see it in your heart to employ me again, I'm sure I could make good use of it for you."

"I'm sorry, Herring, this is interesting, but meaningless to me. The Great Aerodrome is complete, except for testing the engine. I'm not going to throw away ten years of my life and a great deal of money to copy the ideas of two bicycle mechanics who happen to be good kite-flyers. Here is fifty dollars. I'm buying your silence about this meeting, and nothing more."

Langley thumped the carriage wall and the driver pulled over. Herring leaped out without a word, skidding on the sheet of frozen rain. Langley had done him in again, ignoring the priceless information he had given him. He shoved the fifty dollars into his pocket. He would go back to work for Chanute, for as long as that lasted. Blast all scientists! They were all the same, all crooks looking for an easy dollar.

CHAPTER
21

Back at Kitty Hawk, the weather had turned perfect, with the winds sculpting the hills into new forms, providing new ridges to cross, new currents to combat, but most of all steady winds that blew up those beautiful hills all day, averaging about thirteen miles per hour. The glide distances picked up, with Wilbur consistently going over 550 feet, and Orville, improving all the time, working his way from 360 to 505 feet. In two days they made more than 250 glides, their backs and legs weary from hauling the glider back up the hill, their hearts soaring with the knowledge that not only did they have a glider that flew well, but that they knew how to fly it. No more upper wing turns, no more well digging, just long satisfying flights that felt like you were sliding down the broadest banister in the world, rushing down the slopes, tasting the salt in the sea spray, passing over the brush, and finally setting down in a satisfying shower of sand. Sometimes they would be gliding when the ferry to Ocacroke Island would come by, and they could see people standing at the rails, waving their handkerchiefs, not believing what they were seeing. It made them feel good.

Orville's letter-writing to Katharine had dropped off, and Lorin had returned home already with most of the news, but he closed his last letter with a paragraph that said it all, writing, "We have gained considerable proficiency in the handling of the machine now, so we can take it out in any kind of weather. Day before yesterday, we had a wind of 16 meters per second or about 30 miles per hour, and glided in it without any trouble. That was the highest wind a gliding machine was ever in, so that we now hold all the records!

The largest machine we handled in any kind of weather, the longest distance glide, the longest time in the air, the smallest angle of descent and the highest wind!!! Well, I'll leave the rest of the 'blow' until we get home."

He reread the letter and realized that Pop wouldn't approve—it came close to bragging, and the Wrights were against that. But there was no way he could not say it; Katharine deserved to know how well they were doing, she had put up with so much from them while they were sewing up the glider. Besides, it was true, every word of it. They had put up with the wind, the sand, with Herring and Chanute, with boring food and cold quarters, not to mention the danger, the very real danger, and they had triumphed. It was all right to tell what they were doing, he hadn't exaggerated. They had all the records!

They broke camp with no reluctance, storing Chanute's "gift" gliders and their own beautiful 1902 glider in the rafters of the shack, hoping that next year's storms would leave it standing. Back in Dayton, one of Wilbur's first tasks was to write Chanute, and tell him that they had made a record flight of 622.5 feet, staying in the air for twenty-six seconds. As he finished the letter, Wilbur realized that it was only three years before that he had written Chanute, asking for information as to where they might find a good place to glide. In three years they had gone from know-nothings to experts.

Now the fourth year would be decisive.

PART THREE
SUCCESS

Few men during their lifetime come anywhere near exhausting the resources dwelling within them. There are deep wells of strength that are never used.
Admiral Richard E. Byrd

CHAPTER

22

Glenn Curtiss paused after he leaned his bicycle against the wall of Taggart's foundry, catching his breath. It was only six miles from his shop to the little settlement of Bath, but he had ridden fast, conscious that he was getting out of shape. His businesses were taking too much time, and he had not ridden in competition for months.

The foundry was run by a versatile farmer, John Kirkham, who had built a woodworking shop and planing mill to augment his meager earnings from his hundred-acre holding, then added the foundry onto it when he discovered there was a demand for castings and forgings. The rambling establishment marched chronologically from the deep green fields behind toward the road—a stone farmhouse that must have been built in the early 1800s; a variety of utilitarian buildings for storage and shelter scattered around a weatherworn barn from fifty years ago, everything made from wood, some painted, some just scoured by the wind; then the large woodworking shop and planing mill, new, built of wood but with a surprising number of windows on three sides. The last building was bigger than all but the barn: the wood and stone foundry, with a huge central chimney and big double doors able to admit a carriage. Kirkham's son, Charles, was always about, playing with the tools.

Curtiss had made his first trip more than six months ago, arranging for Kirkham to cast engine parts to his design. John had demurred at first, arguing that it was too complex for his shop, but Glenn persisted. He preferred having someone he could trust and work with close at hand to trying to do things by correspondence with someone in a big city. This was going to be a cut and fit operation, and he needed to have his hands on the product.

It turned out to be a good working relationship. Kirkham would take Curtiss's drawings, which were pretty rudimentary, and analyze them from the points of view of both the foundry man who would cast them and the machinist who would have to hone them and turn them into working parts. They learned together, for while Curtiss was more than willing to listen to Kirkham's suggestions, he was persistent about keeping the parts at a minimum weight consistent with the stress they would have to endure. Usually Kirkham would suggest an inexpensive way to get the results—a thicker web, stronger cast brace, a larger hole for the connectors—and Glenn would consider it carefully before coming back and asking for another look at something lighter, even if it was more expensive.

Curtiss had Kirkham begin planning the second set of castings even before he and Neff had finished polishing and assembling the first set into the original Curtiss motorcycle engine. Its single-cylinder was placed dead center in the frame of a Hercules bicycle, and drove the rear wheels with a V-belt. A muffler the size of an oatmeal box hung on the front of the race, nicely positioned to burn your leg if you were not careful dismounting. He retained the standard pedal and gear combination, both for easy starts and when the engine chose not to run.

Practically everyone in Hammondsport turned out to watch him test the motorcycle—there was no question when it was running, for the noise was deafening even with the muffler, breaking the normally quiet dozing of Park Square. He realized almost at once that he had made the first engine too large. It had more power— and much more noise—than he needed.

Curtiss took a set of heavily revised drawings to Kirkham for the second batch of castings after he had put fifty hours of test time on the first motorcycle. While it would cost time and money, throwing away much of what Kirkham had already done, he knew that the second engine could be made smaller, lighter, and much more salable. While Kirkham was manufacturing the revised engine, he put in another two hundred hours of test time riding the first motorcycle, constantly improving it, and more importantly, seeing what had to be done with the second one to make it easier for the average rider to handle.

The second engine was, as Neff pronounced it, "sweet," singing its powerful single-cylinder song through the same size muffler as the first one to keep the noise level down. It was not as powerful as the first engine, and didn't need to be; its smaller size and lighter weight made the second motorcycle much easier to handle. Somewhat to his surprise, Curtiss sold the second machine to a man from Pennsylvania who had been riding on the road to Hammondsport in a carriage. Curtiss had passed him once in his long circling rides around the town, and on his second circuit the man was ready and waiting, leaping out to flag him down. He examined the motorcycle closely, and insisted on purchasing it on the spot at a price Curtiss could not refuse. A few months later, the man, a true believer, opened a dealership for Curtiss motorcycles.

Glenn had always talked his business moves over with Lena, but hesitated now. Poor little Carlton, only eleven months old, had died in February, and she was still desolate. He found her sitting as she often did, in the baby's room, on the little couch where she had spent so many nights awake, listening to her baby's labored breathing. He sat down, slipping his arm around her and brushing the hair away from her face with his hand.

"Lena, darling, would it upset you to talk a little business?"

She nodded, forcing a smile. The long painful months of her baby's life had taken much out of her, and she knew she had to force herself to get back to normal. She was already doing more around the house, cooking bigger meals, trying to forget. But she always drifted back here, to this couch in the sad little room with its empty crib.

"You know we've done very well with the bicycle business, and even with the tack business. I never thought we would have as much money in the bank as we have now, and you probably did not either."

She nodded again.

"Well, I want to switch over, out of the bicycle business, and go into building motorcycles full time. Motorcycles are more fun, and the margin on them is so much greater. I think we've got the best engine in the world for it, your uncle and me, and I just know there's a market out there. I'll tell you, if someone else had built this motorcycle, I would want to buy one no matter how much it cost. It's just better than anything out there, better than anything I've ever seen. It's lighter, it's faster, it's—"

Lena reached up and put a finger on his lips. "Glenn, if you think it's right, you do it. You've never been wrong yet. And I want to help, I want to get involved, I've got to get over . . ." Sobbing, she buried her face in his shoulder, unable to say the rest out loud.

Within a month, Curtiss had his shop converted to a motorcycle factory. It was just a long wooden building, a coal stove at one end, the walls lined with benches, one side filled with machine tools, the other for assembly. In the middle a line of Curtiss motorcycles marched, progressing from a beefed-up bike frame hung on straps from the ceiling down to a finished motorcycle at the end. They called it the Hercules, but it had the Curtiss name in the distinctive cursive script that Claude Jenkins, one of his employees, had designed. Curtiss soon had six workmen, all from Hammondsport, and all earning more than they would have in the wineries. They were glad to be associated with this twenty-four-year-old ball of fire who was making a name for himself not just in Hammondsport, but all around the area.

Business exploded; by May he had to open a second shop thirty miles away in Corning. Orders poured in from across the country for motorcycles, and even more for just the Hercules engine, which was lighter and more powerful than anything on the market. He knew that eventually he would have to expand and incorporate to bring some capital to the business, but for now he just wanted to hold onto it tightly, maintaining control of the engineering and the quality. Engineering was not exactly the right term, and he knew it; neither he nor Neff were professional engineers, nor was Kirkham. But they all understood machinery, and were good with their hands, and that was what they needed now.

Curtiss was bemused by his success, telling Lena, "Honey, I don't know what we are going to do with all this money. It keeps coming in, you know that, you are keeping the books. We've got to keep expanding; I want us to get telephones in the shop and in the house, and I'm going to buy an automobile, soon as I can figure out which one is the best."

Lena was at last becoming strangely content. Glenn had understood about not having any more children, and she was fulfilled by the responsibility he gave her. She liked everyone in the shop, and enjoyed compliments paid to her as she rode past in the special wicker sidecar that Glenn had built for her on a special brilliant red motorcycle. She was not happy—she did not think she would ever be truly happy after Carlton's death, but she knew Glenn needed her, and that had to be enough.

It was just the reverse for Glenn. The more the business prospered, the more things seemed to go his way, the more he wanted to get back into racing—motorcycle racing. There was a gut competitiveness about him that making money and meeting payrolls did not fulfill. He was only twenty-four, and he wanted speed and the rough-and-tumble competition of the dirt tracks where he could test his new ideas.

Buffalo had been by far the biggest city Curtiss had ever seen, but his urge to race took him to Brooklyn in September, where the New York Motorcycle Club was holding a huge meeting.

Curtiss rode down on his latest motorcycle, a small valise tucked behind the seat, following a careful regime for breaking in the new two-cylinder V-2 engine on the trip. He would run five miles at thirty miles an hour, then five miles at forty, and so on up to sixty, then back down, in five-mile increments. It took time, but he'd learned in the past that a good break-in period saved problems later.

He took two days for the trip, stopping in Binghamton to talk to a large foundry there that had quoted him some excellent prices to not only cast but manufacture the engine for him, under his own quality standards. That was a stretch for him—he did not want to surrender that much control, and the size and bustling atmosphere of the Susquehanna Foundry intimidated him. But he needed volume, and Kirkham had already peaked in the number he could deliver. The foundry manager was a tough-talking little Swede who obviously knew his business inside out, and finally convinced Curtiss that he would keep quality up. Glenn quietly decided to see if he could decentralize, keeping the research and engineering and some manufacturing in Hammondsport, but contracting the rest out. He was spreading himself too thin already.

Frank Neff had steered him to the Kearny Hotel in Brooklyn, but he had trouble when he insisted on taking the motorcycle up to the room with him, afraid that someone might steal it from the yard at the back where carriages and a few automobiles were parked. The hotel clerk was a feisty Irishman who stood behind his registration desk with a monarchical air, constantly polishing the desktop as a bartender wipes a bar. He brooked no nonsense from anyone, and flatly refused to let Glenn take his motorcycle inside. He offered a compromise: he would set up a cot in the yard where Glenn could sleep. Reluctantly, Curtiss let his motorcycle stand in the yard, covered by a canvas he found in the corner. No one bothered it.

The races turned out to be a disappointment. Glenn was used to finishing first at whatever he did, but there were no motorcycles like his among the competitors. They were all huge machines with big displacement engines, some having four cylinders, and they were simply too powerful for him to beat. The best he could do was second in a time race, and third in a finish race. He was not satisfied, but he had learned a lot, and his Hercules motorcycle had gained a lot of attention. After he was back, a flood of letters came in inquiring about purchasing the motorcycle or the engine, including a letter from an aeronaut who apparently wanted an engine for his balloon. That was strange; Curtiss could not conceive how you could use an engine in a balloon, but it was not his problem; if someone wanted to buy an engine and put it on an apple pie, he'd sell him one. Then he remembered Augustus Herring, who had written a few letters after their meeting in Buffalo, but then stopped. He would be pleased to learn about the new motorcycle engine—it would be just right for a flying machine.

CHAPTER
23

The world works in mysterious ways. Tom Baldwin had sold his Stanley Steamer back to its original owner at a bargain price to get money for the trip to Paris. The owner, James Fitzgerald, had contacts in Paris with members of the Automobile Club de France, and gave the Baldwin boys letters asking that they be introduced to Alberto Santos-Dumont.

"For God's sake, Tom, be on your best behavior over there. These people are friends of mine, and if I introduce you, I don't want you getting into any fights."

"Fitz, that's a terrible thing to say. Sam and I will be good boys. I just wish we spoke French. How about you coming along and interpreting?"

Tom was not serious. The last thing in the world he wanted was Jim Fitzgerald traipsing along, watching everything they did. But Fitzgerald must have been waiting for the opportunity, for he leaped at the chance, saying, "You're on!" as he ripped the letters of introduction out of Tom's hand.

In the end it worked wonderfully well. The Automobile Club de France had been founded in 1895 by the Count de Dion, and was a magnet for successful French industrialists. Three years later the Automobile Club had spawned the Aéro Club de France, with many of the same members. Fitzgerald's French friend, Pierre Lissarague, was a member of both, and promptly introduced the three Americans to Ernest Archdeacon and Henri Deutsch de la Meurthe, both of whom were determined to see France first in flying machines as it had been first in balloons and dirigibles.

Both men were very well-to-do, and both had created substantial prizes for aviation feats. Newspapers under glass on the walls of the Aéro Club told the story of Santos-Dumont's great flight of October 19th, 1901, when he flew his Airship No. 6 from St. Cloud to the Eiffel Tower and back in just under thirty minutes. Santos-Dumont, who was also immensely wealthy—few in the Aéro Club were not—had collected the 100,000-franc Deutsch de la Meurthe prize for his feat, then immediately made the grand gesture of giving half the prize to the poor of Paris, and half to the crew who had prepared his dirigible. Neither of the Baldwin boys was able to read or speak French, but they had no difficulty in converting 100,000 French francs into twenty thousand American dollars, and they immediately wanted to meet the Brazilian.

Fitzgerald had been warned that Santos-Dumont was a cold, reserved man who was difficult to know, and he admonished the Baldwin boys to be very quiet and reserved. He could not have been more wrong, for when de la Meurthe took them to the flying field where Santos-Dumont was supervising the work on his Airship No. 7, the tiny wisp of Brazilian was utterly gracious, eager to meet the Baldwins because he was planning on taking his No. 7 airship to St. Louis, to compete for the prize at the 1903 World's Fair.

The Baldwins were stunned by the dapper appearance of the twenty-seven-year-old Santos-Dumont. He was at his flying field to work, but he was dressed so beautifully that the might have walked off a magazine cover. Santos-Dumont spoke some English, but as he showed the Baldwin brothers around the huge wooden hangar, he spoke in French, letting Fitzgerald translate, telling Tom, "I want to be sure what I tell you is correct, and my English is not always perfect."

All three Americans were stunned at the sight of the beautiful dirigible Santos-Dumont was building. Airship No. 7 was a pencil-slender, 150-foot-long cylinder that held some 1,250 cubic meters of hydrogen and was powered by a Clément four-cylinder water-cooled engine that was supposed to deliver sixty horsepower.

They fell into a pattern, with Santos-Dumont speaking and Fitzgerald translating, the Baldwin brothers interrupting with questions as they walked.

"He says this is his racing machine and that it will go seventy kilometers per hour." Fitzgerald added in a whisper, "That's about forty miles an hour."

"It is expensive; it takes three thousand francs just to inflate the envelope, and then fifty francs a day to keep it inflated."

Tom did some quick figuring; not too bad, six hundred dollars to fill it and then about ten dollars a day to top it off. He thought it might have been more. Maybe hydrogen was cheaper in France.

"Ask him about the danger of having an internal combustion engine and using hydrogen."

Fitzgerald was better at listening to French and translating it than translating English to French, and it took him a moment.

"He says it is very dangerous, of course. One mistake and boom, you are dead. But he says that he will sling the engine in the car very far below the envelope, perhaps as much as fifteen meters— almost fifty feet. He says that gives him stability, and almost rules out an explosion."

That night in their hotel room, Tom began sketching out his own version of a dirigible. "We cannot compete with little Santy Dumont, Sam, not in spending. He must have fifteen thousand invested in that dirigible."

"Yeah, and look at the size of the shed he stores it in, and the crew of people he's got working for him. We have to come up with something smaller."

"What do you think that Clément engine weighs?"

"Well, I didn't see any radiator, but if he's getting sixty horsepower, it has to weigh maybe six pounds per horsepower. So with the radiator and the plumbing, maybe four hundred, four hundred fifty pounds?"

Tom whistled. "Wow. And I'm not getting any lighter. Santy can't weigh much over a hundred pounds, and I go twice that. We've got to find us an air-cooled engine, one that's a lot lighter than anything I've seen over here."

"Yes, and you have to start laying off the booze. You are as round as our old balloon."

Both men were tired of French food and not understanding the language, and Tom had behaved pretty well until one night when he disappeared. He was gone for two days, submerged in the pleasures of the left bank, and when he reappeared, sheepish, out of money and, for a few days, intimately concerned about his health, Fitzgerald was understanding.

Fitz was enjoying himself immensely, seeing old friends and making new ones. The Aéro Club environment appealed to him, along with the caliber of the people it attracted, the best in France and all very ardent and very vocal patriots. He was pleased when Archdeacon arranged a trip for them to Germany to see the Zeppelin works. It was sort of a consolation prize, for when Archdeacon had tried to get permission for them to visit Chalais-Meudon, he was, to his surprise, brusquely refused. He explained it to the Baldwins as "military secrets," tapping the side of his nose with his finger.

Sam and Tom both liked Germany, particularly the food and the beer, but they spent only a few hours in Friedrichshafen at the Zeppelin works. Count von Zeppelin was ill and not receiving visitors, and the short tour of the works by one of his assistants convinced them that the German concept of flight was far beyond anything they were thinking about. Sam took one look at a scale model of the LZ-1 that the count had flown in 1900, and said, "This is way out of our class, Tom. There's nothing we can learn here. Let's get back to California, and see what we can come up with."

Fitzgerald wanted to go back to Paris and spend some more time with Santos-Dumont, but Tom put his foot down.

"Fitz, we're not your prisoners, damn it! We've been good, we haven't embarrassed you too much, and you've been really good to us. But it's time to get back. I haven't had a drink of bourbon in a month and I'm getting tired of foreign food. All I want to do is get back to the good old U.S.A. and get started on a dirigible. You heard Santos-Dumont talking about going to St. Louis and winning a prize? I'm damned if he will, not while we've got time to build an airship of our own."

"What do you mean 'we?' "

"Why Fitz, you don't think we'd leave you out? We're letting you in on the ground floor as our first investor, and you'll get your share of the prize money in St. Louis."

It was what Fitzgerald wanted to hear. The balloons the Baldwins had flown had never appealed to him and he had no desire at all to jump out of one in a parachute. But Santos-Dumont's dirigibles were exciting and he wanted to get into the field, with the Baldwins if he could, but without them if he had to.

"Tell you what. I've got some land over in the valley back home. I call it a ranch, but it's mostly just a few cows and a lot of empty acreage. There is a ranch house, shielded from the wind by a little range of hills. You come on back and build your dirigible there, I'll put up a big building for you, and we'll be partners, the three of us. I'll put up the money. I'm not as rich as Santos-Dumont, but I can help you swing the dirigible and the engine, and whatever hydrogen it takes. The only stipulation I have is that you let me fly in the dirigible when it's finished. Not in St. Louis, maybe, but afterwards, out in California. I'd give anything to take that dirigible on a tour of San Francisco Bay."

They shook hands, and Fitzgerald left to book their trip back home.

CHAPTER

24

He took a certain pleasure in arranging a meeting with Augustus Herring, not because he wished to see him, but because he knew it would make Samuel Langley so unhappy if he knew that he was doing it. Herring had asked to see his wind tunnel, and Albert Blohm liked to show it off. The tunnel was forty feet long, six feet high, and six feet wide, and winds, straight as an arrow, could be sent down it at twenty-five miles an hour. He had spent a considerable amount of money and an immense amount of time on the construction of the tunnel, and now was perfectly satisfied with it. It was his springboard to scientific fame; he saw it catapulting him into the seat that Langley now occupied as secretary of the Smithsonian Institution.

Herring had appeared thirty minutes early for his appointment, and was sitting quietly in the little waiting room outside Blohm's spacious office at Catholic University. The academic setting appealed to Herring, and he was busily engaged reading through one of the copies of *Scientific American* that he found spread on the library table. Blohm's office had two doors, and he took time to crack the second one and to peer at Herring, trying to get a sense of his mood. Herring seemed perfectly at ease, except for his leg, crossed over his knee and jiggling with the speed of a clock pendulum. Blohm noted that his well-cut brown suit was frayed and a little soiled, but he had a fresh collar on and his well-worn shoes were shined. A white handkerchief was carefully folded in his suit pocket, making him every inch the impoverished gentleman. *He's trying, poor beggar. He probably wants a job.*

Blohm walked to the other door, and emerged smiling, hand extended. "Mr. Herring! I've heard so much about you from Mr. Chanute and Professor Langley! What a pleasure to meet you."

Herring looked frightened, staring into Blohm's eyes, trying to tell if he was mocking him. Blohm saw the fear and went on, running his sentences together.

"You must tell me about your powered flight! You are the only one to achieve flight under power so far! How did you do it? Won't you have some coffee with me? We'll go in here, in the laboratory, and I'll show you my equipment."

Herring soon succumbed, as most people did, to Blohm's charm. He was starving, and the prospect of coffee and a roll buoyed his spirits. Within moments, he was chattering away about his two powered flights in his two-surface machine, Blohm drawing him out with sensible questions.

"A compressed-air engine? Did it have sufficient power?"

"I had a tank that allowed me six hundred pounds of air pressure. That was just enough for about twenty seconds. I would have preferred an internal combustion engine, of course, but that was beyond my means." He started nervously and smiled, "That's the way it is with most things—beyond my means." As soon as he said it he regretted it. He owed nothing to this man, and if he had inherited money the way Blohm had, he would have done far more with it. Herring had received the income from a small trust, adequate when he was single, but not enough for his family and his experiments. The recent years of hardscrabble living had eroded his self-confidence, and he found himself making apologetic statements when he did not need to do so.

Blohm ignored the remark, and Herring went on, describing both flights in detail, embellishing them only a little, emphasizing how close he was to building another two-surface machine, and how he knew where he might get an engine this time. His listener was a perfect audience, keeping his coffee cup filled, pushing the tray of pastries to him, nodding. Herring became expansive; it was good to talk to someone like Blohm who understood exactly what he was saying, and would listen. Still he knew he had to restrain himself, to not speak of the patents he held, the papers he had published, the talks he had given. If Blohm knew about these, well and good. If he did not, he would find a way to let him know later, if things worked out. The thoughts sobered him and he ground to a halt.

After waiting a moment, to see if he was going to go on, Blohm spoke. "Well how is it, Augustus—can we be on a first name basis?—how can it be that Mr. Chanute has not given you more support, or Professor Langley even? We are all in this together, and I cannot understand how such a contribution as yours could go overlooked. If I did not know the two worthy gentlemen, I would say 'professional jealousy,' but surely that cannot be the case."

Herring helped himself to another roll, finished his coffee, and let Blohm pour him another before he spoke. "No, Albert, certainly not." He paused, liking being on a first name basis with this capital fellow, who understood so much. It gave promise for the future. "No, they are both too big for that, and they have done so much. It was fate. When Mr. Chanute came to witness a flight, my engine was not working properly. I think he believes me, I know he believes me, but he has not seen me fly himself, and therefore cannot swear to it." He bit off the end of the roll, conscious that he must be giving the appearance of a starving refugee but not caring—they were on a first name basis—and went on. "And in regard to Professor Langley—we have what lawyers call 'irreconcilable differences,' I'm afraid."

Blohm laughed and said, "Yes, most people have irreconcilable differences with the good professor, you are not alone. But let me show you my pride and joy."

Herring felt comfortable with Blohm, who obviously enjoyed talking about his huge tunnel with someone who understood the technical sophistication it represented. There was nothing like it in the world; even Eiffel's famous wind tunnel was nothing compared to it in size, and certainly not in instrumentation.

Blohm took Herring to a panel where there were dozens of gauges, unremarkable in themselves, but noteworthy for the tiny increments of pressure that they measured. "Believe it or not, my instrumentation is sensitive to differences of a millionth of an atmosphere."

A light went on in Herring's mind. This man was frittering away a fortune on nonsense! What possible difference did such sensitivity make? All you needed was some surface area, a curved airfoil, and an engine to drive it through the air. Good Lord, even those bumpkins the Wrights knew this. Suddenly he felt superior to Blohm, then realized that he would have to curb himself, to keep on being subservient, to work to get whatever was possible from this meeting.

"Let me demonstrate." Blohm sat Herring at a control panel with a window looking straight into the tunnel. Inside was a huge cylindrical shape. "That is Count von Zeppelin's next dirigible. He has been kind enough to ask me to use the tunnel to measure its drag."

Herring was confused. "I would not think drag would be a problem with such a streamlined shape, at the speeds at which it flies. It simply bores through the air."

"You are very right, my friend, except in one respect, and that is what my tunnel measures. There is a tremendous skin friction to a Zeppelin—or to a flying machine, for that matter—and no one has considered it before. Everybody thinks in terms of the flat-plate resistance of a surface—that's why our friends, the Wrights, lie prone on the wing when they glide. But that's only part of it, and for a dirigible, that's the least of it."

Blohm had the gigantic fan turned on, and as the model Zeppelin quivered in the rush of wind, he pointed out the instruments, showing just how the skin drag rose over the length of the dirigible, reaching a peak just before the surfaces converged at the tail. Herring was about to ask how close the comparison could be, for the wind tunnel model was made of a shiny, hard-surfaced wood, while the real thing would be covered with a fabric, painted, but still more porous and flexible than wood; then he realized it was the wrong question. Despite his instinct to criticize, Herring, for once, understood that it was time to be dazzled. Blohm and his wind tunnel opened up so many vistas.

"Have you tested any airfoils in your tunnel?" he asked.

"Yes, of course. I've run tests on Lilienthal's airfoils, and I suspect that his tables are wrong. I've put a model of that foolish effort of Ader's in here, to no purpose; it clearly has no future as a flying machine."

They moved back to his office, and Blohm asked, "Correct me if I'm mistaken, but did you not go with Mr. Chanute to North Carolina to visit the Wrights?"

The coffee in his cup was cold, but Herring finished it off, nodding as he drank.

"Well, what do you think? Are they working in the right direction?"

Herring composed himself. He desperately needed to convert this opportunity to income somehow; he needed money, and he needed it now.

"Almost certainly. I think they have gone beyond all of us, myself included. I'm not certain that they know it themselves. Let me show you some notes and drawings I made while I was with them. In confidence, of course."

"Of course." Blohm took the worn, leatherbound notebook from him and studied it intently, asking an occasional question as to a term or an abbreviation. After almost an hour he handed it back.

"You are absolutely right. They are ahead of everyone." He paused just a beat and went on, "Except of course, for our dear professor across the river, and they are perhaps ahead of him as well. What do they have for an engine?"

Herring shrugged. "Nothing. They are talking about going to automobile manufacturers and getting one."

"Small chance of that; they need something that weighs no more than two hundred pounds."

"Yes, I think they know the problem; they are talking about building one themselves."

Blohm suddenly felt very weary with Herring, who obviously was not being treated well by life and probably deserved not to be. "Then they are beaten. The professor has a wonderful engine man, Charles Manly, and he is making progress. I believe the professor will fly his Great Aerodrome before the end of the year, if not sooner."

Herring made his pitch. "If I had the funds—just a few thousand dollars—I believe I could build a larger version of my two-surface glider, and fly it with an internal combustion engine, perhaps by as early as September."

"If the Wrights cannot get one, where will you get yours?"

"I have a friend in New York who is building a very lightweight engine."

"His name is not Gustave Whitehead, is it?"

As keyed up as he was, Herring laughed. "No, not poor Gustave and his carbide engine. My man lives in Hammondsport; his name is Glenn Curtiss. I can get one of his engines for perhaps three thousand dollars; another two thousand for the glider, and a thousand for living expenses, and I would be ready to go by September."

Blohm momentarily toyed with the idea of giving him the money.

It was a bagatelle; he could give him ten thousand and not feel it. But there was an eager, desperate hunger about Herring that was off-putting. If he gave him the money he would not go away, he would want more of his time and soon enough, more of his money.

"I'm sorry, Augustus, but I cannot. I wish I could."

"Well then, was the information in the notebook of any value to you? Could you let me have something, just a loan, on the basis of what you learned?" There were tears in his eyes; he was begging, he hated it, and Blohm hated him for it.

"No, Mr. Herring, I'm sorry. The information is useless to me, and I suspect to anyone but the Wrights."

Herring noted that he was not "Augustus" anymore, just "Mr. Herring." "Wait just a moment, please." Fear raised his voice a notch, and Herring flinched as he spoke. He reached into the shabby valise he carried and brought out the copies he had made of the wind tunnel calculations Wilbur Wright had sent to Chanute. It was his last chance. If these did not appeal to Blohm, he was finished.

"Please look at these. These are copies of measurements Wilbur Wright made of airfoils placed in their wind tunnel. Their tunnel is of course nothing compared to yours, a little six-foot long box."

Blohm examined the papers, his eyes going over the long list of tables quickly, comprehending the scope of what had been done. It infuriated him. This Wright fellow had generated more data with his little six-foot box than had ever flowed from the monstrous wind tunnel that he had created. And he was not sure that he could duplicate these results, despite the size of his tunnel and its elegant instrumentation. Wilbur Wright had gone directly to the heart of the problem of flight; it was mathematically beautiful, and he despised him for it, and his brother as well.

For the first time in years he suddenly became a fan of Professor Langley. He was not going to let two bicycle mechanics from Dayton stumble across the secret of flight, especially not using some breadbox of a wind tunnel. If they did, one of them, Wilbur perhaps, on the basis of these papers alone, might succeed Langley as secretary. And that was not going to happen, not while he lived.

"Who else knows you have these papers?" Blohm asked, assuming at once that Herring had taken the material clandestinely.

Herring did not answer immediately. If he told him that he had offered them to Langley, it might diminish their worth in his eyes, but if Blohm took the papers, paid something for them, and then showed them to Langley, he would find out the truth.

"Only Professor Langley; I showed them to him. Mr. Chanute has no idea—he would be furious. But I don't believe Professor Langley understood their importance. He has a bad opinion of me, and I don't think anything I'd tell him would really register."

Blohm thought, *A bad opinion, eh? Small wonder, you miserable little thieving turncoat.* But he smiled and said, "Well, Augustus, I believe we can do business together. I'd like you to take this information, and use it in creating a new glider, one of your two-surface models, but larger. You were at Kitty Hawk. Did you see how the Wrights were controlling their glider?"

"Yes, it's the old Mouillard patent, you know, a flap on the wing to act like a drag-brake, changing the angle of attack to cause a turn. Mr. Chanute helped him patent the idea in 1896. It's nothing new."

"What patents do the Wrights have?"

"To my certain knowledge, none. I heard them joking at Kitty Hawk about how their father is always pressing them to get a patent."

"Good. All right, Augustus, I have to go now. What would you say to an initial stake of one thousand dollars, and a monthly stipend of three hundred dollars? As things develop, and you need more money for the engine and so on, there'll be more."

This golden flow of words stunned Herring; he had been hoping for a fifty-dollar payoff. This was a dream come true.

"Wonderful, thank you so much!"

"We'll have no contract, just an understanding between gentlemen. Either one of us can terminate the arrangement at any time. And it must be kept secret! I do not want either Professor Langley or Mr. Chanute to know, and certainly the Wright brothers must never know."

Herring's delicate composure failed; he fell to his knees and grasped Blohm's hand. "Thank you, thank you, I will not fail you."

Physically sickened, Blohm pulled Herring to his feet, and said, "One more thing. I will need to know more about this Glenn Curtiss and his engine—its size, its weight, its output. I need to know that soon."

On Blohm's desk was a most flattering letter from Mrs. Alexander

Graham Bell. She had asked him if he would like to assist the great inventor in a project to build a flying machine, and she also wanted to know if he knew anyone who was an expert in lightweight engines. The letter had troubled him, for before Herring's visit he was going to have to say no to both her questions. He certainly did not want to subordinate himself even to Alexander Graham Bell, and after the fiasco of referring Stephen Balzer to Langley, he could not pretend to anything about engines. Now, if what Herring had to say was real, and he believed it was, he could at least give her the name of the engine man.

Blohm patted Herring on the back, saying, "Now you must go. And since you are working for me, we are no longer on a first-name basis. I would not wish to give our little secret away. Give me your address, I'll have a check mailed to you today."

As Herring wrote his address on an envelope he blurted, "Mr. Blohm, I hate to ask, but could I perhaps have a few dollars advance? I'm quite out of funds, and I need money to get home."

It was almost too much. Blohm did not say another word, pressing some bills into Herring's hand and steering him firmly out the door.

On the street, Herring composed himself, looked quickly at the money Blohm had given him, almost thirty dollars, and thought, *Now for a real meal, and then a telegram to Glenn Curtiss.*

CHAPTER

25

Carrie had barely gotten their luggage packed away in the attic when Wilbur and Orville launched themselves into preparing for the 1903 season. The success of their last glider was so great that they were determined to build and fly a powered aircraft before the next year was out.

One of their first decisions came about by accident. They'd received another in the endless letters from Chanute, in which he talked about Langley's Great Aerodrome in one paragraph, and their 1902 glider in the next. The problem was that he had confused the 1902 glider with the 1901 version, and straightening him out was going to require a long letter from Wilbur to explain the differences.

"You can hardly blame him for not telling them apart, Will; to a lay person they look pretty much the same."

"He's no lay person, Orv, he's been at this longer than we have."

"Just the same, we ought to do like Langley, and give this year's machine a name." Then snickering, he added, "How about 'A Really Great Aerodrome?' "

Wilbur didn't laugh; he never did after Orville had a good idea. They *should* name it. They spent the day tossing names back and forth and by evening had settled on a simple one—the Flyer. From now on, the flying machine would be called the Wright Flyer.

Getting busy on the Wright Flyer meant splitting up their time, with Orville addressing important problems with the bicycle business—he jokingly accused Katharine of just ignoring the store's parts inventory—while Wilbur wrote to ten different engine manufacturers, specifying that he wanted an engine that would deliver between eight and nine horsepower and weigh no more than one hundred and eighty pounds. He had looked into many engine and automobile catalogs and didn't believe he would get a positive response.

He was right. Most of the manufacturers considered his letter a frivolous request and ignored it; those that chose to respond assured Wilbur that there was no engine available that would meet his specifications. The results did not surprise Wilbur. He had started designing the engine even before he sent the letters off, and had chatted with Charley Taylor about the possibility of building an engine.

Between the two of them, they had the components pretty well specified. They built a detailed wooden mock-up that enabled them to lay out the parts and design the crankcase casting so that it would provide support for the other engine parts. Both men were very conscious of weight control, estimating how heavy each part would be. Then they made up a test cylinder that they ran on shop power, just to see how it worked.

Charley smoked about twenty inexpensive cigars a day, each one an affront that the Wrights had to overlook. He was simply too valuable, both as a master machinist and as a constant source of common sense. He worked in the shop with his brown hair brushed back, big, flowing mustache drooping down, eyes concentrating on whatever he was doing, deadly serious while he was working, but able to laugh the instant he put his tools down. Charley felt he had a little leeway with the Wright boys; his wife's uncle owned the shop the Wrights were renting, so in a way, he represented the landlord. It made Katharine dislike him. She said he was too forward and not respectful enough, and talked more than once about firing him.

There was no chance of that. Charley had helped build their wind tunnel for them, and ever since then had been itching to help with the flying machines. They had held him off a bit because he was so valuable with the shop, but now things had changed, and they needed his skill to build the engine that others would not. It pleased him, and he was not shy about expressing his opinions. He had listened when Wilbur outlined the engine specifications—four cylinders, four-inch stroke and four-inch bore, water-cooled, weighing two hundred pounds or less with everything attached—all the accessories.

"Its got to run smooth, Charley, it can't be like one of these rough-running automobiles you hear in the street, backfiring away. We're going to use a chain drive to run the propellers, and that means the engine has to be smooth or it will shake the machine apart."

"If you are going to meet your weight specifications, Wilbur, you are going to have to do something pretty radical for a small town foundry."

"What's that?"

"Make an aluminum casting for the crankcase. Its risky, and we may have to buy a few of them to get one that won't warp, but otherwise we'll never keep it under two hundred pounds. Just no way to do it otherwise."

Wilbur was disturbed. Aluminum was not exactly new, and some automobile manufacturers were using it as crankcase material. Still, it bothered him. "I hate to try something new like that; it's tough enough just building an engine. Would aluminum hold up? How would it work with the expansion differentials between aluminum, steel, and iron?"

"You let me work on it. I know the foreman, John Hoban, down at Buckeye Iron and Brass; let me talk to him about it."

Wilbur had reluctantly agreed. They had the time and the money to try two and perhaps three times with an aluminum crankcase. If it really worked, it would save as much as forty or fifty pounds, maybe more. If it did not, then they would have to go to steel, and just accept the weight. As it turned out, John Hoban was enthusiastic about the project, and got them a special aluminum alloy that was ninety-two percent aluminum and eight percent copper. It was the lightest, strongest, toughest metal he could find, and he told Charley that both Pierce Arrow and Peerless were experimenting with it for their engines—and they were the best in the business.

While he was waiting for Hoban to cast the crankcase, Charley turned the cylinders from fine-grain cast iron, threaded at the top and bottom so that they would fit into the crankcase on one end, and a water jacket could be fitted on the other. A cast cylindrical valve box, with both the inlet and exhaust valve, was installed on top of the cylinder.

The informal way they started off was maintained while they worked to get the engine running. No one drew any plans. Wilbur would sketch an idea on a piece of paper, and Taylor would pin it on the workbench and follow it.

The noise level in the shop doubled over the weeks as Charley, cigar stuck in the side of his mouth, sculpted the crankshaft from a single billet of high-carbon tool steel that was thirty-one inches long, six inches wide, and one and five-eighths inches thick. Charley drew the contours of the crankshaft directly on the steel, then went through a mechanical, maniacal routine of positioning the crankshaft, depressing the huge drill hundreds of times, squirting oil on the bit to cool it, letting the rising whine of steel against steel grind almost to a halt, then stop, move the crankshaft billet a tiny fraction of an inch, shift his cigar, and pull the drill bit down again. The combined stench of burning oil and Charley's cigar permeated the shop, and newcomers would involuntarily gasp when they first walked in.

Despite the odor, it was a winning routine. As Charley worked he went through two different stacks of boxes, one after another. One stack held the small black cigars he favored; the second contained an endless supply of drill bits. Over time the crank gradually emerged, just as a sculptor coaxes a statue from a block of marble. Charley used a chisel to peel through the holes he had drilled until he could pull the rough, metal-flecked crankshaft free from its steel womb. He placed it on the lathe and turned it lovingly, smoothing it down, balancing it out, transforming it into a burnished steel blue gem weighing but nineteen pounds and machined to a tolerance of one-thousandth of an inch.

When he was ready, he called Wilbur and Orville in, showed his gleaming prize to them, then put it in a rig he had built that allowed it to rotate as it would in the engine. He spun it, and it whirled noiselessly, running for a long while before coming to an agonizingly slow stop, swinging back and forth, demonstrating its perfect balance. Wilbur spun it, and then Orville did, and when it had at last come to a halt, Will clapped Charley on the back and whispered, "Good job, Charley." That was the highest praise in the Wright shop, and it meant a lot to Charles Taylor.

Compared to the ordeal of the crankshaft, boring the holes where the cylinders would be mounted in the aluminum block was straightforward, with the steel bits biting easily into the aluminum. There was more labor in the smaller parts, the "innards" as Orville called them—the pistons, valve guides, rocker arms, intake valves—all the parts that had to move together so precisely and with such timing to enable the pistons to suck in the gasoline–air vapor mixture, compress it with an upward stroke, have the ignition fire at the top of that stroke, driving the piston down while another was serving up its ration of fuel. Charley turned jeweler with the smaller parts, machining them, matching them up, putting them together, then taking them apart and redoing them. The only parts he purchased were stock items such as nuts and springs, and he even machined some of these; everything else flowed from his lathe and drill press. As much as Katharine disliked his manner, she would still come down to watch Charley work, his big coarse hands, scarred from a dozen accidents, guiding the parts together, then taking them apart and sanding some minute transgression with oiled blue fine-grain sandpaper. When he was satisfied, he would first weigh the polished part, to be sure it matched the weight schedule Wilbur had set up. Then the part would be wrapped in a sheet of oiled paper and placed in a shop cloth on the shelf over Wilbur's bench.

In designing the engine, Wilbur deliberately kept everything simple. There was no carburetor; fuel ran from a can suspended above the engine, down a pipe to drip, and vaporize over the hot surface of the crankcase before being sucked into a cylinder on its intake cycle. Dry-cell batteries provided the spark to start, but after that a magneto took over. Lubrication was strictly splash-type internally, with any external parts getting loving attention from an oilcan. Cooling was done by convection with a tall slender radiator built from flattened metal tubes. A twenty-six-pound solid cast-iron flywheel was deliberately oversized, to help keep the engine running smoothly, and was heat-shrunk onto the crankshaft.

The engine was like the flying machine: perfectly focused on the task at hand, and without one ounce of weight or one hour of time lost on anything not directly involved in getting into the air.

Charley puttered and puttered, but finally allowed that the engine was ready for run-up on February 13th. He took his time starting it, and when it roared into action, the noise was deafening—they could not use a muffler, it would eat up too much power. Faults showed up instantly, with the cooling being inadequate and the engine not running nearly smoothly enough. After tinkering with it all evening, they ran it up the next day, only to have raw gasoline accidentally drip on the red-hot bearings, freezing them and bringing the engine to a shattering halt that fractured the crankcase.

Charley grinned at Wilbur. "Guess we better ask Hoban to cast another crankcase." Wilbur did not grin back, wondering what Langley's engine was doing at that moment.

There was certainly not a lot to grin about when it came to power. They were having a terrible time with the propeller design. The propeller was as crucial as the engine, for it would translate the engine's horsepower into thrust.

"You know, Orville, this is the first time the Dayton Library has ever let us down."

They had spent days in the stacks, going through engineering manuals, and more time in the periodical section, looking in vain for articles on marine propellers. Ships had been using propellers for almost a century, yet there was not one reference to marine propeller design to be found. Wilbur, as was his custom, wrote away to some prominent boatbuilders in the east, but all but one of the letters had gone unanswered. The one reply, from a good-hearted man in Bath, Maine, stated only that he knew of no textbook on marine propellers; in his own experience, propeller design was done on the basis of experience and intuition. It was a pleasant letter, but no help.

There were some problems they could solve themselves by intuition. They knew their engine would be turning at about 1,100 RPM, and that would be much too fast for a big propeller to turn, so they would need to gear it down. It was a familiar concept: all their bicycles had gears, and they knew where they could get the sort of heavy chain that would stand the power of an engine. But there was no way to guess the shape of the propeller. Or rather propellers, because they planned to use two almost from the start of their discussions. Two propellers would generate more thrust, and keep their diameter down to a reasonable size.

Pictures showed them what had been done in the past with propellers on dirigibles. Santos-Dumont's dirigible had what looked like big flat paddles mounted on a shaft, more like a double-headed flyswatter blade than a ship's propeller, with its broad, curved surfaces.

"The problem is it's not like a wing; you just cannot tell where to start thinking about it."

Orville thought about this for a moment, his mind visualizing the passage of the glider wing through flight, turning the wing in his mind. He waited a minute, not wanting to contradict Will—he didn't like that—but, finally unable to contain himself, said, "Will, that's just it. A propeller is a wing, but instead of sliding horizontally through the air, it's rotating through the air, spiraling along like a bullet, thrusting forward. It's not a screw digging into the air, it's a wing throwing the air behind it. A wing shoves the air down; the propeller throws it backward. Don't you see?"

Wilbur Wright saw immediately and his emotions were mixed. On the one hand, he saw exactly what Orville meant. He was right: the propeller *was* just a wing, and they knew how to design wings. On the other hand, he wished it had been his idea. He knew it was small and petty, but Orville was changing things. The flying machine used to be Wilbur's alone; then, because he needed Orville and he was sensitive, Wilbur made a point of being inclusive when talking about "our flying machine" in all the correspondence, giving Orville equal credit. And now, he was beginning to deserve it; he'd thought of the movable rudder and now this. They seemed to be moving closer together on the flying machine, almost merging, as if they were just one person instead of two.

"Will, did you hear what I said? I said the prop—"

Recovering, Wilbur interrupted him. "Bless you, Orville, I heard you and it was just taking me a few minutes to realize what a great idea it is. You are getting to be a regular Ben Franklin when it comes to inventions! You thought of the moving rudder and now this. We know what to do with wings, all right, and if we have to, we can run some more airfoils through the wind tunnel. But I think this licks the problem, right here and now."

They made a test rig and began trying some propeller shapes, using airfoils that had been effective in their wind tunnel tests. It was immediately evident that testing a propeller standing still was not like flying a propeller through the air, but they had to accept the difference. Wilbur generated page after page of notes, trying to optimize the propeller for length, pitch, and airfoil.

In the end, they held their breath and followed their intuition, creating two propellers, each one made up of three one-and-one-eighth-inch thick laminations of West Virginia white spruce glued together and then shaped with a hatchet and a drawshave. They were eight feet six inches in length, and seven and one-half inches wide at their widest point. Wilbur estimated that they would have an efficiency of about sixty-six percent. The propellers were mirror images, designed to rotate in opposite directions to counteract torque.

The drive system was familiar to them. They used a sprocket on the engine and one on each propeller, chain driven and with a 23:8 ratio so that the propellers would turn about 350 to 400 revolutions per minute while the engine was turning at 1,080.

While they were working out the propeller problem, the weeks passed with Charley struggling to improve the things they now knew were wrong with the engine, particularly the cooling.

CHAPTER

26

Bishop Wright often came down to watch Charley work, admiring his deft hands, and thinking about perhaps having him remove the porch the boys had put on the house and replacing it with a little arched entryway. He disapproved of Charley's cigars, but even so, watching him was a welcome relief from the long hours he spent in his study, writing letters and building arguments against his opponents, many of them men he had picked himself for promotion and honors.

Life was not treating the bishop as he had hoped. Instead of the church rallying to his common sense call for justice, he was still an outcast, treated politely enough, but kept outside the inner circles. Inwardly he was certain that it was not power that he sought, but justice, simple justice that would recognize how shabbily he had been treated.

Then there was Katharine. The girl was an absolute pearl, running the house as he wished, even getting Carrie to serve a decent meal now and again. But she was holding something from him; he was almost certain she was still involved with that Cleaver boy. The real, overwhelming fear was that she would run away and leave him alone in his old age. He could live with the boys, of course, and they would treat him well, but it was not like having a woman around the house. He would not ever go to live with Roosh, no not ever, nor Lorin either, if he could help it. But what he wanted, what he deserved, was Katharine here, right in this house, doing what her mother did so well, protecting all of them. Wilbur and Orville needed her too, just as much as he did.

He was so sunk in thought that he did not feel Orville's gentle taps on his back. Finally Orville tugged his arm, and signaled him to move outside, where Wilbur was waiting.

"Pop, I want you to know we've been listening to you, and I want you to mark this date down in your notebook. It's March 23rd, 1903, and we are going to apply for a patent, today. Here's the paperwork."

The bishop was touched; the boys were moving out from under his control, and as much as he hated it, he was glad to see they were trying to please him, to show him they cared. Even if Katharine did not.

"Now we're not going to try to attempt to patent a flying machine. I don't think the Patent Office will accept a patent on a flying machine until they believe it has flown, and we cannot tell them that. Yet! But we can patent our control system, and that's the heart of everything we do."

"That's smart, boys, you need to have a patent, but when the flying machine flies, you ought to patent it as well. And you've got to keep it secret; don't let anybody, not even your friend Chanute, come around. He might not want to steal your idea, but he'll blab— Lord knows he knows how to talk!—and some smart crook will grab your idea and run with it. And maybe even improve on it, that's the problem, what if they take your ideas and turn them something better. Why . . ."

He was off and running and the brothers knew it; their timing had been wrong, they should have told him just before lunch, when Carrie's call could have broken it up. Wilbur could see inside the shop at the big clock on the wall. It was quarter after eleven. Well, there would be no stopping him, Carrie wouldn't be calling until noon, and in the meantime, they'd have to stand and listen and nod their heads.

CHAPTER
27

It was not until May that Charley had the second engine running properly on the test stand, putting out sixteen horsepower for a little while, then dropping off to twelve and running steady at 1,090 revolutions per minute. They weighed the engine and it came out at 161 pounds; when you added all the accessories, including the tubular radiator, water, and fuel, it was a shade over two hundred. Charley was pleased with his handiwork, glad to have salvaged victory from defeat, and the Wrights were pleased with Charley.

And they were very pleased with the extra power. They had planned for eight; twelve horsepower gave them a margin that they used in part to strengthen the wings and the framework, especially the propeller installation. Wilbur took notepaper and sketched out the new parts he wanted. Charley was now building all the many metal parts that would hold the 1903 flying machine together, and every day getting further away from any interest in bicycles. Once, after Charley gave some broad hints about learning to fly the machine, Orville whispered, "We've created a monster."

It turned out that Charley was the second monster they had created, the first one being their old mentor Octave Chanute. Orville heard a strangled scream and bounded up the stairs to find Wilbur by his bed, gibbering with fury, a thin film of saliva coating his lips, his face pale and hands trembling. He shoved a paper into Orville's hands and said hoarsely, "Read this."

It was a copy of a speech by Octave Chanute, the translation sent to him by the great man himself, totally unaware of the havoc it might cause in the breasts of the Wrights.

Chanute had returned to visit his beloved birthplace, France, and there in April had given a long lecture at the Aéro Club de France to a fascinated crowd of French would-be aeronauts. He was a revered figure, honored for all he had done personally in aviation and in communicating news about flying machines from all around the world. Chanute had been invited to give his talk by the man who now stood next to Ader in French flying machine circles, Captain Ferdinand Ferber. The captain was a hopeless romantic who would not have minded becoming the first man to fly, but wanted more than anything for a Frenchman to have the honor, even if he could not. Ferber had made a crude copy of the Wrights' 1901 glider, not knowing that it was an aeronautical dead end rejected by the Wrights themselves, and blissfully unaware that he was a totally incompetent craftsman who captured neither the heart of the Wright machine, its wing-warping mechanism, nor its soul, the beautiful, economic quality of Wright craftsmanship.

Ferber wanted Chanute to ignite a patriotic fervor in France by revealing just how far the Wrights had advanced, and how unlikely it was that France could overtake them without a vigorous national effort. Chanute was flattered, and his speech took on a flavor that it might not have if the Wrights had been present in the audience. He began with a description of his long experiments with gliders, his work with Herring, and even examined the short, fruitless experiments of men like Huffaker.

As Orville read the first part of the speech, he wondered what was bothering Wilbur. There was nothing new here, not even Chanute's elaborate tribute to the successes that Langley had gained in flying his smaller Aerodromes, or his speculations as to when the new full-sized man-carrying Aerodrome would fly.

It all became clear as Orville reached the part where Chanute's ego took full control of his mouth. Chanute spoke at length and in the warmest tones of the Wrights as his colleagues, young men that he had trained and who were executing his ideas in an admirable way. For the Frenchmen following his speech so closely, it was clear that Chanute was the fountain from which the Wrights' ideas flowed, and that the successes they might attain stemmed solely from his generous nature and brilliant mind.

As he finished reading, Orville began to laugh. Wilbur jerked the speech out of his hand, saying, "What are you laughing at? The man has made fools of us and, just like Pop said, is telling everyone what we are doing."

"That's just it, Will, that's what so funny. He's given this big speech, telling all he's taught us, and he hasn't told them a single useful thing. Look at this answer he gave to a question about how the wing-twisting mechanism works. He says, 'To regulate lateral equilibrium, he operates two cords which act on the right and left side of the wing by warping and simultaneously moving the rear vertical rudder.' Two cords? Where did he get that? He was there, he saw us fly, he had all the time in the world with the glider. And he still doesn't know how it works."

Wilbur did not laugh. "But Orv, just this might be enough to ruin our getting a patent, even if it's wrong. If you disclose publicly what you are doing, I think that keeps you from patenting the idea. Besides, I don't like the idea of him encouraging some Frenchman to try to beat us. It is bad enough to have to worry about Langley."

"Well, you're right there. He'll get them all excited, and they have some rich people there. Santos-Dumont, for one. But I still think it's Langley we've got to beat. Poor old Chanute, he thinks he knows what he's talking about, and it sounds good to others, but he still has never caught on to what we're trying to do. I'll bet that Augustus Herring knows—he never stopped writing the whole time he was at Kitty Hawk, and he is a bright man. If Chanute—or Langley for that matter—knew how to use him, how to get his brain into action, they might be flying today."

"Well, Chanute doesn't have to know what he's talking about, he can ruin us if he just inspires someone else. I've got a bad feeling about this. And you know what's the worst part?"

Orville shook his head.

"The worst part is that we cannot even complain to him, we'll have to eat this and keep on smiling. He's been too nice to us, too helpful to have a real quarrel. There's a word for him that I can't quite dredge up, something that begins with an n."

"Naïve?"

"That's it. Chanute is naïve, and we just have to put up with it. Imagine that, a sophisticated, educated man like him being naïve. But for the Lord's sake, don't let Pop see this speech, or he'll give us another one of his own. Besides, we've got other worries."

They sat silently for a while, and Wilbur spoke. "You know, Orville, Pop has always been disappointed in us because we are really not good churchmen like he is. But what he doesn't understand is that there are different kinds of callings. I truly believe that we were called to aviation as Pop was called to the ministry."

Orville did not respond, not wishing to hurt Wilbur's feelings. He did not feel that way, not at all. He was devoted to this current task of building a flying machine, but when they had done that, he wanted to stop. Especially if they made some money, he'd just like to set up little laboratory and fiddle with things, make small inventions, toys, maybe. And he wanted to do it on his own; he wanted his brother off doing something else, not in his laboratory, not in his house. But he knew Wilbur was different. It was a calling for him, and he had embraced building a flying machine as he might have embraced the priesthood. He wondered how Wilbur would react later, when they had flown their Flyer and made their money. Would he be able to handle life after the flying machine? Orville wasn't sure.

CHAPTER
28

They stood side by side, Langley's white hair flowing, Manly leaning forward, intently reading the instruments, both men wearing earmuffs to dampen the engine's roar. On the test stand his beautiful engine stood, running at its peak RPM, the beautiful noise singing out silken-smooth, no vibration, no backfires, just smooth raw power.

Manley jotted something in his waste book, the notebook that Langley insisted be maintained, and held it up for the professor to read.

52 horsepower!!!!

He took the notebook back and wrote, *I'm going to throttle it down—it's on a 10-hour run, and I'll just let it cruise at about 30 horsepower.*

Manly looked at what he'd written and liked it. Let it cruise at thirty horsepower, that should get him.

When he held the book up, Langley smiled and nodded, then pointed to the entrance to the "fuel cell," as they called the engine run-up area.

Once outside the building, Langley placed both hands on Manly's shoulders and looked him in the eye, for once at a loss for words.

"My boy, you have done wonders. Are your instruments correct? Are we sure about fifty-two horsepower? It seems almost unbelievable."

"Professor, with all modesty, we have the best engine in the world in terms of power for weight, and I think it will be the best for durability and endurance, too. You saw how smooth it was; you could have balanced a coin on the top cylinder."

Langley hesitated a moment; that was going a bit too far, but he chalked it up to Manly's natural exuberance after so many months of failure and disappointment.

"When can you install the engine in the Aerodrome?"

"Within a few weeks. I had a dummy engine made up to check how everything fits, but I'll need to install the engine and run it, driving the propellers to see how everything works."

Langley considered his schedule; he was busy all through the summer. "Do you think we could have everything set up and ready to fly the end of July? That's really the first time I'll be available."

Manly had worked for Langley too long not to pad his schedule a bit. If anything went wrong, and the Aerodrome was not ready by July, there would be hell to pay. He took time, pretending he was considering what needed to be done.

"Sir, I'm sorry, but I think about the end of August will be the best we can do and be safe. We still have to test the launch mechanism and tune it for the weight of the Aerodrome."

Langley nodded. "Let's say September 1st then, just to give you a margin. We'll fly on September 1st, 1903—a good date for school-children to remember."

As the weeks went by, Manly realized just how lucky it was that he had padded the schedule. The vessel that Langley had selected to use to launch the Aerodrome had to have an entirely new catapult launching system built into it. The boat was enormous, able to house the fully assembled Aerodrome along with eight workmen and the military guard the War Department was now insisting on. There was a complete workshop, and the top deck had an eighty-five-foot launching track mounted on a turntable so that they could always launch into the wind. The catapult was spring operated, and so powerful that it was going to hurl the Great Aerodrome from a standing start to twenty-two miles per hour in just one second!

The catapult frightened Manly, not as a launch mechanism, but for its potential energy; he worried that someone would be killed or seriously injured if they were not extremely careful.

The only thing that gave him pleasure was the graceful, almost eerie beauty of the Great Aerodrome itself. It was beautifully executed, its framework a lacy structure of very thin tubular steel. Assembled, its huge tandem wings spread almost fifty feet, and had an area of more than a thousand square feet. From almost any angle, the Great Aerodrome looked like a fully rigged ship. The wings were supported, top and bottom, by a man-of-war's worth of wires that ran from various pickup points on the upper and lower surfaces of the wing. From there they ran to kingposts mounted strategically down the length of the center structure, which consisted primarily of two thin-walled steel tubes just two and one-half inches in diameter. The engine was mounted in the center, driving two rear-facing propellers, each seven feet long, through a transmission system. The propellers were not unlike the sails of a Dutch windmill, cloth stretched over wood and reinforced with guy wires as the rest of the machine was. As Manly walked around the Great Aerodrome he would pluck the bracing wires, letting them resonate like a violin string. Sometimes, if he plucked too hard, he could see the wing's wire-thin leading edge quiver in response.

The Great Aerodrome was unquestionably a remarkable achievement, Langley's crowning glory. And his too, perhaps; he had contributed the engine and he would fly it. If they were lucky, if the weather was good, if the catapult worked, if the airplane flew, and if he lived through the flight, Charles Manly would be world famous. What then? He did not speculate. It was enough to be the man who flew the Great Aerodrome.

In July, they moved the houseboat forty miles down the Potomac to a point opposite Widewater, Virginia, and halfway between the Maryland and Virginia shores. For the newspapers around Washington, this was the story of the century, and a group of reporters gathered, setting up a primitive camp on the riverbank of the Potomac, getting diarrhea from the bad food and picking up malaria like many of the crew of the floating workshop did. It was a pesthole, and the reporters began to take things personally, making sharper and sharper observations on the Aerodrome, on Langley, on the "ark" as they called the houseboat, the weather, and everything else that displeased them.

Then the professor decided do another test, this time of a quarter-scale model that had flown before, in 1901. It was inexplicable to Manly, as it would prove nothing and just cause them endless delays in preparing for the Great Aerodrome's first flight, but he thought it must be just to give the reporters something to write about besides their malaria.

The quarter-scale model was perfectly executed and had a miniature gasoline engine for power. Manly positioned himself in a boat well downstream from the houseboat to watch the flight, and to retrieve the model when it landed.

The press was notified, and at 9:30 A.M. on August 8th, the model was launched, taking off well, but flying only about three hundred yards before its engine failed and it hit the water. Manly had mixed emotions; the sight of the little Aerodrome coming toward him was moving, as beautiful as anything he had ever seen. But when it made a little half-turn to the right and disappeared into the river, he had a sudden clutch of fear, seeing himself inside the Great Aerodrome and suffering the same fate.

The model was destroyed when they pulled it from the river, and Manly had a tough time explaining to a reporter from the *Washington Star* exactly what it was that had been accomplished. He passed off the crash as an error of a mechanic in overfilling the gasoline tank, but the press reaction was negative. If the full-sized Great Aerodrome did four times as well as the quarter-size model, it would still be a colossal failure.

The fiasco with the quarter-size model had only one good result. The professor left the camp, and gave Manly full authority to make the first flight in the Great Aerodrome whenever he felt the machine and the weather were suitable, whether Langley was present or not.

The delegation of authority placated Manly, who knew that the August 8th test flight of the model was irrelevant. It just cost him time that he could have used trying to figure out how to make sure the propellers stayed on the shafts of the Great Aerodrome. Blades had broken twice, and once an entire propeller went spinning across the deck; if it had hit someone it would have killed him. Langley blamed the weather, but Manly knew the failure came from the way Langley had insisted on attaching the propellers to the drive shaft. It was exactly the way he had done with his models, but it was not adequate for the full-scale Aerodrome, not when it was powered by a fifty-two horsepower engine.

As the hot summer days wore on, the problems of launching a flying machine from a houseboat grew more pronounced. The humid weather caused the wing ribs to deform and the propellers to warp. A sudden storm dragged the houseboat from its mooring, tearing up auxiliary equipment and sinking the little fleet of boats that served as transports to and from shore.

September 1st passed without becoming a national holiday as Langley had hoped, but the Aerodrome was finally ready to fly two days later. The reporters were notified; boats had been placed at several points to speed to the rescue of the Aerodrome and its pilot if anything happened; and photographers were spotted along the shoreline with special telephoto cameras, to record the flight from several angles and thus derive all possible data from it.

To reporters watching through telescopes and binoculars, Manly appeared ready to fly, with goggles placed up on his forehead and wearing a cork-filled life jacket. He checked the Aerodrome carefully, inspected the catapult, and then crawled to stand upright in the little pilot's car. There he had the limited controls the Aerodrome possessed. The cruciform tail, balanced at the rear, could be moved up and down. The rudder, to turn left or right, was near him, in the center of the Aerodrome. And Manly himself stood upright at the pilot's station, ready to chauffeur the Aerodrome on its flight.

Manly gazed ahead of him at the river; there was no landing gear, just some flotation devices to keep the Aerodrome from sinking when it came down on the Potomac. He hoped the wind would not drift him over the land—if it did, the landing could be a disaster.

The minutes ticked by and the great moment for the Great Aerodrome had finally come. The only problem was that the engine would not start. The entire stock of dry batteries used to start the engine were ruined from the damp weather. After forty minutes of trying substitute batteries, the wind rose slightly, and to the jeering of the reporters, Manly crawled out of the pilot's station, calling the flight off. As he walked around the Aerodrome, trying to work off his frustration, one of his deck crew made a small a passing joke about "I thought these were dry cells but I guess they are wet cells," and the normally mild-mannered Manly had to be physically restrained from striking him. Manly did not think it was funny at the time but laughed to himself later—they *were* all wet cells, when what they needed were a few dry ones.

The engine's failure to start turned out to have been a blessing.

After the flight attempt was given up, Manly made a close inspection of the Aerodrome, primarily to give himself something to do and keep his mind off the failure of the engine to start. A close look at the wings revealed that the damp had softened the glue that held them together. It would take a month or more to repair them, and then another week at least before he could try again. The future national holiday had slipped into October.

CHAPTER

29

Alexander Graham Bell flopped down in the deep grass, exhausted from a morning spent battling the relentless pull of his kites, his arms aching with the strain. He had started off at seven o'clock, well nourished on Mabel's usual stout breakfast, and had flown for five solid hours until the wind came up and made it unsafe. Now he was starving again, his hands sore from handling the reel and the guidelines. Seated in the kite house, he shared with his two helpers the hearty picnic lunch she had packed, talking over the morning's flights. Then, alternately dozing and writing in his journal, he waited another two hours, hoping the winds would subside. Instead they picked up, so he stowed the kites, dismissed his crew, and walked back up to *Beinn Breagh*, content with the day's work.

Despite his scientific caution, Bell had to admit to himself that he was utterly delighted with his tetrahedral kites. The very first one was a relatively small affair, only sixteen winged cells, each one made up of four four-cell assemblies. It had flown impressively from the start, taking off with an ear-piercing whistle without even having to run to get it airborne. Only about a yard wide and a yard deep, the bright red kite flew better than any other type of kite he had ever built before, and he knew he was on to something.

There followed a string of triumphs, as he built one larger tetrahedron kite after another, some in standard single configuration, and others that were built in tandem, like the wings of Langley's Aerodrome. The first of these was so large that Bell could fly it only in calm weather, which meant he had to put his helper, Gregory Cafferky, on a galloping horse to get it airborne. The reel system for the rope was attached to a special rig built into the saddle. Once airborne, Cafferky would transfer the reel to Bell. The tandem kite flew beautifully in the lightest of winds. It was so successful that Bell immediately built another to be flown over water. It was equipped with two floats at each "wing" tip, the floats also built in the tetrahedral manner.

Without much imagination they called it the "Floating Kite," and Bell and his two helpers had four fine flights, with easy launches, each rising to the limit of the reel. Cafferky worked with another lad, Henry Myers, to help Bell with the flying, with Myers acting as a photographer as well. Bell kept a meticulous written record of all his activities and he insisted that all the kite flights be well documented with photos. The kites were covered in red silk so that they would photograph well.

On the fifth flight of the Floating Kite, the breeze that had been accommodatingly moderate turned suddenly into a squall that lifted both Cafferky and Myers almost four feet into the air. They let go in a panic and the kite pulled the three-eighths-inch manila rope off the reel in a rush, climbing rapidly at a forty-five degree angle until the rope broke. The kite stalled in midair, changed its attitude to slightly nose-down, and glided down to land without any damage at all. It was obviously Aerodynamically stable, besides being able to generate a tremendous amount of lift. To Bell, its success seemed very like that of the model Aerodrome that he had watched Professor Langley fly in 1896. Perhaps they were both on the verge of solving the problem of flight.

The kite flying was unlike most of the experimental work Bell had done in the past, where the usual pattern was one failure after another for many long months until there was suddenly a breakthrough. The kites were just the opposite—they had flown well from the start, and each one led to improvements featured in the next. An almost uninterrupted series of excellent flights had led Bell to patent his designs. While the structural layout of the kites formed the primary basis for the patent, one of his most important claims was that as the kites increased in size, they decreased in weight per square meter of surface area. He knew this was revolutionary; with every other flying machine, the results were usually the opposite; the larger they got, the heavier load each square meter of surface had to take. The discovery bothered him a bit, reminding him of

"Langley's Law," which had argued that the power to maintain a flying machine in flight diminished with its speed. He had known by inspection that this was false, and now he was postulating something that sounded perilously close to it. Yet he knew his figures were correct, and knew where the advantage was obtained: smaller kites demanded more structural material per square foot than did larger ones. If he took the trouble to reduce the size of the aluminum structural members of the smaller kites, he could probably reduce the difference in performance, but there was no point in it, for they served his purpose well built just as they were.

That night, on one of the typical long evenings they spent before the massive stone fireplace in the study, Bell was moved to admit a new ambition to his adoring wife, who, of course, had known it all along.

"I cannot deny it, Mabel. I want to build a powered flying machine that will be as useful as a dray truck, and I want to be first."

"Dear Alec, of course you do. But you have to be reasonable. You cannot be the first in everything, and you cannot do everything alone."

As usual, Mabel was on target, referring obliquely to two facts of life. One was Professor Langley, already well on the way to his first flight, and the other was her plan to get him some useful assistants.

They knew each other so well that he understood exactly what she meant. And he also knew very well that where once the kites had been a hobby, they were now an obsession, and every success increased its intensity. Langley, still his friend and greatly admired, was the archrival, the one man that might beat him in the race to be the first to fly.

Bell patted his wife's hand as he plunged deep into thought. The very idea of Langley and his Great Aerodrome was acutely discomforting to Bell. Langley had started his experiments almost twenty years before, so it was understandable that he was forging ahead now. But a visit to Langley's shop had confirmed his suspicions about the structural integrity of the Aerodrome. It was just too fragile, almost as if it were built of wire-supported soap bubbles. Even if it flew—and if young Manly were on board chauffeuring it, he prayed that it flew well—it was a dead end. There was simply no way that so fragile and delicate a machine could be put to any utilitarian task, or even to fly at a great speed. Yet it did not matter. If Langley's machine made the first successful powered flight, he would go down in history as the first to fly, even if the Aerodrome never flew again.

In contrast, his tetrahedrons were strong, able to take a vicious smack into the ground and come away with little damage. They were modular and could be assembled in almost any size, remaining as strong as ever, and, relatively, growing lighter. That meant they could be powered to fly swiftly, perhaps as much as sixty or seventy miles per hour, carrying large loads through the sky, free of roads and railways. There were some control problems that had to be sorted out, and these would occupy him for perhaps another year. Even though they had the inherent stability that he sought, they responded quickly to tugs on the ropes guiding them. This meant they would respond to some sort of onboard control, a rudder aft of the main body perhaps. And while Langley had frittered away the last two years attempting to get a lightweight engine, a large tetrahedron would be able to accommodate a heavy engine if necessary. As he considered the problem, he realized that heavy engines might even be desirable for the workhorse kites, those carrying freight, for they would be more dependable, able to stay in service for many years.

Bell planned to tackle the problem of control next, and then to work on the choice of power plants. Smiling to himself, he thought, *Or to have someone work on these problems as Mabel is working on me.*

It had been almost a year since his wife had first proposed the idea of a consortium of young men to help him with his experiments. As always, she had done it tactfully, diffidently, and when he erupted in protest—the last thing he wanted was a bunch of youngsters hanging around the house—she had quietly backed off. Like most married couples, they both knew the game they were playing. She had advanced the idea again on several occasions, timing it when he was in a particularly good mood, usually after a successful series of flights. They both knew that his resistance would wear down because it was undeniably a good idea. The question was when, and who the young men were to be.

Mabel Bell had a line on a bright young man already, one she knew Alex would be happy to have. He was John McCurdy, just seventeen, and a student at the School of Practical Science at the

University of Toronto. John was a Baddeck boy, the son of A. W. McCurdy, who had served as Bell's secretary for many years, doubling as a photographer. A. W. was a brilliant man himself, with many patents in the photographic equipment line, but he knew how to step back and let Alec have center stage at all times. It had been a wonderful relationship, and having young John join them when he graduated would be like a homecoming. It was early, though, and Alec was still not quite ready to have assistants on hand. In the meantime, she would go on looking, and he would go on pretending not to notice.

CHAPTER
30

Y ou know, we should have taken pictures on the way down on this trip, so we could give a little travelogue when we get back."

"Yep, we're getting to be experts. It took me about a week to get here from Dayton the first time; this time it was a breeze."

The Wright brothers had left Dayton at 8:55 A.M. on September 23rd, traveling down to Elizabeth City so that they could catch the Ocracoke steamer immediately after they arrived. This got them into Manteo on Roanoke Island at 1:30 A.M. They had arranged for a gasoline-engine–powered launch to be waiting there, and it whisked them to the Kill Devil Hills, arriving at 1:00 P.M. on the 25th. It was a record, just under fifty-one hours of bone-jarring fatigue with nothing but a hard deck to sleep on, but nonetheless a vast improvement over the first trips. The main thing was that they packed plenty to eat on the way, no longer forced to rely on the shipboard cuisine of Israel Perry or Captain Midgett.

Much of their equipment and the material for the new buildings had been shipped ahead, including some sophisticated instrumentation that had been surprisingly expensive, but which they purchased anyway. They had a new French anemometer and a good camera, with a tripod and a big supply of glass plate negatives and a set of batteries for starting the engine. The main components of their 1903 flying machine would not arrive for more than a week, as they wanted to have a new building built in which to assemble it.

The Kitty Hawkers greeted them, if not as royalty, at least as honored old friends. They had taken to the idea of the Wrights and their flying machines, and the Dayton influence was seen in subtle ways around the village. The most notable, perhaps, was the general store which now stocked a far wider variety of canned goods and groceries than had been the case on their first visits. The grocer confided that the locals were now calling for the same "delicacies" that the Wrights had introduced: such luxuries as canned corn, canned tomatoes, and on rare occasions, corned beef. There were other examples as well. Bill Tate now had a stove like the Wrights had begun using, and Dan Tate had rigged up some carbide lighting. Bill was preoccupied with some political problems, and he let the Wrights know that Dan would be substituting for him most of the time. That was not the best of news, for while Bill pitched into the work for the love of it, Dan was a little more inclined to do it for the money— or not do it at all, if he didn't happen to like the task.

The sense of community welcome helped allay the dismay from the sight of their old camp, damaged by a ninety-mile-per-hour "nor'easter" that had swept the Outer Banks in February. It took half a day to uncover the sand from the foundation and another half-day to move the building back onto it. Fortunately, the 1902 glider tucked away inside the battered building had survived the blow virtually intact.

Both men were conscious that the new flying machine would be bigger, heavier, and much more powerful than anything they—or anyone else—had attempted to fly before. To get ready for it, they knew they needed to practice on the 1902 glider, and they juggled the work on the camp to take advantage of any good flying weather.

They planned to fly the 1903 machine as a glider first, not using the engine and propellers until they were familiar with its characteristics and the way the control system functioned on the much larger machine. Over the four years of their experiments, they had made several changes in the operation of the controls. These were a continuing bone of contention between Orville and Wilbur, one of the subjects where their usual bickering took a hard edge that told each of them to back off before the fight became serious.

In Orville's view, Wilbur was the culprit, always modifying the operation or the placement of the controls, looking for ways to make them more efficient or perhaps just to save a little weight. Orville complained that changing the way controls moved could cause a problem if the operator had to make a quick decision; he might react in the way he had been trained on a previous machine.

Wilbur allowed that a good flyer would not have any trouble, the implication being that he, Wilbur, would have no problems, while Orville, with his lesser skills, might. It took all of Orville's self control not to point out Wilbur's first "well-digging" crash the year before, when instead of using the new hip-movement system to control the machine, he had pushed in vain with his feet against the spot where the control for the wing-warping used to be. Last year they had changed the operation of the front rudder, with the movement of the control just the reverse of what it had been the previous year, and Orville wanted to keep it that way. Wilbur, for some reason, had wanted to change it back, but Orville was adamant— no changes in the way the controls worked!

The matter was delicate because they were used to joking routinely in a similar way over other problems. Their jesting arguments had become a means by which they entertained their visitors, a bit of comic showmanship that enlivened their long hours of work. But this was different; this was one of those subjects—like Katharine— where joking was not allowed.

As was their custom when tension built they plunged into work, and the brand-new building was a challenge, for it had to be large enough to let them move around as they assembled their new flying machine—the Flyer. They had help on the construction work from the lifesaving station, and an idea that Katharine had suggested did them a lot of good. Earlier in the summer she had gone through the photographs they had taken of local people, asking about them, trying to get an idea of what they were like. Then she suggested that at some point they should mount copies of the photos and give them as gifts. It was a stroke of genius, and shortly after they arrived, Orville wrote to her, asking that the mounted photos be sent.

The lifesaving people led an austere life, and the thought that these important visitors "from up North" had taken the care to frame their photographs was much appreciated. They were more ready than ever to help with the new building, which quickly took shape, solid on its foundations and parallel to the old structure. The new one was a giant, forty-four feet long and sixteen feet wide, with the eaves set at nine feet. Each end had a door hinged at the top. It could be propped open so they could get a good breeze through, with lots of light, when the weather was right. Outside they braced the walls with stout two-by-fours, angling them deep into the sand, all the while hoping that there would be no more ninety-mile-per-hour winds.

The weather was good on Monday, September 28th, and they stopped their work on the building to carry the 1902 glider to the one-hundred-foot "Big Hill." Its appearance had changed markedly since their last visit, sculpted by the relentless winds. The ridges which undulated up the hill like lapping waves were now positioned at a different angle and seemed to be a little higher and closer together, worrying the Wrights that they might find some differences in the reaction of the wind, which was gusting from twenty to thirty miles per hour.

The new ridges didn't seem to make any difference in the way their glider handled. After an hour's gliding, the gusts ceased and a steady thrusting wind enabled them to stay in the air, almost hovering, over one spot on the ground. This was an enormous boon, giving them the kind of sustained practice they wanted with the controls, and saving them the long hauls back up the hill. On one flight, Wilbur "soared" for almost half a minute without covering more than fifty feet over the ground, the Flyer held steady by the invisible hand of the flowing wind. Orville was close enough to watch Wilbur's quick, almost imperceptible movements of the forward rudder with his hand control, and the slight quick shifts of his hips as he controlled the angle of the wingtips. At the end of one flight he told him "Will, you're like one of those fellows who keeps a whole bunch of plates spinning in the air at the same time, running from one to another, giving a touch here, a touch there, keeping everything going. And the look on your face—utter concentration. I was wondering what would happen if you suddenly had a bird or a bug fly into you."

"I guess I'd drop the plates. It would probably be a bug; the way my heart was pounding, I think the birds would be frightened off."

By day's end, they had lost count of the number of glides, but were gratified that flying was indeed like riding a bicycle—once you knew how, you did not forget. Yet both men knew that they were rusty and needed to do better, and they were still fretting about this when the schooner *Lou Willis* tied up at Kitty Hawk. Captain Midgett had brought them their new flying machine. With a lot of help, they managed to get the crates inside the new building before a torrential rain started.

The weather was bad for the next five days, with winds steady all day at thirty miles per hour suddenly leaping upward as night fell, pulling at the tar paper on the roof and threatening to turn their shed into an impromptu flying machine. Inside their living quarters, things grew steadily worse as water ran through on the floor, leaving swirls of wet sand behind it. When the roaring winds reached a peak, they could hear the tar paper roofing beginning to rip, and Orville went out, his mouth filled with nails and carrying a hammer. Wilbur held the ladder as Orville climbed to the roof, the wind tugging at him, threatening to throw him off as he pushed the tar paper down and hammered it into place, hitting his fingers about as often as he hit the nails. The next day they found out from the weather station that the wind had peaked at seventy-five miles per hour about the time Orville was attacking the tar paper and his fingers.

The brothers were accustomed to bad weather at Kitty Hawk, but the enforced idleness bothered them. The new machine was still in crates, and there was nothing they could do until the storm stopped and they were able to do the finish work on the new building. They would have been considerably comforted had they been aware of events taking place to the north, on the Potomac River.

CHAPTER
31

Charles Manly saw October 7th, 1903 as having two tremendous advantages for the first flight of the Great Aerodrome. The first was that the weather was clear and the wind light; the second was that Professor Langley was in Washington on business.

Manly had been delegated the authority to fly when he thought best; he had also been urged to fly as soon as possible, for the great boat on the Potomac with its large staff was expensive to maintain. Perhaps more importantly, the newspaper reporters were waiting for the flight like a flock of vultures. Their living conditions were poor, they were sick of the food they were getting and their reportage was becoming more and more acerbic, as if Langley were personally to blame for their discomfort. The War Department was also restive: it had sunk $50,000 into the Great Aerodrome, and hostile congressmen and cartoonists were already taking potshots at the implied waste in investing in so impossible a dream as a flying machine. Langley was all too conscious that besides the $50,000, he had siphoned off, quite legally, another $23,000 in Smithsonian funds and grants to sustain the effort. Time was running out and he wanted results whether he was there to see them or not.

The professor had a deep and abiding faith in Manly. It was well justified, for the young Cornell graduate never hesitated to sacrifice his time or his interest in furthering the Great Aerodrome. Today was no different. First, Manly inspected the main frame of the machine from bowsprit to the Pénaud tail, all 58 feet 5 inches of it. He worked from the rudder forward, picking his way along the catapult track, peering up to check the fittings. The huge wings were attached to the mainframe by four triangular pyramids of guy posts, two on top and two on the bottom. As usual—he was beginning to think it a bit of superstition—he touched the guy wires to hear them sing and to see the vibrations ripple outward through the entire wing structure. The Great Aerodrome's wings extended out over the sides of the elaborate launching structure that was built on top of the huge houseboat on which it floated. As Manly strained to check each feature he recalled that one of the reporters had written that it looked like a "wedding cake built by a carpenter," referring to the layers of wood bracing that supported the catapult and the Aerodrome.

Manly next went down and inspected both the platform and the catapult mechanisms. He had talked to each of the crew and was sure that each one knew his duty. For their part, they liked him—something that could not be said of Langley. The workers admired the way Manly had brought the engine along, finally coaxing fifty-two horsepower from it. They also liked the courteous way he treated them, always acknowledging how much they were contributing. When Langley came on board he ignored them except to bark an occasional order. In contrast, the "engine man" as they sometimes called him knew them all by their first name, and was even aware of their family situations.

Manly, a small man of about one hundred and thirty pounds, had his usual life jacket and goggle costume on, embellished today by a barometer sewn into his left trouser leg, so that he could measure the altitudes he reached. He was nervous because he was uncertain how the controls would operate in flight, and increasingly aware that when the flight ended he had better be over the river, or he would be in trouble.

Manly glanced at his watch. After all the years of effort, it was time. He had personally checked the engine, pulling it through so that the pistons all had a chance to move and clear any oil that might have seeped into the cylinder heads. Then he primed it, climbed into the cloth-covered pilot's car, and gave the signal for start.

When the engine roared to life he felt a deep, overwhelming rush of pride. This was his contribution; he had raised it from an eight-horsepower pup to this smooth-running dynamo. He checked it quickly, and saw that it was delivering its full fifty-two horsepower.

The engine was like his child, talking to him, the roaring noise bouncing off the deck, the vibration from the transmission and the propellers shivering the entire structure of the Great Aerodrome.

Manly stood in the flimsy pilot's station and moved the control wheels. One moved the Pénaud tail, just up and down, no lateral movement. The second wheel moved the rudder. He placed his hand on the throttle and nodded to a crewman stationed forward on the boat to fire the rocket that was the signal for the photographers and reporters lining the shore. Tugboats and rowboats were strategically placed downwind from the boat, and the tugs all blew their whistles to alert anyone who did not see the rocket.

His next nod was the signal to release the catapult. Manly was jolted backwards as the catapult and the spinning propellers hurled the Aerodrome along the sloping track. He grabbed for the sides of the pilot car as the Aerodrome tilted downward, throwing him forward over the engine and rudder controls. He went with the Great Aerodrome as it, in the words of a reporter, "simply slid into the water like a handful of mortar."

The swift trip had been a blur to Manly, naturally disconcerted by the snap of the catapult, something he had never experienced before. As he struggled to get up he saw only the turbid muddy waters of the Potomac rushing toward him. Manly was just part of the mortar for the first twenty feet of the descent, but as the machine splashed into the river, he grabbed the nest of wires above his head and pulled himself free. The Aerodrome, not so great now, sank beneath him to settle on the shallow river bottom. Manly saw that part of the wreckage was above the surface, swam to it, and waited to be rescued.

As soon as they had stopped laughing the reporters started writing. The story was not as good as it might have been if the Aerodrome had actually flown, but it was certainly better than writing about damp dry cell batteries and an engine that would not start.

Disappointed and angry, Manly faced the reporters alone. He did not wish to talk at all at first, but they persisted, offering their own ideas of what had happened, and these ranged from an error on his part to an anarchist plot. Desperate, he felt he had to come up with something that was reasonable and would prevent them from putting their own crazy interpretations into print. He finally blamed the crash on "improper balance"—whatever that meant.

CHAPTER
32

Back at the Smithsonian, Ross Robbins had the temerity to enter Langley's office without knocking, barely able to suppress his glee at being the bearer of bad news. The *Washington Star* had phoned Langley, asking for a statement, and Robbins was relaying the request. Langley listened with consternation, seeing his reputation going up in smoke as the Aerodrome had gone down in the water. Robbins later noted to his bureaucratic colleagues with some satisfaction that it was fully three minutes before Langley inquired about Manly.

"He is fine, sir, not injured at all. Just a little damp around the edges. The *Star* reporter asked him what had happened, and he told him that the Aerodrome was out of balance."

Langley was too distraught to catch the levity in Robbins's reply. "He told them what? It couldn't have been the balance, it was something else. Get the *Star* on the line for me."

The professor went out to Robbins's desk—he refused to have a telephone in his office, too distracting—and took the line.

"Langley here. The important thing is that Mr. Manly was not injured. I've analyzed the reports, and I believe that a section of the launching track must have caught one of the Aerodrome's guy wires. We will repair it and fly it again, soon."

It was a purely off-the-cuff comment, based on no information whatever, but couched in terms that spared the Great Aerodrome from failure. He had toyed briefly with speculating that the operator might have made an error, but realized that he would need Manly for another attempt.

For the following week, all across the country, cartoonists and editors had a field day with the accident and with Langley's explanation. There were genuinely funny cartoons that showed the Great Aerodrome as the proverbial handful of mortar, and sober editorials castigating the War Department for having spent $50,000 of the taxpayers' hard-earned money on so obviously foolish a project. Professor Langley never went to vaudeville shows and so was spared the plethora of wicked jokes that sprang up in that arena.

Now the reputations of Langley, the Smithsonian, and the procurement officials in the War Department all depended upon successful repairs to the Great Aerodrome. Charles Manly, who might have been forgiven if he had quit, embraced the task of rebuilding the machine, dredged with a great deal of damage from the Potomac.

Langley had been magnanimous, not once berating Manly for the failure. Instead he asked, almost humbly, "Manly, my able friend, when do you think you will have the Aerodrome ready to fly again?"

"Within sixty days. Without fail, within sixty days."

The professor did something very unusual. He took Manly's hand and shook it.

CHAPTER
33

At Kitty Hawk, the Wrights worked feverishly on the assembly of what they called their "whopper machine" in letters to Katharine. By mid-October they had completed the entire upper wing. They had rarely commented previously on the aesthetics of their machines, but it was obvious to them both that this one surpassed everything they had done in the past. It was undeniably a work of art, beautiful in its proportions and in the way the muslin clung to both surfaces. They had changed the shape of the wing profile so that it was thickest at the very leading edge and tapered to a narrow point at the rear, giving it a very refined appearance.

Orville pulled Wilbur aside once, tugging him to the 1902 glider and having him sight along the edge of the wing. Then he brought him back, and did the same with the new wing.

"I see what you mean, Orville. This is really much more like the wing of a bird in soaring flight; using a flatter main spar makes all the difference."

"It's bound to make a difference in flight, Will. Less head resistance, for sure."

As the machine came together they commented favorably on its appearance again, the first time on the shape of the wing struts, which were smoothly rounded, and again on how well the double rudder had turned out. The 1902 glider had needed only one rudder, but this machine was powered and they would need all the rudder surface area they could get. Even as they commented on the double rudder, the same thought occurred to them: they were talking too much about how pretty it was; it would jinx them if they kept it up. From that point on they never made a comment about the beauty of their flying machine, but they both felt it. It was like a thoroughbred horse, lean and sturdy, without a single part that was not vitally needed.

They were still in a state of mild self-congratulation when Dan Tate brought in their mail from town. It included a newspaper that gave them their first news of the failure of Langley's Great Aerodrome.

As Wilbur read the paper he yelled "Orv, come in here! Langley's gone bust!"

Each man read the article twice without speaking. Dan Tate was pretending to be busy in the corner, fiddling with the fancy French percolator they had purchased to make their coffee, and they didn't want to appear to be gloating in front of him.

Orville spoke first. "Like a handful of mortar, eh? Wonder what happened?"

"Says here that something snagged on the launching mechanism, a catapult. I'm sure glad this Manly fellow got out without being hurt. That was a pretty good fall. Could have broken his neck, easily." Both men knew that within days they would be in the same situation as Manly, and that their necks would be on the line.

There was a related article that soberly laid out Langley's long quest for flight and speculated on the amount of money that had been invested in the experiment. The fifty thousand dollars from the War Department was well known, but the article hinted that Langley had received almost as much from the Smithsonian. It went on to quote a source, who had asked not to be identified, who stated that there was at least twenty thousand dollars invested in the launching mechanism alone.

Wilbur whistled "Twenty thousand dollars. Orville, get out your pencil and paper. I want you to figure out how much we've got invested in our 'launching mechanism.' "

"Don't need any paper. The big cost is lumber; we've got at least two dollars and fifty cents invested in the two-by-fours that we'll use for the launch rail. Then we've got the three bicycle hubs we use, two on the flying machine, one on the rails. They retail for about fifty cents each, so that's another dollar fifty. I guess you could say we've got four dollars in the launch mechanism, give or take a little, and not counting our labor."

Wilbur went to the box where he kept his notebook and leafed through it. It contained entries on everything they had expended since 1899, starting with their first experimental glider, and counting the cost of their food, railroad tickets, shipping expenses, the engine castings, even the little gifts they had taken back to Carrie and Katharine. It took him only a minute, as he had already run totals on each page, as well as a total for each year.

"Right now, Orville, we've got eight hundred and eighty-two dollars invested in this project. We'll need to spend a little more before we're finished, I'm sure, and we'll need to send the folks down here some trinkets to thank them for all they've done. By the time we're finished, it might be close to a thousand dollars, all told."

Orv didn't say anything for a minute, doing some mental calculations of his own to come up with a joke.

"Well, Will, one thing's for certain. If we fly this machine, and it slides off Kill Devil Hill into the sand like a handful of mortar, it will be a lot cheaper mortar than Langley used."

They looked around. Tate had gone out the door, and they both burst into laughter. When they had stopped, Wilbur took note of the date of the paper—October 8th. At the rate they were progressing they would have their new flying machine ready for some gliding tests by the first of November. He called to his brother. "How long do you think it will take Langley to get his machine repaired and ready to fly again?"

"Can't tell much from the pictures; it looks like it was badly damaged. 'Course he probably made some spare parts ahead of time. And it depends on how many people he has working on it. Hard to say how long it will take; what do you think?"

There were pictures in the newspaper of the Aerodrome before its launch, one taken during the catastrophic dive into the Potomac, and two after the crash. Wilbur considered them carefully, and hazarded a guess. "If they really work hard, they might be able to do it in four or five weeks. Like you say, it depends on what they had built up as spare parts. You know what that means for us, don't you?"

Orville shook his head.

"It means we don't have time to test this flying machine as a glider. We are going to use the engine right from the start, and the first time we fly it, it will be for real. No glides, just a powered flight."

His brother was silent. This was not like Wilbur, jumping ahead like this, not doing everything carefully, orderly, safely. It would be a tremendous risk just to get in the flying machine and start the engines and go.

"I don't know, Will, we haven't been working like that. Even when we just change controls, we work up to it testing one control at a time. And powered flight will be a lot different; there will be the stress on the framework from the engine and the propellers running, and we have no idea what the effect of the wind from the propellers will have on the rudder."

"You're exactly right, Orville, but what if we wait and Langley flies first? What happens to our patents then?"

Orville knew very well it was not patents that Wilbur was worrying about. He wanted to be the first to fly; he'd spent four years learning how, and he didn't want Langley to take it away from him. There was no doubt he was right about the timing. If they tested it gliding, it would be the end of November before they could get the engine in it and fly it. By then Manly might have figured out what went wrong and fixed it, wasting all their four years of hard work.

Finally he said, "It's all right with me, Will; if that's what you think, that's what we'll do. Even then it will be close; I don't see how we can be ready much before November 1st and he might still beat us."

"Well, we better get going, before our mortar hardens!" They laughed again, but not so hard this time.

As the days passed, the worries grew, for the Flyer came together much more slowly than they expected, because of its more sophisticated construction. When they began to assemble the wings into a structural unit, they had to force the struts into position because the tight muslin covering had moved the sockets slightly out of place.

Things picked up after they gained the welcome assistance of George Spratt, who came to visit on October 23rd. George was quietly competent, and he immediately lifted their morale with the funny stories that were being told about Langley, telling them with such good humor that it did not seem like they were testing fate by laughing at their rival.

George being there also gave them an excuse to fly the 1902 glider again, and Orville dazzled them on the 26th with a world record for glider flying, staying airborne for sixty-one and a half seconds. Spratt was duly impressed, for he had been able to stay with the glider for the entire flight, running along beside it as Orville kept it almost stationary over the ground, virtually soaring in the sweet updraft that rolled up and then over the Big Hill. That night Spratt could talk of nothing else, convinced at last that the Wrights would fly this very year.

But it was not until November 5th that the Flyer was finally completely assembled and they could test the engine and propellers.

They had moved the Flyer outside its assembly building, not bothering to hook up the rear rudder yet. Wilbur went over every detail of the engine installation, checking the fuel, the cutoff switch, the gear to drive the chains that drove the propellers. Finally he said, "Let's crank her up."

The engine had to be coaxed into starting, and then burst into life, running roughly, not backfiring, but threatening to, the timing apparently slightly off.

Orville suddenly yelled, "Cut it off, Wilbur," but before his brother could move, the propellers broke loose from their shafts.

George Spratt called, "Anybody hurt?" The propellers swung slowly around.

Wilbur inspected them closely, turned and said in a flat voice, "Those dang lock nuts let go; that gave the propellers a little play on the prop shaft and that tore it loose. The engine's vibrations probably did not help."

"We can't repair the shafts here, Will—we've got to get them back to Charley."

The three men conferred briefly. The smash-up was going to cost them ten days, at least, to get repairs. Spratt was more than a little fed up with the cold nights and the recent shortage of groceries, and he volunteered to get the propeller shafts back to Norfolk, from where they could be expressed to Charley Taylor to be rebuilt. He also volunteered to nose around and see if he could find out how the repairs on Langley's Aerodrome were coming.

The day after Spratt left, Octave Chanute arrived in camp. Chanute took the news of the propeller failure easily, saying, "Such things are inevitable when you get into using motors. I much prefer gravity for power, but you've gone beyond that."

The distinguished engineer was now more than seventy years old, and the brothers were amazed at the way Chanute endured the bitter cold winds of the Kill Devil Hills to watch them fly their 1902 glider. As usual, he was full of generous plans for the Wrights' future. First, he was going to have them rebuild his oscillating-wing machine and fly it for him. He had already tried to buy the Ader flying machine and bring it to America for them to perfect, but the French let it be known that it was not for sale. It was obvious that Chanute believed that if the Wrights tried to fly the Ader machine, they would be successful. It was flattering, but ridiculous.

Chanute was delighted with the performance of the 1902 glider, applauding them with obvious sincerity. But it perplexed the Wrights that at the same time, he was somehow unable to make any differentiation between what they had achieved and Ader's abysmal lack of success. In his mind, that brilliant engineering mind, the two were both flying machines, equal in every respect, even though one flew and one did not. And while he approved of every aspect of the Flyer, even its name, it was obvious that he did not see any particular potential in it. In Chanute's eyes, the Flyer was no different than their 1902 glider or his *Katydid*, or for that matter Lilienthal's gliders. It was absolutely imponderable.

Two lines of Chanute's arguments depressed and worried them. The older man pointed out that Langley's engine, at fifty horsepower, was four times as powerful as theirs. Then he computed the expected power loss of the Flyer's propellers to be between twenty and thirty percent. If he was correct—and they worried that he was—this meant that they were really only going to get thrust equivalent to eight or nine horsepower from their engine, just as they had originally calculated before they had added on the extra weight of strengthening the airframe.

Then Chanute went on to say that they had figured everything much too closely.

"You've left too little margin for error. You've got just enough wing area, just enough power, your propellers are just large enough.

What happens if you've miscalculated with just one of these? You won't fly, you'll sink into the sand."

As he spoke, the Wrights looked at him, uncomprehendingly. He was not being cruel; this was an utterly dispassionate appraisal, as if he were checking out a bridge built by natives in some African backwater. He meant no harm, he was talking to them as to a freshman engineering class, not patronizing, just sharing his knowledge. The prospect of a successful flight, which seemed so certain when they left Dayton, now suddenly seemed quite diminished.

The Wrights did not ask Chanute directly about Langley's progress on repairing the Aerodrome, although it was the information they wanted most. Chanute had brought down photographs of the October 7th mishap and used them for the most part to confirm his own views that Langley's basic mistake had been to simply scale his models up. He might have known how the Aerodrome repairs were coming, but if he did, he took care not to reveal it. The Wrights realized that who was first did not matter a great deal to Chanute; he was in the position of being a facilitator in either case, and would go on encouraging them and others as he had done in the past.

The Wrights did not blame him for this, but they could not change their own feelings. They wanted to be first to fly, for a number of reasons, not least the possibility of making some money. But there was also the sheer fantasy of being the first in the world to do something that had been considered impossible for so long. And for Wilbur, there was another factor. He wanted to be first, but he wanted to be first with a flying machine that would leave a legacy. There was no way that the Aerodrome could do that; if it flew first it might actually delay the general acceptance of flying machines. Or so he convinced himself.

CHAPTER
34

The Aerodrome was coming together, more slowly than Manly wanted, but faster than the workmen thought was possible. He was driving them and himself at a furious pace.

Salvaging the engine had been simple. Manly had disassembled it, to be sure that nothing had been ingested while it was underwater, and upon reassembly it ran as it always did, like a twenty-one jewel, fifty-two horsepower Swiss watch.

The central structure of the Aerodrome had been damaged in the recovery operation, but it too had been rapidly repaired. Manly was suddenly aware that the usual conversation and hammering in the shop was absent; the building had become quiet. The workmen had all left, sidling out through the side entrance, and that meant only one thing: Professor Langley was on the way in.

He waited, standing in the pilot's car until the professor was at his side.

"How is it coming, my dear Manly?"

"As you see, Professor; the center section is ready, and the wings are under construction. With luck, we'll be ready by the first of December."

"You've done marvelously well. I'll always be grateful to you."

"I'm glad you are here; I was just going through the control operation, and I wonder if we've placed the rudder in the right position. It seems to me that it would have more purchase, more leverage, if it were farther to the rear."

Manly had been leaning forward, operating the rudder control, and failed to see the look on the professor's face. "Another thing—"

Langley interrupted him with, "Damn you, sir. How dare you question how 'we've' placed the rudder in the right position? This is my machine, I designed it, I had it built, and I placed the rudder where I wanted it, based on years of experiments. How do you have the effrontery to say 'we've' placed?"

Manly was appalled. He meant no disrespect, but he wanted respect for himself.

He hopped over the pilot car and stood by Langley, staring up at him.

"I'm sorry if I've offended you, Professor. Perhaps you'll understand more about the rudder when you fly the Aerodrome next December."

Manly walked to the shop's side entrance, slammed the door behind him, and walked through a crowd of cheering, laughing workmen. One shouted "That's telling him, Engine Man!" while from inside the workshop Langley's voice was calling "Mr. Manly, come here at once!"

Late that afternoon, Langley's carriage pulled up in front of the Georgetown building where Manly kept an apartment. A contrite Professor Langley emerged, his arms loaded with flowers and a huge box of candy. He knocked humbly on the door, and when Manly appeared, fell on him with cries of apology.

Charles Manly was a kindly man, who rarely swore. But as Langley embraced him he thought, *You hypocritical bastard, no wonder the men hate you.*

It was a painful interview for Langley, who, when the apologies were over, started off a technical discussion by agreeing with Manly about the placement of the rudder.

"The rudder will be all right as it is for the first flight. We'll learn something, and the next Aerodrome we build will have rudders placed where you suggest. And we will call the next one the Langley-Manly Aerodrome!"

The concession stunned Manly. It went far beyond anything he had imagined, and, as he had known he would, he agreed to continue to supervise the reconstruction of the Aerodrome and to fly it when it was ready. He still had faith, for he had seen the quarter-scale Aerodrome fly, and it seemed to him that the Great Aerodrome should fly as well. If it did, he wanted to be at the controls—such as they were.

CHAPTER
35

The joys of Kitty Hawk paled in the winter, and the bleak November winds and weather did nothing to increase the Wrights' morale. Charley Taylor had done a good job repairing the prop shafts, but the sprockets were still loose, and with the engine still running a little rough, the chains and the propellers were jerked about, causing Wilbur to quickly cut the switch. Orville went to their tool kit and pulled out a can of Arnstein's Hard Cement, a stellar seller in their shop, for it kept bicycle tires glued to their rims. He applied it liberally to the nuts holding the sprockets tight. They let it dry overnight, and from then on the nuts stayed tight. Pleased by the results, they joked about it as they did with everything that worked well.

"We can use that Arnstein's cement for anything; next time you get a toothache, Wilbur, let me know. I'll slap some Arnstein's in there and take care of it."

"Well you better keep it on hand for your neck, if you pull another one of your crashes in the Flyer."

By November 27th they felt they had the engine running smooth enough to try a test flight if the weather broke. The next day, Wilbur heard Orv give a low whistle.

"Lookee here, Will. This prop shaft is cracked."

He pointed to a hairline crack that ran down the steel tubing.

Wilbur sucked in his breath. "Good thing you found it here and not twenty feet in the air. Well, that's it for hollow prop shafts. We've got to make them out of solid steel."

Shifting nervously, Orville said, "I don't trust Charley for this one, Will. I'm going to go back and machine these myself."

Will nodded, knowing that Orville was lonesome for Katharine, and the shafts were just a good excuse to go back.

"Yeah, you might as well, Orv. We're getting on each other's nerves not having enough to do, the separation would do us good. How long will it take you?"

Orville gave it some thought and said, "I'll send Charley a telegram to get the spring-steel stock. If he has it on hand, I should be able to start back around December 8th. If these shafts work—and I think they will—we should be able to try a flight by the 11th or 12th."

The bad weather left with Orville, and Wilbur spent a pleasant week watching the birds and chatting with the Kitty Hawkers, who had taken to dropping in around dinnertime to keep him company. Back in Dayton, Orville got a welcoming home dinner from Katharine and a scowl from Charley when he told him that he was going to machine the prop shafts himself.

"No criticism intended, Charley, its just something I want to do."

"If it's not a criticism I don't know what it is. You're practically telling me I don't know my way around a machine shop. If you'd listened to me, you'd have used solid steel to begin with."

There was some truth in Charley's remarks. He had talked about solid steel shafts, but Will had overruled him, saying they were too heavy. But as the week wore on, Charley came around, and by the sixth, he was back to his usual cheerful self.

Which was more than could be said for Charles Manly.

CHAPTER
36

Professor Langley had long given up hopes for secrecy, so the second test was arranged to take place at Arsenal Point, just south of Washington, where the Potomac and the Anacostia Rivers join together. The river was well coated with ice and a raw twenty-mile-per-hour wind made handling the big wings of the Great Aerodrome difficult.

Charles Manly was having second thoughts as the Aerodrome came together, for everything reminded him of that miserable October 7th when he had crashed. By mid-afternoon the Aerodrome was assembled, waiting in its catapult on top of the revolving platform, its wings flexing in the wind.

Manly's gloom was reinforced by the palpable distress in Professor Langley's face. The professor had Albert Blohm hanging on him, as usual. Both men were closely escorted by an equally worried-looking colonel from the War Department, whose next promotion probably depended upon a successful flight. The foredeck of the boat had a few of Langley's friends and a half a dozen people from the Smithsonian, talking and laughing with a forced gaiety that fooled none of them. Everyone knew that Langley's reputation as a scientist and an administrator would be decided within the hour.

"What do you think, Mr. Manly?"

"Professor, the weather is bad, and the wind is gusting. If we had more time, I'd say we should postpone it. But I don't see how we can. Let's take a chance."

"I hate to take chances; it's not my way. But you are right, we can't afford to postpone the flight. If you are willing to try it, let's get underway."

The experience of the last flight dictated his outfit; Manly was wearing long underwear, a life vest, and tennis shoes. As he picked his way into the pilot's car, Langley and his friends debarked in small boats, to watch and hope.

The engine started—Manly had been hoping it might not—and sang its regular stout fifty-two horsepower song. The transmission worked well, if noisily, and the seven-foot-diameter propellers made their usual clomping noise. He made a few movements of the controls, checking their response. He waited gravely for a full minute, rehearsing in his mind what he would do if the Aerodrome flew— and what he could do if it did not. Then he signaled for the catapult to be released.

The Great Aerodrome sped down the sixty-foot track, its wings beginning to collapse as soon as speed built up, crumpling even as it was launched off the end of the catapult into an inverted turn that plunged it straight into the Potomac.

The shock of the fall was nothing like the cold jolt of the icy water as Manly was carried down below the surface, his life jacket snagging on some crumpled tubing. Terrified, his breath already short, Manly struggled out of the jacket, striving upward only to find the surface blocked by ice. Panic set in and, lungs bursting, he forced himself to turn and dive back down toward where he hoped he would find a hole in the ice.

Standing next to Langley, Blohm did not hesitate a moment, pulling off his coat and shoes and diving into the water, swimming strongly under the ice searching for Manly.

In the meantime, Manly had popped to the surface, gasping for air and already chilled to the marrow. He was picked up by a boat and transferred to the houseboat, where they wrapped him in blankets and gave him whiskey. Blohm was sitting next to him, not so violently chilled, but still needing warmth and whiskey.

Manly suddenly sat up, still wrapped in the blanket, and screamed, "That goddamn no good sonofabitching Aerodrome is the biggest piece of—" They shoved another glass of whiskey in his face, for the professor was coming down the stairs.

Manly spat the whiskey out and went on, a string of blasphemous curses that no one had ever heard him use, or even thought he knew. Blohm listened with admiration; Manly was better at cursing than the French soldiers back at Chalais Muedon!

Langley listened to him for a full minute, nodding his head as if it were a sermon, then said only, "Mr. Manly, you have failed me." He turned and left, with Manly launched on a new series of curses.

The newspapers fell on Langley and the War Department like hyenas on a particularly juicy carcass, and where the tone had largely been jesting after the October 7th crash, with a few serious editorials thrown in, this time humorous comments were in the minority. The essential thrust was that Langley was a fool who had stolen government money to waste on an impossible project, not once but twice, and that very fact made the government the biggest fool of all. A few columnists were kind enough to give Charles Manly credit for his courage in trying a second time, but for the most part, the reviews were coldly hostile. Somewhat surprisingly, no one mentioned Blohm's rescue attempt, which annoyed him.

The newspaper articles and editorials hurt Langley terribly, particularly when, a few months later, articles began to appear in scholarly journals that questioned his scientific judgment, by inference calling into question all that he had done before in other fields. It was all but unbearable.

Albert Blohm realized that to salvage anything from this debacle, he would somehow have to make it bearable for Langley.

CHAPTER
37

On his way back with the prop shafts, Orville picked up a newspaper in Elizabeth City and was delighted to see the story of Langley's final encounter with the Potomac. There was nothing malicious in his glee; he had no hard feelings for Langley, and only the deepest sympathy for Manly, but it meant that all the problems with the propeller shafts had not harmed their chances. If the Flyer could fly, they would be first—and he knew in his bones the Flyer could fly.

The newly machined prop shafts, an oily blue-black and perfectly balanced, went in on December 11th, and the subsequent engine run-ups were satin smooth.

"I think the steel gives the prop shaft a little added mass, makes it run true." Orville was inordinately proud of the two steel shafts he had turned. "These made Charley green with envy; gave me a little kick to see him fuming!"

"You have to remember, Orv, Charley wanted us to go with solid steel in the first place. I overruled him and it's cost us these last three weeks. If old Professor Langley's machine hadn't done another nosedive, we'd be in trouble."

The wind was too light to fly on the 12th, but the Wrights took the Flyer out and ran it down the track, to see how it would work. On the 14th, the wind was still light, and Wilbur waited until after lunch to tack up a large red flag on the side of the hangar. Life was boring down at the lifesaving station, and they kept a telescope trained on the Wrights' camp most of the time. When the red flag was displayed, they knew the boys were going to fly and needed some help. Within minutes, five of the lifesaving crew were on hand, along with a flock of their children.

With seven people working and a couple keeping the kids away from the Flyer, they laid out their two-by-four launching track. It was one hundred and fifty feet long, and they called it the "Grand Junction Railroad."

It was almost three o'clock when Wilbur won, by the toss of a coin, the right to try to make the first flight.

Orville came up to Wilbur before the engine start.

"Everything OK, Will?"

"I don't know—I'm feeling like I'm going to a wedding or a funeral, I don't know which."

"Let's make it a wedding, Will, we've got no time for funerals."

He walked away. There was a little problem with the engine start, but then the Flyer launched, Orville running alongside for just a bit until it was going too fast for him.

It was going too fast for Wilbur, too. His hands clammy with sweat, he pulled back on the elevator, and the Flyer lifted up then settled back down, hitting the ground no more than sixty feet from the end of the rail and fracturing one of the elevator supports. Wilbur lay prone on the wing, too stunned by the quick turn of events to shut off the engine until Orv came running up.

"What do you think, Will, was that an official flight?"

"Not a chance. I was behind it all the way, overcorrecting. It's different than the glider somehow; the front elevator is way too sensitive. I just put in too much nose up control and wham, there I was. Let's fix her up and try tomorrow."

The repairs took longer than they had expected, and over the course of the next two days they planned the next flight with great care, Wilbur exhorting Orville to stay calm and not overreact to the controls, Orville telling Will that he was no chicken like him, pulling back on the front rudder control like it was a horse he was riding.

The weather was pure Kitty Hawk nasty on December 17th: clear, cold, and with a vicious cutting wind that made flying seem impossible. They tried to start the day as normal as possible, dressing as they always did with white shirts, the patented celluloid collar, and a tightly done tie. They divided up the chores, each one eating breakfast separately. Around nine o'clock they stood together, facing the wind, tasting the salt spray, and watching the endless procession of waves curling against the beach. They both felt the strange combination of happiness and melancholy that Kitty Hawk evoked in them. They were glad to be away from Dayton, out from under their father's thumb, but they were getting tired of pursuing this dream, this Sisyphean hope that rolled back from them, day after day.

"I know how Professor Langley must have felt. Sort of desperate, afraid to make a try and afraid not to."

"Well, Orv, I'm desperate, too, and I'm more afraid of not trying than trying. Time's running out. We better make a try today if we can."

The wind died down a bit and they put the red flag up. A little after ten o'clock five men walked into their camp. One was W. C. Brinkley, a lumber buyer they knew in Manteo—he had provided a lot of material for their buildings. Then there were the regulars from the lifesaving station: John Daniels, fresh-faced and eager to please; Will Dough and Adam Etheridge, both with drooping black mustaches and looking enough alike to be brothers, but totally different in temperament, Dough being volatile and happy-go-lucky, Etheridge dour and gloomy. Tagging behind them was young Johnny Moore, a bright young lad who was probably doomed to a career as a fisherman, and who had once confided in Orville that he wouldn't mind having a chance to glide in "one of them flying machines."

The Wrights had moved the Flyer into position, laying a section of the launch track ahead of it and moving it along, then laying the track for takeoff. In that wind, the seven-hundred-pound flying machine was not easy to handle, susceptible to being blown over. Wilbur tenderly prepared the engine, sitting squat on its four little legs, priming each cylinder, checking the battery box for power and placing it in position, then taking one last walk around to check all the fittings, the propeller sprockets, everything.

Wilbur marched to a propeller and Orville went to the engine. At Orville's nod, Wilbur spun the propeller and started the engine. The two brothers shook hands—not a usual gesture for them, and held just long enough to see that their emotions were involved. Then Orville snaked through the wires to lay prone, his hips in the saddle, his left hand holding the front rudder control, his right the lever that slipped the line holding the machine to the rail.

Wilbur held up his hand, cautioning him to wait. There was one more important task to be delegated. John Daniels was given some instructions on how to operate the camera and to snap the shutter as soon as the Flyer left the rail. The odds on getting a picture were low, but they had to try.

At 10:35 A.M., Orville moved his right hand; the line released and the Flyer moved forward, Wilbur running along the right side, able to keep up in the twenty-seven-mile-per-hour wind that slowed the Flyer down but also helped it get airborne. Orville had not gone down the track more than forty feet when the Flyer lifted off and John Daniels snapped the shutter. Wilbur had halted as the Flyer swept by.

Lying on the wing, Orville was operating on two levels. On the one hand he was paying attention to business, consciously trying not to overcontrol, but still doing it, darting the front rudder up and down, the aircraft following in a rapid wave motion. On the other he was singing with exultation; he was flying, he was the first in the world, there was no Langley no Chanute, nobody that could take this glorious leap into flight from him. He was still singing and still overcontrolling when the flight ended just twelve seconds after takeoff, nosing into the sand, 120 feet from the starting point.

Orville cut the engine as Wilbur ran up.

"Was it a flight, Will?"

"You bet your boots it was a flight! We did it, Orville, we did it."

The boys from the lifesaving station were screaming; they knew what they had seen, and it proved to them that the Wrights—their Wrights, their personal friends—were not just some crazy men from Dayton, they were inventors, they were bringing history to Kitty Hawk.

The two brothers stood for a moment by themselves, their shoulders touching, both of them gazing at the Flyer, then, turning to look at each other and smiling. Orville said it, but they were both thinking it: "I wish Pop could have been here."

They carried the undamaged Flyer joyously back to its starting point, and Wilbur had everybody crowd into their little shack to get away from the biting cold for a few minutes.

They went through the routine again, this time with Wilbur taking his turn, determined to do better than he had on the 14th, determined to do better than Orville had just done. But at the moment of takeoff the joy of flight overtook him, and cautious as he was on the front elevator this time, he still was overcontrolling, bouncing down, frustrated but happy after just twelve seconds. The wind had dropped off, so his path over the ground was longer, about one hundred seventy-five feet.

They were getting expert at the routine, if not the front rudder, and only twenty minutes later, Orville put in a wavy fifteen-second flight that went almost two hundred feet. This time he had time to experience a rare sense of self-congratulation; he and Wilbur had done it, it was truly flying and no one could tell where it would lead—maybe to the Moon.

It was noon when Wilbur tried again, absolutely determined not to overcontrol. He got off swiftly, shaking off any feeling of joy or of satisfaction, concentrating on flying for a long fifty-nine seconds and covering 852 feet before crashing into the sand, just as he had on the 14th, smashing the front elevator. It did not matter. This was flying for real.

The trip back was tiring, with the wind blowing and the sand soft under their feet, but Orville was proposing a fifth try, this time a real flight, all the way down to the beach, to the weather station. That would shake the boys up, and it would make a great story to telegraph back to Dayton—they'd flown down to send a wire!

As they talked, an errant gust of wind got under the left wingtip of the Flyer, tossing it in the air. Johnny Daniels, the photographer, leaped at it and was flipped with the wing, just as the engine tore free from its mounts, crashing through struts, grinding the Flyer up internally as the wind wrecked it on the outside. Daniels emerged from the wreckage shaken but unhurt.

Disappointed, but still elated from the morning's triumphs, the Wrights supervised stowing the mess that had been their beautiful Flyer back into the hangar. They had lunch, then walked to Kitty Hawk, talking earnestly the entire way, telling each other over and over about each flight, from the flyer's view and from the watcher's view, almost unable to believe that their four-year quest had succeeded.

They had planned on success and now they had it. Before they left, Wilbur had carefully instructed brother Lorin on what to do when (not if) they flew. He was to take the telegram they would send to the local papers and to the Associated Press. They had already prepared a description of the Flyer to go along with the telegram.

At the Weather Bureau station, they joked with Joe Dosher, the first man in Kitty Hawk who had ever heard of the Wrights, telling him that they had intended to fly down, but got interrupted. Then they composed the telegram to their father.

CHAPTER
38

The Western Union telegram from Orville had been altered by the time it reached Bishop Wright, now reading:

```
176 C KA G8 38 PAID                              Via Norfolk VA
Kitty Hawk N C Dec 17
Bishop M. Wright
7 Hawthorne St
   Success four flights thursday morning all against
twenty one mile wind started from Level with engine
power alone # average speed through air thirty one
miles longest 57 seconds inform press
   home ##### christmas.
                                      Orevelle Wright
```

Carrie had received the telegram and raced up the stairs two at a time, knowing what it must mean, and hovering as Bishop Wright opened the envelope. He read it aloud, then with a huge smile yelled, "Praise the Lord" and fell to his knees in prayer. Fear that the boys would hurt themselves—maybe kill themselves as that German feller had done—had haunted him each year they had gone to Kitty Hawk and he had never said a word, but he had prayed, oh how he had prayed, not for their success so much as for their survival. And now he had both! The boys had lived through their dangerous experiments and had triumphed. He continued to pray, seriously and fervently, in the concentrated manner that revealed his years of deep devotion to his God, and his certainty that he was communicating directly with Him.

Not knowing what else to do, Carrie dropped to her knees and bowed her head, praying also, giving thanks that all the hard work she had witnessed was fulfilled. It made her proud to work there. Bishop Wright, utterly absorbed in his prayer of thanksgiving, did not notice her, and she stayed until she heard the front door open— Katharine was home. The bishop heard her as well, and called to her.

"They've done it, the boys have done it! They've made their flying machine work!"

Katharine flew up the stairs and read the telegram, pressing it to her bosom and laughing out loud.

"I can just see them, all dressed up down at that forlorn spot, being real calm about everything, but inside, just boiling over with joy." Katharine, by now accepted as the family's general manager, sprang into action, telling Carrie what to buy for the big welcome-home dinner, and gathering up the telegram and copies of the descriptive material Wilbur had prepared to take to Lorin.

Her first stop, though, was the telegraph office, where she sent a wire to Octave Chanute, surely the man who deserved to know first. The boys might have suspicions about his comprehension of what they were doing, and Pop might doubt his honesty, but there was no question that he had mentored them, helping them along with information and encouraging their approach. Besides, he was such a delightful gentleman, always quick with a compliment, and never forgetting to send flowers after a visit. Her wire to Chanute began with "Boys report" and then gave the same information as "Orevelle's" wire—and the same misinformation as well, repeating that the longest was fifty-seven seconds. She did not know that it had been fifty-nine seconds, nor that it would have been much better for publicity purposes to have read "one minute."

Lorin, whom Orville had jokingly called their "press officer," conducted his duties with the usual high level of mediocrity that seemed to characterize his approach to life. His brothers had wanted a dignified, low-key announcement, one that would be picked up not only by the press but also by engineering journals, and they had previously written a very careful—if not technically revealing—

description of the Flyer to go with the telegram. But Lorin's visit to the paper that should have cared most, the *Dayton Journal*, was frustrating. He literally ran in waving the telegram in the air to see his friend, Frank Tunison, the local Associated Press representative.

"Frank, by golly, the boys did it. Look at this telegram."

Tunison, who affected the world-weary air fashionable among newspapermen whose career had topped out at a middle level position, read the wire and handed it back.

"Fifty-seven seconds, eh? If it had been fifty-seven minutes, it might have been a news item." He didn't bother to read the descriptive material.

Lorin thought he was joking. "Frank, the boys flew a flying machine, no one has ever done that before. Look at Langley, he spent a whole bunch of money and failed, and our boys did it for peanuts and succeeded! You can't just ignore this!"

Tunison leaned back in the brown wooden swivel chair, propped one foot on his crowded desk and said, "Watch me."

CHAPTER
39

The boys were still in camp, still elated but suppressing any show of it, disassembling the badly wrecked Flyer, when their photographer John Daniels battered on the door to their shed, yelling, "Boys, you're on the front page in the newspaper, let me in."

Rushing in, he spread a copy of the *Norfolk Virginian-Pilot* over the bent wing of the Flyer, the nearest thing to a table in the crowded shed.

There it was, in black and white "and being read all over," as Orville said later:

FLYING MACHINE SOARS 3 MILES IN TEETH OF
HIGH WIND OVER SAND HILLS AND WAVES AT
KITTY HAWK ON CAROLINA COAST

The story that followed was even more imaginative than the headline, giving a totally inaccurate, fanciful description of the Flyer and quoting Wilbur as saying "Eureka" after the flight.

The brothers looked at each other. "Orv, I don't know whether to laugh or cry."

"We might as well laugh; you have to give them credit for a good imagination. But don't worry about it. Lorin will get the right story into the Associated Press, and people will understand. I doubt if anybody will pick up this story; it reads just like Edgar Allan Poe's hoax on the balloon flight across the ocean."

"I hope Lorin can save us, but I think we will be living this down for years, because people will believe it is what we told the press."

"Will, no one that knows you will ever believe you said 'Eureka.' 'Consarn it,' maybe, when you are feeling angry, or maybe, 'Orville cut that out,' but never 'Eureka.' "

"The problem is that only a few people know me—most will believe what they read in the newspaper. Well, we'll see."

Orville was wrong. By the time they got back to Dayton, someone in the Associated Press had latched onto the *Virginian-Pilot*'s fantasy and condensed it into a four-hundred-word story that flashed around the United States and even crept into the more sensational foreign newspapers. For the next ten years, the *Virginian-Pilot*'s version of their flight would haunt them, as one opponent after another "disproved" it to show that the Wrights were charlatans.

The newspapers might have failed them, but the first night of their homecoming was everything it should be, with Bishop Wright presiding as the patriarch, dispensing his blessings and his prayers on Orville, Wilbur, and all his children equally. Katharine had helped Carrie with a magnificent dinner—well-done porterhouse steaks, a delicacy unknown in Kitty Hawk—and apt to stay that way—and all the milk they could drink.

The next day things began to sour just a bit as Wilbur had a heart-to-heart talk with Lorin.

"Can't you go down and see Frank, and show him the headlines from the *Virginian-Pilot*? He doesn't want the Associated Press running a false story, does he? How could he have turned you down in the first place?"

Lorin squirmed. He had failed, and although it had not been mentioned yesterday, he saw the look in their eyes today; even Katharine, usually so caring, was cold. The contrast was too great. Orv and Will had built a flying machine, and he had failed to get the story in the papers. With tears in his eyes he left, swearing that he would make Frank Tunison run the right story.

And it had not taken Bishop Wright long to revert to form. On Christmas afternoon, after church and prayers and the gifts and the big breakfast, he had both the boys in the study, lecturing them as he had for many years.

"Look at this. Three telegrams from Chanute. He says he is pleased with your success, but he is dying to get you to make it public. You boys know why? Because if you make it public you cannot patent your flying machine. He knows that better than anybody."

The term "you boys" struck at Wilbur. He was thirty-six, Orville was thirty-two, and they were still "you boys" to their father. The success at Kitty Hawk had emboldened Will more than Orville and he said, "Father, you are just wrong. Mr. Chanute sincerely wishes well for us. He may not understand all we do, but his heart is in the right place."

Bishop Wright was not sure he understood. It sounded like Wilbur had just contradicted him. His voice rose and he started again, talking faster, "His heart is in the right place, but his hand is in your pocketbook. Let me tell you something about life, Wilbur, you haven't learned it all yet, nor you either, Orville."

He went on and on, each minute adding a reinforcing stroke to the psychological bars that he had spent a lifetime building, surrounding them with his experience, his essential goodness, their inexperience, their tendency to be taken advantage of, their mediocre business success.

"You can't even get a patent application approved. My goodness, what would it take to do that, especially since you've gone ahead and proved you could fly?"

Wilbur thought about explaining the patent rejection, saying that the examiner had suggested that they get a professional to help them, but was overrun with words as his father droned on.

By the end of the first thirty minutes Bishop Wright had reestablished himself as the one leader in the Wright household, beating down any resistance that they had felt, corralling them back into the pattern in which they had spent their lives. They may have flown a flying machine, but they were first and foremost his sons, and they would listen to him.

The bishop was good at bullying. It was not all calls to honor their father, nor was it all downplaying what they had done. He loved the boys dearly, and he built them up in areas where they could be strong and not threaten him, but just as a hunter guides game into a trap, he led them down to where he was strongest and they were weakest: in business experience and dealing with capable business opponents.

"Boys"—the words no longer bothered Will; they were "the boys" to him and always would be—"you've got to keep this flying machine a secret. If you let someone like Chanute, no matter how well meaning he is, find out how you did it, he will blab to the world. That's his place in your flying society: he's never going to do anything himself, but he lives like a pilot fish with you, following you, living on your leavings. It is not the money; I know he's wealthy. He wants the prestige, and since he has all the money he needs, he doesn't care whether you get what you deserve or not. He'll tell everybody what your secrets are, just to keep on being mister big shot aviation authority, and you'll be back selling bicycles."

Orville tried to protest. "Pop, I don't think so. We'll tell him to keep things to himself. You're right about him not being interested in money, but he's told us to get a patent, many times."

"Sure he has. But he knows your application was rejected, because you had to tell him all about it. And what if he makes a lecture in France like he did last year, and gets the Frenchmen all excited again? I tell you this man is like the cannon in the Victor Hugo story, he's loose and he'll crash through your chances for a patent like the cannon crashed around the ship."

It was a three-hour session. They had gone in as Orville and Wilbur, and came out as the boys, resentful but believing that their father wanted the best for them.

Mentally exhausted, physically tired, they walked together over to Lorin's house where the traditional dinner would take place. They needed to talk privately after their grueling lecture, and they couldn't let their father see them doing it.

"Will, I'll tell you, for a while there down in Kitty Hawk, even before the 17th, I felt like I'd finally grown up, that I was going to be my own man. Didn't tell you about it, but even thought about getting my own living quarters, a room somewhere maybe, or even buying a little house out in the country."

Wilbur listened quietly, thinking, *Maybe just for you and Katharine, eh?* but didn't say it. Then he smiled and said, "Let's walk toward Williams Street, Orv; it'll take us a little longer to get to Lorin's. I don't want to run into Pop on the way—I've had quite enough of him already."

They turned away from Lorin's house, walking easily together, their strides matching, clouds of moisture from their breathing trailing back. Will began, "The problem is we can't get away. He knows it and we know it. He's got us in his clutches. I've never thought about moving out, and I know why. He wouldn't let me. He wouldn't let you either. Or Katharine. I'm surprised that Roosh and Lorin made it."

"That's not the only problem. In fact that's not the most difficult problem. The real problem is that he may be bossy, but when he gets done talking, I have to say he's right. That's the hard part. Sometimes I'd just like to get up and say 'You are all wrong, Pop, and I'm leaving,' but I can't because he's not wrong. He's a smart old bird, and he's got our interest at heart. He goes overboard, but you know he loves us, he's pulling for us all the time."

Will nodded. "Sometimes I get thoughts about him I cannot even tell you, they frighten me. But then I realize, just like you say, that most of the time he is dead right. Certainly we have to keep the Flyer secret. And that is not going to be easy, not if we fly here in Dayton next year. But it has to be done."

"It's cold, Will; let's get on back to Lorin, the ace press reporter."

"We have to go easy on him, Orv, he's feeling bad enough as it is."

"Well, maybe just a few jokes to get the evening started, something like, 'Too bad you were not in Havana, you could have kept it quiet about the *Maine* blowing up.'"

Wilbur laughed and dug his elbow into Orv's ribs, saying, "That ought to do it."

The dinner went off well, the bishop quiet because he had his boys in line and because he liked being at Lorin's house; he wasn't asked there as often as he thought he should be asked. The brothers took Lorin aside and finally convinced him that he had done all he could, and that he couldn't be blamed if Frank Tunison did not know a real story when he heard one.

The Wrights got back to business the following day, getting Charley Taylor to start work on an engine to replace the one that had been ruined when the Flyer was blown over, and another one, more advanced, that had some ideas Orville wanted to pursue as an experiment. Things were quietly normal until the 27th when they received an astounding letter from Augustus Herring.

After—briefly—congratulating them on their flight, Herring suggested that it would be wise to form a partnership in which he would have a one-third interest and they would have two-thirds.

Wilbur sat down the letter, his hand shaking. "The audacity of the man. Father is so right! There are sharks everywhere. Who would believe he could do this?"

He went on reading. Herring claimed that his experiments with flight were also successful, but differed from the approach the Wrights had taken. If they combined forces, they would cover all bases. Then the delicate hand of blackmail crept in. Claiming to be the "true originator" of what people mistakenly called the Chanute two-surface glider, he pointed out the similarity in the Wrights' flying machine configuration. His prior claim would be worth a substantial sum to anyone attempting to lodge an "interference suit" against the Wrights—and, he hinted, someone had already offered such a sum to him.

"It's pretty crass, but you have to admire the man, Wilbur. Who else would have the gall to write a letter like that? It will be interesting to see what Chanute has to say about this. And you are so right. Pop warned us about this man, and there's the proof in your hand."

CHAPTER
40

B ack in Chicago, Octave Chanute's feelings were hurt. After sending three telegrams to the Wrights, and then inviting them to speak at the American Association for the Advancement of Science in St. Louis, he had received a terse telegram saying only, "We are giving no pictures nor descriptions of machine or methods at present."

That was rude, very rude, and he expected better of them. He suspected that their father, that litigious bishop, had warned them about giving away any secrets. And there was the problem: they had no secrets to give. They had not created one element in their aircraft that had not existed before, from the superimposed wings that he himself had invented with his two-surface glider, to the turning of the wing tips, which he and Mouillard had patented in 1896. He had urged them to patent the clever way the wires worked within their wing to twist the tips, but that was it. Just the twisting of the wings was definitely not worthy of a patent—birds had done that for millions of years.

He gave them full and complete credit for what they had done, and that was putting together all the elements, all the ideas from others, in a way that worked well. They were first-rate technicians—but they had not invented anything yet. He felt certain that if they took Ader's machine, the *Aole*, the Wrights would find a way to make it fly as well. They were geniuses with tools in their hands—ordinary men without them.

The Wrights' reticence put him in a very embarrassing position. He was well known to be their mentor, and there were several people who were waiting to hear from him. Poor Langley, first of all, of course; the news must have been devastating to him after the debacle of December 8th, but he was a scientist, and he would be glad that someone had flown, even if it was not his machine. He also owed a letter to Albert Blohm, and perhaps, even to Augustus Herring, although he was hesitant to open communications with Herring, who would surely seek to be reemployed. Then he needed to write the Aéro Club de France and to Hiram Maxim. The professional societies also needed to be informed. It was not an easy task, and he wanted to be sure to have the Wrights' approval on what he said.

A few days later, Chanute received a long and folksy letter from Wilbur, giving a fairly detailed description of his short flight on December 14th, and their four successful flights on December 17th. He knew he was being sensitive, but he thought there might have been a little subtle insult in one of the last sentences. Wilbur had written, "Those who understand the real significance of the conditions under which we worked will be surprised rather at the length than the shortness of the flights made with an unfamiliar machine after less than one minute's practice."

"Those who understand," that was the key phrase. It could be taken to mean that he, Chanute, did not understand, and if so, it was a small and mean thing to say. No one knew better than he how strong the wind was, and he had made many a glide himself. If he did not understand, who could?

As much as he admired the Wrights, Chanute wondered if greed was not beginning to cloud their outlook. He wanted to maintain the friendship, but he would be cautious, aware of their change in attitude.

CHAPTER
41

Professor Langley was still deeply depressed from the second crash of the Aerodrome when, on a late December morning, Ross Robbins brought in his coffee and the morning newspapers, trying without success to conceal the smile on his face. The paper on top was folded carefully so that the Associated Press article on the Wright Brothers was on top.

He had put the tray down, adjusted the shades slightly, and left. Langley did not look up. He rarely spoke to Robbins, and then only to make a specific request, since the fiasco on the Potomac earlier in the month. Robbins waited just outside the professor's door and was gratified to hear the explosive "Mother of God" and, following this, some very satisfactory sobbing.

An hour later Langley called him, acting as if nothing had happened, and handed him a message to be delivered personally to Dr. Blohm at Catholic University. Since then Blohm had visited almost every morning, and had earned the nickname "the Great Commiserator" from Robbins's colleagues, for his role apparently was to somehow bring Langley back from the depths of despair into which the Wrights' flight had plunged him.

It was not an easy task for Blohm, who now sat, as he always did, at the professor's left, looking intently into his face, following his every argument and never disagreeing, unless it happened that Langley uttered some measure of doubt about his own efforts. He had never had a great deal of regard for the secretary or his Great Aerodrome, but it had been necessary for his own plans that Langley succeed. He had spent years making himself agreeable to the man, always on call, in anticipation of the time when he could become a candidate to succeed him to be secretary of the Smithsonian. Now these blasted bicycle mechanics from Dayton had ruined everything—and very possibly had killed Langley in the process. He had looked ghastly on the first visit, a man on the edge of a stroke, and he had not improved in the following weeks.

"There's just no hope of getting any funding from the War Department. I've been insulted there, time and again."

Blohm had heard this at least a dozen times, and knew what to say. "They were the ones to blame! If they had funded you properly you wouldn't have had to struggle for so long." He waited—the next salvo would be against the Wrights and Chanute.

"Chanute betrayed me. He encouraged those ignorant Wrights, told them about my experiments, even let them use his superimposed wing. They are mechanics, they have no idea of what they have done, they could not draw a single principle from all of their work."

Blohm did not speak; it was not necessary to speak often, only when Langley stopped to cough or to take a drink of water or coffee. He did not really listen to Blohm's replies, or at least he never responded to them.

Langley droned on, now castigating that poor Charles Manly, who had only risked his life twice for him. As he spieled the old familiar arguments, Blohm thought about the Wrights. They were mechanics, all right, and good ones, but they did not care a bit about the principles of aerodynamics. At the moment they were probably thinking only about making money from their invention.

Blohm had never met the Wrights. He made up his mind to do so. It is best to know your enemy, and they were unquestionably his enemy. His plan had been for Langley to retire in a few years in a cloud of glory. In the course of that time Blohm would have worked his way to be a logical successor. Now Langley's glory was sunk in the Potomac, and from the looks of him, he would not live another year.

Yet Blohm could not give Langley up, could not break with him, not now. The most likely candidate to succeed Langley was Charles Doolittle Walcott, the director of the National Geological Survey. Blohm had made himself familiar with Walcott's background, sensing him as a rival. Doolittle, that was a good name for him, all right. He was not even a college graduate, called himself a scientist because he mucked about in shale deposits looking for fossils. The problem was that he was very well liked, and his only drawback, as far as Blohm knew, was that he had been instrumental in getting the War Department to back Langley's experiments. If Langley had a friend, it was Walcott, and Langley would undoubtedly take steps to name his successor—after all, that was what Blohm had been counting on. Well, things change. Blohm saw his task now as continue to lock in with Langley, and then move on to become a friend of Walcott as well. It was a long shot, and an unpleasant one, for every hour spent with Langley was totally unproductive. Suddenly he realized that Langley had asked him a question.

"I'm sorry, sir. I was thinking of Chanute's perfidious betrayal and my mind wandered. Would you repeat the question?"

"Why don't you finance the next Aerodrome? We could call it the Langley-Blohm Aerodrome, or even the Blohm-Langley Aerodrome, and we could use your wind tunnel to refine the design. You are wealthy, are you not? Why don't you finance it?"

Blohm thought swiftly. Financing another Aerodrome was out of the question, not because of the money, it was a pittance, but because he could not afford to have his name attached to the symbol of failure in aviation. On the other hand, he could not afford to offend Langley.

"I am so glad that you suggested it, Professor. I've thought about volunteering a number of times, but didn't wish to intrude. I would be honored to do so."

Langley sat up, a bright light in his eyes. "Blohm, my friend, you are saving my life."

"But you do me too much honor. The Great Aerodrome was and will always be the Langley Aerodrome. I'll help in every way I can, but I would not presume to add my name to your great contribution."

Langley's eyes, already watery, misted over completely; he fumbled for a handkerchief, then asked, "When can we start?"

"We've already started, Professor. I'll have the models you've made of the Great Aerodrome replicated for the wind tunnel, and within weeks, we'll have the data that will prove that the Great Aerodrome was the first man-carrying flying machine capable of sustained flight. But we have to keep this secret. I don't want the press following us about, and we must not let the Wrights know what we are doing. I'm sure they are litigious, such riffraff usually are."

He had used the two words that would bring Langley to heel, press and Wrights.

"I agree, not a word to anyone, not to the Smithsonian, not to the War Department, not to anyone. When we've flown the next Aerodrome, then will be the time to tell them. We'll give it to the War Department, cost free."

Blohm nodded, thinking that the professor was quite liberal with *his* money, just as he had been with the War Department's and the Smithsonian's. There would never be another Great Aerodrome, not if he had anything to do with it, but it would not be expensive to make tests in the wind tunnel. When the professor began to press him to start building, he would just put him off, claiming one thing or another from the wind tunnel findings. God knew Langley could not understand what the wind tunnel results would be; he could tell him anything. The main thing was to buy a little time, and ingratiate himself with Walcott. The worst thing was that Walcott was only fifty-three, and in apparent good health. That meant his own timetable to be secretary of the Smithsonian would have to be set back ten years or more—unless he could arrange things otherwise.

CHAPTER
42

Mabel Bell realized that she had a crisis on her hands. Since Chanute's letter detailing the exploits of these young Ohio boys arrived, Alec had been in a profound funk, lost in his thoughts. If they had been back at Baddeck, in decent weather, he would soon have regained his spirits flying his kites. As it was, he sat at his desk all day, pretending to read, but really just brooding. His visit to Professor Langely had not helped. Langley was even more depressed than Bell, and neither could make any effort to cheer the other up. When Bell returned he expressed doubts about Langley's will to live.

"He looks like he's already dead. Eyes are dull, his breath is fetid, he did not even bother to be courteous to me; I might have been some salesman off the street trying to get him to buy brushes."

She wanted to say, "You of all people should understand—you are disappointed yourself, and you had nowhere near the time and prestige invested in flying machines that poor Langley did." But she did not. Alec needed to be shocked out of his mood, but not with a sledgehammer.

"Have you thought about meeting with the Wrights? I'm sure they would respond to an invitation from you to visit."

"I couldn't. It would be just too hard to bear. Besides, according to some people, they are just uneducated mechanics, totally uncultured."

Mabel remained quiet. "Some people" meant Albert Blohm, who had been courting Alec ever since they had returned from Baddeck in September. She had been quite taken with him at first; his manners were impeccable, he showed the greatest respect to Alec, and most of all, he let Alec talk all he wanted to, never butting in as some men did. And Alec liked him too, even began talking about using Blohm as one of the key men in the consortium that Mabel was planning. It was official now, they had stopped their little charade, Alec was willing to take some people on board to help him.

But over time her feelings had changed. Blohm was just too nice, too considerate, and just too subtle about his dealings with Langley. When he spoke about the professor, it was always with admiration, but there was also a joking, somewhat cynical tone to his remarks. Alec did not notice, and because he did not, Blohm began to take greater liberties, sometimes openly deriding the Great Aerodrome, and more than once hinting that Langley was out of his depths in aeronautics. He did it in a way that played up Alec's achievements, so that the remarks were palatable, but it was hardly the way a stout supporter of Langley should have been talking.

Blohm was at his worst discussing the Wright brothers. If one believed him, there was scarcely any sin of which they were not guilty, from pirating Chanute's ideas to making false reports on their achievements to some very guarded references about their masculinity, so oblique that he expected her not to understand. It was clear that he had an unyielding hatred for two men he had never met, two men who had achieved great things in what was supposed to be his field. It was inexplicable, for Blohm had never had his reputation at stake as Dr. Langley did, nor had he ever been more than a peripheral figure in the field. Yet it was clear that the Wrights had deprived him of something he wanted.

Within a few weeks, she had pieced it together. As always, Alec was sitting face to face with her so that she could "hear" him, and she said, "Alec, I'm not sure I like that Blohm fellow."

He was so surprised that he spilled his tea. "Don't like him? I thought you were going to brace me up to hire him, have him head our little experimental group."

"I was, for a long time. But I realized that's not his game. He is after bigger things. He wants to succeed Langley at the Smithsonian."

The older man leaned forward and kissed her tenderly on the brow. "My dear, what's got into you? That's so unlike you. Young Blohm couldn't be thinking of any such thing, he does not have the credentials, and he knows it. You are seeing something that isn't there."

"Well, we will see. He's been showing up here every Thursday afternoon, as regular as clockwork, and I don't suppose he'll stop now. But just to let you know, he is never going to be a part of our association, not if I have anything to say about it."

"And you do, my dear, you have complete say. I would never push anyone on you that you did not like." He waited a second, and like any good husband tried to store up a few moral credits. "Besides, I've never wanted the consortium in the first place. Maybe it's a bad idea after all."

She rang for their maid to clear the tea away and said, "The consortium's not a bad idea. Albert Blohm is."

Just as she predicted, Blohm continued to visit them every Thursday, always bringing her a little, perfectly appropriate gift: a handful of violets, some small confection, a book of poems, every one of them something that she genuinely liked. As the weeks went on, however, each recognized something in the other. Blohm saw that Mabel Bell disliked and distrusted him, and he could not imagine why, except that she was just another ungrateful wretch, accepting his presents but not accepting his abilities. In the brief time of his visits Mabel Bell saw that Blohm's personality was undergoing some very unpleasant kind of a change. There was a look in his eye that suggested madness to her, and she began making sure that young Frank McCarty, their husky handyman chauffeur, was in the house on Thursday afternoons. Her husband discounted her fears, which in fact worried him. They might be a possible sign that Mabel was having some problems of her own that he did not even want to think about.

In late April, Bell was telling Blohm about their preparations to return to Baddeck when the younger man asked if he could make a personal request. They had gradually come to be on a first name basis, and Blohm, after fidgeting for most of the afternoon, finally began.

"Alec, this will surprise you, I know, but I wonder if I can count upon you to support me when the time comes. Professor Langley has clearly lost his faculties and his health. I do not believe he will be able to serve as secretary for many more months. If he leaves, I would like you to back me to succeed him."

Bell was shocked, not so much by the statement as by the fact that Mabel, once again, had been exactly right. All of the courtesy, all of the visits, everything had been for this one purpose.

"Why, certainly, Albert, I will consider that. I'm distressed to learn that the professor is in such ill health, but I have to confess that the last time I saw him, the same thought crossed my mind. But you will understand that I'll have to wait until he in fact retires, and even then, it would not be prudent for me to declare for you until all the other candidates are named."

"Are you interested in the position?" Blohm's voice was accusatory, vibrant with a sense of betrayal.

"No, of course not; I'm far too old, and I am no administrator, never have been. But certainly some of my old colleagues will be considered. The Smithsonian will look to Charles Walcott and others like him, don't you think? I'm sure you understand that."

For the first time ever, Blohm interrupted him. "I understand, perfectly. I'm not one of the 'inner circle.' "

Bell looked into Blohm's eyes, and saw what Mabel had seen there, a frightening instability, barely under control. He knew from Blohm's abrupt reaction that the answer was not what he expected—or would accept.

"What are you talking about, what inner circle? We're discussing a possibility that might not occur for years, and I'm trying to be frank."

Blohm recovered himself. "Of course, Alec, I understand, and I appreciate your position. And you are quite right, *Mister* Walcott"— he emphasized the word mister, to highlight the man's lack of formal education—"will be chosen. But I want to be seen as a contender. There's always the possibility that Walcott would refuse. And even if he does not, it would be wonderful for me to be seen as the man recommended by Alexander Graham Bell! Don't you see? It will cost you nothing, it will not injure this man Walcott, and it will be of great help to me."

Bell was guarded in his reply, wondering where McCarty was, hoping that Mabel had him posted outside the door as she had been doing lately.

"Ah, I see. Well, that is something entirely different! But it will cost me something, you know: it will cost me my friendship with

Walcott. He would never forgive me not supporting him, we have been friends for years."

"And what about me? Are we not friends? What am I to think?"

Blohm had leaped from his chair, and was standing in front of Bell. With a visible effort he took control of himself, and said in an almost normal voice, "I just want you to think about it. Perhaps if you think about it, there will be some way you can do it without offending Mister Walcott. I really better go now, and I hope that I have not discomfited you."

The younger man moved rapidly to the door while Bell remained seated in his chair, thinking, *I'll think about it, all right. And I'll think about the murderous light I saw in your eyes. My goodness, Mabel was so right. Again.*

His wife came in the room as soon as Blohm had left.

"Mabel, my dear, I'll never doubt anything you say again! That man is dangerous. I wonder if I should say something to Professor Langley?"

"No, it would be impossible to prove. I suspect the good professor is leaning on Blohm for moral support, and it might kill him to add Blohm to the list of his disappointments. I'm glad we are going to Baddeck soon. From now on, we will not be at home to Mr. Blohm."

PART FOUR
IMPROVING THE BREED

Difficulties always arise from attempts to improve to the point of achieving what is not possible, thereby failing to gain what is well within reach.

J. M. Cameron

CHAPTER
43

The emotions of would-be aeronauts, always high in France, were as mixed as if Chanute had applied an eggbeater to them instead of just a letter outlining what the Wrights had achieved. His account followed a brief notice of the Wrights' flight in the prestigious magazine *L'Aérophile*. It stated a flight of five kilometers had been made in a flying machine powered by a "tricycle motor." Details were totally erroneous, having the flying machine launched from the top of the highest Kill Devil Hill, flying at twenty meters height at twelve kilometers an hour. The short article concluded with yet another call to arms, quoting Ernest Archdeacon and Ferdinand Ferber, and asking rhetorically "if France must be shamed by the Americans?" *L'Aérophile* would continue to report the Wrights' endeavors over the next few years in an artful manner that combined accurate writing with what amounted to a wink and a nudge of disbelief. The editors, no matter how they felt, knew better than to assert the achievements of the Wrights openly, without implied qualification, for many of their readers would have been vastly offended.

The first *L'Aérophile* article was somewhat offset by a corrected Associated Press version of the flight, furnished by the Wrights in early January and picked up by some European newspapers, but even that met with skepticism. Wilbur told the story in a very straightforward manner, but it was impossible for the French to believe his statement about the wind, in which he said, "Only those who are acquainted with practical aeronautics can appreciate the difficulties of attempting the first trials of a flying machine in a twenty-five-mile gale." This statement was regarded as absurd, even an arrogant slur upon their gullibility. It was common knowledge that the first flights of any flying machine would have to take place in a calm, or, at the very least, in no more than the lightest breeze. To claim a flight in a twenty-five-mile gale went beyond the boundaries of belief.

Chanute had long been the unofficial center of all aeronautical information, and his letters relaying Wilbur's account of the flight had unexpected effects. The reactions of the French devotees of flights, the stalwart members of the Aéro Club de France, ranged from epiphany to blasphemy. For the extraordinarily homely and very inept craftsman, Captain Ferber, the news came as vindication: he was not as crazy as others had thought, flying was a possibility. He was also vain enough to believe that his own experiments, as utterly fruitless as they had been, had been a factor in encouraging the Wrights to install an engine in their flying machine.

For other members of the Aéro Club, the Wrights' success was an insult to *la belle* France, on a par with New York vintners using the word "champagne" to describe the sweet sparkling wine they bottled. For the most part the kindliest of them chose to see the Wrights' flight as a mere door-opener, a turn of the key in the lock of aeronautical success, a chance event that left true flight remaining to be achieved by its natural sponsor, a Frenchman. The less kindly openly used the word "liars" to characterize the Wrights.

The highly inaccurate story in the *Virginian-Pilot* became a rallying point. Everyone was eager to point out the inconsistencies in the story, from the laughable nature of the flying machine it described with its "six-bladed underwheel" to push it into the air to its obviously impossible fifteen-thousand-meter flight. And it was easy to twist Chanute's letter, with its sober account of the four flights, into a perfect argument: for what was a twelve second, forty-meter flight? Nothing, a hop, no more. And who could say if the fifty-seven- or fifty-nine-second flight ever took place? The witnesses were apparently American aborigines, uneducated sailors and fishermen who, as Gabriel Voisin, a newcomer to the field, but soon to be a leader, pointed out, would "not know a flying machine from a *pissoir.*"

As tempers flared and patriotism beat within their Gallic breasts, one certain idea emerged. France must be mobilized; there must be a collective effort to right this terrible wrong, to create in France a true flying machine, one that would take its place with the balloon and the dirigible. These were rightfully acknowledged by the world to be French. The flying machine must not join the vast array of inventions such as the steam engine, the steamship, gas lighting, the telephone and others that were invented first in France and then pirated by others. Had there been barricades around the Aéro Club, the loyal members would have flocked to them, pikes ready for the heads of any Wrights to appear.

While emotions boiled, harder, wiser men made plans. They had encouraged lighter-than-air flight with prizes; they would have to do the same with flying machines. More important, they had to begin sharing information, working together without regard for future profits—an impossible dream as it developed.

Once again the great patriots Henri Deutsch de la Meurthe and Archdeacon stepped forward with sizeable prizes, the former announcing the "Grand Prix d'Aviation," twenty-five thousand francs for the first to fly a powered flying machine in a one kilometer closed circle, and the latter promptly matching the amount. There was a veritable scramble across France as the pioneers of aviation, men like Ferber, Robert Esnault-Pelterie, Victor Tatin, and others, were joined by a host of newcomers who no longer feared ridicule for attempting to build flying machines.

It was natural, indeed inevitable, that Alberto Santos-Dumont would be interested in creating a flying machine, but at the moment he was focused on another goal, flying his No. 7 dirigible at the St. Louis World's Fair. Two years before, he had participated in the panel that established the very rigorous rules for the contest. He had helped formulate the rules, and saw to it that they were so rigorous that only he had a chance of winning.

CHAPTER
44

Partnerships are difficult to maintain, and that of Fitzgerald and the Baldwin brothers was more difficult than most. Fitz had put his two-thousand-acre ranch in the Livermore Valley at the disposal of the Baldwins and financed the construction of a dirigible. He had not provided money on as lavish a scale as Tom thought he had promised, and there was some discontent. Sam was trying to use material from their old balloon to eke out the material they had purchased for the dirigible, but it was slow going. They had an engine stand with three different automobile engines, but they were either too heavy or not powerful enough to handle the weight of the dirigible and Tom.

Neither of the Baldwins enjoyed the austere living in the Valley, and both were spending more and more time in San Francisco. This June morning, however, they had agreed to meet with Fitzgerald at the ranch, to discuss the progress—or lack of it—with the dirigible.

"Tom, I don't mind telling you, I've got more than six thousand dollars invested already, and you still can't tell me when you can fly."

"I don't care if it's six thousand or sixty thousand, I can't find anyone who can make a lightweight engine that will do the job. Look at these things up here; you'd think one of them could do it, but the Ford's not powerful enough and they are all way too heavy."

"Well, how did Santos-Dumont do it?"

"Santos-Dumont weighs less than half than I do, and he flies a little runabout with a tiny engine. He can only fly when the weather is good and the wind is calm. If we are going to do show work, it means we have to have a rig that will fly even when the weather gets bad. You know that."

"I know that, and I know something else." He glanced at his watch. "Just listen."

Both Baldwin brothers looked at him, wondering what he had in mind, when they heard a faint *pop-pop* popping that grew steadily louder. In less than a minute they picked up a cloud of dust hurtling toward them, and a minute after that a dust-covered, grinning man pulled up on a motorcycle bearing the name "Curtiss" scrolled on its side.

"Tom, Sam, meet Harry White. I want you to take a look at this little firecracker of a motorcycle of his."

Tom had already burned his hand on the muffler in his eagerness to come to grips with the little two-cylinder jewel he saw before him. He didn't speak to White, just nodded inquiringly, then jumped into the seat and tore off down the road. It was ten minutes before he returned, grinning broadly.

"Harry, thanks so much. Where can I get us an engine like this?"

White handed him a catalog printed on rough pulp paper, already smudged and worn by being folded and carried in his pocket. It bore the words "G. H. Curtiss Manufacturing Company, Hammondsport, New York."

Baldwin scanned the catalog and turned to Fitzgerald. "Bless you Fitz, this is the answer. I'll write today and order us an engine."

He turned to his brother. "Sam, you can get rid of everything we've got here, the old envelope, these engines, everything. We're going back to our factory in Oakland and get started there."

CHAPTER
45

While France was going through a patriotic paroxysm of flight fever, St. Louis was hosting a celebration of the sale the Emperor Napoleon had made one hundred years before to President Thomas Jefferson: the Louisiana Purchase. The St. Louis World's Fair Grounds spread over thirteen hundred acres on the western edge of the city, and a huge city of plaster-coated buildings grew up, with ornate structures celebrating every aspect of one hundred years of American progress. More than a hundred thousand people passed through the magnificent entrance gates every day, and many of these went directly to the Aeronautics Concourse, where the largest aeronautical display in history was promised. A prestigious commission was set up to judge the events, and included none other than Octave Chanute.

An immense acreage had been set aside for aeronautics at the edge of the fair so that flying machines could set off on the elaborate courses that had been laid out for them. At the entrance to the Aeronautic Concourse, hundreds of awestruck visitors were given the thrill of their life every day, riding up in a twelve thousand cubic foot tethered balloon to as high as seven hundred feet in a birdcage-like basket, and getting a view not only of the thirteen hundred acres of fairgrounds but of all St. Louis and a large section of the mighty Mississippi. A star of the balloon ride was wiry little A. Roy Knabenshue, whose specialty was hanging onto the three-quarter-inch hemp cable, starting off about twenty feet below the basket. When the balloon had risen to two hundred feet, he slid down the cable, using heavy trousers and his shoes to absorb the friction of the slide. Then he would ride up another two hundred feet as the balloon continued to rise, and repeat the stunt.

Like most World's Fairs, the Louisiana Purchase Exposition was not doing as well financially as had been hoped. Still, there were funds to pay for the almost $135,000 in prizes which had been established for everything from balloons to "pilotless aircraft." Entries poured in from all over the country, and the fair officials let it be known that forty-four airships, twenty-six flying machines, ten balloons, twelve kites, and one "gliding machine" would be competing. The first man to enter was the eerily enigmatic and ubiquitous Gustave Whitehead, who claimed to have flown for more than one and one-half miles in 1901, and was bringing an improved version of his machine to St. Louis.

Many of the entries were suspect, the wishful dreams of would-be inventors, and as time passed this proved to be true, because one of the entry rules was proof of a flight of one mile, along with an entry fee. But even as entrants dwindled, the hopes of the backers of the fair rose on the appearance of the famous Parisian aeronaut Santos-Dumont. His dirigible No. 7 arrived by rail on June 27th, with a great deal of ceremony and publicity. Santos-Dumont himself inspected the balloon, pronouncing it "almost perfect" after its long ocean voyage. The shining coating of the envelope had suffered a bit in the passage, and he directed that one additional coat of varnish be added to the five already glistening on its long cylindrical hull.

The slight Brazilian and the fair managers were thrown into a fury the following day when it was found that vandals had made twelve one-yard-long slashes in the dirigible's envelope. Santos-Dumont was coldly indignant, boiling inside with a reasonable hatred against Americans—the same thing had happened to him the year before, with a different dirigible, in Boston. He told the police he was not interested in prosecuting the culprit, if they happened to catch one, and told the press that he was going to take the dirigible back to Paris for repairs. He promised to return, but left determined never to do so. Enough was enough.

The heart of the Aeronautic Concourse seemed to go with him. Contestants were dropping out every day, and the only excitement so far was the glider flights of William Avery, who flew a Chanute two-surface machine. There were no Kill Devil Hills on the fairgrounds, so Avery flew his glider from a miniature flatcar mounted on a railroad track. An electric winch hauled the flatcar forward, and the speed propelled the glider into the air. Avery was proficient, and made several glides of more than one hundred fifty feet. Unfortunately, this was not enough to keep the crowds entertained, and it looked as if the big prizes would go unclaimed. There was a flurry of interest when Alexander Graham Bell himself made demonstration flights of his tetrahedral kite, the visitors more interested in Bell than in his multicelled red silk creation.

All fears about a lack of excitement vanished with the arrival of Tom Baldwin and his dirigible, the *California Arrow*. Baldwin's booming laugh lit up the gloomy pits of the Aeronautic Concourse, and when the crowds gathered around his dirigible, his brother Sam and Jim Fitzgerald would conduct tours, pointing out the special features. Those who had not seen photographs of Santos-Dumont's racy-looking No. 7 were impressed; those that had were not. The *California Arrow* was more football than arrow-shaped, its eight thousand cubic feet contained in a fifty-three-foot-long envelope. Suspended beneath the envelope was a long triangular spruce framework, which carried the operator, the five-horsepower two-cylinder Curtiss engine, and the rectangular rudder.

Unlike Santos-Dumont, who slung his engine far below the envelope, the handsome little Curtiss engine was no more than a dozen feet below the bag, but Baldwin stoutly insisted that this was enough. And stoutly was the operative word now with Baldwin, who had ballooned up to two hundred twenty pounds, and was not certain his dirigible would lift him off the ground.

To the delight of the backers of the Fair, three more aeronauts showed up to contend with Baldwin for the prize. The first to arrive was William Benbow, whose *Montana Meteor* was larger and more streamlined than the *California Arrow*, with its seventy-two-foot length containing fourteen thousand cubic feet of hydrogen. Baldwin looked it over carefully, noting that it had a ten horsepower engine, but it was used to drive no fewer than four propellers through an elaborate drive system, losing horsepower all the way.

Then two Frenchmen appeared, reintroducing the international flavor, and promising more serious competition. The first was Francis Coteau, whose airship, the *Touloun*, was approximately the same size as Benbow's, but powered by a huge sixty horsepower engine whose pounding roar made Baldwin's little Curtiss engine sound like a sewing machine. The final dirigible was the huge *Ville de St. Mande*, brought by another Frenchman, Hippolyte Francois (the crowds loved his name). With its sixty-five thousand cubic feet of hydrogen it was eight times as large as the *California Arrow*, and carried a twenty-eight horsepower electric motor that required almost one thousand pounds of batteries.

Tom and Sam had watched the arrival of each new contestant with interest. They discounted the *Montana Meteor* from the start; it was never going to be able to fly against even the slightest wind, for its transmission system and propellers drained power from the tiny engine. For the most part, Benbow, the *Meteor* pilot, had it paraded tethered around the field. They were a little more concerned about the gigantic *Ville de St. Mande*, which was so large that it would not fit in the shed that had been built for it until a gigantic trench, six feet deep, fifteen feet wide, and one hundred feet long had been dug. Then, on being walked back into the shed, something snagged the envelope, and sixty-five thousand cubic feet of hydrogen was released. No one was harmed, but the ceiling of the shed rained sparrows for more than an hour. Peacefully nesting in the roof of the shed, they had been asphyxiated by the hydrogen.

This left the dangerous *Toulon* as the only real rival. Sam came right to the point. "My brother, you are too damned fat. You put your two-hundred-plus-pound carcass in the *Arrow*, and she'll sit on the ground while that Frenchman flies rings around you."

Fitz was glad to agree. "He's right, Tom. We need to find you a substitute, somebody that hasn't been drinking a gallon a beer a day for the last twenty years."

Tom Baldwin was not amused, but he knew they were correct.

"What do you think about that skinny kid that slides down the balloon cable, what's his name? It's Roy something, a kraut name."

That night they located Knabenshue listening to one of the many band concerts that played every evening near the main entrance to the fair. Sam was not subtle, eliciting in the first minute that Roy was twenty-eight, from Toledo, and weighed one hundred and twenty-six pounds. In the second minute Roy leaped at the chance of flying the *California Arrow*.

Knabenshue was a natural. The next morning, with only a little verbal instruction from Tom, he took off in the *California Arrow* and proceeded to fly a huge figure eight in the sky. Two days later he made a thirty-seven-minute flight, crossing the exhibit grounds time and again, and letting the world know that the Aeronautic Concourse was back in business. Newspaper reporters flocked around the *California Arrow,* and Tom and Sam expounded on their advanced dirigible design while Roy told everyone how easy it was to fly an airship.

Late in the evening, Tom came back from a meeting with the fair officials. He felt he had demonstrated the best flying machine, and wanted to claim the $100,000 prize that was offered.

"Did you get the money, Tom?"

"Naw, it turns out that they run this fair like everybody else runs their fair. They agreed we had the best flying machine, but they showed me the fine print in the application. The best flying machine also had to fly at twenty miles per hour."

"Nobody can do that!"

"Yeah, and the bastards knew it all along. The best I was able to get was this—a thousand dollars." He tossed the bills on the table.

Fitz reached for the bills saying, "This will just about cover our travel and shipping costs," when Tom's hand flew out and seized the money.

"Hands off, Fitz. I'm taking this cash back to Hammondsport, New York, and I'm going to build us a new dirigible there, right at the Curtiss factory, and get us a new engine, one about twice as powerful as this one."

Fitz shrugged and Sam rolled his eyes. When Tom made his mind up, that was it.

CHAPTER
46

The Wright brothers knew that 1904 was going to be a banner year for them, with their new Flyer, even if they had not yet made up their mind about participating in the aerial competitions at the St. Louis World's Fair. Chanute wrote to them continually, urging them to enter, and keeping them posted on the other contestants. The one hundred thousand dollar prize for "best flying machine" was immensely attractive, but they were reluctant to enter until they had tested their new version. Their experience in 1901 and 1902 had told them that things were not always cut and dried with flying machines.

Everything they had learned was embodied in the new Flyer, which was heavier and stronger than the 1903 version, and, they hoped, with its engine geared to turn faster, much speedier. They had made the wing flatter, going to a one inch in twenty-five curvature, and this, with the additional power, led them to expect speeds of at least forty miles per hour.

They had mixed emotions about not returning to Kitty Hawk. They loved the place and its people, but flying at home, near their machine shop, gave them many advantages. They had been lucky enough to obtain permission to use a ninety-acre field at Huffman Prairie, an isolated stretch of farmland outside Dayton. It was convenient, for it was next to the Simms Station stop on the interurban rail line that connected Dayton and Springfield. The land was owned by an old friend, Torrence Huffman, who considered the brothers to be strange, if not crazy, but harmless, and the only request he made was to be considerate of any livestock on the property while they were actually flying. Huffman did not expect much actual flying to take place, but there would probably be noise, and that was bad enough. Still, you had to boost the local boys when you could.

While the Wrights were putting the finishing touches to their new Flyer, they kept up their voluminous correspondence with Chanute, who kept them up to date on people he regarded as colleagues but the Wrights saw as rivals. As much as they disliked the idea, there was a sense of mutual disenchantment that both Chanute and the Wrights tried to fight. For his part, Chanute felt that the Wrights were violating the sense of collegial camaraderie that he had sought to foster in the pursuit of flight. He had always called for a great team effort, believing that somehow the flying machine would emerge as the joint product of half a dozen people. The Wrights knew this, but thought it was nonsense; no one else, not Lilienthal, certainly not Maxim, and definitely not Langley had sought to share their ideas with anyone, and they had no intention of doing so.

"You know, Will, the more letters Chanute writes, the more he proves Pop's point. He seems to think we've just taken other people's ideas, put them in a bag like you throw chicken in to be floured, shaken it, and served up a flying machine."

"Well, it is difficult for him. If he couldn't be the father of the flying machine, he was going to be the midwife. Now the baby's born, he wasn't there, and it hurts his feelings. Still, we're going to treat him right, answer his letters and keep him informed on what we're doing. We'll treat him with respect; he has done a lot for a lot of people. Maybe someday we'll break through to him, and he'll get an idea of what it took us to make those four flights at Kill Devil Hill."

It was April before they had their chores done. Instead of shoveling sand they were scything grass, and a shed had to be built. It was really very much like Kitty Hawk without the wind and the wit and wisdom of the Kitty Hawkers.

These differences proved to be a problem when the 1904 machine was finally ready to fly. Instead of genial locals from the lifesaving station, they invited several newsmen to their primitive field to witness the Flyer's first flight in Ohio on May 23rd. Ridiculous stories about their December flights were still appearing in newspapers and magazines across the country, and Wilbur wanted to put these to bed with a demonstration flight. Their only request of the press was that no photographs be taken. They had just about made up their mind to enter the contests in St. Louis, and they did not want to give anything away to the press just yet.

It was then that they found that they really missed the winds of Kitty Hawk. There was a dead calm at Huffman Prairie, and even though they had a long, one hundred-foot "Junction Railway" for their takeoff run, the Flyer merely clattered down the track, making a lot of noise, but not rising an inch off the ground. If the Potomac River had been at the end of the takeoff run, they would have really "pulled a Langley" as one reporter described their afternoon efforts. They tried again three days later, and this time the Flyer hopped "like a gigged frog," as another reporter wrote, for about thirty feet.

The two trials were utterly humiliating and effectively ended local interest in their efforts, not a bad thing in itself. The two brothers slogged on, realizing that there was no point in going to St. Louis if they could not get off the ground at Dayton.

"Orv, it cannot just be the wind! With an eight-mile wind we're getting up to twenty-six miles an hour flying speed at least on the rail. We should be flying."

"It doesn't make sense, Will. Can't you do some of your famous figuring? What's different about this place and Kitty Hawk, aside from the wind?"

Will had to go back to their shop, where Charley was progressing with work on two more Flyers. The trolley car ride was always a good place to think and he sat puzzling on the problems all the way. As he got off at Simms Station on his return he felt his ears pop. *Must be a change in the weather,* he thought. Then it hit him.

The pressure of the air was different here, less dense. Instantly he knew that the differences in altitude and temperature were affecting flying. Huffman Prairie was some eight hundred feet higher, and in May, some forty degrees warmer than the Kill Devil Hills. This made the air thinner, cutting down on lift, engine power, and their patience. That was the answer, no question about it. He should have thought of this; they had known about the relationship of temperature and density since 1901.

Orville nodded in agreement when he explained his idea. "Trouble is, we can't do anything about the temperature or the elevation.

And our Flyer has to work where we take it, not just at Kitty Hawk—not too much of a market there after you sell a few to the lifesaving boys."

"We'll come up with something. I think maybe we made a mistake going to a thinner wing. Next year we'll go back to a deeper curve, like we had at Kitty Hawk."

"Yeah, and we should be able to pep up the engine some, maybe run it a little faster while we're on the track."

There were other problems. Orville had been forced to use the less expensive white pine for wing spars when he could not obtain spruce. It was a costly mistake, for the repeated hard landings splintered one spar after another, and twice just missed splintering Orville and Wilbur, who survived the many crashes without injury to anything but their self-respect. Over time, they replaced the broken pine parts with spruce when they could get it, and the crashes became less dramatic.

Despite Wilbur's insight, it was more than three months later before they gave up and constructed a catapult to get them in the air. They had shied away from it because of Langley's bad luck with the catapult, but there was no way out.

This was a major project and required some thinking.

"Do we know much about Langley's catapult?" It was a rhetorical question; Wilbur was well aware that they knew only what they had seen in the photographs and the little Chanute had told them—and they did not put much faith in Chanute's insight.

"Well, it was spring-loaded, and that's bad from the start, because you get all your push right at the beginning in a big jolt, then it tapers off. That might be what caused the machine to collapse, just like letting a spring on a valve release, bang, it's gone."

Wilbur nodded. "We don't want to use a spring, so let's use gravity. The pull of a falling weight will be pretty constant the length of the run. It won't start off with a big pull to stress the airplane, just sort of ease in, and have a steady pull, accelerating as it goes."

By the time they had finished talking, the brothers knew what to build. The wooden derrick was easy, and they would place it at the beginning of their track, just behind where the Flyer was positioned for takeoff. The first set of weights totaled twelve hundred pounds. Later on it would go up to sixteen hundred pounds.

It took several people from the usual crowd of onlookers to help them raise the weight to the top of the twenty-foot tower. A rope was run through another pulley system, down to the far end of the track and back to a hook on the front of the Flyer. When the pilot was ready to go, he pulled a rope that released the weight, which, falling, pulled the Flyer forward, catapulting it smoothly into the air after no more than a sixty-foot run.

After that the flying season went very well, with both brothers making long flights and making turns in the air. On September 20th, Orville made the longest flight so far, almost a mile in length, and lasting a minute and thirty-five seconds. Best of all he did it in front of the one man who would get the reportage right, Amos Root, who published a journal titled *Gleanings in Bee Culture*. In it he gave the first accurate, if highly emotional, account of Orville's "big hop," and for the next year, faithfully followed their progress, reporting each achievement to a small band of beekeepers. In the meantime, the *Scientific American* resolutely refused to take notice that the most important invention of the twentieth century was being exercised on a daily basis.

There were lots of problems never envisaged at Kitty Hawk. Flying more or less in a straight line was one thing; turning was proving to be another, even after their experience with turns in the glider.

Orville had turned to Wilbur late one September afternoon and asked, "Why is it different making a turn in the Flyer than in a glider? We used to make turns at Kitty Hawk all the time. Now when I turn I don't know where I'm going half the time. I keep slipping down, losing height, or else I climb too much and nearly stall." "Stall" was a word they had recently started using to describe the sudden fall of the Flyer if the nose was too high and flying speed got too slow. They likened it to the way a drill stalled when it was in too deep to turn, sort of a shuddering slowdown and stop.

Wilbur usually used any talk on flying technique to tease Orville about their comparative flying skills. Neither man minded because both knew that Orville was not only a better flyer, he enjoyed it more. It was a job for Wilbur, but a sport for Orville. This time, however, it was too serious to tease about.

"I don't know. I have the same problem. You've seen me out there, stalling in a turn; last week I didn't catch it in time, and busted up the skids when I hit. Remember we were always trying to keep headed into the wind when we were gliding, balancing the glider all the time. Now it's different, we've got a powered machine, and once we are in the air, the wind doesn't have the same effect, the same value for us. We need some kind of gauge, like the inclinometer or something, that will warn us."

Before the first flight the next day Orville was busy fastening an eight-inch-long white string to the front rudder, which they had begun calling the elevator. A nut was tied to the end of the string. Wilbur watched him with amusement, not saying anything. Orville took off and flew the strangest flight Wilbur had ever seen, little short turns to the left and right, some nose-up, some nose-down, gradually getting steeper than they had ever done before. He was glad when Orville landed.

"What on earth were you doing up there?"

"Testing my gauge. Will, when you take off, that string stands straight out. If you are turning correctly, using the right amount of rudder and twisting the wings just right, it stays straight out behind the elevator. But if you are slipping, if you don't have enough rudder applied, the string moves away from the turn. If you are diving, the string moves up. Just sort of keep that string straight and it helps tell you where you are."

Wilbur went up full of doubt and came down filled, once again, with admiration for Orville's native mechanical sense. He didn't want to spoil him though, and merely said, "Looks like that might work. We'll try it for a few days."

The year 1904 had not started out well; by the time it ended they knew they had a flying machine that they could offer the United States Army.

CHAPTER
47

J ust as the Ohio weather rocketed back and forth from freezing cold to stroke-inducing heat, so did the fortunes of the Wright family fare in 1905. For Bishop Wright, things took an unaccustomed turn for the better, for from January on he was encouraged by events in his church. Then, the May general conference of the United Brethren Church accorded him a complete victory; all of his longtime enemies were turned out of office, and his contributions for over thirty years were richly recognized. It was a long, hard-fought battle, and he valued the boys' support; both Wilbur and Orville had stood by him, making trips on his behalf and writing some briefs that were better than any lawyer could do.

The triumph, so long delayed, permitted him to retire at seventy-seven, full of honors and able now to devote himself to the management of his children's affairs, something that he enjoyed second only to running church affairs. There was much to do—the poor lads, successful as inventors beyond all dreams, were hopelessly naïve when it came to business matters. If he was not vigilant—and intrusive, he admitted that, he intruded on them for their own good—they would give the house away. And Katharine—she demanded constant watching too, although she seemed to be coming along, to be more content. At least that Cleaver fellow was no longer hanging about, looking hangdog and flinching every time the Bishop walked in the room.

For Wilbur and Orville, things were much less satisfactory for most of the year. Helping their father had been a distraction, one they gladly endured, but it took weeks of work away from their new Flyer, which was not performing well. Wilbur had insisted once again on altering the control system, and it caused problems. To control the Flyer, it was still necessary to operate the wing-warping with the hips, but the rudder was no longer interconnected. Instead, the rudder was operated with a small hand lever, as was the elevator.

"It's too much to do, too much to think about, Will, and besides, we just got comfortable with last year's controls. Why do we have to change?"

"One word, Orville, and that's performance. The new Flyer will do much better in turns if we put in just as much rudder as we need, and don't let the wingtips decide for us."

Orville had argued long and hard against the idea, but Wilbur had insisted. As Orville had prevailed in the same argument on the 1903 Flyer, he felt he had to give in this time. He would soon regret it.

For some reason that they could not determine, the 1905 Flyer was beset by a series of crashes that saw the skids folded, wings crumpled, struts broken, and the engine shifted off its mount. All were repaired in a few days, and there had been no injuries. They discussed every crash, but there was no pattern, and even Orville did not blame it on the new controls. It was turning out that flight was not some arithmetical exercise, where you added or subtracted to get an answer; rather, it was an involved calculus with so many variables that they were unable to know all of them, much less count or qualify them.

Even straight and level flight was difficult, for the slightest over-pressure on the control for the elevator could cause the nose to rise or fall. When you went into a turn, all bets were off, for the very act of turning introduced new elements into the equation. The wing on the outside of the turn necessarily moved faster than the wing on the inside; the greater speed imparted more lift and more effectiveness to the controls. Then, when control pressures—by moving the hips and pressing on the two control levers—were altered to stop the turn, and roll out of it, all the forces changed again.

Then there was the wind itself; when it was coming straight at you, it was a friend, a helper, adding to airspeed, but from the side or from behind, it was something else again, also introducing factors which could not be predicted before the event nor determined afterward.

It was a gigantic puzzle, one that would have been intellectually fascinating if you were not lying in the airplane with no protection to guard against a sudden crash into the ground.

On July 14th, Orville was having a good flight, making smooth turns that kept him within the prairie dog–infested Huffman Prairie. Flying was never humdrum but now he took the time to check things on the ground—whether the interurban trolley was coming, how many horses were over in the pasture, routine things. As he turned away from the trolley line, he suddenly nosed up, lost airspeed, made the wrong control movement, and was smashed against the earth as the Flyer dashed straight down into the ground at thirty miles per hour. The front end of the Flyer was destroyed, all the struts broken and driven backward, and the engine torn from its mounts. Orville was tossed like a rag doll to one side, laying there and not moving as the crowd rushed across the field toward him.

Wilbur ran to the crash, hoping that the gasoline would not spill on the hot engine, praying that they would not find Orville pierced by one of the arrow-sharp broken shards of the framework, the biggest danger in such a smash-up.

They found him laying flat on his back, eyes closed, conscious, but not wishing to speak. Wilbur crouched at his side, patting his face, checking his pulse, assuring him that a doctor had been sent for. Pale and bruised, he remained on the ground for some time before finally, with Wilbur's help, sitting up. The small crowd that surrounded them let out a collective sigh of relief.

"How are you feeling? Any pain?"

Orville shook his head. "Don't think I've broken any bones, and my head doesn't hurt like it did at first. I think I've been lucky."

In half an hour he had recovered completely; it was a good thing, because there was still no doctor on hand. He sat on the sidelines, under the shade of a wagon that had been driven over to carry him away, watching Wilbur direct the recovery efforts on the Flyer. It was badly damaged, and would be in the shop for a week or two.

As they were driven back to the Simms Station platform, Orville reached out and laid his arm on Wilbur's sleeve.

"Will, you remember our arguments about the new controls?"

Will nodded. He was feeling terribly guilty, suspecting that the changed controls had contributed to the accident.

"Well, I let you win that argument." He didn't go on to say, "And you see what happened." He didn't have to. "Now you've got to let me win this one. I want to show you how we are going to rebuild this Flyer when we get back to the shop."

Will was so relieved that Orville had not been killed that he would have agreed to anything.

"Orv, you do what you think is right, and I'll not say a word."

"Will, that's a promise. Don't ask me what I'm doing or why, just let me do my work. I know how you feel about the Flyer, I know it's your baby, but I've got some ideas I want to try out, without the usual arguing back and forth." Orville did not often have such a margin of moral superiority over Wilbur, and he wanted to take full advantage of it.

The next day at the shop, Orville sketched out on a piece of tablet paper exactly how he was going to change the Flyer. Wilbur started to argue, saw the look in Orville's eyes, and quietly stepped in to begin work.

Both men knew they had reached a different point in their lives; for the past five years they had been thinking in lockstep, one complementing the other. This was different; they were seeing things in a very different way. In the past, it had been as if they were mentally wired together; now there was a split.

On August 24th, the totally rebuilt Flyer III, as they had begun to call it, was brought out. Orville had increased the size of the front elevator by almost half, to eighty-three square feet, and moved it forward so that it was now eleven feet seven inches from the wing. He had done this by intuition; he had not put one figure down on paper, but simply made mental estimates, drawing on his knowledge of the last four years, and most important, of the last flying season. Wilbur still had grave doubts, and was more than pleased to have Orville make the first flight. He expected the additional elevator to be far too sensitive, making straight and level flight difficult and turns impossible.

From the first takeoff, it was obvious that Orville had performed some sort of miracle on the machine. The Flyer suddenly became a docile performer, easy to fly, much easier to maintain a very level flight path, and easy to fly in turns that became ever steeper. The best news, the "proof of the Orville pudding" as Orville called it, was that there were no more accidents or near accidents. Orville had done the impossible: he had made flying routine.

When Orville tried to explain the reasons for the change in performance from the standpoint of practical mechanics, his brother rebuffed him. Instead, Wilbur went to work with his numbers, and quickly determined that the Flyer's stability had been vastly increased by repositioning the front rudder—the elevator as they called it now. He was not sure that the increased size of the elevator had much effect, but absolutely certain that moving it forward had been a stroke of intuitive genius, and he did not hesitate to say so to Orville, or anyone else who would listen.

Flight times started to climb almost miraculously. Where they had been well satisfied with a one- or two-minute flight, they were now going ever longer, from eighteen to twenty to thirty-three minutes, and were seemingly limited only by the gasoline supply. The longer flights introduced a new problem: neckache. Lying prone, the Wright boys had to hold their head up to watch the horizon and the front elevator. It was easy to do on a short flight, but became agony as the flights grew longer and longer. The first thing they did after landing was to roll over and massage their neck.

Longer flights like these could not be hidden, for people going by on the trolley in one direction would see the Flyer still aloft when they came back in the other. The interurban began to be a tourist attraction, with dozens of people, some from far outside the local area, coming out on the trolley. Simms Station became a featured stop, and vendors were quick to pick up on it, offering soda pop and candy.

At long last, the press picked up the flying activity at Huffman Prairie, and soon fairly accurate reports were being carried all over the country. It delighted the Wrights that the *Dayton Daily News* and the *Dayton Journal* engaged in a heated rivalry, one trying to outstrip the other on flying stories. They often saw Frank Tunison, and were uniformly courteous to him, although they were tempted to say, "We still ain't flown fifty-seven minutes, Frank, what are you doing out here?"

On October 5th, Wilbur Wright put in a flight that capped the year's flying. Lying prone on the wing, his neck aching from the strain of looking up at the elevator, the string, and the horizon, he circled Huffman Prairie for more than thirty-eight minutes. It was a world record, and the press was ecstatic, praising the Wrights and loudly condemning anyone who had ever doubted their claims. Octave Chanute immediately wrote that he was coming down to see another great effort. With his usual luck, his visit was marred by a violent storm that prevented flying. Chanute seemed always to just miss out on the big Wright events.

Despite the encouraging flights and the widespread publicity, the Wrights were unable to convince the U.S. Army's Board of Fortification and Ordnance that they had brought their machine to "the stage of practical operation." The Army was gun-shy, not from combat, but from the Langley fiasco. Feeling that they would never be able to breech the walls of caution in the Board of Fortification, the Wrights made successive presentations to the British and French governments. There was obviously sincere interest, and some promises of participation, but all of the contracts were doomed, and doomed, oddly enough, by Wilbur Wright.

CHAPTER
48

In the days following his father's triumph in the United Brethren Church, Wilbur had listened more and more carefully to his father's arguments about protecting their invention. Orville listened also, and agreed as well, but he did not have the profound conviction that Wilbur embraced. Will was certain that the world was out to rob them of their invention, and he was not going to allow it.

Katharine took an entirely different view. One afternoon she had ridden the interurban trolley past Simms Station all the way into Springfield, to meet Henry Cleaver. He took her to Guyton's Drug Store, where the fountain was fabled for its ice-cream sodas and cherry phosphates.

They claimed one of the leather-covered booths, daringly sitting on the same side as if they were expecting another couple, and covertly holding hands.

"How are the boys doing?"

"It's been a terrible summer for them, Henry, dear. I told you about Orville almost killing himself last July. I hate it every time they go out to fly, they are so sure of themselves, and they act so carefree."

"Well, they don't fly very high."

Katharine shook her head. As much as she loved Henry, he still had no idea of what her brothers had done. "No, they don't fly very high, maybe twenty feet off the ground, but they are going thirty miles an hour—a lot faster than that carriage of yours will go—and if something happens they could get killed."

Cleaver quickly retreated—the quickest way to annoy Katharine was to say something that could be interpreted as even faintly disparaging about her brothers. He had seen her light into a reporter on the *Dayton Journal* who had made some joking remarks slighting the Wrights—it wasn't pretty, and it scared the reporter. It scared Henry, too, making him think.

"When are they going to sell their idea and make some money?"

Katharine made a rude sound sucking in the last of her soda through the straw and said, "Sorry. I hit bottom." She was silent for a moment, patting his arm, then said, "I don't think Wilbur will ever sell one of his Flyers. They are like his children, or more, like his wives."

"I didn't get the impression that Wilbur had too much interest in wives." This was dangerous territory, but he was feeling reckless, not flinching as Katharine's eyes flashed another warning.

"No, not so far, but that doesn't mean he won't. Right now he's in love with his flying machines. He's as possessive as you are, as silly jealous about them as you are about me, Henry."

Cleaver did not reply. It was a sore point. Katharine was a grown woman, twenty-nine years old, full of life and promise. Yet she was trapped in that blasted house on Hawthorne Street, and he worried that she would never get away to marry him.

There was another source of irritation. Few people knew they were romantically involved, but many knew that they were friends. Henry's own circle called him "the fifth Wright brother" because he looked so much like Orville—the same build and coloring, and until Katharine had made him shave it off, a similar mustache. When his friends were feeling mean they would refer to Katharine as "Mrs. Orville."

He sought to recover a bit, and in a conciliatory tone asked, "How can he be in love with a flying machine? It's just cloth and wood and metal. It's noisy and dangerous, and so what if it can fly, it can't do anything else."

"I don't know. It's a sickness, maybe. He's captive to Pop's ideas, of course, about spies and charlatans and thieves stealing ideas. But it's more than that. He's gone beyond Father in his obsession for secrecy. And something's happened between him and Orville, I don't know what, but they are not like they used to be."

They walked slowly to the door, hand in hand, then down the

sidewalk to a bench under the trees, placing their backs to the dappled light that flashed through the tall hemlocks. "Wilbur is a businessman, you know, a merchant. He's sold bicycles for years, and a few years ago sold an automobile, even thought about going into the automobile business for a while. You'd think he'd know how to treat a customer. But he doesn't. Listen to this. When he offers a Flyer for sale—and the price is high, believe me—the buyer has to sign a contract without ever seeing it fly, or even seeing it, or even seeing pictures or drawings of it. Wilbur doesn't ask for any money until after the contract's signed, and he's demonstrated the airplane. But no one is going to sign a contract like that. Can you imagine some poor government worker going in and telling his boss that he signed a contract to buy something he had never seen? I think he might make some concessions to the American Army, but not to a foreign government. There have been two times when he thought he had a sale, once to England, and once to France. Both times, they backed out, unwilling to meet Wilbur's terms."

Cleaver laughed out loud. "You can't be serious. No one would buy anything under those terms, especially for something as out-landish as a flying machine. Have you talked to him about it?"

"I'm perfectly serious, and yes I've talked to him about it. But you know how he treats me, with love, but with no idea that I have any sense about anything except running a house. He's a dear boy, but I frankly think he's not normal about this."

Cleaver couldn't restrain himself. He had been angry too long to let the chance go by. "Well he's not the only Wright brother who is not normal."

Katharine stood up, her faced flushed with rage. "I suppose that you mean Orville by that remark?"

"Yes, I do not think it's normal that he is so attached to you. It is just not right for a woman, almost thirty years old, to have her brother so tied to her. Do you know what people call you some-times? Mrs. Orville! And I don't blame them. You should see the way he looks at you."

Katharine fought to keep from crying. "Henry, are you saying that there is an unnatural relationship, that . . . Orville is my lover?"

It was too bold a remark for Cleaver to respond to. He looked down, angry, afraid to say more.

"Well?" she persisted. "So I'm some sort of a pervert that has an incestuous affair with my brother, and a love affair with you, too, is that it?"

"I didn't say that, Katharine."

"No you didn't say it, but you've hinted at it before, and this is as close as you dare to come. Well let me tell you, Henry Cleaver, my brother is a good, pure man, and he would kill you for making a remark like that."

He looked at her and said only, "See what I mean? That's not a rational response, not from you, and killing me wouldn't be rational for him. Goodbye, Katharine."

He rose, leaving her sobbing. It was not the first time that they had parted with her in tears, but she sensed that it might be the last. Henry was a proud man. As she quietly cried, she thought, *My God, I'm just like Wilbur! I'm offering my love on terms no one can accept.*

CHAPTER
49

The wind was whipping off Lake Michigan, rattling the windows of Octave Chanute's sprawling fieldstone home. He sat at his desk, reviewing the letter he had put off writing for so long to the Wrights. He would not have written it at all if he did not believe that the business methods adopted by the Wrights were not only hurting them, but hurting aeronautics in general.

The letter could be a disastrous mistake. Two years ago, perhaps even a year ago, he would have sent the letter without a second thought, confident that the Wrights would understand his motivation and not take offense. No more. The two men whom he had grown to respect and admire so much had changed in the last two years in ways he could not possibly have foretold, Wilbur much more so than Orville, who still seemed to have his head on his shoulders.

He adjusted the lamp over his desk, and picked up the letter to read it again, to make sure there was nothing in it but the hard facts of the last two years.

Chicago
January 31, 1908

My dear colleagues,

The papers have reported that you are "enjoying" weather fully as cold as that afflicting us here; I hope that you are staying warm, and that you and your dear family are well. I'm looking forward to a personal visit, when you will tell me about all the wonderful things you are doing. I want you to remember everything and tell me everything.

But this letter has a very serious purpose, one that may, I fear, impinge on our friendship. It is to tell you of my very great concern about your decision not to fly any more after your splendid achievements of 1905, and to provide you with some information that might be of use to you. If, in the process, I appear to intrude on your private affairs, I apologize in advance.

Our friendship goes back many years, to your first letter in May, 1900, and has been strengthened by many meetings and how many letters— four hundred perhaps? It is this long association that prompts me to review the past three years, and to have the temerity to suggest a course of action for you. I'm very much aware that everything I tell you will be new to you, but it might be that seeing the events recapped might possibly have some effect upon how you view things. And, to be honest, this letter is also an attempt to put our own relations in order. It has not escaped me, nor can it have escaped you, that in recent weeks our letters have become less and less friendly. It hurts me to say so but it seems to me that there have been some from you that I might have interpreted as definitely unfriendly. I hope I am wrong.

We are all engineers. Rather than dress up my comments with a superfluity of words, let me just lay down, in roughly chronological order, some of the events of the preceding three years. Then, if I may, I'll draw some conclusions and make some suggestions that I believe will benefit you. I know that I have no official reason for doing so, but surely the high regard in which I hold you both allows me some little leeway. Before I start, let me say this. If I offend you I apologize, but will not be sorry, for I owe it to you and to myself to be candid.

Let us start with your brilliant, record-setting success in 1905, when you truly perfected a practical flying machine. At that moment in time, you said that you felt you were ten years in advance of any competitor, and I certainly agreed with you. But things have changed. Look at this list, and consider it carefully, my very dear and valued friends.

(1) You decided that secrecy is preferred to further development, and stopped all your flying.

(2) The French offered prizes for developing a flying machine. You refused to compete.

(3) As you have told me, tenders for the sale of your machine to the U.S. Army, and the French, British, and German governments have come to naught.

(4) The estimable Ernest Archdeacon and Gabriel Voisin created

and flew a glider. It is unmistakably derived from photos of your flying machine.

(5) Other Frenchmen followed, all using your gliders as the basis for their work. It should be noted that they are serious men: Esnault-Pelterie, Ferber, and others.

(6) Skepticism mounted on your achievements in many of the most influential journals. I know this does not bother you, but it encourages others! The more the French doubt your achievements, the more they will press on to make their own contributions.

(7) On October 23, 1906, our old friend Santos-Dumont flew for about sixty or seventy meters in a flying machine that echoed yours, even if it was not so controllable. You dismissed this as a mere "hop."

(8) On November 12, Santos-Dumont flew for seven hundred twenty-six feet, and while you agreed that this is not just a "hop," you dismissed it as a basically uncontrolled flight. This may be true—but not in French eyes. To the French, it is "fly first, control later."

(9) Then a year later, you witnessed Henri Farman winning the prize you could so easily have won, flying for nearly a kilometer. And just two weeks ago, he collected $10,000 by flying the required fifteen hundred meters in a circle.

Let me stop here for a moment, and just say that in European eyes Farman is the man of the hour, superseding even Santos-Dumont. This may not be important to you in some respects, but it must be important to you for commercial reasons. Do you believe for one moment that the French government will buy an aircraft from you when it might buy one from a national hero? There would be riots in the streets, my friends.

To this point in this overlong letter, I have tried to convince you that the ten-year lead you had in 1905 has evaporated to perhaps the lead of a year or so. I stipulate freely that the Europeans (as you know, there are Danes, and Britons and others also involved) got their great leap forward by both copying your ideas and taking confidence from your success. Nonetheless, they have moved ahead.

But all this is but a prelude to news that I have that should be of utmost importance to you, and I have it directly from the source, Alexander Graham Bell himself. Despite your clear lead, he is still interested in investigating flight. He has formed a consortium of young men, engineers, to attack the problem. Mrs. Bell is backing *him, and providing the resources from her own considerable wealth.*

He has mentioned four names, only one of which is familiar to me, and that one is Glenn Curtiss. This is a man to contend with! I'm sure you saw the news articles labeling him as the "fastest man on earth," driving a motorcycle at one hundred thirty-six miles an hour. He is an engine man, and he's flown Captain Baldwin's airships as well. Oddly enough, one of the other men in Bell's consortium—he calls it the Aerial Experiment Association—is a Frederick Baldwin, but is no relation to the balloonist. There is also an old friend of their family, a Thomas McCurdy, and a young U.S. Army officer, a Lieutenant Selfridge.

Now, my friends, this is an organization of tremendous potential, as I think you will agree. They will build on what they know you have done, and if they do not find the same path to flight that you did, they may well find another. And their having the Army connection is worrisome for your possible sales to the U.S. government. Selfridge could become their advocate for the flying machines they produce—and they will produce them, I assure you.

I implore you to consider what I've said, and say that to maintain your lead, you must resume flying, in as public a manner as possible. You should seek prizes, and demonstrate your clear lead while you have it.

With the most fraternal feelings, and with the hope that I have not permanently damaged our friendship, I remain your true friend.

Chanute reread the letter, then put it aside. "I'll read it again tomorrow, and if I still feel the same, I will send it. They need to hear this, whether they like it or not."

CHAPTER
50

The Wrights did not like it. For one thing, they had already made up their mind to begin flying again, and now it would appear forever to Chanute as if he had been directing their actions.

"Will, he's gone too far this time. I don't give a hoot that he means well, he has just gone too far."

Wilbur was silent, terribly offended.

They were both alarmed. As much as they hated the letter, as much as they wished to send a stinging reply, there was so much truth in it that they could not easily dismiss it.

"I'll tell you Orv, it's depressing. We've kept him so well informed on everything that the letter must have seemed perfectly reasonable to him."

"Well, I don't mind telling you, this business about Bell and Curtiss worries me the most. Bell is a genius, of course, and I remember Curtiss very well. He is a very intelligent young man, and a wonderful mechanic."

Curtiss and Captain Baldwin had visited Dayton in September of 1906. The four men had gotten along well, with Baldwin explaining his dirigible to the Wrights, and the Wrights being less cautious than usual about showing photographs of their flying machines.

"Funny, that did not bother me so much as the news about Farman. Alexander Graham Bell is a scientist. His association is probably just a research bureau. There might be something commercial coming out of it, but not for a long time. Especially if he keeps on with those tetrahedral kites of his."

"Will, the most important thing is to keep this letter from Pop.

He didn't see it come in. I'll go tell Katharine and Carrie not to mention it."

"That's a little sneaky, don't you think? What if he asks if we've heard from Chanute? He does that, you know."

"Sneaky it may be, but I don't want to sit through a three-hour lecture on it. If he asks, get out the last one we had from Chanute. He hasn't seen it."

"I guess the only bright spot was that we had not told anyone about the way the negotiations with the Army are looking up."

The cumulative effect of newspaper articles and some surreptitious visits to Dayton had finally brought some of the key members of the U.S. Army's Board of Fortifications around to the idea that the Wrights had actually flown. Wilbur had made a personal visit, and his manner—friendly, precise, and fully informed on every detail of his flying machine—finally moved them into action. On December 23rd, 1907, they had issued a solicitation for bids, Signal Corps Specification No. 486, for a flying machine that could carry both a pilot and a passenger for a distance of 125 miles at a speed of forty miles per hour. The machine needed to have an endurance of one hour, and to land without damage.

When Wilbur had read out loud, Orville joked, "We better not let you fly it then, Will—remember the fourth flight in '03?"

The specification went on to say that an intelligent man should be able to become proficient in its use with a few hours' instruction, and that it had to be able to be disassembled so that it could be loaded and carried on a standard Army horse-drawn wagon.

Specification No. 486 had brought jeers and cries of pain from the aeronautical press, who saw no sense in issuing a specification that could not possibly be met.

"We ought to write Chanute, and thank him, and point out to them that the Army believes us enough to write a specification that suits us to a T."

"Bad idea, Will. Chanute would broadcast this to everyone, and then, when we win, someone will protest that we had undue influence."

The press was apparently incorrect about the rigorous nature of the Army specification, for no less than forty-one competitors had made proposals by the time the competition ended on February 1st.

It was much like the entrants to the St. Louis World's Fair. Most of the would-be competitors dropped out when they were required to put up ten percent of the bid price as a qualifying fee. For some this might not have been much, for bids ranged from a few hundred dollars up, topping out at an even one million by an optimist. The Wrights lowered their asking price to $25,000 for the privilege and the honor of serving the U.S. Army.

One other bid was accepted, and the Wrights were not surprised to find that it had been tendered by their old gadfly Augustus Herring, who had submitted a bid of $20,000 and a promise to provide an advanced flying machine of his own design. Because of his reputation for his pioneering work, the Army accepted both his proposal and that of the Wrights. The Wrights did not object; Herring's personality was such that it was difficult to be angry with him, and his proposals were usually so outlandish that they were amusing.

Both Herring's potential competition and the letter from Chanute were forgotten in the delight of the next event to rock their lives. After years of fruitless, mind-numbing negotiation, their agent, Hart Berg, had at last closed a deal with the French government. It was far better than they might have hoped—a new company was formed to build and sell Wright aircraft in Europe. Called *La Compagnie Genérale de Navigation Aérienne*, it would, after the demonstration flights, be paid five hundred thousand francs for delivery of the first machine and twenty thousand francs each for four more aircraft. The Wrights would receive fifty percent of the initial share issue. It was a coup. In "Model T" dollars, as Orville referred to them, it amounted to an incredible $180,000, plus the prospect of millions more over the next few years.

For Wilbur, the pain of parting with a Flyer was eased by his knowledge that many more would follow. Looking ten years younger, and moving as if a great stone weight had been removed from his shoulders, he said, "Orv, this is the best thing that could have happened. I know we are going to do well with the Army, but now the pressure is off. Even if something should go wrong in the Army flight trails, we have this big sale in France. And there will be others, now, I know."

With the news of the French contract in hand, Wilbur went to his writing desk, and wrote the following to Chanute:

My dear friend,

 Although we have corresponded in the interval, I have not properly thanked you for your long and thoughtful letter of January 31st. Never have any fear that any advice from you might be misinterpreted, we value your friendship far too much for that.

 But it was impossible to respond directly to your letter because of certain negotiations that were then going on. Now you know that we have been awarded a contract to participate in a competition for the Army (along with your friend and ours, Augustus Herring). What you might not know is that we have also reached an agreement with the French, and I will be going to Europe to demonstrate the Flyer in the near future, even while Orville prepares to demonstrate another example to the Army.

 Thus you see we have acceded to your advice!

There were a few other paragraphs, dealing with some studies of the wingspan and lifting power of crows before he signed:

With the greatest admiration and respect,
Wilbur

He tossed the letter to Orville, who read it, laughing. "Will, I tell you, all this traveling to Europe has made a diplomat out of you. Why, I can remember a time when you would have written him a scorcher! This is just right, and it will keep him off our back for a while."

CHAPTER
51

The latest news convinced Albert Blohm that he was indeed cursed. A terse note from the law firm handling his finances coolly told him that his once substantial estate had virtually evaporated because of some totally unforeseen stock market losses. He suspected fraud, but there was no way he could tell, as he had trusted them implicitly. Some of the money had been in bonds, a reasonable sum, but the interest was not enough to live on. There was no way out; for the first time in his life, he would have to go to work for a salary.

It was fortunate that he had befriended poor Langley and then, later, Dr. Walcott. The Smithsonian employed him as a research assistant whose task was to catalog the many experiments that Langley had conducted in the South Shed, and more importantly, prepare the twice-crashed Great Aerodrome for exhibit. It was not unpleasant work, but it was far different from running his wind tunnel—another sore point in his current travails.

The administrators at Catholic University had been totally unsympathetic to the news of his financial problems. As soon as he informed them that he could no longer subsidize the operation of the wind tunnel, they had it and its valuable instrumentation removed and the building converted to storage. When he asked if he could store his instrumentation, they told him no; he had no alternative but to send it to a junkyard. It was a cruel, cold blow, but still nothing like the one he had received from Alexander Graham Bell.

Or rather, from that witch Mabel Bell. Blohm was sure that she had sabotaged his chances to be a part of the Aerial Experiment

Association; she had never liked him and she had influenced Bell against him. He would have been perfect, and he understood that they were paying the participants well, as much as five thousand a year.

Well, it was their loss. Instead of getting a man with a genuine knowledge of aeronautics, and with a reputation in the community, they had picked some nonentities, people no one had ever heard of. Curtiss was the exception of course, and he was entirely out of place. He was like the Wrights: a bicycle mechanic turned engine builder, no education, no culture, dirty fingernails, the very things that would repel Mabel Bell.

The final blow was the reappearance of the Wrights on the scene, with their chance for an Army contract, and what appeared to be a golden opportunity in France. He had written them a congratulatory letter and received a very nice reply. They were curious fellows, aloof, but still staying on everyone's good side if they could. Blohm had heard from Chanute of the offer Herring had made for a partnership, and Chanute had gone on to make a point of how courteously the Wrights still treated Herring. He had also praised them for the nice letters they had written about Langley after the professor's death in 1906.

It just reinforced his view of Chanute as a bumbling outsider. What else were they going to say about a dead man that they humiliated—no, killed—with their success at Kitty Hawk? They would have had to be fools not to have been gracious, and as much as he disliked them—hated them—for their success, they were not fools, he gave them that. Speaking to himself, Blohm said, "My life is a shambles. No money, no wind tunnel, and certainly no becoming secretary of the Smithsonian. What can I do to turn this catastrophe around?"

The idea came to him as he had workmen remove the Manly engine and put it in the shop for overhaul and preservation. If he could not beat the Wrights, and he could not join them, he could take away some of their luster by restoring the Langley myth. Their letters about Langley had given him the key. Wilbur had written after Langley's death that it was his encouragement that led the Wrights to attempt to build a flying machine. Wilbur had gone on to say that, "but for an accident on launching," that the Great Aerodrome might have been the first aircraft "capable of flight." That was it, that was the phrase that he would build on, and that would be how the Aerodrome would be labeled when it was put on exhibit.

Blohm knew that he always needed a cause. For years, the cause had been to succeed Langley as secretary of the Smithsonian. That was impossible now. The new cause would be somehow to defeat the Wrights, to take from them the mantle of greatness that he knew they did not deserve. Langley could not do it while he was alive. Perhaps, with Blohm's help, he could do it after his death.

CHAPTER
52

Tom Baldwin annoyed Lena at their first meeting, and managed to keep annoying her from then on. He had come to Hammondsport to buy an engine for a dirigible and had somehow become almost part of the family, Glenn's family, not hers. She knew that Glenn liked Tom, and that it was good business to have him as a customer, but Baldwin was simply too loud, too fond of the local Great Western champagne, and too determined to get Glenn interested in flying machines.

And she knew there was more to it. Prior to Baldwin's arrival, Glenn Curtis had been the number one person in Hammondsport, well known for his engines, his motorcycles, and records he set riding them, but most of all for his factory, where he treated his employees very well. At a time when things were slow everywhere, the Curtiss plant was running both day and night shifts to make engines, and still not keeping up with the demand. Yet when Baldwin began building his dirigibles there, Glenn instantly became number two in the eyes of the townspeople, for the huge man was internationally famous, a celebrity, and the townspeople flocked around him. Every time one of his new *California Arrows* was making its first flight, the whole town turned out to celebrate. Lena tried to tell herself that she was upset for Glenn and not for herself, but she knew that was only partially true. When Glenn was number one, she was the wife of number one, and that's the way she liked it.

The two men could not have been more different in appearance or personality. Glenn was always serious, and appeared severe sometimes when he was really just analyzing a problem. Only of medium height, his erect stature and demeanor made him look taller—until he stood next to Baldwin, who not only dwarfed him, but invariably clasped his huge beefy arm around Glenn's shoulders, so that they looked like a father-son team. Normally standoffish and reserved, Glenn would grin with delight when Baldwin picked him up and whirled him around over his shoulders like a child—as he often did. Maybe it was something he missed in his youth, she didn't know, and she could say nothing, for Glenn liked Baldwin from the start, admiring the jovial extroverted characteristics in him that he knew he lacked.

There was a hard business core under their natural friendship. For Curtiss, the very best thing about Baldwin was that he could tell him exactly what was needed for dirigible engines. For Baldwin, he had found in Curtiss an intelligent man who could translate his needs into smooth-running engines.

Glenn was convinced that there was a market developing for airship and flying machine engines, and he wanted to be able to fill it. It was part a native interest and part good judgment, for he could charge twice as much for a dirigible engine as he could a motorcycle engine. After all, if the dirigible engine broke down you might drift across the country, but if a motorcycle engine broke down you just pulled to the side of the road.

The fire was fed when Baldwin gave him news about the Wright brothers' achievements, carefully planting an idea that he hoped to harvest in the years to come when he turned from dirigibles to flying machines.

Lena had complained about Baldwin to Glenn, but only once. He'd replied in a very reasoned manner, pointing out all the good things that had come from the association. To meet Baldwin's needs, he had created his "wind wagon," a tricycle that had a mount on which various engines could be placed, and was driven by a big propeller. But the best thing had been Baldwin's request for a more powerful engine. Curtiss had created a new V-4 engine that was selling better than they could have imagined, and at a very high profit margin. It had led directly to an even bigger engine, the V-8, which was beginning to sell as well. Yet it was not what Glenn said that convinced her; it was the intensity of his expression and the tone of his voice. It was obvious that this was not a subject that he wanted to discuss again.

It became the custom for Glenn and Tom to go to the annual New York Automobile Show, sponsored by the Automobile Club of America, and enhanced in recent years by Aero Club of America exhibits. It was a business trip, but laden with pleasure, for they saw things and met people that were equally intoxicating to a boy from Hammondsport and a man from Oakland. By 1906, Tom had given up his interest in steam cars and was fascinated by the new eight-cylinder Marmon and the huge, luxurious Locomobile, while Glenn was taken by the Cadillac and the Packard runabout. They debated their choices hotly as they moved from booth to booth, picking up literature and promotional ideas as well.

They finished looking at the cars before going to the Aero Club section of the show, for both men were among the stars there, with some people anxious to meet them, more desiring to sell them things and a few, a very few, wishing to buy. Only three of Baldwin's *California Arrow* dirigibles were on display—last year there had been four. They took up an enormous area, of course, but the Curtiss engine that powered each one was slung underneath, easily visible to the crowd.

Curtiss had met Alexander Graham Bell briefly at the 1905 show, and Bell had made a personal trip to Hammondsport a few weeks later to order a two-cylinder Curtiss engine of fifteen horsepower. This time Bell sought him out, telling him that he had been a little disappointed in how the engine had performed and sounding him out on his views on larger engines. After more than an hour of discussion, he placed an order for a four-cylinder engine of twenty horsepower to be used in one of his tetrahedral kites.

Back home he told Lena, "You wouldn't believe it. He was standing there, huge white beard and all, sort of towering over me, talking to me as an equal. He wears these funny looking tweed suits; looks like he just came over from Scotland. And he asked about you, remembered your name from his visit the year before! I couldn't do that for his wife, I couldn't tell you now what her name was, maybe he didn't tell me. But he was so nice, asked all sorts of questions. And I'll tell you what kind of a personality he has! During the whole time we were talking, Tom Baldwin just stood there, not saying a word. I'd introduced him, of course, but he didn't butt in, didn't interrupt, just took it all in."

Curtiss had leaped back into work at his usual frenetic pace, racing motorcycles whenever he could. Things seemed to be going reasonably well during the following summer because Baldwin was touring with his airships more often than usual, until there came a day she would never forget: June 28th, 1907. Baldwin had a new *California Arrow* that he was testing, and he could not get the engine running to his satisfaction. He would take off, make a turn along the waterfront, then come back, go through the laborious landing process, and chat with Glenn about it. Finally Curtiss said, "Do you think I could fly it myself? If I were up there with the engine, I could tell a bit more about it."

Baldwin agreed immediately—he had been hoping to get Curtiss involved in the actual flying. They talked for a while, discussing how to handle the airship. Curtiss kept nodding, impatient, and finally told the waiting crew to cast off. Within a few minutes he was four hundred feet in the air, engine wide open, the envelope ruffling with the pressure of the twenty-mile-an-hour speed he was wringing from the engine.

After all his years of experience on bicycles and motorcycles, flying the dirigible came naturally to him. He quickly learned how early you had to make the control inputs to anticipate a turn and how to trim it by moving up and down the walkway to get the best speed for an engine setting. He enjoyed the view and the overpowering sense of freedom; he was seeing Hammondsport and Keuka Lake as he never had before. The absence of dust added to his delight—racing a motorcycle was fun, but you ate a lot of dust to do it. He had gone up in the dirigible as a motorcycle racer; he came down as an aeronaut.

The flight had upset Lena; she knew that Baldwin had planned to drag her husband into the flying machine business all along. Glenn denied it, saying he had more than enough to do just making and selling motorcycles, and almost had her convinced when the letter came from Canada. It was a formal invitation from Alexander Graham Bell to become part of the new Aerial Experiment Association, whose motto, Bell told him, was "To Get in the Air." Bell had spoken to him about it before, but Curtiss had never believed he was serious. The letter was indeed serious, indicating that he understood that Curtiss had a business to run and could not spend all his time at Baddeck. Further, he offered a salary of five thousand dollars to compensate for his time as "director of experiments."

Curtiss brought the letter in to Lena diffidently, expecting her to insist that he refuse. She was delighted instead, urging him to go to Canada to see Bell to accept the offer. It puzzled him, but for Lena, Glenn's association with Alexander Graham Bell completely offset his association with Tom Baldwin. Bell, she felt, was a man worthy of Glenn's time and effort, a man he could learn from, and a man who could give him even greater stature.

Glenn left for Baddeck with Lena a very happy woman; Tom Baldwin was not such a happy man, for he hated to see Curtiss's attention diverted to someone else's flying machine.

CHAPTER
53

In Hammondsport, the summer of 1908 was marked by almost continuous thunderstorms, a plague of june bugs and the greatest event in the history of the city, the competition for the *Scientific American* Trophy. The competition was being held in conjunction with Hammondsport's traditional Independence Day celebration on July 4th. Crowds had been pouring in since the previous day, coming on foot, by boat, bicycle, automobile, and a special train that the B&H railroad had laid on. The weather was no better than it had been all month, but the wind and drizzle dampened no one's spirits.

The *Scientific American*, the most prestigious journal in the United States, had long been skeptical of flying machines, and had been especially—and unfairly—dubious about the efforts of the Wright brothers. In time, however, the evidence of the flying at Huffman Prairie became so compelling that the *Scientific American* had not only reversed itself, extolling the Wrights, but established a gorgeous $2,500 trophy for the first heavier-than-air flying machine to fly for over one kilometer in a straight line.

The *Scientific American*'s editors had expected the Wrights to leap at the chance to acquire a trophy that was obviously well within the capability of their Flyer, and were disappointed when Orville Wright wrote to decline, giving as his reasons the forthcoming army trials. Orville was too polite to say that they resented the treatment they had received in the past from the magazine and that competition for prizes was beneath them. They felt that it smacked of huckster-ism, and the Wright Flyer was too profound an achievement to require such tactics. And, of course, they had no wish to expose their Flyer to view so that it could be easily copied.

Fortunately for Hammondsport, Glenn Curtiss had a different point of view. He and his colleagues in the Aerial Experiment Association had with monumental effort and a great deal of their own ingenuity, already copied enough of the Flyer to feel that they were ready to try for the prize on July 4th.

The great national holiday was always celebrated in Hammondsport, but never with the feverish anticipation of the year 1908. The townspeople, who thought they had become accustomed to celebrities with the frequent appearances of Captain Tom Baldwin, and indeed their own Glenn Curtiss, were dazzled by the thought that aeronautical history was being made in a town where wine had long been the only product. Only in the past few years had such modern devices as Curtiss's motorcycles or Baldwin's dirigibles been built there, and they were still getting used to the idea. They were particularly proud of the huge Curtiss factory where many of them worked, with its five buildings sprawling across several acres of land. There was a big boiler and engine room, built separately, with a machine shop on its second floor, a two-story carpenter shop, and a big assembly hall. There had never been anything like it in the area before.

Gossip spread swiftly around Hammondsport, so the average citizen knew that the Wrights had declined to participate, and some expected this, for many believed the Wrights were nothing but fakes. If you wanted the genuine article, you came to Hammondsport, where Glenn Curtiss, the fastest man on earth, 136 miles per hour on the monster motorcycle, was now a flyer.

Almost everyone was also aware that Alexander Graham Bell was not going to be there for the celebration. He had become a popular figure, staying at the Curtiss home, and Lena Curtiss had made sure that she and Mrs. Bell were seen often in the back of Glenn's new Packard. Bell himself made a point to be friendly, and many Hammondsport citizens had stopped him on the street to shake his hand. But the Bells were on their way to their home in Canada, and would miss the great event.

But as swift as gossip was, and as interested as people were, few of the townspeople had yet comprehended just how distinguished a gathering of leading aeronautical figures it was, all eager to witness what amounted to the first public attempt at a flying record in the United States.

The curious thing was that while almost all of the aviation personalities were happy to be there, they were for the most part happy for very different reasons. The aviation crowd had settled, like an elaborately poured *pousse-café*, into a series of layers of self-interest.

Certainly the bottom layer began with the members of the Aerial Experiment Association. A successful flight today would confirm Mabel Bell's wisdom for having brought the AEA into being. It had taken a great deal of effort to persuade Alec that he needed help, and a great deal more to get the right people. Mabel had selected two of its members, John McCurdy and young Frederick "Casey" Baldwin, while Alec had selected the third, Glenn Curtiss. The fourth—and Mabel's favorite—was Lieutenant Thomas Selfridge, who was so confident that the future of the Army lay in aviation that he had sought Alexander Graham Bell out and had himself seconded to work with him. He proved to be a welcome addition and was soon Mabel's friend, even though she had at first been disturbed by the aggressive way he had presented himself. Later Mabel realized that this aggressiveness was part of his strength. Selfridge had been the only one to volunteer to test fly Alec's big kite, and had endured a violent crash and a dunking into the chilly waters off *Beinn Bhreagh*. She had been deeply concerned, but Selfridge had laughed it off, telling her that he would "live forever."

Curtiss was the great surprise. While she could not be attracted to him personally as she was to Selfridge, she was very touched by how accomplished he was in speaking to someone with hearing problems. He told her the story of his sister Rutha, whose illness had been so much like her own, and his proficiency in communicating either with finger language or by speaking so that his lips could be easily read gave him a central position in the group, for he could "translate" for others with Mrs. Bell.

It was a surprise to Alec as well, one that endeared Curtiss to him even beyond his normal reserved but businesslike manner and his undoubted genius with engines. Bell's great life work had been his study of the inheritance of deafness, and he spent many hours with Curtiss discussing Rutha and her medical treatment when they might have been talking flying machines.

The four young men got along better than might have been expected, given their different backgrounds. Curtiss was quite diffident from the start and remained somewhat aloof. He had succeeded in the business world in a way quite beyond the abilities of the others, but they were all college-educated, and he was ashamed that he had completed only the eighth grade. Realizing that his speech and his manners were comparatively unpolished for this elite circle, he kept back, watching the others, and adjusting his own actions to theirs. McCurdy, Baldwin, and Selfridge understood this, and they tried to avoid creating any awkward situations for him.

Most of the initial inhibitions had soon passed, and for the past nine months the four young men had been deeply embroiled in Alec's projects, arguing fiercely at times over technical issues, but also making jokes and engaging in some horseplay. Despite his obvious reservations on some of the ideas the others developed, Curtiss participated as much as possible, given his business responsibilities. On social occasions, he relied on stories of "the other Baldwin," Captain Tom, to entertain his listeners. Tom Baldwin was sometimes there himself, laughing as heartily as anyone, and standing in flabby contrast to the trim, superbly built and immensely strong Casey Baldwin, who had been a star athlete in college.

Casey had done military reserve duty with the Canadian Engineers, a mounted unit, so he felt an affinity for the West Point–trained Selfridge. A Californian, Selfridge had been interested in aeronautics from his youth, and had plotted his course in the military to take advantage of the emerging science. Selfridge was much like Curtiss in his demeanor, being reserved and courteous, but capable of a belly laugh when one of an almost continuous series of practical jokes was pulled by McCurdy, who was most at home with the Bells, his father having worked with them.

For his part, Alexander Graham Bell was less satisfied with Mabel's association. When Selfridge had crashed in his tetrahedral kite, the *Cygnet I,* the four younger members of the consortium had immediately focused on their real interest, a flying machine, using their limited knowledge of the Wrights' work as a starting point. Both Curtiss and Selfridge had written the Wrights, asking for information. Both received rather cool replies that referred them to already published material, including their "U.S. Patent No. 821,393": a clear warning shot across the bow.

It had not deterred them. When the more conservative Casey Baldwin pointed out, "We may wind up with a lawsuit on our hands," Curtiss had responded: "The Wrights cannot shut down flying everywhere in the world just because they've made a few good flights. We've all looked at their patent, it controls twisting the wing-tips. Well, we won't twist the wingtips, we'll do something else."

McCurdy had chimed in, "And if we don't, the French surely will. Not a day goes by but some Frenchman tries to set a new record. If the Wrights want to sue, let them sue Farman or Voisin."

The plan developed that each of the young men could in turn build an "Aerodrome," as they called the flying machines in deference to Langley. They hoped to learn from each one and improve on the successor, compressing the development process that took the Wrights so many years into a few months.

Selfridge did the first design, the *Red Wing*, so called because it was covered with the same material that Bell used in his kites. Earlier in the year, on March 12, Casey Baldwin had flown it on sled-skids off the ice at Keuka Lake. It had not flown well, but its staggering three-hundred-foot journey through the air was in fact a flight. The very next attempt was not, for the *Red Wing* demolished itself in a crash that proved it was not under control. The ubiquitous Augustus Herring learned of the crash, and immediately volunteered his services to analyze the difficulty and suggest improvements, an offer that was quickly accepted. Herring had, of course, wanted to work with the AEA from the start, and now he began to insinuate himself with Curtiss, who still regarded him as an aeronautical genius. They picked up quickly on the time when they had met in Buffalo, and Herring was soon angling for a job in the Curtiss factory.

When his turn came, Baldwin improved on the *Red Wing* with the next design, the *White Wing*. Alexander Graham Bell, smarting somewhat from this diversion of attention from his beloved tetrahedral kites, nonetheless made a critical suggestion, proposing the addition of triangular tips on the upper wings, to operate differentially for lateral control. Four words leaped to their collective minds—"wing warping" and "patent violation"—but they persisted. Like young musketeers, they clanked their engineering swords and swore again not to let the Wrights' patent stand in their way. There had to be more ways into the air than that of the Wrights, and if it came to a patent fight, so be it.

Both Selfridge and Casey made attempts to fly the *White Wing* without much success; it was fitted with a wheeled undercarriage and had trouble leaving the grassy meadows where it was tested. On May 23rd, it was the turn of the old motorcycle and dirigible maestro, Glenn Curtiss, to fly the *White Wing*. In his first flight ever in a powered Aerodrome, he lifted off and flew for more than a thousand feet, making cautious turns, steering it as he might have done a powerful motorcycle. When he landed he had already mapped out in his mind how he would design the next Aerodrome in the series.

The *White Wing* was flown once more, and McCurdy crashed it ten seconds after its faltering takeoff. Curtiss did not mind; he was already at work on the third of the Aerodromes, one that would embody all his ideas.

So it was that all the members of the Aerial Experiment Association were anticipating a successful flight. And so was the next layer of the *pousse-café*, the twenty-two members of the Aero Club of America who had flocked to Hammondsport to witness the event. There was a little tension, for Allan Hawley, the Aero Club president, was a good friend of the Wrights, having once treated Wilbur to a balloon ride on his trip to France. Hawley was convinced that the Wrights' refusal to try for the trophy was both a tactical and a strategic error, but he had to appear unbiased.

Assisting Hawley was another friend of the Wrights, Augustus Post, a dapper, bearded sportsman who handled racing cars, balloons, and publicity with equal assiduity. The story was told of him that in 1900, when his balloon burst over Berlin at three thousand feet, he had escaped by parachute, landing on a rooftop where he found he could peer directly into a woman's boudoir. True or not, it was typical of the dashing Post, who was everywhere on the field at Hammondsport, kissing Lena Curtiss's hand at one spot, shaking Tom Baldwin's hand at another, standing with his arm around Charles Manly at yet another, and always, by the sheerest coincidence, when a photographer was present. At his side, shunning the photographers, but shaking hands with everyone he could, was one of the Aero Club's founders, Albert Blohm, there to represent the Smithsonian and to keep his eyes and ears on Manly, who had recently been quoted on some very anti-Langley remarks.

The contest was bittersweet for Blohm. On the one hand he had to be gracious and friendly to the members of the AEA, despite the fact that he had been prevented from joining them; while on the other, he was going to witness a Curtiss success, and every Curtiss success he counted as a Wright failure. Over the months, Blohm had succeeded in consolidating his hatred so that he now quite be-

lieved that the Wrights—who were scarcely aware of his exis-
tence—were the authors of all his troubles. Blohm wanted revenge,
even if he had to get it secondhand, through Curtiss's success. The
celebration posed a bit of a logistics problem for Blohm, for eager
as he was to meet influential people, he tried to keep himself away
from Herring. It was particularly galling that Herring had already
secured some kind of a consulting role with the AEA. Herring, for
his part, was stalking Blohm as he stalked the others, ready as always
to shake hands, offer advice, and seek a favor.

Lying on top of the Aero Club layer was the smaller contingent
from the *Scientific American* itself. Most of them were quite pleased
with the prospect of the day's events, but Charles Munn, the pub-
lisher, really wanted the trophy to go to the Wrights. When the
AEA had proposed July 4th as the date of the trial, Munn had tried
to procrastinate, to give the Wrights time to think. He had used
the excuse that the trial should be held near some large city, but
Curtiss and Selfridge visited him in New York and in a very straightforward fashion pointed out that Munn's own rules explicitly stated
that the contestant could choose the place of the trials.

At the moment Munn was more distressed than ever. He had
been invited to inspect the AEA's aircraft, and from the first look
saw that it clearly derived from the Wrights' efforts. Munn knew
that litigation loomed, and he hoped the *Scientific American* would
not be a defendant.

This many-layered social *pousse-café* was topped by a swirling mist
of mixed emotions. Lena Curtiss was almost delirious with happiness, proud of Glenn and, as weary as she was of being a hostess
to the other members of the AEA, was nonetheless charmed by
their unfailing courtesy and compliments. They had totally displaced
Tom Baldwin from Glenn's attentions, and this pleased her as much
as it displeased Baldwin.

Captain Tom was not upset about the social aspects; he had some
hard practical facts to consider. He was preparing a dirigible to sell
to the Army at the same August trials where the Wrights would be
demonstrating their Flyer, and he wanted Curtiss to focus his attention on the engine he would use. Baldwin intended to get into flying
machines himself someday, but right now his fame and fortune were
riding on folded cloth and ropes in Glenn's factory, and he was
distressed that his engine had not yet been run.

And then there was Glenn Curtiss himself, moving swiftly around his Aerodrome No. 3, oblivious to the crowd, the celebrities, and anything but the trim of his machine and the hum of his engine.

Hard knocks early in life and years of business experience had made Glenn a realist. He knew that anyone looking at his Aerodrome No. 3 would see the basic similarities to the Wright Flyer. Both had superimposed surfaces—biplanes they were beginning to be called—and like the Wrights' propellers, his propeller faced the rear. Both machines had front and rear stabilizing surfaces. Both were just about the same size and weight. There was no escaping this. But Curtiss pinned his hopes on some essential differences. His big forty-horsepower engine drove the propeller directly. He had a tricycle landing gear, much like that used on his wind wagon, and he didn't need a derrick to get off the ground. Most important, he had Bell's moveable wingtips, which avoided the problem of twisting the wings, enabling them to be built stronger. And they worked just as well, perhaps even better—he hoped.

Curtiss wished that he had the confidence in success that he heard being expressed all around him. It was bad luck to talk about the flight as if it were easy, indeed, as if he had already flown it. The truth was that he had flown the Aerodrome No. 3 only a dozen times, never very successfully. The first flight had been scheduled for June 21st and on that day Alexander Graham Bell had jestingly named the machine the *June Bug*, in honor of the horde of greenish-blue winged beetles nibbling the vineyards at Hammondsport that summer. *Gold Wing* would have been a better name, consistent with the previous two Aerodromes and reflecting the yellow-ochre color that the sealant coat of paraffin dissolved in gasoline had given its wings.

The first hop was over in only eleven seconds. In the days that followed, he had made twelve more straight-line hops that lasted from as little as three to as much as sixty seconds. All told, he had spent exactly five minutes and eighteen seconds in the air, including his single hop in *White Wing*. When they averaged it out, it came to just about twenty-three seconds per flight, not exactly an encouraging statistic.

Despite their disappointment, the AEA members had been afraid that the Wrights might change their minds and try for the *Scientific American* Trophy, so they decided to take a chance. A sixty-second flight would win the prize, and even if they fell short, the attempt would generate a lot of publicity for the association. They were already thinking in terms of manufacturing Aerodromes for sale to the general public. If they won the trophy, they would have a tremendous advertising feature; if they did reasonably well, it would still help. If they failed, or if Curtiss crashed, they were obviously not ready to sell Aerodromes yet, so even that would be a positive result—or so Selfridge, the incorrigible optimist, had insisted.

There was more to it. The very idea of the *Scientific American* Trophy had a gut appeal to Glenn, whose study was filled with loving cups from all the many bicycle and motorcycle races he had won. This trophy was a gorgeous sculpture, with silver winged horses arranged around a green onyx base, topped by a pylon with the globe and an eagle surmounting all. It was supposed to be valued at twenty-five hundred dollars, but it was worth many times that to Curtiss, because of its source, the *Scientific American*. If he won the trophy, he would move in his own mind from the ranks of unwashed motorcyclists to those of engineering professionals.

Shrugging off the demands from his friend Tom Baldwin for more emphasis on the dirigible, Curtiss had spent almost all of the last few weeks obsessively building and improving the *June Bug*. It was built on the base provided by the early AEA airplanes, and it would serve as the foundation for the next Curtiss flying machines he would build, for he was already determined to part company with the AEA—it was too confining to work with a committee. And just as he had leaped from bicycles to motorcycles, so would he move from motorcycles to aeroplanes, as they were beginning to be called. Aviation was in his future—and his future could well be decided today, July 4th, 1908.

The day wore on with an agonizing decline in the weather. The wind rose and the rain came more frequently. The typical Independence Day entertainments were on hand, with plenty of booths featuring games and tents with refreshments. But the expectant crowd began to thin out. Not until a little after 5:00 P.M. did Curtiss signal to have the *June Bug* rolled out from its tent to the starting point. There were many hands to push it to the half-mile track on Stoney Brook Farm, where the testing grounds were located.

The officials began to mill around, with Charles Manly himself leading the party to measure off 3,300 feet, slightly more than the kilometer distance the prize required. Earlier, Manly's private discussion with Curtiss had been a bit disappointing. Manly had wanted to encourage him, but it was evident that Curtiss was in no mood to listen, and it almost seemed to Manly that Curtiss considered him a jinx. He did not understand, but he wished him well anyway, hoping that the clover in the field would be as kind to Curtiss coming down as the waters of the Potomac had been to him.

Unlike the Wrights, Curtiss flew in a seated position, unwilling to trade the experience, the sense of balance, which he had gained in a similar position on motorcycles, for the reduction in head resistance found in a prone position.

Just after seven o'clock, Curtiss signaled that he was ready. A quick check confirmed that the officials were also ready, and Glenn took off in a cloud of dust and smoke, the forty-horsepower engine drowning out the cheers of the crowd. He soon discovered that the *June Bug* was badly out of trim, climbing rapidly to forty feet, and edging ever higher. On the ground, Lena shuddered and looked away.

Curtiss put pressure on the elevator, stopping the climb, but leaving the *June Bug* in a nose-high attitude that generated more drag than the pounding engine could handle. He gradually slowed down and bounced into the earth, one hundred feet short of the marker where Hawley was waiting.

Once again many hands, too many, rolled the *June Bug* back to the starting line with Curtiss issuing sharp commands to take it easy and not damage the fragile surfaces. At the starting point, Curtiss superintended an adjustment in the tail, giving him a little more nose-down trim. This time the flight went well from takeoff, through the bobbing flight where his altitude varied from ten to twenty feet, and speeds up to thirty-nine miles per hour. He deliberately kept low, never flying more than twenty feet off the ground, and then, exhausted, landing in a pasture more than a mile and one-quarter away from the starting point. Curtiss had won the *Scientific American* Trophy, added another one minute and forty seconds to his flight time, and permanently left the ranks of unwashed motorcyclists.

Informed by telegram of the great event, Alexander Graham Bell sent a message to Curtiss, congratulating him, and another to his lawyers, instructing them to get to Hammondsport immediately and patent everything that could be patented on the *June Bug*. He expected to hear from the Wrights in the near future.

PART FIVE
TRIUMPH AND TRAGEDY
AND TRIUMPH

Not in the clamor of the crowded street,
Not in the shouts and plaudits of the throng,
But in ourselves are triumph and defeat.
Henry Wadsworth Longfellow

CHAPTER

54

The news came when, for one of the first times in their life, the Wrights were truly divided. Wilbur was in France, feverishly preparing their Flyer for demonstrations that would fulfill the French contract, while Orville was working with Charley Taylor and Charles Furnas to complete the Flyer he would demonstrate to the Army. The word of Curtiss's triumph had reached both brothers at about the same time, and Wilbur wrote that Orville should send Curtiss a stiff letter immediately. In it, he was to tell Curtiss that the Wright patent of 1906 covered all aspects of adjusting the wing and rudder for control in flight, and offered a license to use the Wright patent on machines built for exhibition purposes. It was a stern letter, but Orville softened it at the end by wishing Captain Baldwin well in his forthcoming attempt to sell the Army one of his dirigibles.

Yet the fact of Curtiss's winning the trophy was only the tip of the iceberg. The real horror was that their long-felt belief that they were five years or more ahead of all competitors had been utterly destroyed. There was no telling the effect that this would have on future contracts in the United States, or in Europe, nor could they judge what sort of a spur it would give their European competitors. The AEA had gone from some short glides in Chanute-type gliders to the *Scientific American* Trophy in less than nine months. The Wrights knew that this would have been impossible if they had not used the secrets that the brothers had spent five years in discovering, secrets that Curtiss and Baldwin must have spied on in their visit. It was such a brazen theft that they believed it would be easy to prove in a court of law.

They were also discouraged by the fact that Curtiss, who had seemed so friendly, could be such a scoundrel, to say nothing of Alexander Graham Bell, whose probity was supposed to be unquestioned. It made them all the more cautious, and the only thing that Wilbur could be thankful for was that he was in France and that Orville would get the full brunt of their father's "I told you so" onslaught. It came, in copious amounts, so much that Orville began spending more and more time at the factory, even taking his meals there rather than returning to his father's unending lecture series.

Both brothers knew that their greatest safeguard would be to sew up the Army and the French contracts with successful flights. They were confident that a public display of their Flyers would put Curtiss's one-mile hop in perspective, although they were both keenly conscious that their attempts to refresh their flying skills, rusty after an almost three-year layoff, had not gone well.

They had brought their 1905 Flyer down to Kitty Hawk in April of 1908, looking forward to a joyous reunion with the villagers, and a quiet place to practice flying. They found neither. The villagers had changed their simple ways, and while they still liked the Wrights, they thought it was time to share their wealth. And far from being quiet, reporters and the growing legions of aviation fans surged down to watch them fly.

They had to make some meaningful changes to the Flyer to relieve the problem of aching necks and to prepare for the demonstrations. They installed side by side seating for two in the aircraft, and once again modified the controls.

The trip went from relatively unpleasant to disastrous in a hurry. Visitors and reporters had hounded them without mercy, and both men had been ill, the bacteria-ridden water of the lifesaving station doing them in.

The old camp was in ruins, and it took weeks before they could begin to do a little flying. Things improved slightly, and on May 14th, Wilbur decided to take the hardworking Charles Furnas along on a flight, making him the first flying machine passenger in history. A mechanic in Dayton, Furnas was utterly infatuated with the idea of flying, and had gladly come down to Kitty Hawk to help in anyway he could. Orville then gave him a ride, not so much to please Furnas—although it did—but to get used to flying with someone, as they would have to do for their demonstration flights.

They soon felt they had regained at least some of their proficiency, but that afternoon, the alteration in controls had once again worked its wicked magic. On what proved to be their last flight of the season at Kitty Hawk, Wilbur had pushed forward on the elevator control when he meant to pull it back, crashing into the blowing sand at more than fifty miles an hour. He was badly bruised, and the Flyer obviously needed a week or more of repairs. They decided to call it quits, hoping that their next flights—at Fort Myer, Virginia, and in France—would go better.

CHAPTER

55

Now the next flights were almost on them. Wilbur had arrived in Paris on May 29th, fully recovered from the bruises of his accident, only to find his business partners sunk in despair. European flyers were making one dramatic flight after another, and with every one, the belief that the Wrights were "liars not fliers" rose. With each rise in that belief, the value of the Wright contract seemed to sink, and the hard-edged French businessmen wanted action. The biggest news was that their archrival in Europe, Henri Farman, had made a flight with the chauvinistic Ernest Archdeacon at his side. The fact that the flight was little more than a straight-ahead hop was lost on everyone—except Wilbur Wright, who knew that a hop was easy, but that real flying, thirty-eight minute Huffman Prairie flying, was not.

Things did not go well in France. The Wrights had negotiated with a highly recommended engine builder, Bariquand et Marre. They issued a contract to build duplicates of the Wright engine, and shipped an original engine as a model, along with all the required drawings. When Wilbur arrived he found that not only had they not built new engines, they had almost ruined the old one. It was the start of a long learning process in which Wilbur's pointed perfectionism would be sanded smooth by *laissez faire* French attitudes on craftsmanship.

Wilbur's frustration with his French colleagues had a curious, almost magical effect on him. The more annoyed he became with them, the less he felt the age-old oppression imposed by his father. At first he could not explain the relationship, but finally he realized that the recalcitrant French were assuming the role his father played in his life, but that there was a significant difference. He was helpless with his father, doomed by long years of practice to acquiescing in whatever he said. With the French it was not the same; as stubborn as they might be, he could and did eventually control them. Each time he had a particularly frustrating encounter—as when he found the original engine had been run without enough oil and was virtually ruined—he sensed that he was shedding the weight of his father's control. It was as if his life were being given back to him at a pace metered by his annoyance with his new colleagues. He was out from under his father's stern gaze now, and he became increasingly determined to break the old bonds, to return to Dayton as his own man.

The feeling of independence had been growing on him, but the first time that he positively identified the strange transition for what it was occurred at a dinner that the Wrights' European representative, Hart Berg, had arranged for him. They had spent a long day arguing with the management of Bariquand et Marre with no apparent results, and the totally frustrated Wilbur and the apprehensive Hart had not exchanged a word until they were met at the door of the Ritz by their hosts, a small group of French Aéro Club members. They were served in a private room decorated so extravagantly with pictures and statues of frolicking nymphs that Wilbur had difficulty following the conversation, preferring to let his eyes wander around the walls of the room.

The too-rich meal had been conducted with the customary French formality, filled with flowery toasts and protestations of esteem. On his previous trip to Europe, it had always been Wilbur's custom to merely wet his lips with the wine, acknowledging the toasts, but adhering to his father's strict admonitions about abstinence. But it had been a particularly depressing day, and Wilbur found that a little of the wine, the merest bit, was escaping his tight lips and going down his throat. There had of course been several wines served, in different glasses, and by the end of the evening he had drunk no more than half of one glass all told. Yet he liked it, the taste, the warmth, and most of all the significance of the departure from his usual habits; it made him feel not so much that he had defied his father as that he had begun to define himself. He had done something because he had wanted too, not because it was what his father demanded.

There was another element as well. He missed Orville—but Orville was not there to be taken care of, to argue with, and most of all, to remind him of the sway their father still held over them. If he were ever going to break free, he would have to do it on his own, and now was the time.

Their agent, Berg, was a godsend that made the trip as pleasant as possible, and shielded Wilbur from much of the anti-Wright sentiment that could be found in every newspaper. He was being billed as a naïf at best and a confidence man at worst, and there was an almost joyous sense of anticipation, waiting for the day that this stiff, awkward *poseur* from America would finally be exposed. Wright sensed that Berg had some agenda of his own when they spent days searching for a perfect site for the trials. Wilbur gradually got the feeling that Berg was showing him the less desirable places first, much as a horse trader shows his inferior stock before springing the one he really wants to sell upon a customer. Finally Berg led them to Le Mans, where they met Leon Bollée, a roly-poly man who had an automobile factory there, and who sweepingly offered space, mechanics, and whatever else Wilbur needed. It soon developed that Bollée was not among the Frenchmen who doubted that the Wrights had flown; he was an ardent fan, and although he knew no more English than Wilbur knew French, they almost instantly became friends for life.

Bollée had sought permission for them to fly from a French military establishment, but red tape intervened, so, as the second best place, he took them to the Les Hunaudières race course, south of Le Mans. Renting the race course was quite expensive, two hundred fifty francs a month, plus fifteen percent of the gate if Wilbur gave exhibitions, but Berg assured him that it was worth the money for it was close enough to attract not only all the necessary reporters, but also the wealthy investors he hoped to find.

A group of patriotic French aviation fans had already gathered, and they protested the selection of Les Hunaudières as being far too small for a flying field. When Wilbur quietly allowed that it would do, their opinion that he was nothing but a *bluffeur* were confirmed. Not even Farman could fly from such a field! If 'Weelbur

Vreet,' as they called him, accepted this field, it meant only one thing. He did not intend to fly at all.

Berg had secured a room for Wilbur at the Hotel de France on June 16th, the day that the crates containing the Wright Flyer arrived at Le Mans. It was a small hotel, with a good dining room, and, while much more expensive than Wilbur had expected, it was good value for the money. As a friend more than as their agent, Berg was attempting to educate the Wrights, to elevate their tastes a bit from Dayton, and the hotel was a good start.

CHAPTER
56

In a life studded with failed friendships, one person had remained true to Albert Blohm, even after his money was stolen away by his former friends on Wall Street. She was Annette, his mistress of many years and who was now Madame Coujade, the estranged wife of an impoverished French army officer. Although their physical relationship (with one brief exception) had ended long ago when Annette had returned to France, Albert had made arrangements for her financial care.

Theirs had been an unusual affair. First of all, they had been passionate lovers without ever pretending to be in love. He admired her for her beauty and quick wit; she liked him for his generosity and his obvious intelligence, but most of all because his servants liked him, and she knew that was a good sign.

They had corresponded after she returned to France, and met once in London for a joyous sexual reunion. Then, when she was thirty, he earned her gratitude forever. She had become pregnant not by him—and was considering an abortion. He had urged her to have the baby, and, at the time still being very wealthy, had established a trust for her and the child. It took care of their living expenses and even made provisions for his education, for she had subsequently given birth to a fine boy. It was the trust, in fact, that later made her sufficiently attractive to Lieutenant Henri Coujade for him to overlook her status as an unwed mother. For a small bribe it was possible for him to create the necessary papers that proved that Annette was a widow, and thus suitable to become an officer's wife.

It was also the trust that allowed Annette to leave Coujade when he began beating her after he drank too much. She wrote to Blohm to thank him once again, and received in return a letter with the first request he had made of her since their time in London. To her it seemed to be simple enough, a favor that she could easily do. He wanted her to seek out this famous American, Wilbur Wright, and seduce him.

It had not been difficult to find him. Wilbur's comings and goings were followed raptly in the Dayton papers, and often in the Associated Press. When Blohm found out that he was in Le Mans, he wrote to Annette, and within the day she had found out his hotel, put her son with an aged aunt, and secured a room in the Hotel de France herself.

In his letters Blohm had told her of Wilbur's habitual shyness, warning that it might be the case that "he did not like women" and that he would rebuff her. He wrote, "But I do not believe this is so. He seems very normal in most respects, from all that I have heard and read of him. It is possible that he is very religious, or it might be that he has a physical incapacity. But see what you can do; if you cannot seduce him, then no one can. And, this is very important. If you cannot seduce him, you must compromise him, you must leave the impression that you have seduced him."

It did not occur to Annette to ask why Blohm was interested in having her seduce Wilbur Wright. She knew that he had suffered many disappointments in recent years, and he had, in the flurry of recent letters, let it be known that he hated the Wright brothers. In reasoning it out she discarded blackmail as a motive; Mr. Wright was not married, and if he had an affair with a Frenchwoman, it would be of no concern to anyone. And after his years of kindness, Albert would certainly not expose her to harm.

In this she was quite wrong. Albert Blohm knew that Lieutenant Coujade had been cashiered for drinking, and believed that he would leap at the chance to become the aggrieved party in a suit against the newly wealthy Wilbur Wright. Such a suit would adversely influence the sale of Wright Flyers, and the thought pleased him. There was another possible dividend, one he was almost counting on. If Curtiss replaced Wright as a primary supplier of flying machines, there would certainly be a place for Blohm, either in engineering, or in Europe as a sales representative who spoke several languages.

Annette was very patient and quite subtle. The day after she arrived, she managed to pass Wilbur on the street, not looking at him at all, counting correctly on being observed by him. Then on two subsequent evenings, she arranged to be just finishing her evening meal at the time when she knew he would arrive for his own supper. This was easy, as he was very punctual, always dining promptly at seven. On the second time, as she left, she acknowledged his smile with one of her own. A few days later, she passed him in the hotel hallway, and they exchanged greetings.

More than a week elapsed before she timed her evening meal to coincide with his. Then, looking very shy and nervous, she sent a note to his table asking if he was in fact Wilbur Wright, and if so, could she please have an autograph for her five-year-old son. He was glad to comply.

They had dinner together the following night, and Wilbur found the experience as warm and pleasant as the very small sips of wine, totaling no more than half a glass, that he now allowed himself with meals.

CHAPTER
57

As obdurate and disagreeable as the U.S. Army had been to the Wrights for so many years, they now found in Brigadier General James Allen, Chief Signal Officer, a rational man who would work with them to define the specifications of their contract to supply the Army a Flyer. Allen, for example, quickly understood that for an airplane flying over a closed course, upwind and downwind, there was a difference in the way you measured the speed. If you averaged the speeds for each leg, you came up with a higher figure than if you averaged the time for each leg, and he was quick to agree to an amendment to the specification to reflect this.

On his return from the agony of the last trip to Kitty Hawk, Orville found that in many ways his world had changed forever. There was a constant stream of visitors to the Wright shop, and the volume of mail had increased a thousand percent. Even worse, he was being pressed for articles for national magazines, and while the payment was good—five hundred dollars from *Century*, for example—writing was not his forte, and he felt ill at ease about it.

His unease was communicated to the "two Charleys," Taylor and Furnas, for they were trying, for the first time, to produce the Flyer in volume, with no less than five being under construction. In some ways it was easier—the machinery could be set up to do a certain set of parts, and then all of that certain set could be made for all five Flyers. On the other hand, this was boring for Charley Taylor, who liked to see the parts march together in the assembly process, and lost interest when he was merely filling parts bins.

They had worked through the first part of July before Orville finally realized that he had asked too much of himself and the two Charleys. It was not going to be possible to smoothly bring all of the Flyers into being at once; they had to start concentrating on what he was now calling the Army Flyer. Once the decision had been made, work proceeded smoothly—much more so than was Wilbur's lot in France.

CHAPTER
58

Wilbur had been beside himself when he first opened the packing crates. The Flyer had been shipped over the previous year, and had gone through customs prior to languishing in a warehouse. Instead of smoothly stacked wing surfaces, elevators and rudders, he found a jumbled mess. At least a dozen wing ribs had been broken, the covering was torn, the radiators were smashed and items that should have been securely fastened, large metal parts like the magneto, had been stored loosely in the case. During its trip to Le Mans they had torn through the fabric and smashed more wooden parts.

Immediately after work, Wilbur dashed off a stinging letter to Orville, accusing him of utter carelessness in packing the Flyer. Later, sober reflection and a joking letter from Orville made him realize that the French customs inspectors were at fault. They had not damaged anything themselves, but after inspecting each and every item, they had not repacked them properly. When the crates were subsequently moved to storage, the loose parts had done considerable damage.

He worked for days, getting ineffectual help from Bollée's mechanics because of both language and cultural barriers. In time he overcame this, in part by taking lunch with them whenever he could. He was dressed, as always, in suit and tie, with a cap, while the workmen wore the traditional loose blue fatigues. The novelty of "one of the gentlemen," a man in a suit, eating and chatting with them, soon earned their friendship.

The engine continued to give him trouble, never more so than on July 4th, when a rubber tube—installed by Bariquand et

Marre—came loose and scalded his arm and side with boiling water. Bollée was there to render first aid, but it was a painful injury that did not heal fully for weeks. He felt worse the following day, when he learned that Curtiss had been winning the *Scientific American* Trophy while he had been writhing in pain.

The obviously painful burn earned him no sympathy with the fans of French aviation; they saw it as probably a self-inflicted wound designed to further delay the inevitable day when Wilbur Wright would at last have to admit that he could not fly. But it did earn him sympathy, much appreciated, from Annette, who helped him dress his burns morning and evening.

He pressed on despite the pain and with a religious discipline that dismayed his French mechanic colleagues, used to a more liberal interpretation of Frederick Taylor's time and motion studies. By August 4th the Flyer was ready, and he had it moved to the shed that Berg had contracted to be built. There were primitive living quarters reminiscent of Kitty Hawk built into the shed.

Wilbur checked out of the Hotel de France a different man, aware that an idyll had ended, and more than prepared to take on the French who did not believe in him, and the father who did.

Although it was not an idyll that ended for Annette, it had been an agreeable time. She had grown fond of Wilbur and respected him, and wanted him to succeed with his flying machine. The French aviators were so rude and insulting in their remarks in the newspapers that it embarrassed her. She knew that Wilbur was not capable of lying; if he said he had flown, he had flown. She left the hotel as well, worried now that there might be more to this business than Albert had told her. She hoped that Albert would not harm Wilbur. She thought she knew that he would not hurt her.

Rain and a concern for his arm, still not healed, forced Wilbur to wait until Saturday, August 8th, before attempting his first flight. His thoughts were filled with memories of his last flight at Kitty Hawk, when a touch in the wrong direction on the elevator control had plunged him into the sand. He shrugged it off. In the intervening two days he had amused himself by using a French-English dictionary to read the predictions in the newspapers and weekly magazines on his inevitable aerial fiasco. One of the prevailing stories was that the Wrights were only circus acrobats, able to keep a machine in the air by the manner in which they could spring from one side to the other, keeping it in balance by sheer physical dexterity.

Berg came in with Bollée at mid-morning. "Not much of a crowd, yet, Wilbur, but an elite one. You have many from the French aerial establishment here. You should hear Archdeacon prattling on about the impossibility of your flying."

"Archdeacon is an ass, as we all know from the papers. Who else is there? Is Farman back from the States yet?"

Berg conferred in French with Bollée before answering. "No, Farman is not here. The most important person is probably Louis Blériot. He is surrounded by his clique, of course, they are nodding agreement with everything he says. The Zens brothers, Paul and Edmond are there, they are staying away from everyone else, I don't know why. There is one chap that Henri here thinks is René Gasnier, the chap whose picture was in the paper yesterday, with the Voisin machine. There are some Russian officers, writing furiously. Most of the rest are journalists—Francois Peyrey is there talking up a blue streak. Everyone is tired of waiting; you would think we had invited them down personally."

Wilbur went to the door of the shed and peeked out. He could see the stands, where, as always, the women and the men had divided into small groups, the women laughing and talking but obviously uncomfortable in their voluminous skirts and huge hats, the men gesticulating, arguing, and alternating eruptions of heights of patriotic Gallic flying fervor with their own gales of laughter.

He turned to Berg and said, "I don't see Madame de Farge, but I hear the needles clicking." Berg laughed, then had to explain the joke to Bollée.

Henri was always jolly, but he sobered up to say, "Veelbur, you've hit it. This is going to be a new French Revolution! But you will be running the guillotine on the pride of people like Archdeacon!"

As the hours passed, Wilbur considered Henri's remarks and liked it better the more he thought about it. He was here to revolutionize aviation, and prove to the world that the Wrights were indeed flyers and not liars. He stole another look out the door, wondering if Annette might possibly be in the crowd.

It was not until well after noon that Wilbur finally appeared, dressed in his usual gray suit and high white starched collar. He helped to open the doors of the shed, and eased the Flyer out so that its tail assembly could be attached. There was a collective gasp from the crowd at the Flyer's size; it seemed huge and immensely strong compared to the French designs with which they were familiar. Archdeacon immediately asserted that this was the last straw, this enormous barn could not fly, and his sally was met with the kind of nervous laughter that signaled a growing unease. Perhaps the Wrights could fly—this was obviously a very well-built machine, and the way the smartly dressed American moved about it, checking its fittings and attachments and making a long series of precise adjustments, added to its credibility.

Wilbur and Bollée knew what the crowd did not. This airplane, so beautiful in the soft sunlight, had never flown before. There had been no time to test it. Today Wilbur would fly it for the first time, still scarred from the boiling radiator water and still remembering his last flight, the crash at Kitty Hawk. And only Wilbur knew that in all his experience, counting all the flights from 1903 on, he had spent less than an hour in the air in a powered flying machine.

Later in the afternoon, Wilbur moved the Flyer to the launching tower, and there was a general outcry of rage at using such a crutch. Once again Archdeacon seized the center stage, pointing out that the tower completely invalidated anything the Wrights might have said or done! He raged that using a tower and a track was not flying, it was little more than a cheap American version of the Roman catapult. You could hurl a stone into the air with such a device, and Wilbur Wright could ride the stone as far as he wished, but it was not flying, not as Frenchmen understood flying to be.

Archdeacon felt a great deal better; the sight of the Flyer had discomfited him, and he now repeated the image of the Roman catapult as the totem of his disdain to whomever would listen. He made sure that he got to several reporters; it was a *bon mot* that would work well in tomorrow's stories.

The crowd had thinned to just the diehards, the would-be aviators, the reporters, and only the most romantic of the women by half past six when Wilbur had the propellers pulled through and started the engine. He had not delayed without purpose. He was not going to fly until the wind, the weather and the flying machine were ready, and they were not ready until now.

After a few popping, backfiring false starts that brought his heart to his mouth, he succeeded in getting the engine to run smoothly as it rapidly came up to speed, growing louder all the time, but not quite drowning out the noise of the propellers spinning and the busy whir of the transmission chains. His helpers, all looking deadly serious as if the entire flight rested on each one of their shoulders, held the airplane back on the track. Wilbur sat for a moment, deliberately working the controls through their full range of movement, checking the elevator control twice, determined not to make the same error that he had made at Kitty Hawk, not here, not now.

Wilbur placed his cap on backwards, settled carefully in his seat, still an unaccustomed position, and signaled that he was about to release the weight, so that those holding the flying machine back would let go. The Flyer accelerated rapidly on the combination of the catapult's smooth pull and the power of its propellers, then leaped into the air.

The waiting crowd believed that an accident must have taken place—any flight they had ever seen had required an endlessly long, jouncing takeoff run at the end of which the Farman or the Voisin or the Blériot flying machine staggered reluctantly into the air, dropping back down to bounce once or twice and then lurching once again upward. This Wright Flyer was like an arrow shot out of a bow, and Wilbur Wright was already hurtling toward the trees lining the far end of the racetrack grounds.

The onlookers had begun a ragged cheer that grew slowly in volume then suddenly turned into a wail of horror. It was obvious that Wright was going to fly directly into the trees, and at the speed he was flying he would inevitably be killed.

At the controls of the Flyer, Wilbur was immensely dissatisfied with himself. He had already made four or five mistakes, any one of which could have killed him, the most serious being repeatedly moving the front elevator the wrong way. He had caught it each time, but now the trees were looming up and with a sharp movement of the controls—handle on the elevator lever to the left to turn, rudder control to the left, elevator control slightly back—he pulled the Flyer into a steep bank that brought it around in a ninety-degree turn. He leveled out, flew straight as an arrow, and then did another ninety-degree turn down the other side of the racetrack, sending it thundering toward a crowd that was now on its feet, screaming ecstatically at the miracle they had just witnessed. No French airplane had ever turned like this, all the Wrights had said was true, he was the king of the sky and they had all been chauvinist fools! Louis Blériot, short, swarthy, ordinarily pugnacious, and long contemptuous of the Wrights, could not respond to questions from reporters, saying that he had not yet digested the immensity of what he was seeing.

As Wilbur made his second set of turns that took him past the grandstand, he did not look at the delirious crowd, nor could he hear its roaring cheers; instead he concentrated on flying the machine, consciously noting which way the elevator worked each time he applied a correction. To the onlookers he appeared like a serene god, sitting upright, staring straight ahead, apparently not moving, his control pressures invisible. Far from being an acrobat leaping about the wing as Archdeacon had predicted, he could have been controlling the airplane by his thoughts alone.

Once again at the near end of the field, Wilbur made another short turn, then came down, touching down lightly and skidding to a halt only fifty feet from the launching tower. Wilbur Wright sat with his hands on the controls and all of Europe at his feet. The flight had been less than two minutes long, but it had changed the crowd forever just as it had changed their world. He made his way from the airplane, the delirious throng surging around him, men shaking his hands, women trying to touch his coat, reporters jostling for a statement, for a word. Wilbur was thinking, "So much for acrobats, so much for 'liars not flyers,' " but he said little, keeping his features composed. His French would-be rivals were less inhibited, each one trying to express to the journalists what it meant to them, what an event it had been, how it had transcended all national borders. It was no shame for France to have been bested by the Wrights; there was simply no comparison, they were not just Americans, they were men of the world!

Berg wanted him to make a second flight immediately, but Wilbur declined. It would be better to carefully check the Flyer over and make sure that nothing had come loose or out of alignment. There was the merest murmur of protest from the crowd when Wilbur indicated the flying was over for the day; they immediately fell back into the delighted buzz that communicated their sense of privilege of having been there on this day of days.

After Wilbur moved the Flyer and himself to the privacy of his shed, the people still hung around the building, cheering, urging him to appear. Instead Wilbur stayed quietly inside with Bollée, Berg having gone back to town for a celebration at which Wilbur was the absentee guest of honor. The two men shared a cold supper that tasted better to Wilbur than anything he had ever eaten in his life.

With this utter triumph, this complete vindication, Wilbur knew that he had moved completely out from under his father's control. He was prepared to return to Dayton and immediately do what Orville had dreamed of doing: establish a home of his own. His father would always be welcome, but as a guest, not master.

Ever the mathematician, Wilbur analyzed the situation, and began to assign weights to the factors that had helped free him. He grudgingly gave five percent to the little half-glass of wine he now took on most days. He felt uncertain about this, hoping it was not, as his father had always predicted, a stepping-stone to drunken degradation. He did not believe it would be. To Annette he cheerfully assigned fifteen percent; he would be forever grateful to her. She had liberated him not only from some of his inhibitions, but also from the threat of hellfire that his father held over him like a weight in his derrick tower. It had been a curious repression. Wilbur did not believe in hell, or heaven for that matter, but he had believed in his father's assessment of what was good for him and what was evil. Annette had not been evil, he was sure of that.

But eighty percent of the reason for his liberation lay in today's flying display. Despite the mistakes that only he knew that he had made, he had been masterful—the reaction of the crowd proved that beyond any doubt. As he quantified the eighty percent, he went through a little litany, a review of the cause and effect that had led to today's dazzling events. He was Wilbur Wright. He and Orville had gone from a kite to today's Flyer on their own. In France, he had assembled the Flyer, and he had made the flights that devastated the French. It was his own doing; he owed his father nothing but his love, but he would no longer permit him to control his way of life. There was something he did owe, however. He owed it to Orville to help him break free of his father, and he would do that when he returned.

Immediately after the triumph, Berg had wired Bishop Wright with a brief story of the great success. Wilbur spent Saturday evening doing everything necessary so that the Flyer could fly again on Monday, ignoring the crowd still milling around outside. As a matter of habit, Wilbur chose not to fly on Sunday, instead writing a long letter to Orville, detailing the flight and the minor mechanical changes he had made that might be useful on the Army Flyer. Then he spent the afternoon reveling in the impossibly gratifying stories in the French newspapers, where the most common headline was simply *Il Vole!*, which even Wilbur could translate as *He Flies!*

After a good night's sleep, he was awakened early on Monday by what sounded like a herd of cattle stampeding by. It was the first of a crowd that would soon number more than two thousand, and would include everyone in France who had thought about flying or who wished to see their newly adopted national hero, that famous Frenchman, "Veelbur Vreet."

"Veelbur" made only two short flights on Monday, the second of which was a figure eight. The effect of the second flight was absolutely devastating upon the other French fliers who had assembled, now as ready to believe as sinners at an evangelist's tent. One of the most prominent and certainly the most beloved of these was Leon Delagrange, who cried "Marvelous" at the top of his lungs, and then gave a reporter from *Le Matin* the headline of the decade when he turned, pressed his hand on the man's shoulder and said simply, "We are beaten."

It was, in fact, Waterloo and Sedan rolled into one for the dreams of the French aviators, and yet it was still utterly glorious, for man could fly, all men could fly, Wilbur had given them the key to the air.

From that point on crowds began to build in number and in elegance. There was nowhere to be in France but at Les Hunaudières, with Wilbur Wright and the new world he offered. He flew longer every day, flying eight minutes on August 13th. On the very next flight his old *bete noire*, incorrect control movements, caught up with him and he crashed into the ground, collapsing the left skid and damaging the wing. The French cheered the accident as wildly as the longest flight, convinced that it proved that their new hero was human, after all, and that was good.

There were some naysayers still. Archdeacon could not forgive Wilbur Wright for humiliating him by succeeding on so grand a scale, and continued to snipe at him. Louis Blériot, mindful of future commercial competition, retracted some of his earlier glowing remarks, and raised some doubts about the range of the Flyer.

These were exceptions, and they were scarcely heard in the clamor of acclaim.

Albert Blohm had followed Wilbur's successes with a sinking feeling. This was not the time to attempt to bring about a scandal; Wilbur was far too popular. He wrote to Lieutenant Coujade, saying that they would have to wait for a while before beginning the divorce proceedings, and sending him one hundred dollars to soothe his feelings of marital outrage for another year.

CHAPTER
59

Tom Baldwin and Glenn Curtiss had been at Fort Myer, Virginia since July, working to transform a greatly enlarged version of the original *California Arrow* into the Signal Corps Dirigible No. 1. Flight tests of the big, 19,800-cubic-foot airship had begun on August 14th, with the portlier-than-ever Baldwin standing at the rear of the catwalk to operate the rudder while Curtiss was at the front, running both the twenty-horsepower Curtiss engine and a large biplane elevator that they now used for altitude control.

The doubled volume of hydrogen had been enough to compensate for Baldwin's weight, but Curtiss was having trouble with his engine and could not muster the full twenty horsepower necessary to drive the billowy, elephantine airship at the required twenty miles per hour. They did average 19.61 miles per hour, however, and passed their endurance flight of two hours with ten minutes to spare. The minor difference in speed was expensive. Baldwin's bid price had been $6,750. The tiny .39 miles per hour speed deficiency—which, as Baldwin wailed, could easily have been a measuring error, a delay in clicking the stopwatch—had invoked a fifteen percent penalty, costing them a whopping $1,012.50. Nonetheless, on August 20th, they finalized the contract by which the Army bought what soon became "Old Number One," the first airship in what Baldwin and Curtiss hoped would become a powerful fleet. Part of the deal was to train operators, and Baldwin gladly trained three sharp young lieutenants, Frank P. Lahm, Benjamin D. Foulois, and Tom Selfridge.

Orville had a grudging liking for Tom Baldwin, but he resented

Curtiss, who had so obviously stolen their patented ideas and used them in the so-called AEA Aerodrome No. 3.

"*June Bug!*" he growled at Charley Taylor. "They ought to call it the *Hum Bug*, for he is humbugging people if they think he has something to sell of his own. He just has no shame, that Curtiss feller."

He liked and respected two of the three lieutenants Baldwin had trained. Lahm was an old friend whose father had helped them numerous times, and Foulois was a feisty little man who was rough-edged and a shade defensive in his attitude, but whose good humor always came through. But Selfridge! That was too much. Selfridge was a member of the Aerial Experiment Association that had stolen their ideas and he, like the other two lieutenants, was also on the Aeronautical Board that was going to pass judgment on the military Flyer.

Selfridge made Orville uncomfortable. He was a little too good-looking, a little too friendly, more than a little too confident, and he weighed too much. At 175, Selfridge was forty pounds heavier than Foulois, whom Orville liked better anyway, and forty pounds would mean a lot on the test flights. The thing that Orville resented most was the way Selfridge constantly pumped him for information, even at the evening social events. Then, to make matters worse, Charley Taylor had let Orville know that Selfridge made fun of Orville behind his back, criticizing his manner of speech, and pointing out flaws he saw in the Flyer. There was nothing Orville could do about it. A protest was out of the question, it would insult everyone in that closely disciplined institution, the Army. He had to give Selfridge the benefit of the doubt. The man was an officer, after all, and his actions would be scrutinized by Lahm and Foulois, so he would probably be fair. Probably. Maybe. Possibly. Fortunately there were two other members, both majors, George Squier and Charles Wallace, and they would undoubtedly have the final say. Orville hoped that Foulois would be selected to fly with him as an observer. Selfridge really should recuse himself, if he were absolutely honorable.

Like Wilbur in France, Orville had no complaint about his accommodations, for he was staying at the elite Cosmos Club, Washington's intellectual center, under the sponsorship of the overly friendly Albert Blohm. Grateful as he was for a convenient place to stay—it was right on the trolley line out to Fort Myer—Blohm worried him. He was much too accommodating and his job at the Smithsonian seemed to be that of keeper of the Langley flame. Orville had also learned from Charley Taylor, who had proved to be a perfect conduit for gossip all over Fort Myer, that Blohm wanted to go to work for Curtiss in some capacity.

Not that there were not problems with Charley Taylor. He and Charley Furnas were doing excellent work, as always, but Taylor was jealous because Furnas had actually flown not once, but twice. To Taylor this was intolerable, for in his view Furnas was a Johnny-come-lately who had not yet paid his dues.

As everyone, including the Army, had expected, Augustus Herring had not made an appearance, sending instead a request for an extension of time, pleading a finger injured in a test of his engine. The Army granted the request, and would do so again, confident that Herring would never bring an aircraft to the competition. He was a gadfly, someone that had to be tolerated for what he had done in the past, and to be watched for what he might do in the future.

Once again, Charley Taylor had the insight.

"You know what they are saying about Herring, don't you Orville?"

Orville did not and Charley went on, "He's put in a bid of twenty thousand dollars, hoping that the Army will pick him as low bidder. Then you'll have to subcontract your airplane to him so that you are not shut out. Pretty slick!"

"Pretty slick!" Orville snorted. "Pretty stupid. Will and I would put a match to the Flyer before we would let Herring get his hands on it."

While the newspapers continued to be filled with news about Wilbur's amazing achievements in France, the three men from Dayton got down to serious work assembling the military Flyer. They were most worried about the engine, for so much depended upon its putting out its full horsepower. The contract called for a payment of $25,000 if the Military Flyer flew at forty miles per hour in its speed test. They would get an extra ten percent for every mile above forty and lose ten percent for every mile under it. Two miles over meant an extra five thousand—two under and it would cost them that amount, plus nasty lectures from Pop and Wilbur.

Fort Myer was the classic nineteenth-century Army fort, with its immaculate green parade ground, tall trees and beautiful old brick buildings. The problem was that it was dangerous as a flying field, and Orville knew it. It was too small, about a thousand feet long and seven hundred feet wide, and bordered by too many trees. The big buildings also had a bad effect upon the wind when it came from the north or the east, making it turbulent and difficult to predict how to lay out the takeoff track.

On September 3rd, Orville spent most of the day preparing himself mentally for the flight. As had been the case with Wilbur, he had not test-flown the airplane he was about to fly, and he was as apprehensive about the new control system as Wilbur had been. He had had a relatively good flying session at Kitty Hawk, at least compared to Wilbur, but he was not comfortable with the new seat and control arrangement, and despite the flights with Charles Furnas, he was concerned about carrying the extra weight—and the possible diversion of attention—of the Army observer. It would take every ounce of concentration he could muster to fly in the confines of Fort Myer, and comments or questions from the observer would only cause problems.

Late in the afternoon, Orville made the first test flight, to the cheers of a crowd of about five hundred people that included President Theodore Roosevelt's son, Theodore Jr. The flight went well at the beginning; Orville made one and one-half trips around the drill field at about thirty-six miles per hour, flying no higher than thirty-five feet. Then he made a hard landing that broke the front skid. Almost every person of the five hundred who had gathered to watch continued cheering as they raced out to the Military Flyer. In France, Wilbur's flight had been an epiphany for many who had thought he was a fake. At Fort Myer, most of the onlookers expected Orville to succeed, and so their cheers, while fervent, lacked the guilty hysterical quality of the French. In Washington, most had come out expecting to see a practical flying machine, and they got exactly what they expected. A few came out expecting him to fail, perhaps even to crash. They had to bide their time. And where the newspapers and magazines in France had gone crazy over Wilbur's flight, Orville's first success was not even front-page news.

In the next few days, Orville made some more test flights, acquiring confidence. On the 9th he made a record fifty-seven minute thirty-one second flight that surprised even him, for it was a world's record, exceeding even Wilbur's longest flight. He then topped this on the very next flight the same day, flying for sixty-two minutes and fifteen seconds. On the third flight of the day, he took his friend Lieutenant Lahm as a passenger for a five minute and nineteen second flight—another world record.

He was joking with Charley at the end of the day, "Well, Wilbur's not the only one who can set records, Charley! We did pretty well today."

Charley did not take the "we" bait. He was not taking any "we's" until he got a flight himself, and he let Orville know it.

"Don't know why you're flying this Army brass around, Orville, when you never give me a ride."

"Charley, you'll get your ride! As soon as we've sold this Flyer to the Army brass you're complaining about. I have to fly with them, I have to make—"

Charley interrupted him with a low whistle. "Orv, you better look at this." He pointed to an eighteen-inch split in one of the blades of the left propeller. He inspected the blade closely and checked the other three blades, which showed no sign of wear or of a potential split.

"We'll have to replace these, Charley. I'll have the new propellers sent out. Do you think its safe to fly with this one tomorrow? I have to carry an observer, and I don't want to cancel if I can help it. Doesn't look good. What do you think?"

Charley responded with his hurt voice. "Doesn't matter what old Charley thinks. You ought to ask that young Furnas fellow, except he's not here working, he's out having a good time."

Shrugging his shoulders, Orville walked over to the workbench, calling over his shoulder, "Stop your complaining. Let's fix this thing and go get something to eat."

He and Charley nailed down the loose piece of the split propeller, and glued cloth over it to strengthen it. Then they had to see to the propeller's balance. It was time-consuming, and Charley had shifted over to complaining about never getting fed before they had finished.

There was no flying the next day, and, when a bit of bad weather came in, Orville decided to take the time to overhaul their engine, even if it meant stopping flying for a few days. To his indignant surprise, their work was interrupted by a visitor: a smiling, if sheepishly hesitant, Glenn Curtiss.

"Mr. Wright, I just came by to wish you luck in your trials. I'm sure you will be successful."

Orville straightened up, carefully wiping his hands on a cloth and checking them before reaching out to quickly shake Curtiss's extended hand.

"Thank you, and congratulations to you and to Captain Baldwin. You've sold the United States Army its first dirigible! I hope you sell many more." *Actually*, Orville thought, *I hope you concentrate on dirigibles and stop infringing on our patent.*

"I see you are overhauling your engine." Curtiss went on to explain how they had been penalized for not achieving the specified twenty-mile-per-hour speed. "I hate to say it, but my engine was at fault. Nothing I could do seemed to get it running right. What do you think makes your engine run so smooth?"

Orville didn't believe what he had heard. Here was his archrival, his patent-infringer, the big engine builder, coming to him on advice for a smooth-running engine.

"Well, as you know, the engines are two different types; I think your lightweight V-4 is good for airships, but our in-line four has a big flywheel, and I think that helps. It's heavy, probably too heavy for you to use, but it suits us."

"You using any special fuels or oils?"

The man was impossible!

"No, just what the Army furnishes, same as you."

Curtiss made some more small talk and left, leaving Orville fuming.

In the following days, Orville made some spectacular flights, including a new record of over seventy minutes, delighting the Army contingent. He embellished this flight with two tight figure eights over the parade ground, then took care to set a record with the most important man on the Army board of review, Major Squier, flying him for nine minutes and six and one-third seconds. He could see that Squier was visibly impressed, especially when Orville landed so smoothly it was difficult to tell when they touched down, and, at the end of their sliding, stopped almost next to the takeoff derrick. When the engine was shut down, Squier pulled the cotton stuffing out of his ear and asked, "Did you grease the skids that time, Mr. Wright? Seemed like we slid in slicker than a pool ball on a table."

In his room at the Cosmos that night, Orville was thinking about how he would tell Wilbur about his "grease job" when there was a knock on the door. A messenger was there, with a letter from Wilbur marked "For Orville Wright's eyes only." He opened it, expecting to find some technical advice, for Wilbur was a master of giving technical advice from a distance. Instead, he read:

Dear Orv,

Please, please destroy this letter as soon as you have read it. You'll see why, but Pop must never see it, nor must you ever discuss it with him.

Orv, I've broken free of him. At last, here I am, forty-one years old, and I'm finally free of Pop! I'm going to come home, and as you talked about one time, I'm getting my own home and I'm going to lead my own life. There is too much to tell you now, but I want you to know I'm going to get you free too!

This doesn't mean I don't love him, you know I do, and I know you do too. But we've got to get away, we have proved ourselves in this world, and the next, too, maybe, but we've got to stop being Bishop Wright's boys, and we've got to stop now.

Don't tell anyone about this, it would sound crazy. Don't even tell Katharine, and I know you keep nothing from her. I'm going to try to get her loose, too, and I think if you help, we can.

Fly safely, take no chances and remember: we are going to be free.

Affectionately,
Wilbur

Orville read the letter twice more before carefully tearing it into tiny bits, putting it into another envelope, crumpling it and putting it in the wastebasket.

He knew exactly what Wilbur meant about wanting to be free. But he knew there was a price to pay, and he was not sure he was prepared to pay it. That price was the relationship with Katharine. What would happen if the household split up? She would certainly have to stay with Pop. What would she think of him, if he left to live in his own house? And there was no point in moving out to go live with Wilbur! That would be as bad as living with Pop.

A glance at the clock by the side of his bed told him that it was time to go to sleep. Tomorrow was the big day. He had to be ready. And, of course, the Army had selected Lt. Selfridge, all 175 pounds of him, to be the observer.

CHAPTER

60

September 17th was windy, and Orville spent the day mentally preparing for the flight, putting Selfridge out of his mind entirely. It had been five days since he had flown, and he always felt apprehensive when there was a long interval between flights. Twice he sat in the Military Flyer and mentally flew around the parade ground, moving the controls as if he were in flight, making doubly certain that he pushed the elevator control in just the right direction. The little drill bothered him, for he never made a mistake while doing it on the ground because there was nothing to divert his attention. Once airborne there were a thousand things: the direction of the wind, worries about the flocks of starlings, the sound of the engine and propellers, the incessant need to adjust the controls to maintain level flight. With Selfridge on board, Orville would have to indicate what he was doing, show him how the turns were made, point out any hazards, make sure Selfridge did not touch any of the controls.

He was concerned about the propellers. The two new propellers had arrived yesterday and were already installed. They were nine feet long, six inches longer than those they had always used. He and Wilbur had argued long and hard about the installation of what Will always called the "big screws." Wilbur had always advised against their use, worried about their strength, but Orville was convinced that the "big screws" generated more thrust, and he would need thrust today.

They climbed aboard the aircraft at five o'clock P.M., Selfridge handing his uniform jacket and hat to a friend to hold for him.

Orville thought momentarily about suggesting that he keep the jacket on—it got chilly when the flight went on—then thought, *No, let the big Mr. AEA birdman get cold, it will serve him right.*

Orville signaled, the weight dropped, and the Military Flyer moved swiftly down the track, rising to twenty feet and beginning the first of three circles within the parade ground. Orv kept the Flyer low, no higher than the second story of the redbrick buildings, and Selfridge seemed at ease, but intensely busy, his eyes moving all over the Flyer, watching Orville making control inputs, then trying to check the wings and the tail to see their reactions. Orv smiled to himself. The control inputs he was making were too small and swift; it would be impossible for Selfridge to watch the control lever move then look to catch the movement of the airplane itself.

As they completed the turn on the last circuit, Orv began to climb, heading toward the lines of white crosses that defined the Arlington Cemetery. He leveled out at about one hundred feet, much higher than he usually flew, and began a much wider, less abrupt turn because he could now fly outside the narrow confines of the parade ground. As he turned he heard *tap tap tap* coming from the rear of the Flyer.

Selfridge heard it too and watched closely as Orville turned to check each propeller. Orv had already decided to land, intending to cut the power as soon as the Flyer was pointed toward the parade ground, into the wind.

In the next instant there were two bumps that signaled trouble followed by a violent shaking and a skidding turn to the right. His heart in his mouth, Orville switched off the power and pulled at the controls, but the Flyer turned, now dropping on its left wing and pulling around into a head-on nosedive toward the ground.

Selfridge was staring straight down, and in the silence, broken only by the sound of the wind in the wires, Orville heard him mutter "Oh! Oh!"

Still fighting the controls at about twenty-five feet above the ground, Orville saw the nose start to come up and had a sudden hope they were going to make it—just as they smashed into the ground by the gate in the cemetery wall and both were swallowed by the blackness.

CHAPTER
61

Like a tide surging into a shallow bay, the ring of spectators converged from all points around the parade ground, racing toward the cemetery, the mounted officers leading the way. A cloud of dust that some feared was smoke puffed up briefly from the Flyer. It lay crumpled, its left wings collapsed flat while the right wings were torn, but still intact, pointing slightly upwards as if in mute protest.

Neither Wright nor Selfridge was moving, and the first people to reach the wreckage worked carefully to remove their bodies. The cavalrymen formed a ring around the site to keep spectators back, one excited officer ordering, "Ride them down if they get too close."

The broken wires and fractured spars impeded the rescuers, whose movements caused the shattered Flyer to shift and creak in a menacing death rattle. Both airmen lay facedown as if they had been flung into the earth by a giant hand, then held there by the flattened wings. The engine had torn loose from the structure and was lying on the wing that pressed on the back of Selfridge's head. Extricating the two men from the wreck was difficult because each time one section was moved to free them, the swaying wires pulled another section down.

They reached Orville first, pulling him out as gently as they could. The awkward flop of his leg told them that bones were broken. Without a word, a dozen hands reached out at once to hold him steady, trying to keep him immobile until they could lay him upon the grass to wait for the ambulances that had been summoned. A heavyset doctor had been watching the flight from his carriage at the road on the side of the parade ground. When the plane crashed he had run with his medical bag across the field to the crash site. Panting heavily, he had to shove the frantic Charley Taylor aside before he could begin attending to Orville.

The other rescuers were working hard to get to Selfridge, still pinned under the wreckage. They finally manhandled the Flyer up and away long enough for him to be pulled out, torn and bleeding. When he was clear, the Flyer was released, dropping a few feet with another crash of snapping wood and wires.

Both men were unconscious, and the three Army doctors already on the scene realized that Selfridge must have suffered a massive skull fracture. They quickly agreed that both men were far too seriously injured to be carried in the rough-riding horse-drawn ambulances that had just arrived. Instead, stretchers were brought, and the two victims were carried as gently as possible to the Fort Myer hospital, with many people assisting in relays.

Sobbing, Charley Taylor watched them leave, partially reassured by the doctor's promise that Orville had not suffered fatal injuries. When the stretcher-bearers were at last out of sight, he began the process of putting the sad remains of the Military Flyer on an Army wagon to be transported back to the balloon shed. He was already planning how to crate it to avoid damaging it any further. Charley knew that the first thing Orville would wish to do when he recovered would be to examine the wreckage and try to learn what had turned an ordinary flight into a disaster.

The usually quiet tan halls of the Fort Myer hospital were pulsating with people, all bathed in the flickering yellow of the newly installed electric lights. The military police had tried to screen visitors, but the halls had filled right up to the doors of the operating room with newspaper people, senior officers, and several congressmen who were giving lengthy statements to the reporters. A hush fell over them when the operating room doors were opened and a gurney was wheeled out, a green sheet pulled over the body. A slender captain, looking deeply depressed, rapped on the wall to get their attention and said only, "Lieutenant Selfridge expired at 8:10 P.M. without regaining consciousness. His principal injury was a fractured skull." No one present took note that Selfridge was the first man ever to die in the crash of a manned heavier-than-air craft.

Some reporters bolted out the door to file their reports, but others waited for the bigger story: the fate of Orville Wright.

Within twenty minutes, the slender captain returned again, this time to announce, "Mr. Wright's injuries are serious, but he is expected to live. He is in a stable condition, and no further reports will be made until tomorrow morning." There was a general run for the door by the reporters, and the rest of the crowd began to file out at a leisurely pace, still buzzing with excited conversations.

The examination of Orville's injuries showed that he had suffered a broken left thigh, several broken ribs, and numerous lacerations. He was in shock, occasionally mumbling unintelligible words. Several hours later, when Orville finally recovered consciousness, his first question was about Selfridge. Told that he was dead, Orville gave an agonized sigh, saying only, "The poor lad, the poor lad."

In Dayton, Katharine was momentarily stunned by the news, then packed quickly, taking the first train to Washington to care for Orville. When she arrived he was still drifting in and out of consciousness but seemed to sense that she was there. Katharine stayed at his side, night and day, and would do so for weeks to come. Neither she nor Orville knew it, but the accident became the defining moment in their lives, one that would move them ever farther from Wilbur and from Bishop Wright. For his part, the good bishop, in Indiana on family business, took the news of the crash stoically, as if he had expected it. The emotionless notation in his dairy was very brief, saying only, "Orville injured. Orville's disaster at 5; Selfridge's death."

CHAPTER
62

The news arrived in France at eight o'clock the following morning. Wilbur Wright was preparing his Flyer for an attempt at the coveted Michelin prize, which promised twenty thousand francs for the longest duration flight made in 1908. He was interrupted by an obviously troubled Berg handing him the telegram with news of Orville's accident and Selfridge's death. Wilbur immediately cancelled all plans for flying for the next week, and began blaming himself for the crash, believing that he should have insisted on returning to be with Orville at the Army trials. He had been too greedy, trying to satisfy the French contract at the same time.

His mind, ordinarily so orderly, was an endless whirl as he rode his bicycle back the poplar-lined road to Le Mans to wait for further word. As he pedaled, a painful series of thoughts revolved and replayed in his head. First he agonized over Orville's injuries, hoping that no infection would set in. Orville was not strong. Typhoid fever had almost killed him and blood poisoning would carry him off for sure. Then he felt sorry for Selfridge, all thoughts of their rivalry gone. This led to the thoughts he and Orville had always banned—just how dangerous flying really was. It was something he had always known, but could no longer ignore. The crash underlined this clearly. He knew he was vulnerable, too, but less so than Orville, for he was always more careful. He had crashed a few times himself, but this was Orville's fifth serious crash, not counting several more where he had broken a skid or a wingtip. The next stop on his circle of thoughts was a return to his deep sense of guilt for allowing Orville to go to Fort Myer alone. Wilbur felt that if he had been there, the accident would not have happened. Yet as the miles passed, he found another, totally unworthy worry ranging through the back of his mind. It disgusted him to be so petty at such a serious time, but he could not escape asking himself, "Has Orville received my letter about being free from Pop? And if so, has he destroyed it?"

CHAPTER
63

Back in the United States, Octave Chanute, who had always had bad luck when he came to see the Wrights fly, remained in Washington to help Katharine. His first action was to ask for an extension of the contract from the Army. General Allen believed that Orville had already proved the Wrights' claims for their Flyer and was more than willing to give them a nine-month extension of time in which to formally complete their contractual requirements.

Before the day was out, Chanute, always the friendly intermediary, suddenly found himself in the midst of a red-hot controversy. Alexander Graham Bell, John McCurdy, and Casey Baldwin had arrived at Fort Myer to serve as Selfridge's pallbearers. On their way to the cemetery chapel where Selfridge's body had been taken to await burial, Bell turned to the two younger men and said, "We ought to drop in and pay a courtesy call on Mr. Wright."

Baldwin, who felt Selfridge's loss more than anyone, except perhaps Mabel Bell, asked, "Don't you think it will seem a little strange if we all go? Perhaps you should go, but not John and me."

"Nonsense; we'll all go."

In the end it did not matter, for the physician attending Orville had already ruled no visitors, and they were turned away. On the walk to Arlington Cemetery, they found that their route took them past the balloon shed where Charley Taylor had brought the mangled remains of the Flyer and had almost finished crating the Flyer for shipment. They glanced in past Sergeant William Downey, on guard at the door, and saw that the top of one of the crates was open.

Alexander Graham Bell's name worked magic, and Sergeant Downey proudly led them inside.

Glancing at the jumbled remains, McCurdy said, "It's a wonder Mr. Wright wasn't killed, too."

Baldwin said, "The wing looks broader than I thought it was; I thought it was perhaps five feet wide."

Without a word, Bell pulled out the tape measure that, with a pocketknife and a notebook, was his constant companion. He inserted it in the case, measured the wing's width, and said, "Six feet, six inches."

Charley Taylor arrived moments later and closely questioned the sergeant; when he found out that Bell had actually made a measurement, he went directly to Katharine, who exploded at the utter treachery of spying on an injured man's flying machine. Chanute, ironically, had lunched with Bell and his colleagues, but when he returned to the hospital, Katharine charged him to investigate what she called "this tasteless crime." He did, somewhat gingerly, not wishing to offend Bell but more afraid to cross Katharine. In time he reported to her that it was probably just an innocent event; Bell only measured the width of the wing, and those dimensions were public knowledge. Katharine would never be sure what they measured, but she would always be sure she could not trust Bell and the AEA—and she was not too sure about Chanute.

On October 12th, Augustus Herring introduced the only light note into the tragedy of the Fort Myer competition when he appeared with an assistant, two suitcases and, delivered separately, a large trunk. Claiming that these constituted a "technical delivery" of his aircraft, Herring gave a brilliant demonstration of optimistic salesmanship. Playing mostly to the reporters, his mellifluous Southern accent conveyed the image of a sincere, good-humored man who was totally honest. He wove his talk into a believable piece with his hands and his movements, striding about as a magician might do, inserting the slightest bit of self-deprecatory humor at exactly the right times. As he talked, he took from his assorted baggage what he said were parts of the two engines he planned to use. They appeared to be five-cylinder radials, not unlike the famous Manly engine used on the Langley Aerodrome, and he claimed twenty-two horsepower for each of them. Then he produced what he claimed to be the key element of his flying machine, the center section, and showed how he would operate the controls. His flying machine could be expanded easily in size just by lengthening its wings, he claimed, attaching them to this center section, and with the largest wings could carry up to sixteen people.

The Aeronautic Board, still stunned by the loss of Selfridge, one of their members and a good friend of every man on the board, did not attempt to counter his arguments, for it was easier just to allow him the requested time. Some of the press had a field day, calling him "the new pocket-size Langley," while others said that it would be safest for all concerned if he just kept his flying machine in the suitcase. But some took him seriously. The prestigious *Harper's Weekly* printed a three-page story that ranked him as an equal to the Wright brothers. That story would provide an impeccable reference for him in several future business deals—including a vital one with Curtiss.

When Katharine heard the story of Herring's "technical delivery," she relayed it to Orville, who laughed for the first time since September 17th.

CHAPTER
64

When the news had first arrived about Orville's accident, Wilbur told Berg that he was going to return immediately to the United States.

"Wilbur, please, you cannot do that. If you do, everything we've done so far will collapse. We don't have investors yet, you know that."

When Wilbur hesitated, Berg went on.

"The best way for you to help Orville is to win every prize being offered; you could scoop up ten thousand dollars in prizes by the end of the year, and twice that if you would try the Channel flight."

Lord Northcliffe had already contacted Berg, telling him that the formal prize for a cross-Channel flight would be announced as one thousand pounds, but that he would give Wilbur another thousand to make the attempt.

"I don't think so, Hart. We've only got the one Flyer over here. After Orville's accident, another crash would just about ruin us, and I don't fancy coming down in the Channel with a bad engine."

Berg had not pressed the issue, and Wilbur, buoyed by news from Katharine that Orville was going to recover, and uplifted by his own reinforced sense of independence, launched an aerial assault on records and prizes. In the next ninety days he set eight world records.

Four days after Orville's accident, Wilbur Wright had shattered the existing world records for both distance and duration, flying for an hour and thirty-one minutes and pocketing a five thousand–franc prize from Aéro Club de France. As he considered the prize, Wilbur realized how far he had come in the world; the single prize of roughly one thousand dollars was equivalent to all of the money he and Orville had invested in their four years at Kitty Hawk. Now, the five thousand francs was what he had heard Hart Berg describe as "walking-around money," just a minor infusion of funds for day-to-day expenses. He never thought he'd think about a thousand dollars like that, nor that it would give him so much pleasure to do so.

As demanding as the flying was, Wilbur drew strength from it. Any ordinary flight required tremendous concentration, but record attempts were even more difficult. There was no time to consider anything but the continuous control inputs needed to keep the flight as smooth as possible, which increased efficiency, and made for higher speeds, loftier altitudes and improved range. When he came down from a flight, he was usually tired, but within moments, he would get a new boost of energy from the consciousness that he was doing what no one had done before—and no one else could do.

But the continual setting of records was the least of Wilbur's attractions for the people of France, who now found him accommodating, smiling, willing to take passengers for quick and dazzling rides. Where once described as "tall, lean, and vulpine"—he had to turn to a dictionary for that one, and was not flattered by what he found—he now was described as "tall, athletic, and aristocratically handsome." He didn't have to look that up and he liked it a lot better.

Berg was delighted that Wilbur was more than happy to meet the wealthy financiers and members of royalty who were making pilgrimages to what had now become a social triumph, a meeting with the great "Veelbur Vreet." Far from being the monosyllabic recluse of the past, Wilbur made every effort to extend himself, even inviting Mrs. Hart Berg to become the first woman to fly in a heavier-than-air machine. Nervous at first, she enjoyed the flight and inadvertently sent a fever racing through the fashion industry. For modesty's sake, her voluminous skirts had been held tight by a rope around the calf, and voila, the "hobble-skirt" was born, and soon no woman of fashion could be seen without one.

Wherever he went, awards, medals and honors showered down on him like rain from heaven, and he was always careful to insist that Orville be included in any citations. At one dinner, where he had been faithfully promised that he would not have to speak, the master of ceremonies used the term "birdman" to praise him, then called him forth to the lectern to "say a few words." When he got there, Wilbur smiled and said only, "I know of only one bird, the parrot, that talks, and he can't fly very high." The chance remark brought down the house and was instantly repeated all over France. It pleased Wilbur to think of it—he did not often come up with exactly the right remark at the right time.

Yet Wilbur did not let his new exuberance get in the way of the serious business of flying. He prepared his record flights with care, being certain, whenever possible, that potential investors were on hand. In doing so he completely changed Hart Berg's working style. For months Berg had hammered at would-be investors, dangling every sort of plum, only to have them back out at the last minute. Now people were scrambling to invest, and his task was to select the most financially worthy of them to "let in on the ground floor." The first of a series of European Wright companies was formed, the *Compagnie Générale de Navigation Aérienne*. Just as the Wrights wished, the new company did not plan to manufacture Flyers itself, but would license their production. The immediate return was gratifying; about $50,000, plus stock and a royalty. Wilbur knew the news would bring a smile to Orville's lips, for it certainly did to his.

By December there was only one more prize worth taking, the Michelin prize that Wilbur had been preparing for when he had received word of Orville's crash.

"What do we need to do to win the Michelin cup?"

Hart responded, "You don't have to do anything. Your September 21st flight was an hour and thirty-one minutes. The best Farman has done is a little more than forty-four minutes. The cup goes to the person with the longest flight of the year."

"I don't know, Hart, I don't like it. The French are coming along awfully fast. I'm afraid Farman will come back and steal the record from me between now and December 31st."

"Don't worry about that so much; what we have to worry about is Farman and Blériot building and selling flying machines in Europe. The French love them because they are Frenchmen. Thank God we got our company going. I don't think we could have done it next year."

"Well, I'm going for two hours. I know Farman can't fly two hours without landing, his engine won't take it."

It was bitter cold on December 30th when he made his first attempt. Hart had tried to dissuade him, pointing out that it was well below freezing, and it would be colder still in the air, flying close to forty miles an hour. Wilbur laughed and took off, flying in the frostbiting cold for an hour and fifty-three minutes before he landed, out of fuel.

"Wilbur, that's plenty. Farman isn't even making an attempt for all we know."

"No, I said two hours and I meant it. I don't care about Farman. I just want to end 1908 with a record no one will beat for awhile."

December 31st dawned cold with snow in the air; it warmed enough to change to a freezing mist, and Wilbur had droned around the triangular course for forty-three minutes when a fuel line burst, spraying him with gasoline and forcing him to land. Hart tried again to talk him into quitting—he had won the Michelin Cup, the 20,000 francs were his already, it was foolish to fly in this weather.

"Come on Wilbur, you'll get pneumonia. Worse, I'll get pneumonia unless you quit."

Late in the afternoon he flew the course for two hours, eighteen minutes, and thirty-three seconds. He landed when the tank was almost dry, his fingers almost frozen, and his spirits better than they had been since Orville's crash.

CHAPTER

65

Everyone in the Aerial Experiment Association had been aware that flying machines were inherently dangerous, and never more so when untrained pilots were sent up in untried machines. Bell had seen his own kites put people in danger, including the poor Selfridge, whose death at Fort Myer had sapped the spirit of the organization.

Mabel Bell kept saying, "The irony of it, the irony of it! He always said he would live forever. And then, to die in a Wright machine. He had such a brilliant future."

Alec was not much in the comforting line; a few pats on the hand and he was back with his notebooks, always thinking about the next experiment. And although there could be no bright spot in the tragedy, he did feel some relief that Selfridge had died in the Wright machine rather than in one of his tetrahedral kites. That would have been truly unbearable.

There was another factor in the decline of morale at *Beinn Breagh*. Bell's cherished tetrahedral kites had courteously but unmistakably been rejected by his young associates as an avenue to flight. They were intent on developing Aerodrome No. 4, the *Silver Wing*. As a result, Bell and Curtiss, while remaining nominally friendly, had finally reached a breaking point. In private conversations with Captain Tom Baldwin, Curtiss complained that while Bell was no doubt a genius, he was immensely impractical and "the poorest man with tools that I have ever seen."

Baldwin stoked Curtiss's discontent, for he was being privately courted by Augustus Herring, who was dangling the prospect of a huge Herring-Curtiss company in front of him, one with a Baldwin Airship Division.

"Glenn, you really have a lot of respect for Herring, don't you?"

Curtiss nodded. "Did you see the article in *Harper's Weekly?* That's the Herring I know. The man is an aeronautical genius, and his patents on gyroscopically controlled aircraft are the way to beat the Wright brothers."

Baldwin's strong suit was not subtlety. He was used to pressing to get his way and he did so now. "Tell me directly. Can you get out from under the AEA? Will Bell let you go?"

"That shouldn't be a problem. I don't want to offend him, but I can't work with them anymore. I'm not used to committees, and the Aerodromes even look like a committee's work. I never did like the way the wings droop toward each other, one curving up, one curving down. Didn't make any sense, whatever good one wing did was cancelled out by the other, and it was hard to build. I'm going to build my own flying machine, one that doesn't have anything to do with the AEA."

"What about the patents Bell is taking out on the *June Bug?*"

Curtiss shuffled the papers around on his desk and came up with an envelope. "This is what Bell sent me; it's his patent application on behalf of the AEA. It's comprehensive. But I've got some ideas on how we can beat it. There's more than one way to skin a cat, the same as with the Wrights. But even if we have to pay them a license fee, I'm going to do it."

"If you break with him, will he give you a license? I don't know what kind of man he is. Do you know him well enough to take a chance on setting up your own company?"

Curtiss sensed that Baldwin had his own agenda. It was all right; he had been unhappy with the AEA all along, and Curtiss was sure that he wanted in on any future plans. "It won't be him who will decide, it will be Mabel and the lawyers. He'll be too involved in the engineering side to worry about patents and lawsuits. But it doesn't matter. I'm going on my own, no matter what. It will be a long time before the patents will be issued, and it would take more time to have them, or the Wrights, sue about the patents. By then I'll be established, and able to fight them."

Baldwin noticed that Curtiss said, "I'll be established," not "We'll be established." It angered and worried him. He was going to have to promote Herring's idea. He would be better off as a part of Herring-Curtiss than just being a customer to Curtiss alone.

A week later, Baldwin met with Herring in Washington. Albert Blohm joined them, wearing two hats. He was a technical adviser, and he had the interest of a Wall Street financier, Courtland Bishop, who was interested in flying. Blohm had sold him a two-surface Chanute glider the year before and taught him to fly it. They had established a strong friendship, and he found that Bishop also believed in Herring's genius. Besides being well connected with a Wall Street firm, Bishop had his own funds, and had told Blohm that he would help Herring if he began a manufacturing firm for flying machines.

Baldwin was surprised and disconcerted to see Blohm.

"Albert, I'll be blunt. You are supposed to go to work for Glenn Curtiss when you finish your job at the Smithsonian. I know that for a fact, Glenn has told me so. I'm surprised to find you here."

Herring spoke. "Albert and I go back many years, Captain Baldwin." Blohm thought, *Yes, we go back to a time when you had to call me Mr. Blohm.* Things had changed.

Blohm spoke up. "I still intend to work for Glenn, if he'll have me. But Augustus has told me of your tentative plans, and it just happens that I know someone who will help finance a Herring-Curtiss company, if I recommend it."

Somewhat reluctantly, Baldwin asked, "What is your deal, Mr. Herring? What do you have to offer Glenn? He's already got a big factory going—he told me he made more than one hundred twenty thousand dollars profit last year on motorcycles. He can get financing, I know."

Herring started to speak, but Blohm interrupted. "I'm sure he can. But on what terms? Many people will think that he'll have to pay the Wrights a royalty on every flying machine he sells. That means lower profits, and who knows what the Wrights will want to charge? But I've been assured that with the Herring patents to protect us from the Wrights, we can get excellent financing. You may have heard of my colleague, Courtland Bishop. The question before us is how do we approach Glenn?"

Baldwin thought it over. Bishop was well known; if he was coming in, then it would be a very solid business deal. "Well, it can't be me. I know Glenn doesn't have a high opinion of my business judgment, and I can't say I blame him. It shouldn't be you, Mr. Blohm, you are going to work for him, so you can't be giving him financial advice. I know he has great respect for you, Mr. Herring. I think you should approach him, and soon."

Blohm spoke up. "The one thing we've got to remember is that we are doing this in Glenn's interest. He'll be much better off with Mr. Herring's patents and adequate financing from Courty Bishop. I don't think the Wrights will be able to compete with a combination like that."

CHAPTER

66

Katharine and Orville had arrived in Paris on January 12th, 1909, Katharine still bubbling over with details of their ocean voyage to whoever would listen.

"Who would ever have believed that Orville and I would ever get to Europe together? And the people on the liner, the *Baltic*, they could not have been nicer. They all knew who Orville was and treated him like a king."

Wilbur nodded, smiling, delighted to have them in France, but shaken by Orville's hesitant walk. His brother moved slowly, in evident pain, using two canes, watching the sidewalk or floor very carefully to be sure he did not misstep. Katharine clung to his arm, supporting him, but her eyes darted everywhere, taking in the taxis, the kiosks, the people passing on the street, caught up in the sheer joy of being in France.

Madame Berg was on hand at the Ritz to greet them, and she easily persuaded Katharine to go shopping with her. As soon as the door closed behind them, Wilbur and Orville fell into an intense discussion of the accident.

"Tell me again what it was, Orv."

"Well, it's pretty much like I told you in the letter. The longer propeller was not strong enough; it flattened out a little from the centrifugal force, and when it did, it moved just far enough to tear a stay wire loose on the rudder."

He took a piece of paper and made a quick sketch, although Wilbur knew very well exactly which wire he meant.

"Then the rudder fell on its side, and that threw the airplane into a nosedive—it was acting like the forward rudder does, only in reverse. I was tugging on the front rudder control and nothing was happening, but when I started moving the rudder controls, the nose started up."

Orville was ashamed of the accident, but proud of his flying. If he hadn't, in just a split second, interpreted what the rudder was doing, and moved the controls to raise it, he'd have died with Selfridge. He kept his eyes fixed on the table, waiting to hear Wilbur's opinion.

"Well, we can fix the propeller, and we can route the stay wires a little further away from the arc of rotation. I think it was a one-in-a-million chance accident."

Relief flooded through Orville. Wilbur was accepting his analysis. He'd expected a long and contentious argument.

"The only thing that saved me was that the nose started coming up. If it hadn't, I'd be six feet under back in Dayton."

They were silent for a while, both conscious of how Orville's survival was also a one-in-a-million chance. Then Wilbur asked, "And what do you think of our dear friend from Chicago?"

Orville sighed. "It's so strange. No one could have been nicer to me at Fort Myer. Mr. Chanute personally got the extension on the contract from General Allen. He did everything he could for Katharine, of course. But he still doesn't understand what we've done."

"Here, look at this. It is an article by Paul Renard, based on a letter from Chanute. Berg had it translated and typed up for me."

Orville read through the two pages quickly, then slammed his hand on the table.

"This is outrageous. He tears apart every claim of our patent and then, get this—" he read aloud, " 'But the Wrights' most important merit lies in their application of a motor to a glider.' "

Orville laid the letter down. "How many times have we told him that the engine was the least important element? And how many times have we explained the controls to him?"

"Too many. But you have to remember that his name is on that absurd patent of Mouillard's and he has never agreed that our system is different. I don't think he is senile; he is just being consistent."

"You're more forgiving than I am. I think he's thinking about lawsuits down the line. Letters like this could destroy our patent claims in court. I think we ought to have a showdown with him, once and for all."

"Orville, you've gotten feisty since you had your accident."

There was another silence, and Wilbur could wait no longer. "Did you get the letter I sent to you at the Cosmos Club? The one about breaking away from Pop's control?"

"Yes, and I destroyed it, too, just like you asked."

It was Wilbur's turn to sigh with relief. "Well, what do you think?"

"I think that things change. I'm glad you feel you've broken away and the good Lord knows I've wanted to. But things changed with me on September 17th. The only thing I want to do now is get back into the Flyer at Fort Myer and sell it to the Army. If I can do that, believe me, I'll break free and I'll never have to leave Hawthorne Street to do it. Pop's not my problem, not anymore. My problem is getting back in the Flyer and doing everything the Army wants done. When I hear them say 'Sold,' I'm going to be free of all my worries. Including Pop!"

There was silence for a third time. Wilbur understood exactly what Orville was saying, perhaps better than he did himself. The crash at Fort Myer came when Orville was establishing himself, setting a new record on practically every flight, breaking even the ones Wilbur had been setting in Europe. He had almost completed the Army requirements to buy the Flyer. Once that was done, they could have started their own factory for manufacturing Flyers in quantity. The crash put all that in jeopardy, and the trials had to be done over.

But if Wilbur saw that Orville's crash had freed him from Pop, changing his focus, he saw also that the same crash threatened his own sense of breaking away. It was not enough that he break away from Pop and leave home—Orville and Katharine also had to be freed. And it did not seem as if either wanted to be. There was more to it than Orville said. He and Katharine were mighty thick, too thick to break away independently. The thought depressed him, and he was glad that he had to leave Paris soon.

The terms of the French contract that Berg had worked out required Wilbur to move his operations south to Pau, near Toulouse, and there teach three French officers to fly. Pau was a beautiful city, all white and pink stucco houses with brick-red tile roofs, but it had fallen on hard times since King Edward had selected Biarritz as his favorite French resort. He had taken the royal clientele with him, and the city fathers were delighted to have the most famous celebrity in France there to teach flying.

They selected a beautiful flying field, six miles from the city, and then spared no expense building an excellent hangar, far nicer than any Wilbur had ever had, complete with living quarters. Katharine and Orville had remained for two days more in Paris, taking in the sights, then came down to live in a fantastic suite at the Metropolitan, the best hotel in Pau, all compliments of the city.

Katharine had become a magic lightning rod for the Wright brothers; when she was present, the press clustered around her, turning her into the princess of aviation. Unlike her brothers, she loved chatting with the reporters, and prepared for interviews so that she would say something quotable. Her natural grace charmed the French, and her ease with everyone from shipping magnates to the king of Spain led them to believe that she must have come from an immensely wealthy family, used to consorting with royalty. She even laughed and made light of the widespread exploitation of the Wright name, as songs, poems, clothes, tools and even food were named after the Wright brothers.

As thoroughly as she was enjoying herself, Katharine also saw, as Orville and Wilbur did not yet see, that there was another French revolution underway, this one in aviation.

"I think you really should try the Channel flight, Wilbur. If you don't, I'm sure that good-looking Latham boy will."

Wilbur shook his head. "He flies an Antoinette, and I don't think he can keep the engine running more than twenty minutes at a time. I'm more worried about our little copycat Blériot. He's adopted wing-warping without a by-your-leave, and he's making longer and longer flights."

Orville chimed in. "And don't forget Farman. He is really forging ahead. Don't tell Berg, but if we don't sew up Germany and Italy on this trip, and maybe England as well, we are going to be out of business here next year."

There was no need to tell Berg; he had been saying the same thing to Wilbur for months. Wilbur went to Italy in March, to do demonstration flights and teach two Italian pilots to fly. The contract netted $10,000, but its real purpose was to pay the way for Berg's syndicate to make a deal in Italy. Orville and Katharine followed along behind, luxuriating in Rome's Hotel Britannia—somewhat more ornately done than 7 Hawthorne Street—and meeting the tiny King Victor Emmanuel III at the airfield at Centocelle. There followed what amounted to a royal progression back to England, where the crowds were more constrained, and it was easier to conduct business.

While they traveled, they never stopped worrying about their French rivals, whose flights were continually headlined, but they were blissfully unaware of the competition Glenn Curtiss was creating in America.

CHAPTER
67

G lenn Curtiss had still not "put her in a brick house" as her father
had promised. Instead they lived in a huge white rambling two-
story house that was beyond anything her father could have dreamed
of. Glenn, except for his monomaniacal devotion to work, had been
an almost perfect husband through all the years of their marriage.
He had taken care of her, sustaining her when the baby was lost,
and understanding that there were to be no more children. In return, Lena had worked hard to be a good wife and business partner,
and felt that she had made some real contributions to the big Curtiss
factory that spewed out motorcycles, engines, and even dirigibles,
of all things. And now Glenn was gambling it all on the word of a
man she had never liked, Augustus Herring.

"I cannot believe you would do this, Glenn! You are putting up
everything we have, our business, the land, the factory, even our
house! And what are you getting in return? A few scraps of paper."

Glenn was patient. She could not be expected to understand high
finance. "Lena, trust me on this. This is a fantastic deal for us. We
are getting money and shares of stock in what will be the greatest
aviation company in the world!"

"How much money and how much stock?"

"We get sixty thousand dollars, half in cash, half in a mortgage.
We get one hundred sixty shares of preferred stock and four hundred shares of common stock. It probably amounts to close to three
hundred thousand dollars, all told."

"And what does Herring get?"

Curtiss was slower to reply in this. "I don't know exactly, it's mostly common stock, maybe two hundred thousand dollars worth."

Her eyebrows, which had been rising, shot up. "How about your patents? And your share of the AEA patents?"

"They are part of the deal."

She was too shocked to speak, then reached over and tapped her finger on the top line of the first paper in the stack. "And why is it called the Herring-Curtiss Company? You are putting up all the assets. What is he contributing, and why does his name come first? You are far better known."

"Not in aeronautical circles, I'm not. Herring is a famous, well-respected man, and he is putting up his patents. Without the patents, we couldn't go into business, we'd just be subcontractors for the Wrights. And he's arranged for the financing. We couldn't have done this without him."

"Who has the most stock? Who has the last say?"

"Well, Herring has the controlling interest, but it had to be that way, for the same reason his name went first. Investors will have more faith in him."

Lena burst into tears. "Glenn, you are blind. The man has hypnotized you. You've got a factory that earned a clear profit of one hundred twenty-five thousand dollars last year. I don't know how much it's worth, but it has to be worth half a million dollars, with all the land, and the equipment, and our house. You are turning this all over to a perfect stranger for a few thousand dollars and a lot of promises. I don't understand why. We are doing fine here; we don't have to make airplanes, and we don't need to be a minority partner in our own business."

Glenn's jaw worked, a sign that he was becoming angry. "Lena, stop it. I've done well in the past, and I'll do well with this. I've had Courtland Bishop look over the finances, and he is investing his own money. And even if you don't like Herring, I do. I've known him for years, and he is the smartest aeronautical engineer I've ever met."

Lena saw the look in Curtiss's face and composed herself. "Let me ask one more question, then I'll shut up. You've already made this deal, there is no sense in my being angry about it. But have you looked at his patents yourself, and are they something that you need?"

Curtiss flushed. "No I haven't, that was Bishop's job, and he looked at them to convince the other investors. But Herring has explained them to me several times, and I know they are what is needed."

"I said I'd shut up, but I have to ask. What is Professor Bell going to say?" Glenn was silent, looking hangdog. He knew how much Lena enjoyed the association with the Bells. They both liked her, and she liked showing them off. Lena was not snobbish, but she had not always been treated well by the Hammondsport "elite." It was an innocent bit of payback, and now he had ruined it.

"He is not happy with me at all. He thinks I've let them down, and I have. But I could not stay with the AEA, it was choking me. They will never do anything much with Tom Selfridge gone. It's time for them to fold up shop. It's a shame, but that's the way it is."

Lena didn't say anymore. Crying softly, she turned away, certain that Glenn was making the biggest mistake of his life—of their lives.

Confident that Lena would come around when she finally understood the magnitude of the new enterprise, Curtiss turned his attention to his latest opportunity. The Aeronautic Society of New York had asked him to build a flying machine for them, for five thousand dollars. It would be the first that he would make entirely on his own, without the constraints of Bell and the AEA.

An utter realist—except when it came to Herring—Curtiss knew that his new machine would look even more like the Wright Flyer than did the AEA Aerodromes. He pinned his hopes on an innovation of his own, placing the ailerons in-between the upper and lower wings. This avoided the problem of twisting the wing surfaces, as the Wrights did, and, he hoped, might possibly be outside their patent.

The new flying machine took shape quickly; it was smaller than the AEA Aerodromes, and covered with white rubberized fabric that had been tinted with yellow ochre. He and his shop superintendent, Henry Kleckler, did most of the work, following through on the ochre motif with the yellow varnish used on all the woodwork, and while the factory name was a proud Curtiss Number One, it was called, inevitably, the *Gold Bug*.

Before the *Gold Bug* was finished, two opportunities loomed on the horizon. The first was another try for the *Scientific American*

Trophy. The second was to compete in what was touted to be the largest aviation event in history, a week-long air show at Rheims, France, in August, 1909. The main event was the Gordon Bennett Trophy, with a five thousand–dollar prize. Curtiss decided to try for both, and immediately set his factory to work building a special aircraft for the race in France.

The rules for the *Scientific American* Trophy had been changed to match the rapid advances in aviation, and now the trophy would be awarded for a flight of twenty-five kilometers. They had added a tough specification: the flying machine would have to land within three hundred yards of the takeoff point.

Curtiss prepared for the attempt on the *Scientific American* Trophy by flying at an Aeronautic Society air show at Morris Park. The flying qualities of the newly named *Golden Flier* (the Aeronautic Society had thought *Gold Bug* too reminiscent of Edgar Allan Poe) were far better than that of the *June Bug* and, he was convinced, of the Wright Flyers as well. The mid-wing ailerons worked perfectly, enabling him to make low, tight turns around pylons just as he used to do on his motorcycle. He felt so comfortable flying the *Golden Flier* that he actually took his hands off the big control wheel to wave at the crowd as he passed.

On July 17th, Curtiss sat upright in the seat of the *Golden Flier*, almost ready to tackle the *Scientific American* Trophy, and thinking how far aviation had come in a single year. The *Golden Flier* was smaller, lighter, and much more powerful than the *June Bug*. He had switched to a four-cylinder, water-cooled engine in the *Golden Flier*, and now the engine would run until the fuel ran out, never over-heating as it always had in the *June Bug*.

It was 5:20 A.M., nearly time to go. He carefully checked the controls, turning the large, automobile-style wheel to the right and left to check the rudder, pushing forward and pulling backward on the same control to move the elevator. The big innovation was the shoulder yoke; if he leaned to the left, the left mid-wing aileron went up and the right mid-wing aileron went down, causing a bank to the left; the reverse was true for the right. Moving all three controls in a single fluid motion was so similar to the banking turns he had made while motorcycle racing that it came easily to him.

Despite the early hour, a crowd of more than three thousand had gathered, the men all in suits, most wearing straw hats, the women in their customary flowing skirts and huge headpieces. Charles Manly was again the official judge, and he had provided his sister with numbered placards to show the number of laps Curtiss had flown.

The *Golden Flier* flew beautifully, with Curtiss keeping low, never getting above thirty feet off the ground, and making sharp turns around the flags that marked the course. Twelve laps would cover twenty-five kilometers, winning the trophy, but Curtiss flew nineteen, covering more than twenty-five miles. At the postflight celebrations Curtiss announced that if anyone exceeded his distance, he would take to the field again to be sure the trophy was his. Then he asked to be excused, saying, "I've got to get busy on the machine that will win the Gordon Bennett Trophy!"

CHAPTER

68

The summer had passed quickly and gloriously for the Wrights, and never more so than in their return from Europe. They managed to avoid a parade in their honor in New York, but were brought to Washington for a meeting with President Taft. Then they had to endure the elaborate Wright Brothers Home Day Celebration that had been a year in preparation and was scheduled for June 17th and 18th. The Wrights had tried to quash the event, claiming that they had to prepare their Flyer for the military trials at Fort Myer, but no one would take no for an answer, from Governor Harmon to the mayor of Dayton.

The Wrights responded to the long, bombastic speeches of the politicians and the heartfelt cheers of the Dayton crowd as they had to the celebrations in Europe, with becoming modesty and a measured style. Bishop Wright made the invocation, but after that sat quietly, obviously proud, waving occasionally to friends, but in general keeping out of the limelight. Their old friend and judge, General Allen, presented the Congressional Medal that had been awarded them, and Governor Harmon gave them the Ohio equivalent.

Through all the festivities, Orville made a point of not speaking publicly; he would smile agreeably and talk to anyone privately, but made no public statements. Wilbur, by now well experienced in public speaking, would make short and often clever speeches in response to the praise being heaped on them. Katharine would deal with the press and public in a one-on-one manner, charming everyone and keeping her brothers protected from all but their oldest friends.

The parade did eat into preparation time; the Flyer had been sent on to Fort Myer, and the day after the big parade, they caught the ten o'clock train to Washington. It was the first chance they had to talk since their return, and Orville wanted to make an immediate point.

"Wilbur, if it's all the same to you, I want to do all the flying at Fort Myer. I feel an obligation to do it, and I know the area already."

He had other arguments mustered, but Wilbur responded, "I think you should. I'll concentrate on keeping everyone away from you, answering the questions, trying to set up discussions for later on business matters, but you focus on the flying. This may not be the most lucrative contract in the world, but it's the most important to us."

Their reception at Fort Myer was like another homecoming parade. It was obvious that General Allen and the Aeronautic Board were glad to see Orville in such apparent good health, and the general atmosphere was more of a coronation than a competition.

It did not last, of course. When wind kept them from flying, disappointing the contingent of congressmen who had gathered to watch their first flights, the Washington papers sniped at them, saying they were ungrateful, undiplomatic, and uncaring. The Army officers, even Orville's favorite, Benny Foulois, became impatient with the constant delays. Some began imputing fear of failure to Orville, and the first flight on June 29th didn't help. The Wrights, with their eternal tinkering, had created yet another new control for the rudder, and he flew only forty seconds on the first hop, unsure about the setup. Things rapidly went from bad to worse, with a hard landing breaking a skid on the second day of the trials, when the engine failed.

The sudden silence startled Orville, who immediately thought of the crash the year before even as he banked the Flyer around for an approach to the field. Too low to have much choice, he landed straight over a thorn tree that snagged his wing and slammed the Flyer into the ground.

He was still sitting there, not hurt, but shaking from the emotion of the near-disaster, when Wilbur arrived. After checking him over, he asked, "Orville, you still want to do all the flying?"

Too upset to speak, Orville nodded his head.

"Well, this one will take a few days to fix. I think you'll have to go back to Dayton, if you are up to it. I need to stay here and talk to the lawyers about protecting our patents."

Orville returned fully recovered five days later, and flew again on July 12th. While outwardly as imperturbable as ever, both the Wrights were beginning to feel the pressure. Their feelings were similar to the summer of 1905, when they were having so much trouble with their Flyer. But now, just as after the crash in 1905, everything seemed to come together, and Orville began to make one record-setting flight after another.

Their efforts kept getting little jolts that spurred them on. On July 26th, they were relegated to the back pages of all the news-papers as the headlines blazed with accounts of Louis Blériot's flight the previous day across the English Channel.

"Well, the picture looks like he used his Model XI for the flight. Berg told me that he had copied our wing-warping exactly."

Orville replied, "Great! Another case for our patent attorney." He stood up, and shouted, "What kind of people are these who would simply steal our ideas, without any apologies? It is no different than using a gun to hold up a bank."

"I'll tell you what kind of people they are. They are like Glenn Curtiss. Look at this."

He tossed over a letter from Curtiss, congratulating Orville on his record-setting flight and talking about his own activities. It was his last paragraph that was the killer, and Orville read it aloud: "In regard to patent matters, I want to suggest that if you contemplate any action that the matter be taken up privately between us to save the possible annoyance and publicity of lawsuits and trial."

For once Orville was speechless—but not for long. "This is too much. The man steals the entire idea of our Flyer, steals our patents, and then says he wants to save the publicity of lawsuits and trials."

Wilbur nodded. "Well, there will be lawsuits, Mr. Curtiss can be sure of that."

It did not help matters when they learned that Curtiss had won the *Scientific American* Trophy for the second time on July 27th. The annoyance was offset by Orville's carefully executed flight with Lieutenant Lahm on the same day, exceeding by twelve minutes the Army's requirement for a one-hour flight with a passenger.

On the 29th, Wilbur and Orville had another one of their in-creasingly rare heart-to-heart talks. It started when Wilbur inquired about Orville's health, and his plans for "the big flight" the next day, when he was scheduled to carry Benny Foulois on a ten-mile round-trip across country to Alexandria.

"I'm ready, believe me Wilbur, I'm ready."

"And how are you feeling inside?"

"You mean about breaking free? Well, it's not like you and Pop. I can tell by the way you act when you're with him that you are free of him. He knows it. He doesn't like it but he knows it. He's eighty-one now, and I think he'll be content just having me and Katharine to run, and maybe running Roosh and Lorin a little bit when they come around. But I think you are home free."

"Doesn't it bother you that he's going to go on dominating you, hanging over the house like a blanket?"

"Ah, I'm used to it, Wilbur. My life changed back here at Fort Myer last year when I crashed. I've told you that, and it just put things in perspective for me."

Orville was quiet for a while, seeing that Wilbur did not understand, or if he understood, didn't approve. The real problem was that the change in his life changed things with Wilbur, too. They had been like one for so long, and now it was becoming clear that when Orville thought or spoke about breaking loose, becoming free, he wasn't just talking about the feeling of guilt from the crash. He also meant getting free from Wilbur, something that his brother had never contemplated, something he could never understand.

There was no loss of affection or concern. Orville knew that he would gladly lay down his life for his brother. It was just that life was moving on for him, away from Wilbur, away from flying machines for that matter. He knew that there was no way to say what he felt in a way that would not devastate Wilbur, and he didn't try. His brother would learn over time, there was no need to have a confrontation, particularly now, immediately before the last big flight of the Army trials.

"As for me, if I make that flight tomorrow, and the Army buys the Flyer, I'll be free, too, just like you, not from Dad but from the curse of having crashed with Selfridge on board. That was hard on me, Wilbur, not just getting hurt, but having that man's life on my conscience. I know it couldn't be helped, but it's been gnawing at me."

Both men were silent. They had functioned almost as one since those first experiments in 1900. For almost ten years now they had been so close that they could work for hours without a word, then spend hours arguing furiously.

Wilbur's face was white, his hands shaking.

"There's more to it than that, Orv. What's happened to us? We used to be closer than twins, closer than Siamese twins, and all that's going away, we're changing. Maybe my getting free of Pop wasn't a good idea after all. Maybe we were destined to let him run us till he died."

A sense of relief flooded Orville. Wilbur was seeing it, he was getting it. Maybe this would be easier on both of them than he thought it could be.

"Well, we were like that because we had to be to figure out how to make a flying machine. We never could have done it if we hadn't been. That's why no one could do it until we showed them how. It took that."

He fumbled for a word and Wilbur supplied it.

"Communion. We had a communion, Orv, and you're right, it was solving the problem of flight. Now it's different. And you've moved away. You are so close to Katharine that you don't need me, you don't have the time for me anymore. And that's fine."

It wasn't fine and they both knew it, but there was nothing they could do about it.

It was raining lightly on the morning of the "big flight," but the crowds slowly gathered, and by the middle of the afternoon, almost eight thousand people packed the parade ground.

Orville had asked for and received Benny Foulois as his observer for the flight. They had established a good relationship from the day Foulois came in their shed at Fort Myer, carrying a wadded-up ball of cotton waste and wearing coveralls that had every pocket filled with screwdrivers, wrenches, and pliers. He was there to work and they took him at his word.

As they worked, Foulois asked good sharp questions that showed the depth of his interest. He wasn't just interested in learning to fly, he wanted to know why the machine flew and what every bit of equipment was for.

Because of his experience in mapmaking, Foulois had been selected by Major Squier to lay out the course for the speed test. The Wrights liked the businesslike way he went about it. The ten-mile course would run south, parallel to the Potomac River, from Fort Myer to Shooter's Hill in Alexandria, Virginia. Shooter's Hill was a one-hundred-foot rise in local elevation where the cornerstone for the George Washington Masonic Memorial had recently been laid.

Foulois sent two officers, Major Charles Salzman and Navy Lieutenant George C. Sweet, to Shooter's Hill to act as official observers. He arranged for a temporary field telephone and a telegraph line to be made available for them. They took the liberty of setting up their equipment right on the Masonic cornerstone, causing a minor disturbance with Masonic officials a few days later when they found out about the "desecration."

Foulois asked that two balloons be used for the trials, one to be flown at the halfway point, and one at Shooter's Hill. The two officers were to signal the exact time that the Flyer passed over the start point at Fort Myer, then record the exact time of its arrival over Shooter's Hill.

They had talked with Foulois about the previous year's accident with Lt. Selfridge, and Orville showed Foulois the changes that had been made to the propeller and the rigging, assuring him that it wouldn't happen again. Foulois was not worried; he had faced much more dangerous situations fighting in the Philippines, and he had confidence in Orville.

"Benny, this should be a perfectly routine flight, but if there are any problems, I'll pick out a field and land in it. If there are no fields, I'll pick a clump of trees and land in the top of them."

Foulois did not say anything, but he knew that on the route he had chosen there were few fields and lots of trees. Nodding, he climbed through the rigging into his seat at Orville's left, a walking instrument panel, with an aneroid barometer on one thigh, a compass on the other, two stopwatches on a chain around his neck. An Army map of Virginia, one that he had personally updated from a Civil War original, completed his ensemble.

Foulois grabbed the edge of his seat with both hands as Orville used the foot pedal to bring the engine up to full speed, then released the wire holding the Flyer on its track. It shot forward, gathering speed, then began a climb to 125 feet, far higher than Orville typically flew.

Always conservative, Orville made two circles of the field before coming down its center, speed built up, to pass over Wilbur, standing with a stopwatch and a signal flag. As they passed over, he waved the flag, and punched his stopwatch; in the Flyer, Foulois started his own watches running.

The flight went smoothly, despite a little turbulence that made Foulois uneasy. Orville was continually occupied with small control corrections, but in the back of his mind, in the recesses where he kept his thoughts of Katharine, there began a delicious interplay of sensations. He was proving to the world, again, that the Wrights had conquered the air, and he was proving to Katharine, and his father and even Wilbur, that he was more than capable, he was formidable. It was an intoxicating sensation—he'd never felt it before, not even at Kitty Hawk on his first flight, not ever. He turned and smiled at Foulois, and Foulois jumped—Orville had never smiled at him before.

They turned sharply around the balloon at Shooter's Hill while crowds of spectators waved from below. On the way back Orville quickly tapped Foulois on the arm and pointed up, Foulois jumping a little, then smiling with relief. With a little back pressure the Flyer began to climb until Orville leveled off. Foulois checked his barometer and held up four fingers—they were at four hundred feet, a new altitude record. Below their vision expanded, they could see west to the Shenandoahs and east to a glistening body of water that Orville could not identify.

Orville traded altitude for speed as they neared Fort Myer, letting the Flyer accelerate as they descended, to flash across the parade ground finishing point at more than fifty miles per hour. As they passed the starting tower, Foulois clicked his stopwatch for the last time, grinning as he nodded his head enthusiastically to Orville. They landed easily in a cloud of dust, and the U.S. Army had just purchased the world's first military airplane.

The crowd, sensitive for once, held back, letting Wilbur reach the Flyer first. Scarcely recognizable with the huge grin on his face, he shook hands with Foulois briefly, then grabbed Orville's outstretched hand and yelled "Orville, you are free!!! We are free!!!"

Foulois wasn't sure what it meant, but it obviously touched both the brothers, who held their handshake for a long time before breaking loose to accept the congratulations of the crowd. As they did, he noticed something very different. Instead of moving in lockstep, arms almost linked as they had always done before, they allowed the crowd to separate them, each one holding court separately with admirers and reporters. Then he saw Katharine, face flushed with pleasure and pride, emerge from the pressing throng to be at Orville's side.

AFTERWORD

O rville had averaged 42.583 miles per hour on his qualifying flight, earning a bonus of $5,000. Benny Foulois would eventually have the Wright Military Flyer sent to him in San Antonio, where he taught himself to fly, corresponding with the Wrights. He later rose to be chief of the Army Air Corps.

Orville and Wilbur had much to attend to, for their contract also involved teaching three Army officers to fly. Over the next two years they did well financially, from prizes and the founding of the American Wright Company in November 1909.

Wilbur found that while he was free from the pressure of his father's oversight, he was now captive to the pursuit of the patent suits they instituted against Glenn Curtiss and foreign aviators and manufacturers. Wilbur would become as obsessed with patent fights as he had been with the creation of the flying machine, but there was a great difference. In his monomaniacal pursuit of a flying machine, his efforts were rewarded, step by step, with success. Even though almost all the judicial decisions were favorable to the Wrights' cause in the patent fights, there were no immediate material rewards, nor did there seem to be any likely future material rewards from them. When Wilbur died of typhoid fever in 1912, it was seen by some of his intimates as almost a blessed relief to him.

Orville lived with his father and sister Katharine until 1913, when they moved into a comfortable mansion, Hawthorne Hill. Designed by Orville himself, it featured many mechanical innovations in the plumbing and heating systems that symbolized Orville's change in interests. He continued to participate in aviation, but only in a peripheral way, lending his name to causes he thought worthwhile. He himself made no other significant contribution to aviation, but occupied himself as he always said he wanted to do, with a variety of inventive projects. These, which included some toys that were sold commercially, kept him busy in the small but well-equipped laboratory he had built.

On April 3rd, 1917, Bishop Wright died at the age of eighty-eight, and Orville became the head of the family. For the next nine years he lived in happiness with Katharine at Hawthorne Hill, dispensing largess to his surviving brothers, Reuchlin and Lorin, and to their children. Then Katharine dropped a bombshell. She had secretly been seeing a widower, Henry Haskell, for more than a year, and they were married on November 20th, 1926. Orville was furious and refused to speak to her again until the day of her death, March 3rd, 1929. He brought her body back to be buried in the Wright family plot.

The great inventor, half of the most brilliant aviation engineering team in history, lived quietly until 1948, when he suffered a heart attack in his office and died shortly thereafter in the hospital.

Glenn Curtiss's life took many different turns. When the Wrights' patent suits forced the discovery that Augustus Herring actually had no patents to protect the Herring-Curtiss firm, the firm quickly lapsed into bankruptcy. Every one of Lena Curtiss's predictions had come true; Curtiss lost everything.

In the course of the patent suits, Curtiss also lost a bit of his dignity. He was persuaded to undertake the restoration of the Langley Aerodrome, to prove that it had flown before the Wright brothers had. Extensive changes were made to the Great Aerodrome, and it was flown in a few hops off Keuka Lake. The Smithsonian was thus able to claim that the Langley Aerodrome was the first flying machine "capable of flight," and gave Curtiss some questionable ammunition for the patent suits.

Orville Wright responded indignantly, and, unable to obtain satisfaction from the Smithsonian, sent his original 1903 Wright Flyer to the Science Museum in London for exhibit, a rebuff to the Smithsonian Institution that was not redressed until 1948.

Fortunately for Curtiss, the bankruptcy of the Herring-Curtiss firm did not stop him; his reputation and energy allowed him to form a new firm, the Curtiss Exhibition Company, which made money giving air shows around the country. The success of this company enabled Curtiss to establish the Curtiss Aeroplane and Engine Company, which became the largest manufacturer of aircraft in the United States during the First World War. The war had also brought an end to the patent dispute issue, when the need for increased production of aircraft dictated that a cross-licensing agreement be made available to all manufacturers after payment of a standard fee.

When the war ended, Curtiss knew that the demand for aircraft would fall off and he transferred some thirty-two million dollars in assets from aircraft manufacture into investments. He became a prime speculator in Florida real estate development, and reportedly ran his already considerable fortune into an even larger one.

Curtiss's old *bête noire,* Augustus Herring, had one more game to play. After remaining in relative obscurity for years, Herring pulled a brilliant stroke in November 1918, when he called a meeting of the board of directors of the supposedly defunct Herring-Curtiss Company. A new board of directors, favorable of course to Herring, was elected, and a $5,000,000 lawsuit instituted against Curtiss. Herring lost the first lawsuit in 1923 and died of a stroke in 1926. But the suit went on, and in 1928 an appellate court reversed the decision. While negotiating the settlement, Glenn Curtiss died of a pulmonary embolism. Herring's family subsequently received $500,000.

Tom Baldwin became an accomplished pilot of Curtiss flying machines, and eventually headed up some of Curtiss's many businesses. Baldwin, who had awarded himself the imaginary rank of captain, rose to be a genuine major in the Balloon Corps during the First World War.

Octave Chanute, who might be said to have started the Wrights on their way, became increasingly difficult, obstructing their patent suits with statements that he believed to be true, but which were not. The Wrights properly took umbrage, and there was an exchange of ever-sharper letters until shortly before Chanute's death in 1910.

Albert Blohm undertook as a crusade the denigration of the Wright brothers, and spent a lonely lifetime doing so. He remained prominent in all the aviation societies, and even secured a position at the Library of Congress, but his one mission in life was to smear the Wright brothers' claim to be the first in flight. Oddly enough, very few people took exception to his actions; he was simply regarded as one of the unusual, unpleasant facts of aviation life, a nice enough fellow with the exception of his imponderable hatred of Orville and Wilbur, two people who had never done him any harm, but had done the world a great deal of good.